THE
MARK
OF THE
WOLF

BOOK OF SECRETS VOL. I

Also by the author:

<u>Mundus Occultus Stories</u>

Bad Trip

Ozark Mountain Nightmare

The Mark of the Wolf

Book of Secrets Vol. I

JS Groves

Scorpio Moon
2018

First Printing: January 2018

ISBN 978-1-947116-02-3

Scorpio Moon
Kansas City, MO

DEDICATION

First and foremost, this book is dedicated to the Muses. O you daughters of Zeus, my eternal thanks for your unending song in my ear. Aromatics and libations I offer you.

Secondly, this book is dedicated to Dionysus, for without wine and madness, I could never have persevered. Io Iachos! Io Bromeos! Io Zagreus!

Next, this book is dedicated to everyone who has listened to me talk non-stop about this novel and all the related stories for the last decade, particularly my partner Audrey. Thank you all, especially those who looked at the very early drafts. Without your support, I might have given up years ago. Also, thank you all for not killing me when I didn't shut up.

Inevitably, this book is also dedicated to my pre-readers and amateur editors who helped put a polish on the final draft: my mother, Kathy; Audrey, again; Charlie; Rose; Steven. Thank you so much.

Finally, this book is dedicated to Marissa and Lance, whose first novels made print before mine. You beat me to the punch, you fucks. Mad props.

--JS Groves

PROLOGUE

Burning Eyes

C.2200 BCE

The people watched in horror as Dream Leopard dragged the boy from the hut they shared.

They cried out in protest and confusion:

"What are you doing, holy one?"

"He is your son, your apprentice!"

"How has he wronged you?"

"What crime has he committed against our people?"

But they would not approach Dream Leopard, and he would not be swayed.

"The boy sees secrets that no one should know," the priest cried out, whipping the boy with a lash of woven vines. "He does not abide by the spirits. He attempts to command them. He dreams of commanding you, of commanding me. He wishes to be a king, as they have down the great river and beyond the mountains above us."

He whipped his apprentice until he could struggle no longer, until he reduced the boy to a weeping pile of rags and bones. Then, when the boy could no longer flee, Dream Leopard fetched a burning brand from one of the cook fires. He rolled the boy over onto his back and sat on his narrow chest, leaning in close to the boy's face.

"You see too much," Dream Leopard said in a voice too low to carry. "More than any mortal should know. No one should know the path to another man's glory or disgrace. No holy man should seek the power you seek."

He blew on the brand, stoking it hotter.

"Let this teach you," he cried in a voice loud enough to be heard by all who had gathered around them. "Do not mock our ancient traditions by turning them to evil purposes."

So saying he stabbed the red-hot brand first into the boy's left eye, then his right. He pulled sacred salt-ash from a pouch at his waist and ground it into the boy's burned, bleeding eyes. Finally, he stood and let the boy crawl away, where he found shelter in the arms of his mother's family.

2

"Shelter him if you can stomach him," said Dream Leopard, "our ancestors admire compassion. But from this day forth he has no name."

The boy, named Jkor until that moment, collapsed into the arms of his aunts, who carried him back to their hut where he tossed and turned in restless, fevered sleep.

Sliding in and out of consciousness, the boy did not speak for weeks. Instead he dreamed. He dreamed of walking through familiar jungles and foreign ones, of following the Great River downstream until jungle gave way to grassland and grassland gave way to sand. He dreamed of great mountains, built of sunbaked brick and vast stones moved from their native rock by human hands to the banks of the River. Each of the mountains held countless secrets and promised to reveal them to him, if only he would come.

Tales of Dream Leopard's cruelty spread far. Healers came from nearby villages to apply poultices and pray over the boy who had been Jkor. Finally, when the moon had waxed and waned and waxed again, the boy began to whisper in the ears of those who tended to him.

"Expect a great catch on the third day of the new moon," he told one cousin. "But take only your most trusted friends on that hunt with you. When you return, the headsman will look favorably upon your interest in his daughter: ask for her hand as soon as you return."

All who did as he advised prospered: their hunts were successful, their harvests plentiful, and their alliances bore noble fruit. No one failed to notice this. Nor did anyone fail to notice that those who disdained him, those who opposed his family, those who continued to support Dream Leopard, saw their game vanish before their eyes, their crops wither, and their wives turn barren.

"I should have killed him," Dream Leopard was heard muttering more than once.

"Perhaps," his new apprentice said to him, a year after he-who-had-been-Jkor was maimed. "But it is too late, now. His blood has not poisoned him. He is blind, but he has healed.

Your standing has not. Fewer people come to you each day. We should leave."

"We cannot leave. Where would we go? Who has been putting these ideas in your head?"

The apprentice looked away and did not answer. Dream Leopard sat back and crossed his arms, wondering if he had any allies at all left among his people.

That night, the apprentice strangled Dream Leopard in his sleep, and left his body in its bed to lie.

Come morning, the apprentice crawled across the village on hands and knees until he reached the hut where he-who-had-been-Jkor sat on his bench awaiting those who would come to him for advice.

"Burning Eyes," the apprentice addressed he-who-had-been-Jkor. "Our former master was a festering wound at the heart of our village, hungry with jealousy. It was out of jealousy for your vision that he blinded you, and out of jealousy and fear that he never truly instructed me in the priestly arts. The path to justice has come to me in my dreams, and I have followed it. I have come to you to ask that you take me as your apprentice, and to take the place that would have already been yours if not for our former master's jealousy."

The blinded youth sat quietly for a time, his face serious.

"Take me to the body. I will dispose of it properly."

Burning Eyes had not stood under the sun in three quarters of a year, or walked farther than the tight circle around his hut. The trek across the village was tiring. It was also silent: no one spoke to them. No one helped them. No one impeded them, either.

"I will need you to bring me things. Place them where I tell you. Then go. I will keep him from becoming an angry ghost. His death curse will not follow you or harm our village."

Each of the items Burning Eyes named was to be found in the holy man's hut. The apprentice found them all, then left as instructed, tying a reed across the doorway to indicate that no one was to enter.

All day and all night, Burning Eyes chanted and prayed and made mystical gestures. He dressed the body and bound it

4

in the reed blankets on which Dream Leopard had slept. At dawn he called for assistants to dig a hole in the woods, then to guide him there by touch as he dragged the body, himself. He continued to chant and pray as they buried the body.

"Why do we not burn him, as is proper? Will not animals come to disturb this grave?"

"In a year's time, we will burn him. Nothing will disturb him, not even his own restless spirit. This rite will assure him the peace in death that he never found in life."

And it proved true: though many came to leave offerings on the grave – for Dream Leopard had been well-loved, before he had gone mad – it remained untouched. In the meantime, Burning Eyes took over Dream Leopard's role as holy man: taking his hut, his apprentice, and his tools, as his own. All that had once been so violently denied him was now his.

Years passed. Holy men, shamans, and priests came from all around to seek the council of Burning Eyes. Some traveled for entire cycles of the moon just to ask him how their ambitions could be achieved. And he answered them all.

Still the dreams came, as they had from the beginning: ever more clear and demanding. A golden, burning chariot rose as the sun, shining over a dead and blasted desert, cut by a great river. From the banks of that river sprang a village bigger than all the villages he'd ever seen put together. In the middle of the dried mud dwellings rose stone buildings so massive that, were it not for the knowledge imparted by the dream, he would not have recognized them as the work of men. In one such man-made-mountain, the son of the sun ruled over his people with the aid of his holy men. In another, secret, temple a group of nine sorcerer-priests and seven witches guarded and cared for a sacred object in a stone box. He could see it, shining with power and calling to him through the box, but it was like nothing he had ever seen: like a length of cloth rolled around the sticks that had been fixed to either end. It whispered in his mind, promising the secrets of the universe if only he would release it from its vault.

One day, at last, he woke with the voice still in his head. He did not know where it was, not exactly, but he knew the direction in which it lie. He did not hesitate or consider. He packed one satchel with his tools, another with supplies stolen from the village larder. The object, the power, called to him, and he could no longer deny it. He could do nothing but answer.

It was still night. Not even the hunters had risen yet. He walked out of the village and into the dense jungle.

The village itself was so familiar that he needed only his memory and his cane to find his way. The jungle, though, was an alien place of trip hazards and pitfalls. At first, he stumbled and crashed through the tangle and brush, but he quickly learned some of the jungle's secrets, and new applications for his own. Although he could not see the trees, he could sense their lives. By the end of the second day he had learned to dodge most hazards of root and branch, and to sense the general lay of the earth beneath his feet by the life that teemed over it.

Food became a problem. On the eighth day of his journey, his carefully hoarded supplies ran out. He could not seek solace from friendly villages, even if he had known where one might be. Once word spread of his disappearance, as it had by now, none would remain. Though he was respected, he was also feared, and to vanish in the night as he had, stealing food, would conjure only greater fears. He could dowse for water, but without the eyes and skills of a hunter he could find little else. He could find some plants without eyes, but not many. Still the beacon called, and somehow he found the strength to follow.

After a few days without eating it began to seem as if the call, itself, was sustaining him. Every night he dreamed of it, sometimes getting flashes of sand or hills or jungle or swamp... land he would travel through but which he would see only in his dreams.

Burning Eyes traveled, stumbling between the green spirits of the trees, for so long that he lost track of day and night. The sun rose and set at its own pace; he rose and collapsed at his. Instead, he marked the passage of time by the waxing and waning power of the moon. The moon was near to full when he left his village and it waned, waxed, and waned

6

again before his bare feet and his nose told him that he was leaving the familiar jungle for a wetter, rotting place: the dangerous, evil swampland that bordered his people's lands a little north of east.

For the first time in half a moon, he sensed the lives of humans in the distance, at the outermost edge of his perceptions. They were not exactly in the direction of the calling mystery, but his people had no allies among the swamps, and there was some chance that he could seek food and shelter there. As he drew near, he could feel the presence of a powerful witch, and when he slept he felt the reign she held over the dreams of her village. She fluttered, beautiful and terrible, around the edges of their sleeping minds. To his surprise, she sensed his watching presence. Her attention turned from the dreams of her people to focus on him and, for a moment, he saw her as she saw herself, rather than through the eyes of her people. The differences were confusing, and all he was certain of before she stepped back from his dreams was they were kindred spirits, of sorts: powerful and ambitious.

When he woke he was troubled. Only Dream Leopard had ever been able to sense his presence in the dream world. It was unheard-of that a witch be so powerful a dreamer. She had been absurdly masculine in the minds of her people – nose pierced and arms scarred in the manner of their warriors. Clearly she had used her magic to seize power as a priest, the presence of which he could not sense, to demand a masculine role in the rule of her village. It would be a risk, begging succor from her and her people, and he spent some hours attempting to consult the spirits on the matter. Hunger and the call clouded his mind, however, and in the end he was left with only his exhausted mortal wits to aid his decision.

Burning Eyes was not very far from the village when a hunter came close enough to pick out from the lives of the trees. The huntsman stalked him for nearly an hour before shouting at him to stop, in a barely recognizable accent. Burning Eyes stopped. There was no way he could physically contend with a warrior. He tried to divine the other man's ambitions and sense out the best approach to control him, but the witch-woman had

7

affixed him with some sort of charm. All Burning Eyes could detect was the psychic scent of her, obscuring that of the warrior.

"Who are you," the warrior demanded. "What village do you come from?"

"I am Burning Eyes, a holy man from more than a moon's travel to the south and west. I follow a dream quest."

He knew where the warrior stood and he turned his sightless gaze upon the man. It was laughable how many were unnerved by his stare. There was a long pause before the warrior replied.

"Our priest wishes to speak with you."

"Take me to her."

PART I — BITTEN

Coffee and Cigarettes

THURSDAY, AUGUST 27TH, 1998

"Tobacco," one young man said as he measured herbs into a small round box, "is traditionally attributed cleansing properties, just like the others."

His appearance was dramatic: six feet tall, with straight black hair that flowed down his back, halfway to his hips, and hid the multitude of piercings in his ears but not the barbell in his brow or the ring in middle of his lower lip. He wore a collared black cotton shirt, and his baggy pants were covered in pockets. His dark clothes and hair made his ruddy face seem paler than it was. A pair of silver pendants hung from his neck. The herbs came from the multitude of pouches hanging from his belt and wallet chains.

He loomed over the other two from his perch at the top of the stairs leading up to the building next to their favorite coffee shop. The sun had passed far enough toward the horizon that the shadows were beginning to lengthen, but the concrete steps were still hot to the touch and the steady Kansas wind provided only small relief from the summer heat that they pretended not to feel.

"Myself," he went on, "I just use it to make the smoke smoother. Throw in some white sage and lavender, though, and you have a nice herbal warding. I also like to add mugwort to help me see a little more clearly into the spirit world. I recommend you get the herbs from the co-op and the tobacco from the pipe shop in the antique mall – the best bang for your buck, if you will. Sans 'baccy, it works just as well in a brazier."

He put the lid on the box and twisted it a few times.

"Is that the same grinder you use for the... other stuff?" The second boy asked, a little nervously, earning a laugh from both of his companions.

He was blond and small, tanned from yard work and hours at the pool. He dressed in a ubiquitous jeans-and-tee-shirt ensemble, and tended to fade into the background whenever possible.

Sitting at the low end of the stairs, with his shoulder pressed to the concrete wall that divided the stairs on which they sat from those that descended to the coffee shop, he had crane his neck to see his friends where they sat above him, one behind the other.

"Hell, no, Jake. I don't take my paraphernalia out in public." He opened the grinder and pinched half of the contents into a waiting roller, producing a cigarette-shaped tube of herbs with a snap. "Hey, Aaron, you still got my light?"

"Yeah," the third boy said. He threw the Bic back over his shoulder without looking and the first boy snatched it from the air with barely a glance. Aaron's hair was rich brown, hanging just past his shoulders and framing his olive face with graceful curls. His pants were tailored, and his shirts usually silk. A single silver ring pierced the lobe of his right ear and a five-pointed star hung from his neck.

"Good catch, Dom. How do you two do that?"

Aaron laughed and Dominic grinned as he lit the cigarette.

"Practice," Dominic admitted.

They were his closest friends, but Jacob often felt like the odd man out. Where he was small, quiet, and nondescript, they were tall, loud, and flamboyant. Everyone at school and his parents' church said they were gay. He wondered sometimes if they were together, but had always been afraid to ask.

As Dominic pulled on his cigarette, a thickness that had nothing to do with the smoke seemed to gather in the air. It grew slowly, filling Jacob's head with the strangest sensation of disconnectedness. Finally, Dominic took a particularly deep drag and blew out a thin ring of smoke. The pressure vanished with a tingle. Aaron and Dominic both relaxed visibly. Something else about the feel of the afternoon changed subtly, but he couldn't describe it in words.

"I know you felt it that time," Dominic said. It was in Aaron's eyes, too, but he almost always let Dominic be the one to tell Jacob the things that he didn't want to hear. Jacob shrugged and looked away.

"It's your turn to get coffee," Aaron decided, pulling a fiver from his pocket and waving it at Jacob. "Black forest mocha."

Dominic snatched the five and replaced it with a ten before passing it on: "Green chai, hot."

Jacob gave them a sour frown, but he was in need of his own refill anyway, so he took their money and went down and inside to order their drinks.

His attention drifted around the room while he waited in line and on his order. Small sounds and movements drew his attention from one corner to one table to the next. There, a couple was quietly fighting – no one else could probably tell, but he could. There, a girl trying to channel whatever was in her head through her hand and onto the pages of a sketchbook. There, a boy high out of his mind and sipping coffee while he watched everyone in the room. There, a woman having an exceptionally unpleasant conversation with an exceptionally unpleasant man – she was tall, wiry, with heavily muscled arms, in ragged jeans and layered tee-shirts; he was taller, slender, soft-bodied, with eyes like ice and an air about him that made Jacob feel physically unsafe. Something about her was stunningly familiar.

His sister Ricki was waiting for him by the time he made it back outside.

"You're late," she said, tapping her foot.

He checked his watch, carefully synchronized with hers and their father's every day or night before they went out. He wasn't, but that was beside the point.

"That drink is not coming in my car," she said.

"Do you want it down your dress, instead?"

"You wouldn't."

"And I'm not going to spill it in your car, either." He handed Aaron and Dominic their drinks. "I'll see you guys later."

They stared after him for a few minutes, watching Jacob's shoulders sink lower and his head bow farther each step he took. Dominic caught himself grinding his teeth, and took a deep breath to calm himself.

"I don't like her," he said, to no one in particular.

"The whole fucking fundie lot of them can fuck off and die," Aaron said. "That would be nice."

Dominic closed his eyes and took another deep breath.

"I take it we just missed Jake." The voice came from behind him.

"Yeah," Dominic said with a sigh. "How's it going, Amber?"

A glance over his shoulder told him that she'd brought Jennifer, as usual.

"Good," Amber told him in a voice that was entirely too chipper. Bracelets rattled as she pushed the hair back from her eyes. She was wearing one of her almost-but-not-quite-see-through peasant tops, and a flowing patchwork hippie-skirt that she had probably made herself. "How about you guys?"

"Great, until Ricki the Hellbitch showed up," he told them with a shrug. "Anything fun and interesting happen since last we met?"

Jennifer shook her head, adjusting her pastel blue sundress as the evening wind played with the hem. "Only if you think decoding Latin text is 'fun and interesting'."

The two girls were a study in contrasts. Amber was shorter, blonde with natural voluminous curls, curvaceous and busty. Jennifer was tall and lithe, athletic bordering sinewy, with straight brown hair that rivaled Dominic's for length. When they didn't know he was watching, Dominic liked to try to decide which of the two was better looking. It was a subject which required a great deal of study.

"I do, actually," he said. "What are you working on?"

"Homework, mostly, but I've also been trying to read the original Aeneid to see if it's any more interesting than the translations I've been offered."

"It's not," Dominic said, shaking his head, "trust me. You should check out Gnaeus Naevius."

"Who? What?"

"Roman dramatist from the Punic Wars. I'll lend you a copy. How about you, Amber?"

"Well," the other girl drawled, putting on her very best 'cute face', smiling and batting her eyes as her shoulders moved back and forth. "I've been going out with my boyfriend. Last night we went to dinner and saw that new vampire movie, *Blade...*"

"So," asked Aaron, sounding mildly irritated. "Are we ever going to meet this mysterious boyfriend? Or even hear his name?"

Dominic perked up. This should be good.

"Eventually," Amber answered in a coy tone. "I'm trying to get him to come to our pagan group meetings, but he's always busy."

"And a name?" prompted Jennifer.

'Amber's stringing Jennifer along, too?' Dominic thought. *'That's unusual. They're almost inseparable.'*

"Alex."

That got Dominic's attention.

"Alex?" he demanded. "As in our Alex? Alexander fucking Dixon?"

Amber answered with a nod, a smile, and a deep blush. *'How the fuck did I miss that?'* The three of them had been hanging out and smoking weed together since the beginning of their junior year. Sure, Alex was hard to read, but Amber was an open book with large print! She'd been talking about her shiny new boyfriend for nearly a month, and he'd not caught a whiff of it off of either of them when they were together. The marijuana must be affecting his perception more than he wanted to admit.

"Alexander Dixon," repeated Aaron in a cold voice. "It's bad enough that he got you two on his habit. Now you're going out with him?"

"Jesus, Aaron," swore Dominic, ignoring the glare Jennifer gave him for his blasphemy. "What's your beef with him? You and Jacob talk about Alex like he's some kind of monster. I mean, sure, he's an atheist, but...?"

14

"Fuck," Aaron said, standing up and brushing the wrinkles out of his pants. "Do whatever you want."

Storming off when he didn't want to talk about something was one of Aaron's least attractive qualities, as far as Dominic was concerned, and he had a tendency to do it whenever the subject of Alexander Dixon came up.

"Well, Jen," Dominic asked, turning his attention to her, "you've known them for half of forever. Do you know what's up?"

The taller girl shrugged. "Not really. I know that Alex, Aaron, and Jacob were all friends when they were little. Them and Anthony Domiano. All our families used to go to the same church, back before Reverend Baker came and it turned into the Rapture Baptist. There was some kind of fight. That was when Alex and Anthony's rivalry started, and Aaron and Jacob haven't been friends with either of them since. But that's all I know."

Dominic nodded. He'd known that much already. He'd asked Alexander, too, but the other boy had refused to talk. He would always say, 'Ask Jake or Ron.' Only Alexander ever called Aaron that. He was also one of the few people to call Domiano 'Tony'. It hurt Dominic a lot that neither Aaron nor Jacob trusted him enough to tell the story behind the three-way feud between themselves, Anthony Domiano, and Alexander Dixon. Obviously, it had something to do with Aaron's coming out of the closet, but it seemed like there was something more to the story. From the outside, at least, it looked a lot more personal than simple homophobia.

"Well," Amber said. "We were just stopping in for our latté fix. You want to walk the strip with us?"

It was tempting, but he did have the finishing touches to put on his first essay of the year and zero-hour weights class in the morning. Wouldn't do to let his grades slip now.

"Nah, you girls have fun. I'm gonna get home."

The Seer

There were nine of them: three women and five men flanking a
powerfully built man a few years older than the rest, all dressed
in leather and steel. Black chaps and jackets studded and
spiked at the seams and at the cuffs, heavy chains rattling at
their hips. They tore down the streets of urban Chicago on their
motorcycles, taking up both lanes, weaving in and around the
cars of terrified local drivers, deeper and deeper into the old
city, laughing and whooping back at the angry shouts and
honking horns they provoked. Finally, they skidded to a halt on
a block of tall brick buildings with storefronts on the ground
and offices and apartments stacked on top of them. One by
one, they parked where they could: in between cars, on the
sidewalks, in planters, in alleys.

    Their destination was a hole-in-the-wall bar, visible from
the street only as a neon blue guitar, an illegible wooden sign,
and a flickering lamp over a set of precarious concrete stairs
descending below the level of the sidewalk. The door at the
bottom of the stairs bore another wooden sign, which
proclaimed the establishment the Blue Mojo Bar & Grill. A
bouncer – a man of only medium height but with biceps as big
as his thighs – sat just inside the blocked-open door, and let
them pass without question.

    The Blue Mojo was ill-lit by a half dozen blue-coated
florescent lamps mounted above the bar and hanging from the
ceiling over the pool tables at the back, and by three pillar
candles at each table. The air was thick with smoke. The crowd
was well mixed: artsy-looking white kids mingling easily with
the working-class Blacks and Latinos locals. The bartender was
a hard-looking woman with a square frame, heavy gauge steel
earrings, and tattoos instead of hair. An old, tinny recording of
John Lee Hooker played while a half-dozen young men
scrambled over the stage, setting up for the night's
performance.

    The leather-clad gang radiated violence and hunger, and
those they passed moved as far out of their way as they could.
The leader, for the older man was clearly that, wore as much

steel as the others combined: heavy links of chain wrapped around his shoulders and in loops around his writs and waist, spikes up the arms of his jacket and down the legs of his pants. Tattoos of flames crawled up his neck from under his stained A-shirt and the heads of wolves snarled from the backs of his tattooed hands. His short hair was going gray at the temples and in his thick beard.

He sniffed like an animal at the smoky air, and his eyes scanned the room like he was looking for someone in particular. His gaze settled on a dark corner, where an old man leaned casually over an ashtray and a tall glass of amber liquor.

The old man was thin and small boned, darkly black-skinned, his tightly curing white hair cropped close to his skull and his clothes layered and torn. The shadows seemed to cling to him, thicker at his table than in the rest of the bar, and his blind white eyes almost seemed to glow. The old biker gestured to his followers, half of whom went to lean on the bar while the others followed him to the old man's table.

"Are you the one they call Django Bones?" He asked in a hard voice. He wasn't angry, just unaccustomed to speaking gently.

"I am," the old man answered in a thick drawl, turning toward the grizzled biker. The old man's milky eyes were so penetrating that he had to remind himself that no one could see through cataracts that thick. There wasn't even the faintest shadow of an iris. "Sit."

He sat, and one of the women who had settled at the bar brought him a drink. The smell of potent marijuana and good bourbon hung thickly around the table and the old man took a long drag off of his joint while the larger man took a long pull from his beer.

"I'm told you're a powerful seer."

"I am." Bones wasn't bragging, just stating the fact.

"Tell me what I've come for."

"Testing me costs extra." He might or might not have been annoyed; it was hard to tell.

"If you're a poser, it's gonna cost you."

"You didn't come here to threaten me, Michael. Not all the way from Los Angeles." The seer's drawl clipped most of his words in half, but drug out Michael's name and that of his city by an extra syllable each.

Michael paused. He hated mystics. It was bad enough that his pack even needed a shaman. They always knew too much and they never gave it to you straight.

"My shaman is dying and his replacement can't find an heir of his own."

"Can't find or can't make?"

"Either," Michael growled.

Those blind eyes were fucking creepy, and Michael used his drink as an excuse to look away. It wasn't like the old man could see him break eye contact, right? Django Bones seemed to stare at him for several long minutes. He took another drag off his joint before answering in that distant voice seers used when they were putting on their show.

"In the morning, you and your pack will take I-55 south and my man will meet you on the road. You will know him when you see him. He will lead you to a restaurant in Kansas City where they will know you for what you are and make a point of leaving you alone. You will find a girl there, my man will point her out to you, and one of you will Mark her. Wait. Watch. Keep quiet and out of sight. Before three moons have waxed and waned, you will have the shaman you need."

The stress on the last four words somehow conveyed to Michael that the old man knew exactly what he needed in a shaman. If the price didn't turn out to be too high, this might work out alright after all.

"And your price?"

"Afterward, I will require one of your pack to serve me for a time."

"When? Who? How long? For what?"

"At my convenience. One of your women. For however long I need, for whatever I may require."

Michael laughed. "You think you can handle my bitches, grandpa?"

An unseen force seized Michael by the throat. He struggled against it, tried to pull away, but the grip was too strong. Spots appeared in his vision and the world swam as blood and air were cut off from his brain.

The corner they were sitting in brightened as all the shadows condensed into a glowing-eyed man-shape, its too-long arm stretched over the old man's head and across the table to throttle Michael.

"I'll not dignify that with an answer, boy," said the old man. "Show some respect."

Michael stopped struggling and the shadow-hand released him.

It had been twenty years since anyone had the stones to call him 'boy', but with those red eyes staring out of the solid shadow above him, Michael wasn't going to make an issue of it.

"Whatever you want."

"Be on the highway before noon."

The dark figure vanished and the shadows settled back over their corner of the room. The old man was wearing a small, cruel smile as he raised his glass to toast Michael and his pack. Michael took the hint and went for the door.

"Tell them to have their fun," he growled to his second. "You and I are going back to the motel."

Michael stalked back out the door. He was waiting with his motorcycle running by the time Big Hugh caught up to him. Hugh started his own bike and followed Michael onto the road without question. The motel was eight miles away, and they stopped on a dark stretch of road halfway there, pulling into small alley between two tall brick buildings.

"The seer knows what you're really after," said Big Hugh. "You think this'll go down like he says?"

Michael wasn't sure, but that was always a problem with mystics and informants. That was why he'd gone so far from home: to keep the conflict of interests to a minimum.

"Old Bones has a rep. They say his Sight's so clear that he can't lie. But you don't have to lie to leave something out."

Hugh nodded his agreement. "The Wolf King of Kansas City has a rep, too."

Michael growled at the very name. Wolf King. He refused to believe a single man could be powerful enough to dominate every monster in an entire city. Good thing no one had ever tried that shit in LA. There'd have been war to make the race riots look tame.

"If we're gonna go there, Michael, we better pay our respects. I don't wanna die if it turns out the stories are even halfway true."

Big Hugh didn't believe the stories, either, but he was cautious. That was why he was second. In this, though, Michael would be cautious, too. He already owed a favor to the seer. He didn't want to piss off the most powerful werewolf in the country, too.

School Haze

FRIDAY, AUGUST 28TH

Dominic was doing yoga on the exercise floor as his classmates began trickling in, giving him odd looks or pretending he didn't exist as best suited each of them. Half the class had been here last semester, too. You'd figure they'd have gotten used to it by now. The fact that some muscles in the human body couldn't be stretched without looking silly was no reason to neglect them – and if they wanted to see something really mind-boggling, there was always the sixty-year-old, three-hundred-pound woman who'd taught him these stretches in the first place.

Unlike most of the people who took zero-hour weight lifting, Dominic was no athlete. But his father had eventually convinced him that the ancient Greeks had had the right of it: a healthy mind required a healthy body. At least he'd had Alexander to entertain him last semester. This year the martial artist was in sixth hour weights.

"Some people sweat, Dom," his friend had pointed out. "I don't like being stanky all day."

Unlike Alexander, Dominic had no problem with the public showers. He had been attending the clothing optional pagan festival circuit with his parents' coven for as long as he could remember. He really didn't suffer from any sort of body-shyness, much less the neurotic self-consciousness of his peers.

"Doesn't that hurt," Jennifer asked, not for the first time. She had come up from behind while he was in his Half Lord of the Fishes pose. His left foot was tucked under his right buttock, and he had placed his right foot on the outside of his left knee. His torso twisted so that his right hand rested on the floor behind his back. He held his left hand up in the air with its elbow braced against his upraised right knee.

"Not if I'm doing it correctly," he said, turning to look at her and to get in another good back stretch while he was at it. The position probably looked even more painful than the last and might strike the weak of heart as obscene. Jennifer shuddered, looking away, and he did his best not to grin.

The PE coach showed up to let them in to the weight room, at last, and the usual fight over the radio ensued. Dominic and Jennifer just shook their heads, heading for the sit-up benches. It wasn't like any of the people shouting for this station or that knew what good music was. They had managed fifty sit-ups each by the time a station was negotiated. Last year, the coach had eventually decided to rotate stations daily – one station, Monday, a different one Tuesday, and so on. Dominic wondered how long it would be before he remembered and re-implemented that solution.

"I brought Gnaeus Naevius for you," he said to Jennifer as they moved on to the bench press. "It's my dad's copy from college, though, so try not to let it get any more beat up than it already is."

"You know I take good care of books, Dominic."

"I do. I'm just saying: my ass is grass if anything happens to that old paperback. Dad'll roll me up and smoke me."

She laughed, almost dropping the bar. "Fair enough."

Amber meandered in with the bell, a usual, by which time Jennifer had already set herself up at their table. She smiled warmly at the smaller girl, patting the seat beside her.

"Hey," she said.

"Hey, yourself," Amber said back with a smile of her own, immediately pulling her sketch pad from her patched and battered backpack. To warm up her fingers, she began doodling a maze of Celtic knots and flowers. "Good day, so far?"

"So far," Jennifer agreed. "You?"

"Mostly," Amber said with an overly dramatic sigh. "Starting the day with algebra is just not my idea of a good time."

Jennifer hid a smile behind her hand.

The chatter died down to a murmur as Mrs. Wren made herself known, bustling in from the supply room that doubled as her office. She was a short, pale woman, growing plump as

she approached middle age, her face usually split by a smile.
Her mousey hair was done in a multitude of short braids; they
hung loose today, each capped with a colorful glass bead. She
greeted them all warmly, gliding from one table to the next with
a grace that always caught Jennifer by surprise, and offering
helpful comments on the work she'd seen them doing the day
before, then turned them loose again on their projects. They
should be at least half done, she reminded them, and ready to
be turned in at the end of class Monday – giving them the
chance to take their pieces home over the weekend, if they so
desired. She then sat herself down behind the desk at the front
of the class and pulled out her own sketch book, turning on her
stereo and setting them loose to "do Art."

Jennifer sighed a little at the musical selection. It was
that Led Zeppelin CD again. When she came back from lunch,
Ms. Wren would be red-eyed and extra smiley. Which meant
that Amber probably would be, too.

The murmur of conversation returned to its former
volume, accompanied by the grind and clatter of tables and
chairs as everyone moved to their cubbies to retrieve their
project drafts and then to the supply rack for materials.

"So, when's the next full moon?" Jennifer asked as they
settled in with their pieces and supplies. The assignment was to
draw or paint a landscape, a place of comfort remembered from
childhood, done in chalk pastels. Jennifer's was an image of
her grandfather's farm: the red barn in the middle of a green-
gold field against a blue sky streaked with white clouds. She
was proud of it until she looked at Amber's.

"Next weekend," Amber said, tying her hair up with a
scrunchy. "Saturday the fifth."

Amber had taken a little liberty with the subject – at
least, as far as Jennifer knew, Amber had no particular
childhood connection to the train tracks by Burcham Park – but
her rendition was evocative. Rusty tracks stretched across a
dark wooden bridge over a creek, vanishing into a stormy
horizon.

"Will you guys be doing your moon thing then?"

"Of course. Would you like to tag along again? You know you're always welcome."

"Yeah, I would like that. It's so peaceful out there."

"Now, your assignment for this weekend," Mr. Saunders explained as he walked down the row passing out worksheets, "is to finish reading chapter five of your textbook and answer both the review questions in that book and the questions on the paper I'm handing you now."

Amber took the page and glanced it over. *'Lots of who, what, when, and where,'* she observed. *'Not very much why.'* Still, she diligently dug her text from her dying backpack and flipped it open on her desk.

"This is important material for the section we'll be starting Monday, so take your time," Mr. Saunders continued, now settling back behind his desk. "You have twenty minutes left before the bell. Feel free to work together in small groups."

"Hey," Jacob said, scooting his desk closer to hers. "So I hear it's you and Alex these days."

Amber smiled and blushed, letting her blond curls fall in front of her face.

"Yeah," she said. "Did you hear from Dominic?"

"Of course. Why didn't you tell us sooner?" he asked, sounding a little hurt.

Amber gave him an odd look – half guilty, half sour. "Because you and Aaron hate him."

"We don't hate Alex..." Jacob hedged, holding his hands out.

"Aaron sure does, and you won't talk to him. You don't even like Dom or I to talk about him when you're around. What happened between you guys?"

"Ask Alex."

"He tells me to ask you and Aaron!"

"Then ask Aaron."

"He just storms off!"

Jacob looked away. "I don't want to talk about it."

24

Amber sighed.

"You guys are my friends," she said. "I want to understand."

"You can't understand. You weren't there. You didn't see it happen." He shifted in his chair, looked away, and sighed. "I'd tell you if I'd tell anybody, Amber. But we don't talk about it."

Amber tried to glare at him, but it was useless. For one, she was perfectly aware that her glares tended to come off as pouts; for another, Jacob was refusing to look at her. Jacob really was a master of the guilt trip – you'd figure he'd been raised Catholic, not Baptist. Sometimes he didn't even have to say anything. She sighed again, turning her attention to the worksheet in front of her. It was already half-covered in doodles: flowers and sigils and geometric patterns. Her hands did the strangest things when her mind was elsewhere.

She tried to focus on the assignment. She only had tonight to do her homework: tomorrow she had an all-day date with Alexander. Dominic would be joining them some time that evening, and she knew from past experience that she didn't do her best work after a day of such adventures.

Their spotters called out the reps in stereo:

"... Twelve ... thirteen ... fourteen ... fifteen."

Exhaling slowly, they allowed their arms to drift backward, dropping the barbells into the waiting hands of their spotters. They kept their breathing steady, their arms limp at their sides, while the spotters added another set of weights.

"Two hundred and thirty-five," Alexander panted, flexing his cramping fingers. Neither tall nor short, he was stocky, compact, and soaked in sweat. Shoulder-length black hair clung to his brown face and neck, itching furiously.

"You ready?" his rival egged him on. Anthony was a tall, powerful-looking boy with his brown hair cropped close to his skull. "Not giving up, are you?"

From across the room, Anthony looked half again the size of his rival. On the scale, the difference wasn't so clear.

"Always. Never."

The spotters were done.

"Ready?"

"Go!"

"One... two ... three ..." the count continued upward, both boys straining visibly. The count had slowed by the end and their breath grown ragged, but both made it to the target fifteen.

Again they let their arms fall limp, taking deep and measured breaths while their spotters adjusted the barbells.

"Two hundred and forty-five," Tony announced.

"On your count," said Alexander.

"That's quite enough, boys," the coach interrupted. "No need to hurt yourselves, now. Let someone else have a turn at the bench."

Alexander growled and clenched his fists. His arms burned. So did his lungs. He should not be upset to have this contest interrupted. Even if he didn't lose, he was going to hurt himself. Sitting up, he met Tony's eyes. They shared a look, Tony's face as carefully neutral as his own. Tomorrow they'd continue the challenge. For now, though, they would rest their arms. Tony went for the sit-up benches, so Alexander took a spot in line for the leg press. He let his mind drift while he waited.

He had the house to himself, tonight. Charlise would go home with one of her friends after school. She hadn't said so, but she always spent the night away while their parents were out of town. She would call from the pay phone at school and there would be a message waiting on the answering machine by the time he got home. He was meeting up with Amber in the morning, and Dominic would be joining them in the evening with a new bag.

He wondered if Amber had gotten around to telling anyone about "them" yet. He'd felt just a little silly keeping things on the down low around Dominic. The boy was gay for

God's sake, what did he care? He knew that Dominic wasn't the issue, though.

'*Jake and Ron are the issue,*' he thought. '*She's terrified of their disapproval.*'

It was his turn at the machine, and he loaded up the weights before settling down on his back. He glanced briefly at the toned legs of the girl in line behind him, visible just out of the corner of his eye, but refrained from sneaking a peek up her gym shorts.

'*I guess I understand,*' he thought to himself, his mouth making a sour twist as he pushed, careful not to lock his knees. '*They've disapproved of me for years and it still gets to me sometimes.*'

Aaron had a mighty glare, and Jacob's disappointment was even more cutting. What really got to him, though, was remembering the fear in their eyes that day. Amber thought she could help reunite them, but she didn't know what she was working against. She couldn't know until Jake and Ron were ready to do a little of the bridge-mending, themselves.

The weights clanged loudly against themselves, and Alexander was chagrined to realize that he'd let his temper slip. He was clenching his jaw and he'd locked his knees under two hundred and forty pounds of iron.

'*Focus, dumbass. You have to fucking focus.*'

They met on the east lawn, near one of the huge trees that dotted the yard, shading the east side of the building and somehow softening the brick facade.

'*I ought to know what kind of tree this is,*' Jacob chided himself as Aaron approached. For a moment he felt a cold, sharp wind, but it passed before he could even shiver. '*Not much of a witch, am I?*'

"Hey, Jake."

"Hi, Aaron."

They stood together, watching the curb and waiting for their bus. Some days the buses were all there waiting in a bright yellow row, all but blocking the narrow road. Usually at least one or two of them were late, but today it seemed that they all were. Waiting, students milled around the yard in small groups that seemed to orbit one another. A hundred little cliques hovering close to those that most resembled themselves. Almost no one actually stood alone, but there were a few misfits tucked into corners and leaning against the trees.

There, at the south end of the building today, hovered the hicks. Dressed in jeans and boots, flannel or rude tee-shirts, they were a combination of lean and strong that was hard to find in the student population - the product of actual labor. Some sported cigarettes tucked behind one ear, others spat entirely too often. Between classes they were known to gather in the hall near the gyms.

Elsewhere, a half dozen boys and girls dressed in black made a circle that pointedly excluded the world. Heavy wallet chains, technically a violation of the school's "weapon" rules, had come un-tucked from deep pockets, some hanging as low as the knee. The only splashes of color to be found were blue or red, more often as hair die than on tee-shirts. One boy even had the balls to wear a skirt to school, the way Dominic sometimes did downtown or out at the Sanctuary. Jacob really didn't understand the goth kids. If you went so far out of your way to look different, of course people were going to treat you differently.

The band kids, easily the most diverse-looking clique, gathered near the south parking lot, not far from the practice field. Excepting Aaron and Dominic, all of Jacob's friends were there ... but he wasn't a band kid, and he just wasn't comfortable around them when they were around the rest of the band. Another fold of which he wasn't a part.

The rest, clannish and alienated as they were, all looked a great deal alike. Some were richer, others poorer – mostly poorer; the preppies had generally migrated to Free State High when it opened last year. Jeans and tee-shirts, skirts and blouses or tops. A few still wore shorts, despite the changing season, a refusal to acknowledge Nature that he had never really understood. Some of the girls were just showing off their legs, sure, but the boys?

Jacob knew a few of them, at least. Jen, talking to some girl from the Lutheran church his family went to once a month, when Mom got tired of the fire and brimstone they preached at the Rapture Baptist. Anthony Domiano, the bane of Aaron's existence, watching the girls from a distance. Dominic was already gone, probably home an hour ago.

At the north end of the school, young men in dark suits were passing out little orange Bibles, preaching for some church or another. Usually it was the Latter Day Saints or the Gideons, but you just never knew.

"Something on your mind, Jake?" Aaron asked. "You look distracted."

Jacob shrugged. It was hard for him to focus, sometimes. The world just kept tugging at him, first this way then that.

"Sorry," he said. Then: "You heard about Amber and Alex?"

"Yes." Aaron made the word an epithet.

"I don't like it either. I know it's not our place, but... he still scares me, Aaron."

"He should scare you. He's a violent maniac. Everyone's seen his fights with Tony." Aaron's mouth turned up in a sneer. "He gets off on it, Jacob. You can see it in his eyes."

Jacob nodded. You could see it in his eyes. You could see it in every line of his body, in the way he walked, in the tournament medals he pinned to his book bag. Alexander Dixon was a predator, just like Anthony Domiano. The difference was that Domiano was a scavenger, preying on the weak; Dixon liked to hunt other predators.

Jennifer was at the street corner, waiting for her ride, when Margaret Dunn approached her from behind.

"Hey, Jennifer, how're you doing?" Margaret was almost as tall Jennifer, herself, but with softer features and more muscular limbs. She wore her hair loose, tumbling in waves down to her waist, and somehow managed not to tangle it in the brass buttons of her cutoff overalls. Her voice was warm and genuinely friendly, a little to Jennifer's surprise. *'I thought I was on everybody's prayer lists since it got out that I spend my Full Moons with Amber.'*

"Oh, hi, Mara," Jennifer said, cautious but hopeful. "Mostly good, I guess. Very busy."

Margaret smiled, moving to stand at Jennifer's side. "Me, too. You were right. The AP classes are hard, but they're worth it."

"I'm glad to hear that. I'll admit that it's hard on the social life, though. I almost never see you except at church, and I always have to leave so quickly. Are you trying out for the track team again this year?"

"I haven't *officially* decided yet," said Margaret, making air quotes, "but probably. I really enjoy it. Why, are you thinking of taking it up again?"

"Maybe," Jennifer said, shrugging. "It's been, what, three years? I've been lifting weights, but I fell off the running wagon. I'm not really in the right kind of shape, anymore. But I do miss it."

"We could practice together," Margaret offered, moving around a little farther to look Jennifer in the eyes.

"Sure," she said. *'Maybe I didn't entirely trade one group of friends for another.'* "I'll think about it. I'll give you a call tomorrow."

"But not this weekend," Mara said, hands raising to her mouth. "I'm sorry. I've got a date."

"A date? Congratulations. With whom?"

"Anthony."

Jennifer blinked, and tried very hard to keep her face neutral.

"Anthony Domiano?"

"Yeah. He asked me out on Monday. He was so sweet, I just couldn't say no," Margaret said with a smile. "Oh, there's my ride! See you Sunday!"

"Have fun," Jennifer said, waving goodbye. *'Poor girl's in for a surprise when that mask falls off.'*

The Wolf King and the First Fool

The pack hit the south-bound highway an hour before noon, thundering down the blacktop with little concern for speed limits or traffic law. Michael led the pack, flanked by Caleb and Big Hugh, followed by the bitches while the junior members held the rear. Old Bones had assured them that they would recognize his man on sight. Michael didn't doubt it, but he didn't know what to expect, and that made him nervous.

They were halfway out of Chicago when another motorcycle thundered onto their stretch of interstate. The bike was obviously custom: shining white, detailed with chrome, the front wheel chopped out a good three feet, and the handlebars swept so far back that the rider almost lounged atop his machine. The rider, himself, was so tall that he might not have been able to sit on a bike that hadn't been made just for him. Long black hair and a long black coat flowed out behind him, snapping in the wind. For a moment, Michael thought about driving him off the road to steal the bike and that fly leather jacket, but then the man turned his head. Michael flinched, just a little, but Caleb swerved to the far edge of the road, his face distorted in terror. Just this once, as Michael stared into those glowing red eyes, he was willing to credit Caleb with prudence instead of cowardice. He'd only seen those eyes once before, but Michael would never forget them. Being throttled by a shadow while staring into those eyes was the sort of thing no man should ever forget.

The creature – Michael didn't think for a moment that it was a man – pulled ahead of them with a mocking smile. They followed him for almost an hour, until they were well outside the edge of Chicago proper and were about to pass into the wasteland of rural Illinois, when he pulled onto an off ramp that dumped them almost directly into the parking lot of a squat, windowless greasy spoon. The building was of square cinder block construction, painted a sickly green that had not improved as it faded in the sun, and marked with the name Mama Grimm's in red across the wall to the left of the door. The seer's creature waited just long enough for them all to pull

up in the lot behind him before going inside. It was being
seated by a surprisingly attractive waitress when Michael
followed through the door. He waved the junior members to sit
wherever they wanted. Big Hugh and Caleb followed him to the
black-clad creature's table. Under the potent odor of the food,
the place stank of spilled beer, piss, and stale blood.

"Burgers," Michael told the girl. "Beers."

She glanced at his men, who nodded, then turned to the
creature.

"I require nothing," it said. The creature's voice
surprised Michael: low, smooth, melodic. He'd expected
Vincent Price, not James Earl Jones. The creature sat in the
corner with its eyes closed. It sat perfectly still, seemingly
without breathing – Michael could not even hear its heart
beating. It moved only when one of the younger wolves had the
strange notion to launch a straw wrapper in the creature's
direction, snatching the flying paper out of the air with two
fingers and placing it carefully on the table without otherwise
acknowledging that anything had happened.

"Check," he shouted at the waitress when they were
nearly done. When she left to get it, he turned to the creature:
"So what's the plan, bub? Where are we going?"

"Kansas City," it said. "I'll lead you when we get there.
Are you ready?"

"Waiting on you, buddy."

A look of mild annoyance crossed the creature's face,
drawing a strong stench of fear from Caleb. Michael wondered
if there was something Caleb could sense from the creature, or
if he was just a pussy. If Ruger had been well, it would have
been fine: he'd just have asked and been done with it. Caleb
couldn't be trusted.

"If you must address me," the creature said coldly in that
mismatched voice of his, "I am the Monster."

Monster. Huh. *The* Monster". This was going to be an
interesting trip.

They were back on the road in ten minutes. They didn't
stop again until they took the I-64 / US-40 exit to St. Louis.
They hit another greasy spoon on the Illinois side before

following 64/40 to I-70 and over the river westward. Another three hours of hard riding put them in Kansas City, where the Monster lead them through downtown into the old train yards and to a surprisingly upscale-looking steak house in a refurbished building just off the highway. They parked close together in the lot by the restaurant.

Michael looked to the Monster, his jaw tight.

"The one you must Mark will be here within the hour," the Monster said. "We should make ourselves comfortable."

Michael grunted, then gestured to his junior members. "Stay here until I get back. Follow our recruit home if you have to. We'll go pay our respects to the local authorities and meet you back here."

The Monster smiled.

"You will find the Wolf King's court in a warehouse club just past the arena," it said. "It will be difficult to miss."

Michael spat. "Heidi, you come with us. Lonna, keep this lot under control."

He watched his pack follow the Monster into the restaurant, then restarted his bike and pulled back out onto the road. Hugh, Caleb, and Heidi followed at his heels.

It didn't take long to find the club where the Wolf King held court. The fleet of sports cars and motorcycles in the lot and the hugely muscled men guarding the doors were dead giveaways. The bouncers weren't werewolves, but wore St. Lazarus crosses around their necks and carried monster-killing van Helsing guns in shoulder-holsters and huge knives on their belts. An alliance with the Cult of Lazarus would explain how a single werewolf could own a whole city. Too bad that wasn't an option for Michael. The Lazarites required their stooges to live quieter lives than he was interested in.

The front door led to a coat room where they were disarmed by two big men in muscle-shirts that read 'SECURITY' and a short, slender man in a suit and tie. The suit, armed with a clipboard, looked each one of them up and down. He stared Michael in the eye for long enough that it was almost a challenge. Michael was about to throw the first punch when the smaller man nodded subtly.

34

"Welcome, sir, to the Wolf King's court," he said. "Please, make yourselves comfortable."

The security guards stepped aside.

The place was huge. Stepping through the door, it looked like the club took up the entire ground level of the warehouse. The ceiling was ten, maybe fifteen feet high through most of the place, but it opened up over the dance floor and the stage. Michael and his pack wound their way through an insane mix of werewolves, mortals, and... *other things* wearing human faces. The patrons were dressed and undressed in an incomprehensible variety of suits, ethnic costumes, leather, latex, and Renaissance Faire garb. The lighting was so dim that most humans would barely be able to see where they were going and who they were with, except over the dance floor, which seemed like daylight in comparison.

Michael led them through the crowd, only about a third of which gave way in the manner to which he was accustomed. One woman – dressed in see-through white with an evil-looking snake wrapped around her waist and shoulders – had the nerve to growl and bark at them playfully. He turned to growl back but saw, in the corner of his eye, a look of terror across Caleb's face, and the sound died in his throat. The woman smiled and the snake watched them as she glided away. He had the strangest impression that the snake was the brains of that operation. He shuddered, leading his pack to the edge of the floor.

"Heidi," he said, "flag us a waitress."

A pair of DJs manned the stage, free styling together, and a man sat on a throne above and behind them, flanked by two burly men in chain mail vests, with a naked woman curled at his feet. The Wolf King was a small man, maybe five-foot-six, and slender. He wore a suit that even Michael could recognize as expensive, and gemstones glittered on his fingers in the bright light that centered on the throne and stage. The bodyguards were werewolves, and the naked woman powerfully other than human, but the might of the Wolf King's Mark flooded the room, suffusing everything and everyone on the dance floor, flowing over him and his pack.

From a hundred feet away, the Wolf King met Michael's eyes, and suddenly he knew that the DJs and the dancers on the floor all beat in time with the Wolf King's heart. He could feel the power drawing him in, feel it reaching out to his pack, urging them to join the beat, to match their hearts in time with his and dance, feeding the Wolf King's power with their own.

A woman in a red Chinese dress came up to the throne from behind, pulling the King's eyes from his, and the feeling passed; Michael's heartbeat was his own again. Holy shit. Mortals weren't allowed to be that powerful, were they? The Wolf King turned back to him, but didn't grab for his mind again. He just nodded and went back to watching the dancers.

Heidi had just gotten ahold of a server when the woman in the red dress came up to them.

"My Master is ready to receive you, now. Please follow me."

"What?"

"You know, I am sure, that the Wolf King interviews every wolf pack that comes into the city."

"I'd heard," he admitted grudgingly.

"Follow me," she said again. "The waitress will know where to bring your drinks."

Feeling less and less comfortable by the moment, Michael gestured for his pack to follow with him. He'd known he wouldn't be top dog, here, but having this little control over the situation made him nervous. He hadn't expected to be railroaded the moment he stepped through the door.

The woman in red led them around the dance floor to a flight of stairs sheltered in the shadows behind the throne, up and through a winding hall of unmarked wooden doors. One of those doors let into a large office with two executive chairs facing the teak desk, behind which sat another throne. There was a brown leather couch to one side, facing an ornately painted wall on the other.

The left panel of the wall depicted a blasted black wasteland with a red-gold, hermaphroditic goat-horned figure overlooking scenes of people doing great evil; the right panel showed acts of love and kindness watched over by a smilingly serene woman, like the portraits of Mother Mary he'd seen in his youth, except that she was naked and blue. The panel in the middle, although less active, was even stranger: a sword driven into the ground, towering over a field like a great cross; to one side, cast in night, a man hung from a tree while his ghost ascended into the sky; in the opposite corner a man came out of a cave, glowing to match the sun rising above him, mocked by a demonic figure while a woman watched them from atop the cave. A crucifix hung above the couch.

"The triptych is beautiful isn't it?" the Wolf King asked as he came in from behind his throne.

"What? The painting? It's interesting, I'll give it that."

"It represents the three aspects of the Lazarite faith. Each set of figures to the sides represents a sacrament or a blasphemy. The center panel depicts the core mystery."

Michael almost said 'religious folks are crazy', but, as he turned to look at the King, he saw that the small man was wearing a jeweled crucifix as a tie tack. It was too fancy just to be for scaring off vampires.

Michael gave him a slow once-over. The Wolf-King's suit was the precise same golden-brown as his hair, which he wore slicked back from his forehead. A diamond sparkled in his left ear to match the gems on his fingers. In person, his presence was not so great as it had seemed on his throne, though he did not seem so quite so small without his gigantic guards towering to either side of him. Maybe the chair was magic, or the floor enchanted. Although he smelled clearly of werewolf, and Michael could see the Mark shining clearly in the Wolf King's eyes, he did not smell like enough power to have affected everyone in the club the way he had.

The Wolf King might or might not have the personal power the rumors claimed, Michael decided, but he had the loyalty of every monster from here to the door and there wasn't going to be any getting out alive if it came to a fight.

"Sit," said the Wolf King.

They did.

Michael and Hugh took the big chairs, leaving Caleb and Heidi the couch. Caleb settled himself against the right arm of the couch with a lazy ease – more ease, Michael observed, than in the presence of the Monster – his white teeth flashing a smirk in his brown face, an idle hand pulling his bobbing black ringlets of hair back from his eyes. Heidi sat as far from Caleb as she could manage, trying to watch both him and the King at the same time.

"Welcome to my court," said the man behind the desk. "I am David Hower, the Wolf King of Kansas City."

"Michael, boss of the Fifth Street Devil's Club. My second, Big Hugh; my shaman, Caleb; my girl, Heidi."

"Welcome, Lord Michael, Masters Hugh and Caleb, and Ms. Heidi of the Fifth Street Devil's Club." Their names sounded strange when he said them so formally.

There was a light tap at the door. The Wolf King gave no signal that Michael could see, but a waitress came in with their drinks, then vanished.

"Now," the Wolf King continued, "although it pains me, I must bring us to business with unseemly haste. You must accept my apologies, but your arrival is ill-timed. I have another appointment tonight which is quite pressing. Please, is it business or pleasure that has brought you to my city?"

For a moment, he thought about lying, and the Wolf King's eyes went hard. The power in them welled back up. For a moment, Michael thought he wasn't going to have the chance to answer, "Business."

"Ah. I see," he looked them all over again. "I assume this is not the entirety of your pack?"

This conversation was not going in a direction he was comfortable with, but the Wolf King was too powerful, his Mark too overwhelming. It was hard for Michael to hold his gaze and harder still to avoid his questions. Whenever he even began to think of lying or evading, the Wolf King's power would flare and his eyes would begin to fade from pleasant, smiling brown to hard gold.

His first impulse was to brag, to exaggerate the size and strength of his pack. His second impulse was to play it the other way, to deny that there were any others. His chest tightened. It was hard to force words past his lips. When he

38

finally succeeded, the words that came were not the ones he had intended.

"No," he said. "The rest are out on the town."

"Michael of the Fifth Street Devils Club," the Wolf King said, "please, do not attempt to evade me. What are you and your pack doing in my kingdom?"

"We're looking for an apprentice for Caleb," he said, before something else could come out. "Seer told us to find her here."

"You were seen riding into town with the Monster, so the seer must be Django Bones."

"Yeah."

The Wolf King's eyes narrowed and a low growl escaped his lips.

"Tend to your business as quickly as possible, Michael of the Fifth Street Devil's Club. It would be terrible for all involved if the Monster were to have time to grow bored here in my city. It would be more terrible still if you, yourselves, were to disturb my peace."

He let the silence lie, pregnant with threat. Any other werewolf, even so far from his own home, Michael would have attacked for the insult. But he knew who would win. Looking into those ever-more-golden eyes, Michael realized that the Wolf King, alone and without his entourage, could devour his entire pack.

"Now, what tribute have you brought me?"

Suddenly they were back on ground that Michael understood. He looked over to Heidi. The girl stood, five-foot-two balanced on boots with five inch heels, dressed in ratty jean shorts and her club jacket, over a half-shredded fishnet bodysuit and nothing else. Bleached blond hair hung low down her shoulders and in front of her eyes. She swished over to the desk, nervous, but more afraid of him and Caleb than of the Wolf King.

"For you to play with while we're in the neighborhood."

Heidi made it as far as half way around the desk, then stopped when she met the Wolf King's eyes.

"How... traditional," the Wolf King said slowly, looking her up and down from her delicate triangular face to her small, boyish breasts, and down her skinny legs. For a moment, he thought the Wolf King would refuse his tribute and that there was going to be war, but just when the silence had drawn out too long, the door opened behind them and the Wolf King said: "May will see you out. Come back for your girl when you leave town. Do not bring the Monster."

Animals

They must have been making out on the couch when he
knocked. That was the most reasonable explanation for
Alexander's tousled hair and the smirk he was wearing when he
finally opened the door.

"Got time for the candy man," Dominic asked with a
smirk of his own, "or are you ... busy?"

"I don't know what you're talking about," the other boy
said, his smile dialing up to a shit-eating grin. Alexander stood
about four inches shorter than Dominic, but he was just as wide
at the shoulders, and as dark as Dominic was pale. Dixon was a
born athlete and, from what Dominic had heard, there was no
doubt that Alexander could fight. He also had the lovely habit
of running around in shorts and tank tops that did everything
to show off the rippling muscles of his arms and legs. Dominic
could have lived without the violence, but Alexander was
straight, and it was silly to be too picky about your eye-candy.

Dominic followed Alexander into the living room, where
Amber was in her usual position: lounging across the love seat
with her head resting on one arm and her legs hanging off the
other side. Alex fished a wad of bills from his pocket and traded
them for the dime bags in Dominic's, then settled himself
against Amber's legs rather than taking his own traditional seat
in the recliner. Dominic relaxed into the abandoned throne.

"Where's Charlie?" Dominic asked while the other boy
examined and consolidated the contents of the bags.

"Staying at her friend Lisa's house, like she usually does
when our 'rents are out of town."

"Cool."

Satisfied with his purchase, Alexander fished a black
DARE Frisbee from under the couch and a pack of Zig-Zags
from his pocket and went about rolling them a pair of joints.
Dominic didn't bother to criticize his technique: Alexander
would either get the hang of it eventually or give in and buy a
rolling machine. Or a pipe.

While he worked, Amber pulled her legs out from where they were squished between Alexander's back and the couch and settled them across his lap, forcing him to balance the improvised tray on her knees.

"Shall we walk?" Alexander asked, holding up a pair of reefers. They were a little bent and twisted, but they did look better than the last set.

"Absolutely."

"Let's go to the creek this time," Amber suggested.

"Sounds like a plan," Dom said with a shrug.

The bikers were staring at her. Five of them, three men and two women, dressed head-to-toe in leather. Spikes stuck out from their clothes and faces at all angles. They ate steaks, and empty beer bottles covered most of their table. They had been staring at her since she and Anthony had first walked through the door an hour ago and she'd been staring back for the last twenty minutes. Anthony Domiano was so busy staring at her chest that he still hadn't noticed.

"...and then", he went on, "there was the time José and I jumped that little rat Mathews in the locker room with a coupl'a wet towels. Hadn't actually heard anyone scream like a little girl before."

His idea of conversation had begun with long-winded accounts of his victories on the track and football teams. Around fifteen minutes ago it had moved to the various ways he, José Martinez, and Richard Wailings enjoyed tormenting those smaller and weaker than they.

'I bet those bikers could teach him a thing or two about violence,' Margaret caught herself thinking, much to her own shame.

"My youth minister says that devil worship is on the rise, and we need to be careful. Some of the girls on the squad say there's a coven in the school, and I think that faggot Pohl is the head warlock or whatever."

42

'*Heaven help me,*' she thought, '*now he's moved on to religion.*' She was Christian, too, but the deepening conservatism of the local Evangelicals frightened her. What part of 'judge not' didn't they understand?

With the bikers, but sitting a little to the side, was a tall, pale man whose shining black hair hung down past his waist. He was dressed in black silk and velvet, with knee-high boots of gleaming polished leather. He was beautiful instead of handsome; Margaret's friend Andrea would have called him 'bishonen'. To Margaret he somehow seemed the most terrifying of them all.

"Hey, baby, are you are you going to eat the rest of that?"

Had he really just called her 'baby'?

"No, I'm ready to go when you are." Her appetite was quite dead, thank you very much. The steak was good, she'd give it that, but she'd never come back. She'd also never speak to Domiano again, much less go on another date. Her interest in the male sex as a whole might be in the morgue. She endured his continued stares and those of the leather-clad criminals across the room, and when he was done with her ribs and the beer the waiter had forgotten to card him for, she was more than glad to be on her way. The bikers' eyes followed her out the door.

He went on parroting his youth minister's paranoid delusions about satanic cults and the homosexual agenda as they took a city road out of the Bottoms and back on to I-70 West, barely pausing for breath during the forty-minute drive home. Although there were no lights behind them, she imagined that she could hear the roar of motorcycle engines over the grumbling of Anthony's pickup truck. Anthony dropped her off at her doorstep, a mile and a half east of Lawrence proper.

"You should really come to church with me, tomorrow, Mara," he was insisting for the third time since getting back in his truck. "Reverend Baker gives very moving sermons."

"No, Anthony. I always go with my family, and this weekend is my brother's birthday."

"Oh. Are you sure?"

"Anthony," she said, gentle but firm. "Don't push." For a moment she was afraid he would to try for a goodnight kiss, so she hurried to let herself out of the truck.

"Goodnight, babe," he called to her as he drove off. For a second, as his headlights passed over the trees that hid her yard from the county road she thought she saw a gleam of chrome, and when the sound of his truck was gone she could hear the low rumble of motorcycle engines clearly. Margaret wasted no time fleeing to the safety of her parents' house.

———————

Dominic sat in the big leather chair across the coffee table, looking like he was trying not to pass out. Alexander lounged on the couch, enjoying his high and the feel of Amber's head resting on his chest. Unconsciousness might not be too far away for him, either. With his parents out of town and his sister at a friend's house, fading out right here wasn't going to be a problem. Amber made her happy-kitty noise and snuggled closer against him.

"Well, guys," Dominic said in that slow, careful way of the very stoned. "I think it's time for me to fly."

"Drive safe," Amber admonished him just as slowly.

"Yeah," Alexander added. "Don't get dead."

Dominic Richardson visibly gathered himself, checked himself for wallet, watch, and keys, and strode out the door with a look of determination on his face. They started laughing as soon as the door closed behind him

"Did you see that face?" Amber giggled.

"Dom makes the best faces," Alex agreed, wheezing with laughter.

"Especially when he's high."

When the giggles finally faded, Alexander Dixon grunted and pulled himself out from under her as gently as he could. She grumbled a little, but let him get up to lock the door and put away the paraphernalia.

"Coffee or sleep," he asked, glancing at the clock. It wasn't even midnight.

"Coffee," Amber purred as she stretched. Alexander knew she didn't do it solely for his benefit, but he sure enjoyed the view she presented on his way to the kitchen. This new bag was a little more potent than he was used to; the familiar ritual of grinding and starting the coffee helped bring him back down to earth.

He perched himself on one of the bar stools that hovered around the central island. Amber plastered herself to his side, playing with his hair and fingering the edge of the shirt. He didn't usually like to be touched, but he was getting used to it. By the time the coffee was done perking, he could almost string two thoughts together.

Alexander disentangled himself from Amber to get their coffees.

"Alex," Amber asked as he pulled a pair of novelty mugs from the cabinet, "Why don't you ever come to the pagan group meetings?"

He sighed.

"Because I don't want to deal with the shit everybody gives the rest of you."

She scowled at him.

"Alex," she said, "that's cowardly."

"No," he said, pouring their coffee with slow, stoned deliberation, "it's practical."

She crossed her arms and stared hard at his back.

"Besides," he reminded her, handing her the purple leopard print mug, "I'm agnostic at best."

His own mug was black with a yellow cartoon smiley face.

"But," Amber insisted, "you believe in the magic."

"Sort of," he said, hiding behind his coffee. "I believe in *ki*. But not the Goddess or the Law of Three."

She sighed, and slurped her own coffee.

"Please," she said. "Just for me? Just this once?"

"Alright, alright. I'll come."

"Thank you," she sang, pressing herself against him again.

"But not this Monday," Alexander blurted. "I have to test for my next rank at the dojo."

"Oh."

"I promise I will come next week. That's when you do your full moon thing, yeah?"

"The ritual's Saturday. Your sister's thing is that night."

"Oh, right. Her exhibition. Damn."

"But we'll talk about it the Monday after."

"I promise."

Somehow, Dominic made it home without drawing any police attention. The marijuana haze rendered the county roads surreal, and he devoted all that remained of his wits to staying in his lane. It was a pretty good bag. Once back within city limits, he was more comfortable; he knew all the unwatched side-streets back to his house. He managed to park his car so his parents wouldn't know how fucked up he'd been and made it up the back stairs to his balcony without falling to his death.

Aaron was waiting for him on the bench by the door, staring sullenly into the sky, arms stretched over the back of the bench with a cigarette held loosely in his right hand. His left leg was crossed casually over his right, pulling the fabric of his pants just tight enough to emphasize the bulge of his crotch. The moonlight gave his pale skin an ethereal glow and made his hair a cascade of shadow across his face. Unlike anyone else Dominic had ever known, the moonlight brought out Aaron's aura: shimmering silver, except for the pale green of life at his core and the tendrils of ghostly white that wove through him and tasted like a graveyard.

'Fuck,' he thought, 'I am way too high to deal with this.'

"What's up, man?"

"We haven't talked since Thursday," Aaron said, eyes fixed heavenward. "I wanted to apologize."

Dominic waited. He knew Aaron far too well to accept that as the apology. After a few moments of silence, the other boy rose gracefully and glided over to Dominic, stopping just far

46

enough away that he couldn't feel Aaron's breath on his face, and meeting his eyes with that seductive, hypnotic way he had when he wanted something. Dom held the gaze, trying not to let it have its intended effect, but he knew he was lost when Aaron leaned in and, placing his hands on Dominic's hips, whispered in his ear: "I'm sorry I've been so angry since I heard about Amber and Alex. I know Alex is your friend."

"I thought we broke up."

"When do I ever mean it?" Aaron asked, pressing himself against Dominic's body.

"Every single time," he said, giving up and leaning into the embrace. "Maybe more."

SUNDAY, AUGUST 30TH

The howls came from every direction, from near and far. They weren't the high, chattery wailings of a coyote – Grandpa had taught her to recognize that sound when she was little – or the familiar, sporadic calls of her neighbor's dogs. They were deeper, throaty, intertwining.

Closing the windows did not close them out. They called to her, somehow, a force that tried to draw her up out of her bed and into the night.

There were a half-dozen voices among them, at least, and they continued without pause until nearly three in the morning, when the noise ceased abruptly. The howls didn't fade off into the distance, didn't lose voices one by one. At exactly 2:45 the howls stopped, like they had all realized they had somewhere else to be.

Four hours later, she was in her Sunday best and piling into the family car, then on her way to church. Her brothers were squeezed into the back seat beside her and trying to wrestle each other out of their seat belts and onto the floor, as usual. Brian Junior and little Paul weren't doing their sex any favors in her eyes: they should both be old enough to sit quietly on a Sunday, at least. Her parents didn't seem to notice that she wasn't her usual cheery self. Maybe the howling had kept them up, too.

The Holy Cross Lutheran Church was an immense building of white stone walls, glass windows, and pale concrete accents. Shining steel crosses, mounted on marble stands in the yard, halfway between the wrought iron gate and the front door, stood guard over Pastor Mary's gardens. Usually just being in sight of the building was deeply comforting. Here, Margaret felt personally sheltered by God's hand.

Today, though, she had the frightening impression of being watched from the shadows. Movement flickered in the corner of her vision, something dashing down the garden path. A shadow on four legs, with gleaming green eyes. A dog? A wolf? It was too big to be either. Doyle's line came to mind, as always in Grandpa's voice: '...*an enormous coal-black hound, but not such a hound as mortal eyes have ever seen ... its eyes glowed with a smoldering glare.*'

She shook her head, tried to convince herself it was just the lack of sleep.

Her father liked to arrive to services early. It gave him the chance to talk to the pastor by himself, sometimes. It let him see who else liked to show up really early, and who liked to show up at the last minute. His own little social experiment, he'd told her. The usual crowd of elders and pillars was waiting: the widow Mrs. Pennington, who'd been coming every Sunday without fail since she was sixteen; John Stamen, who saw himself as the unofficial leader of the congregation; the Gundersons, who liked to talk about the good old days when the rites were in Latin and the sermon in German; Samuel Royce, who was endlessly agitating for the church to join the Missouri Synod and give up their support for women's ordination and the inclusion of gay men and lesbians.

Standing near the pulpit, speaking to the pastor, was a man Margaret had never seen before. Pastor Mary left him to make her rounds as the last-minute wave began, but Margaret's eyes stayed on the stranger. He was of middling height and build. His robes were elaborate, with a hood and a stole, two overlapping sashes, and three layers of cape, but unadorned by

48

jewels or embroidery. Curling sidelocks and a long ponytail poured out from under a skullcap, his hands were hidden in black gloves. He had a sharp square nose, and his skin was golden-brown and weathered. His beard was close-cropped and, like his hair, beginning to go steel gray.

"My children, my friends," Pastor Mary began when the last stragglers had settled in. The man hovered a few feet behind her. "I'm surprised and pleased to tell you that we'll be having a guest speaker here, today. I studied under him at seminary, and he's touring the country talking about the dangers of fundamentalism. Please, everyone, Father Joshua Owen Masters."

As he stepped to the pulpit Margaret was struck by his charisma, his presence. When he placed his hands on the podium the silence was complete. People even seemed to have stopped breathing. With his eyes alone he captured and held that dead silence for several long seconds.

"Welcome, faithful children, to this house of God." His words, although softly spoken, filled the room. People started breathing again. "I have come to speak to you of an unpopular and uncomfortable subject. Fundamentalist religion is on the rise in today's world, and with it yet another resurgence in the belief that we are on the very brink of the Last Days. The Battle of Armageddon approaches, they cry. See how the world wallows in sin. See all these strange people with their strange ways invading our country. See our children turning away from Christ to practice witchcraft and homosexuality. They scream at us: 'The world will end tomorrow!'"

His voice rose slowly, at first, but the last five words came out in a full-throated roar that echoed in the silence that followed them. Margaret's heart raced, and she caught herself raising her hand to her chest.

"What people really mean, however," Masters continued, once more calm, "when they speak of the end of the world, is the end of the world as they know it. Fear of change, fear of the new and different are the very root of fundamentalist thought."

His eyes roved over the crowd as he spoke, and he gestured with ever-increasing fervor.

"The modern conservative Christian, based on his equally weak grasp of Biblical and historical truths, has come to the conclusion that he knows which passages in this arcane and labyrinthine tome –" here he raised, one handed, the huge Bible that Pastor Mary kept on display at the pulpit – "that God 'really meant'. They quote quite selectively from Leviticus and other books to prove their points, but in their examination of the fine print they miss the major passages."

Margaret sighed, relieved. Masters' words, so directly counter to Anthony Domiano's ranting last night, resonated with her deeply. Would he speak of the covenants? Of Grace? Though it was silly and vain to think so, so far the sermon felt as though it had been written for her personally.

"The world – God's world, shaped by His hand – is far from over. But dark times are, indeed, coming. You, the faithful, must be vigilant." Now she felt betrayed. How could he speak of dark times coming, now, after having condemned conservatives for their cries of prophetic doom? "The comfort of your lives has made you complacent, and you cannot see the signs of the times... or even the writing on the wall."

Increasingly animated throughout the sermon so far, now Masters stilled behind the pulpit, raising to his full if modest height, and stared directly at Margaret as he spoke.

"Wolves stalk outside walls of this very house, lying in wait for one of your own, but you cannot see them because you are blinded by the modern world. You see what you expect to see and in the name of your holiness and your sanity, you deny the evidence of your eyes and ears."

'Wolves?' A chill ran down her spine, and it was almost as if she could hear them howling in that very moment. The intensity of his gaze conjured that of the bikers at the restaurant last night, and the terrible pale man who had sat among them. Then he turned his attention to the congregation as a whole, addressing them, perhaps, for the first time.

"In the coming years, much of what we hold as truth will be proved heresy, and much of what we believed heresy will be revealed as truth. Christianity will be sorely tested in the decade to come, as the worst of our brothers escalate their war

50

against the world. If you are to survive the dark times ahead, you must be true to your faith and true to yourselves, but you must not let the truth blind you to what must be done and who your allies must be."

———————————

It was the second time Amber had awoken in Alexander's bed, and she found it only marginally less disorienting than the first. One wall, hidden behind a thick blue curtain that cast the entire room in a strange light, was nothing but windows; the opposite wall was an elaborately decorated bookshelf, half full of books, papers, statues and figurines. The other two were white, with pale wood paneling that came up almost to her waist. The bed sat in the middle of the room, at least ten feet of floor lay between the edge of the mattress and any given wall, and the waxed hardwood floor was protected from the furnishings by several large, red, mock-Persian rugs. It was hard to think of a starker contrast to the closet-sized room she had in her mother's apartment.

Alexander was on the floor, doing push-ups. It was his moving that had woke her.

"Do you do that every morning," she asked after watching him for several minutes, "or just on the weekends?"

"Every day," he told her as he switched to sit-ups. "My body, my temple."

"Wow. I didn't realize." He wasn't wearing anything but the boxer shorts he'd gone to bed in, so she took the opportunity to really admire the way the muscles played under his skin. "You don't preach like most health nuts."

"If I were a real health nut," he grunted at her between reps, "I wouldn't smoke pot."

She didn't count, but he must have done a hundred before he switched again, now to stretches. She wondered if he knew what effect he was having on her. Alexander was almost too muscular for Amber's taste, but watching his body move and flex as a faint sweat beaded on his brow...

51

'Is it getting hot in here, or is that just me?' His skin was dark and smooth, a warm sepia color and almost hairless below the neck except for a narrow trail of glossy black hair from his belly button to under his boxers, so she had an almost unobstructed view. For a second, as he finished his final stretch, she thought the boxers were going to give up the last of his secrets, but he bent too far forward, and she was robbed.

Margaret stumbled away from the sermon, unable to shake the strange and unsettling feeling that it had been meant for her. What could that possibly have meant? What could any of it have meant? Dark times are coming... heresy revealed as truth. Pastor Mary had never brought in such a frightening speaker before, but the way she introduced him... there was no mistaking the awe in her voice. Who was he? She had introduced him as "Father", a title largely reserved for Catholic priests. Why was he preaching here, in Kansas, among Lutherans?

There was a bench in the garden where she liked to sit and pray, and she found herself there without having really thought about it. One of the great crosses cast its shadow at her feet, but the symbol of her Lord didn't offer its usual comfort. Her heart was still racing and her mind kept jumping back and forth between the preacher's words and the howls that had kept her up last night. It was insane, of course. There were no wolves in Kansas. But today, neither her rational mind nor her faith could drive back her fear.

"Our Father, who is in heaven," she began, trying to calm herself with the familiar Lord's Prayer. "Hallowed be your name..."

She didn't have the chance to finish. A snarl came from the bushes in front of her, drawing Margaret's attention, and a great black dog stepped out only a few feet away. The dog was bigger than any dog she'd ever seen before, or even heard of. Its eyes were gold and held a haunting, almost human awareness. It lunged. She screamed, holding her hands up to guard her face.

It knocked her backward off the bench. It caught her arm in its maw and crushed it effortlessly. She screamed. Why would no one help her? The dog savagely shook her broken arm and the pain almost drove her into oblivion. The only thing holding her to consciousness was the malignant light in those golden eyes. She could not look away.

Jennifer was walking toward Margaret when the dog struck. She froze in horror as blood sprayed and Margaret began to scream. The monstrous canine was almost the size of a person and, to Jennifer's dismay, it seemed that the entire congregation was as frozen as she was. Margaret's family had gone white with fear, and her brothers were screaming, too. A few of the elders fainted, and almost everyone else wore dead masks of shock and horror she knew matched her own. A few, herself included, managed faltering steps in Margaret's direction, but no one seemed to know exactly what to do.

Only the guest preacher, Masters, stood calmly: his face was frightening and cold beside Pastor Mary's ashen horror.

"Help," Margaret managed to choke out at last, "Oh, God, someone help me, please!"

From where she stood, trembling, Jennifer could clearly see both Margaret and Father Masters, and in the liquid crystal slow motion that had begun the moment Margaret first screamed, she saw his face change from cold to what she could only describe as ... ecstatic. Radiant. She felt a presence, again, as she had when he had spoken at the pulpit, but she did not see him move. Without passing the twenty yards between the door where he and Pastor Mary stood and the shadow of the cross where Margaret lay screaming under the beast, he was suddenly at her side. The skirts of his robes billowed and his long hair streamed back as if a great wind had risen around him and she saw the flash of silver spurs on his heels as the square-toed motorcycle boot slammed into the dog with a savagery to match its own, lifting it a good three feet off the ground.

"Back, beast!" the Father commanded in a ringing tone that carried even more power than that with which he had mounted the pulpit. From nowhere she could see, a long knife appeared in his hand. "Back!"

Miraculously, the dog let Margaret go, turning and running from another kick and leaping over the six-foot-tall stone wall that surrounded the church.

Time returned to its normal pace. Sound returned to the world. Suddenly there was chaos. Half the congregation was screaming. Hopefully someone was calling 911, but Jennifer's brain simply shut down.

This wasn't happening. It was impossible. Dogs that big didn't exist and old preachers could not run faster than she could see, much less kick said impossible dog hard enough to lift it off the ground. Said old preacher did not wear motorcycle boots and carry a Bowie knife, and no one wore spurs in this day and age!

More time must have passed than she realized, and someone must have had their head on straight, because the sound of sirens filled the air and Jennifer could move again. She wanted to go comfort Margaret, see if she was even awake, but a crowd had surrounded her while Jennifer stood in shock.

Consequences

Alexander dropped Amber off outside the apartment at quarter of eight, kissing her goodbye quickly before speeding off to his aikido meditation class. She clambered up the stairs as quietly as she could, ever conscious that the walls blocked sound like thin waxed paper. Holding her breath, she turned her key in the lock with practiced stealth. Slipping inside, she held the knob and leaned on the frame to muffle the sound of the latch before silently depositing her shoes in the rack by the door.

Her mother's work boots were in their place on top of the rack; at least they hadn't kept her late today. It had been a good enough job until they'd put her on third shift for complaining about the other manager's sexual harassment of several employees.

Rebecca Lee was waiting up for her. She was still in her work uniform, rumpled and sweat-stained, her face slack with exhaustion and stress lines crinkling her eyes at the corners.

"So, was Alex staying the night at Jennifer's house, too?"

Amber flinched. She was caught: red handed, dead to rights. Grounded for life.

"Do you have anything to say for yourself?"

"Well, you see, when you pour hot water on Jen she turns into Alex..."

'Baleful' wasn't really adequate to describe her mother's glare.

"I should have known this was going to happen the first time you came home smelling like pot."

"You knew?" Amber demanded, shocked. Then: "Wait, how do you know what weed smells like?"

"How do you think you happened," her mother snapped, then sighed. After a pause she said, still angry but calmer, "You realize I'm more disappointed in you for lying to me than for sleeping with him, right?"

"We didn't...."

Her mother's tone went back to cold and sharp: "So you're telling me you slept on the couch?"

"Well, no..."

"But you haven't had sex yet?" Her mother sounded a little hopeful, but mostly skeptical.

"No!"

Rebecca shrank back into her chair, the righteous wrath going out of her with heavy, tired sigh.

"Well, that's something at least. You're thinking about it, though?"

"Yes," Amber squeaked, ducking her head and blushing down to well below her neckline.

"Oh, God, Amber. I know you're getting high, you have this crazy witchcraft thing I don't understand, and now you're thinking about having sex? Can't you learn from at least some of my mistakes?"

"Oh," Amber demanded bitterly, "so now you're saying I'm a mistake, again?"

"Yes! That doesn't mean I don't love you – I do! I love you more than anything else in this stupid, shitty world – but, yes! Getting pregnant when I was seventeen – your age, Amber, think about it! – was a mistake that destroyed every dream I had!"

Amber wanted to have a witty comeback, a biting retort, but she couldn't choke anything past the sob welling up in her throat.

"I'm not telling you never to have sex," Her mother looked at her with pleading eyes. "You are old enough to make that decision, I suppose, and too old for me to teach you anything you're not willing to learn, but... Please, please, please! ... Don't be stupid about it?"

"Mom?"

"I'm not saying I condone any of it," Rebecca said, her face hot, her finger raised. "But you're old enough to make your own decisions. Just, please... I love you so much, and we're not doing that badly, but... I was higher than a kite and way too young when I got pregnant with you, and I've never seen your father since. Don't fuck up like I did. We're barely making it right now, and I don't have anyone to help support you like your grandparents do us. Don't throw your life away."

LIBER DOMINICI VOL.III SUN 30 AUG 1998
He slipped out while I was asleep.

Of course.

At least this time I didn't make a liar out of him again by making him promise to stay. He says he's not allowed to stay out all night. I might believe that if he ever hesitated, even a little bit, to stay out late.

I don't know if it's worse when he leaves while I'm sleeping, or if it's worse when he doesn't even wait—just takes what he wants, then leaves while I'm still cuddling.

Why do I put up with this shit?

Is it just because he's so damned pretty? Because he's the only cock-loving Goth I know? Because he's the only Pagan my age who can keep up with me in ritual?

I used to love him so much. I thought he loved me, too. We've done things together that I've never even read about. Our synchronicity was so strong last year that we started sharing dreams without even trying. But he just keeps getting colder and colder. I can see less and less of his aura.

I still love him.

But that's not enough.

I'm done with this shit.

Fucking done.

TUESDAY, SEPTEMBER 1ST
Margaret awoke to the rhythmic electronic noise of a heart monitor. She'd never heard it before in the real world, but anyone with a television would have recognized it. She was lying on her back, propped half-up by the uncomfortable cushions of the hospital bed, with tubes and wires trailing from her right arm and a strange dead weight holding down her left.

All of her hurt, just a little bit, and the world was fuzzy around the edges. Outside her room, she could hear two men talking.

"So, what do you figure really got her?"

"Don't know, but it weren't no dog, that's for sure."

"That's for sure. Ain't no dog alive can bite through a person's arm like that. Both bones, sliced clean like a knife."

"Girl's lucky to still have her arm."

A nurse shooed them away but didn't check on her. She was left with the electronic monitor noises and her own fuzzy, confused thoughts. She did remember a dog, vaguely, if a dog could have the Devil's eyes. Those eyes were all she could remember, besides the pain, shining like golden lanterns of evil. She was so thoroughly drugged that she could barely move her head, and no other part of her body even tried to respond to her pleas.

There was no television, no radio... nothing to distract her from the moaning of people on the other side of her curtained 'privacy' and the rhythmic noises of her various monitors and drips. She lay there for what felt like forever, staring at the ceiling and hoping that something – almost anything – would come to distract her from her drug-fuzzed view of the lights and her increasingly clear memory of what had happened.

She didn't want to remember. The sermon, the demon-dog. The pain and the blood. The nightmares of dying and killing that had woken her.

Eventually, a nurse came.

"You're not supposed to be awake yet," the woman said, giving Margaret a tired side-eye while she changed the IV bag and checked the machinery.

"I can't move," she whispered. "Could you turn the TV on for me please?"

"I'm sorry," the nurse said. She didn't sound it. She looked at Margaret with a sort of suspicion. "This is the IC unit, there's no television. I'm going to get a doctor to check on you. Are you in any pain?"

"No. Everything's fuzzy."

"Good, that's the morphine. It should be keeping you asleep. I'll be right back with a doctor."

———————

THURSDAY, SEPTEMBER 3RD

The day hadn't been a good one so far, not by any stretch of the imagination. Dominic still wasn't talking to him. He had given Aaron a brief lecture about "making up his damn mind" before storming off. Last semester Aaron would have spent the day looking forward to make-up sex after school, but this time Dominic might have actually meant it. His mind had been in all the wrong places, and he was pretty sure that he'd bombed his third hour math test. Only math, and only the first test of the year, but...

The waxing moon had his skin itching with power, making it even harder to think, harder to keep his mind where it belonged. Anywhere but his relationship with Dominic. It happened every month: the closer the moon came to full, the more clouded his senses got and the harder it was to think about anything.

Dominic said he needed to learn to ground almost as badly as Jacob, but it was only a problem for two or three days before the full moon, so Aaron dismissed it as that much more of Dominic's "I've been at this since I could walk" bullshit. Being raised pagan didn't make Dominic an expert on anything but his mother's coven. It sure as fuck didn't give him the right to tell Aaron and Jacob how to work their magic. Even if it probably would be for the best if Jacob, at least, listened. His own gifts, on the other hand, had never hurt him, so he couldn't be fucking up as bad as Mr. Experience liked to imply.

Grumbling silently to himself, he dropped his math book in his locker, trading it for AP chemistry and his lunch. He slammed the locker closed, and something slammed into him from behind, mashing his face into the unforgiving metal surface.

"What'cha doing, faggot?" came the mocking voice from behind him as he slid slowly to his knees. "Lose your balance?"

His head rang from the impact, but he was not going to take this lying down. Using the wall of lockers for support, Aaron got back to his feet and turned to face Anthony Domiano's familiar smirk. José Martinez and Richard Wailings, his ever-present goons, held Anthony's flanks secure but they didn't look like they were going to join in today. They would, however, stop Aaron if he tried to run. No chance of anyone intervening, of course. Probably not even the teachers, unless Anthony got rougher than usual.

"Fuck off, Tony," Aaron spat. "Don't you have anything better to do? Torture kittens, maybe? Pull the wings off of flies?"

"Nope," said Anthony. A quick boxer's jab slammed into Aaron's ribs and knocked him back against the lockers with an echoing crash. "Beating the faggot out of you is God's good work."

The next punch hit him in the gut, left him coughing and sputtering on the floor until Anthony dragged him back to his feet just to throw him back against the lockers.

"You can't beat it out of someone, Tony," Aaron said, coughing. Not that being rational ever did any good. "You're just born a certain way."

"Not what my minister says," Anthony countered, raising his fist for a good right hook. Aaron turned away, braced himself for the punch, but it never came. Instead, Anthony's face smashed into the locker beside him, hard enough to dent the door and make a crash that they probably heard up in the principal's office. Anthony tried to struggle back to his feet, but José landed on top of him before he had the chance.

"This is the second time this week, Tony," came the hated sound of Alexander Dixon's voice. "You have a shallow fucking learning curve."

Aaron looked up from the tangled pile of Anthony and José. Alexander was standing, posed, where Tony had been a moment ago. Richard Wailings was watching him nervously, one hand cocked back, but looking at his fallen friends out of the corner of his eye.

"You want some, too, Richie?" Alexander asked.

"Who appointed you lord and fucking master, huh," demanded Anthony.

Alexander laughed as Anthony and José found their feet.

"Same to you, Tony," he said. "Because if you really think you're doing God's work, you're even dumber than you look."

"Is there a problem here, boys?" Long after there was any need for him, Vice Principal Grant chose to make his appearance. He knew what was going on, of course. He had to, unless he was even more stupid than those shallow, wide-set eyes made him look.

"Of course not, Mr. Grant," Alexander Dixon and Anthony Domiano said in unison without breaking eye contact.

"That's Dr. Grant, boys."

"Of course, Dr. Grant," said Anthony.

"Glad to hear it," the Vice Principal said condescendingly. "I'd hate to have to expel our star football player and the boy who should be our star wrestler."

"When you sponsor a judo team," Alexander said, "I'll play on it."

"Wrestling's an American sport."

"It's Greek, actually."

Dr. Grant's expression darkened, but Alexander was no more afraid of him than he was of Anthony, José, Richard, or anyone else. There were days when it seemed like Alexander Dixon believed that he was invincible. The way his eyes burned with inner fire, Aaron could almost believe it, too. It just made Aaron hate him more.

Dr. Grant waited until Domiano and company had departed before leaving Aaron alone with Alexander.

"Are you all right?" Alexander asked.

"I don't want your help," Aaron hissed. "I've never wanted your help."

Alexander sighed, and in that happy moment before the invincible mask fell back into place, Aaron could see he'd really hurt the other boy.

"If you ever thought it was just about you, you're even dumber than Grant and Martinez," the shorter boy said, turning on his heel and stalking off.

Harvest Moon

SATURDAY, SEPTEMBER 5TH

Jennifer watched her friends form a circle in the moonlight. Dominic stood over a small altar-table in the center, facing Aaron at the north point, with Jacob standing to his right and Amber to his left. They had placed bamboo torches to light the cross-quarters. A small fire burned in the cauldron on the altar, where it sat between a smoking cluster of incense and a silver goblet of wine. Aaron, Amber, and Jacob each held an unlit taper candle and stood with their heads bowed. Dominic held his hands outstretched, a silver dagger in his right hand and a sickle-looking blade in his left, his own taper tucked into the sash of his skirt. All four were bare-chested and liberally anointed with glitter-laden ceremonial oils that gleamed and sparkled in the torchlight.

"Behold," Dominic cried, his voice echoing across the lake. "We gather to honor the fullness of the Moon. Blessed is She, the eye of our Goddess, and blessed are we in Her light and Her love."

He knelt to the altar, trading his sickle for a few sticks of the incense, then stepped back from the center so that he was just a little farther from the altar than the others. Facing outward, he waved the incense back and forth three times then thrust the dagger through the tendrils of smoke. He walked the quarter-circle to stand behind Jacob with his right arm outstretched, always pointed directly away from the altar, with a tension in his arm that suggested he was cutting something thicker than just the air.

"Spirits and Powers of the East," said Jacob, his voice barely reaching Jennifer as he lit his candle, "Creatures and beings of Air and intellect, we bid you come to watch and guard our Circle."

When Jacob had finished his invocation, Dominic again waved the incense back and forth, repeated the stabbing motion, and continued walking the circle to stand behind Aaron.

63

"Spirits and Powers of the North," the grim boy called in a commanding tone, lighting his candle with a well-palmed match. "Creatures and beings of Earth and life, we bid you come to watch and guard our Circle."

Jennifer's other friends had often wondered how she could be comfortable even watching such a heathen ritual. They weren't small-minded enough to call it Satanic, at least not to her face. She did have a little trouble explaining it to them, or even herself.

Dominic repeated the incense and dagger motions again, and moved on to stand behind Amber.

"Spirits and Powers of the West," the girl invoked, her voice filled with awe. "Creatures and beings of Water and emotion, we bid you come to watch and guard our Circle."

Another waving of the incense and thrust of the dagger, Dominic completed his trip around the circle.

"Spirits and Powers of the South," he called, voice again echoing over the lake. "Creatures and beings of Fire and passion, we bid you come to watch and guard our Circle."

With a final wave of the incense and thrust of the dagger, Dominic closed the sacred space. Although tonight was not one of them, there were times when Jennifer could almost see the line of their circle, a curtain of nothing that shimmered and curled like a thin wall of mist around their rites.

Sometimes she could even sense a presence like what she felt at church. She had never admitted either of these things to anyone, of course. It was not the presence of her own God, she was certain. Equally shining and benevolent, it was somehow different in tone and texture. She could not explain how that failed to shake her faith.

As usual, she felt obliged to bend her head in her own prayer. She did not pray in words – even the prescribed Lord's Prayer usually felt hypocritically grandiose to her – but simply opened herself to the presence of her Savior. Tonight, as it had for the last week, the 'answer' she felt was different. Jennifer did not suffer the hubris that God spoke to her, but when she prayed she could usually feel an answering warmth, the love of a distant but devoted father. Now, though, it felt like an echo:

faint, but closer. This did not shake her faith, either, but it did confuse her. The dissonance had been particularly strong last Sunday, during Father Masters' sermon and when Margaret had been bitten. The words of Father Masters had been deeply moving to her, and frighteningly prophetic in light of the attack.

As always, Dominic stepped back to the edge of the circle he had drawn. One at a time, each of the others stepped forward to kneel at the altar for a moment before resuming their places at the quarters.

Jacob went first, plucking a square of cloth and two vials of herbs from the grass around the altar. He measured the herbs into a stone mortar and chanted as he ground them with the pestle, then poured the mixture onto the cloth. He added a trinket from his pocket, too small for her to see clearly from where she sat, and bound it all up with a string and a prayer.

Amber went next, poking the brazier to life before sifting a different collection of herbs onto the coals. Jennifer knew what this offering was: Amber always burnt rose, willow, and St. John's wort, asking the Goddess for success in love. Jennifer wondered, '*Doesn't Alex count?*'

When Aaron knelt at the altar, he cut one of his fingers with a small knife and flicked drops of his own blood in each of the four directions and into the brazier. He pulled an airplane bottle from his pocket and offered that to the directions and the fire, as well, and a little more directly onto the ground. He drank what remained and bowed his head for a long moment before returning to his station.

Last, as always, Dominic made his own offerings of herbs, wine, honey, and incense from the collection of vials hidden around the altar. His movements were slow, his gestures meticulous and solemn.

Their private rites and offerings finally complete, Dominic produced a loaf of bread and a wine-sized bottle of beer. He opened the beer, filled the chalice, and passed it and the loaf around the circle. Each of them drank and broke off a chunk of bread before passing on the 'cakes and ale'. Beer and bread went around the circle a half-dozen times, the four witches laughing and talking too quietly for Jennifer to make out a word.

When they had all had their fill of bread and thrown the rest outside the circle as offerings, they finally brought the ritual to a close. Dominic walked the circle in reverse, each of them thanking the elements for their presence and biding them, "go if you must, stay if you will. Merry meet, and merry part, and merry meet again."

Jennifer stood and brushed the grass from her skirt. Grabbing the cooler of un-ceremonial snacks and beverages, she went down to join the others as they migrated to the campfire they'd set up before they started the ritual.

Amber flounced over to join Jennifer just as she was settling onto the waiting picnic blanket. It still embarrassed Jennifer a little to see her friend running around half-naked, although she'd come to enough of these moon rituals that much of her remaining embarrassment was about her own jealousy over Amber's larger breasts. Jennifer wasn't really sure if Amber was a nudist or an exhibitionist – probably the former, since Dominic and Aaron liked boys, right? – but, either way, Jennifer didn't have whatever it took to go running around-half naked, herself. Dominic had said more than once that consideration for her was the only reason he wore clothes out here at all, and Jennifer was half afraid he wasn't joking.

"So, how's my Jen?" Amber asked, reaching into the cooler for the lighter, domestic beers they both preferred.

"Mostly good," Jennifer said, taking the offered bottle and opener. "It's been a long week, though. Three essays, two tests to study for, a book report to write and a chapter of my history book to read."

"You silly AP people. Why work so hard just to lower your GPA?"

"College credit. Pride. And I like working my brain."

Aaron and Jacob were still hanging out by the altar, talking quietly, and Jennifer could see Dominic's pale back retreating into the woods. He always wandered off right after ending the ritual. He said he was meditating, but she figured that what he was really doing was getting high. At least he had the good manners not to do it around the rest of them.

"How about you?"

"Good," Amber answered, lying back on the blanket. "Alex took me out to dinner last night. We went to Fifi's. It was good."

"And school?"

"I hate it. I don't know how I'm going to make it through college."

The land currently known as Cybele Sanctuary had drawn religion to itself for some time. It had been a Baptist camp before converting to pagan use, and it had served some other Christian denomination before that. It had also, Aaron believed, attracted its fair share of Bad Things over the years. The ghosts that always hovered at the edge of their rituals were proof enough of that. They never came to the edge of the Circle: the spirits hovered past the edge of the firelight, just close enough to watch. Just close enough to drink up some of the energy and extend their half-lives. Just enough to become a little more... real.

There were stories about what some of those Bad Things might have been, where some of the ghosts had come from. He'd never heard anything from reliable sources, but there were always rumors. A teenage boy lured out to the land and never heard from again, his car dredged out of the lake. Animal sacrifice and Satanic rituals dating back to before the Baptists got their hands on the land. A mobster hang-out in the '20s. Sexual abuse of children under all the owners. No proof of any of it, but that didn't keep the neighbors from believing everything. The neighbors particularly enjoyed believing all of it now that the land catered to heathens and nudists.

There was a spot, on the north edge of the lake, where spirits and the dead gathered in the greatest numbers. A concrete slab that might once have been a foundation, cracked with age and weather, radiated a subtle sense of unease.

67

Someone had told him, once, that the slab had supported the altar block under the Baptists, and that it had been tipped, cracked, and re-consecrated when the current owners had taken over the land. To Aaron, though, it felt more sealed than consecrated. Standing on top of it, he felt as though he were on the lid of some arcane cage. He liked the feeling. He liked how, standing there, he could see and hear the dead more clearly.

Usually the spirits just babbled and wailed, but they seemed particularly active tonight. Something had them excited, and it wasn't just the ritual he and the others had performed. They were trying to tell him all about it, he realized. They drew even closer, swirling and yammering.

If only he could understand them.

She would never have known the difference in the waking world, but here in the dream she knew that they were not dogs, but wolves. They stalked her night and day, haunting her from the shadows and from beneath parked cars. They called her name as she stumbled through unfamiliar streets of her dreamscape.

"Margaret. Come to us, Margaret. You belong to us now. Margaret...."

She tried to run, but she couldn't escape. The wolves paced her easily, one running circles around her to show his disdain, another emerging from the shadows to follow her casually down the middle of the road. She called out for help, but there was no one in the deserted city to answer her cries.

"You can't run from us, Margaret," they howled, "you're one of us now!"

Every street she turned down, they chased her. Houses blurred by, blocks blurred by, whole cities, and a spark of desperate fury ignited in her belly. It grew as she ran, anger slowly eating away at fear until she seethed with such a rage as she had never felt before. Her heart pounded. She had never been so aware of her own blood. Damn the wolves. Damn them all to hell for tormenting her. How dare they mock her?

She'd tear them limb from limb. She would break their bones
and devour their flesh! Damn them! Damn them all! She
hated them!

The rage, the hatred, the fury… they consumed her flesh
as she ran. Her bones broke and reformed, her muscles
stretched, tore, and healed, and the fury burned brighter until it
consumed everything she was. Her life and her thoughts and
her dreams were stripped away, leaving nothing but the fire and
the rage.

She wanted to share her pain with the world – a world
consisting not of individuals who had somehow wronged her,
but of a great, monstrous and many-faced Them who
threatened her by their very existence.

Presences appeared at the edges of her awareness and
for a moment she moved to attack, before recognizing that they
were somehow familiar. They were like her: burning against
the world.

She found herself running through the woods. The
wolves were no longer chasing her, but running with her.

She was hungry. They would hunt.

SUNDAY, SEPTEMBER 6TH
"I'm free."

Caitlyn had been camped out here for more than a week,
but tonight was the first time she said it aloud. She'd begged
them for almost two years – her handlers, the Elders, and even
the Queen, herself, in one bold moment – to let her out, to let
her go back to a normal life. To leave behind the politics of the
Court and the groves. To set aside the death and the slaughter;
to no longer answer to the Order of Herakles.

At long last they had relented. At long last, she was free.

Last night some kids had been performing their own
ritual to the moon and she'd been tempted to join them.
Instead, though, she had simply sat, as she did now, in the grass

below the Sylvan Grove, and listened to the silver song of their rites. With a little luck, though, she'd encounter them again.

Casting aside all thoughts of the past, all hopes for the future, she stood and looked up at the moon.

She stood in the moonlight at the shore of the lake, below her favorite of the various groves hidden around the trails, and raised her arms up to the moon. She opened herself to the light of the Moon, to the breath of the Air, and the life of the Earth. Fire burned along her spine, as it always did when she worked magic, and she reached out with her mind to quench herself in the cool Water of the lake.

She let it fill every part of her, every cell, every molecule... then let it spill over back into the world, and tried to let it take with it all the hurt she had suffered since the last moon, all the pain she had seen and endured. And last, as she had never before dared, she tried to let it take all of the blood she had spilled and cleanse all the wounds she had taken. She tried to wash herself clean of the last five years, but it wasn't enough. She gathered more, more, always more, trying first to banish it in the Moonlight, then to wash it away with the Water, then scour it with the Earth, and finally sear it away with the Fire of her own soul. For hours she stood there, bathed in the light of the moon and bare to anyone and anything that might pass by, and tried to cleanse herself of the death.

When the sun rose, at last, it found her on her knees, sobbing into her hands, not one drop of blood washed clean.

Secrets and Shame

MONDAY, SEPTEMBER 7TH

The dream had been so vivid, she was surprised to find herself in her bed.

'*Something's wrong.*'

Her whole body tingled with an almost-pleasant ache, like she had spent half the night running instead of sleeping. She had the strangest idea that she could still smell the blood, earth, and grass of the dream, still taste the iron tang of blood in her mouth. The clock projecting onto the ceiling told her that the alarm hadn't yet gone off and wouldn't for another hour.

'*What's out of place?*'

She was naked. Not just naked, but sweaty and dirty. Her hair was matted and tangled, not the in the tidy braid she always wore to bed. Her sheets had been thrown to the floor and she was lying atop the shredded remains of her nightgown.

"What?" Her voice cracked, and her tongue touched something sticky on her teeth and lips. Something thick, smelling of copper and tasting of iron.

Margaret threw herself from her bed into her bathroom to spit the blood from her mouth. Leaning over the sink, she spat and coughed with enough force that she almost threw up.

She stared in horror at the red mess in the sink. For a moment she thought she had coughed the blood up all over her hands, but the blood was dried and caked under her cuticles and nails, and spattered all the way up her forearms. Her reflection in the mirror was even more frightening. Dried blood at the corners of her mouth and dotting the hollows under her eyes. More dried in her hair and in her nose. This time she did throw up.

When she was done, she realized that something else was terribly, impossibly wrong.

Her cast was gone.

Her arm didn't hurt. There was no half-healed wound, no scars. No evidence that it had ever been so badly broken that the doctors had warned she might need titanium splints and that even then she might not ever use it normally again. No evidence that the attack had even happened.

She stumbled into the shower and turned it on full blast, as hot as it would go, letting it pound through her hair and down her body. Painfully hot rivulets made their way down her face and she was afraid it was going to scald the skin from her flesh... almost wanted it to, to be rid of the blood. She grabbed her loofah and scrubbed herself fiercely. Long after it had all washed down the drain, had all been scoured from her hands and her face and her hair, had all been rinsed from her mouth by the too-hot water, she still scrubbed harder and harder, trying to purge herself of even the memory of it. She didn't stop when she'd scrubbed herself raw, or even until several minutes after she'd begun to bleed, when the blaring of her alarm in the other room somehow brought her back to awareness of the world.

Margaret turned the water from hot to cold and collapsed to the floor of her shower stall, sobbing uncontrollably as the water washed her own blood down the drain after the rest.

She would have to turn off the alarm, she realized dimly after a while, before someone came to check on her. Margaret stumbled out of the shower, wrapping herself in her robe with no thought of how she would get the blood out, later, and slammed her hand down on the clock. It crunched and went silent.

'Shit,' she thought. '*How am I going to explain that?*'

She stood there, shaking and staring at the broken clock until she heard a voice at her door.

"Mara, honey," it was her mother, even more chipper than usual, "are you up yet?"

"Getting dressed, Mom," she said listlessly.

"Alright, but your brothers are going to eat your breakfast."

One foot after the other, she forced herself back into the bathroom. Hopefully, there was still a first aid kit under the sink. She'd had it for years, from back when she had to fix up

72

her friend Raechel after a run-in with her step-dad, before the State had finally done its job. It was, but when she shucked the robe to try to clean up the holes she'd torn in her arms, there was no evidence that she had been bleeding. No evidence that anything had ever been wrong except the missing cast and the blood still under her nails. Well, that was one less thing she was going to have to explain to anyone. One more thing she was going to spend the rest of her life not thinking about, ever.

She put on underwear mechanically, crawled into a pair of jeans and a comfortable tee, then hid it all under her favorite Lawrence Lions hoodie. She found the cast under the bed while looking for her shoes, cracked but mostly intact. She couldn't stuff her hand back into it. How had it come off?

'Don't think about it, just make it through the day.'

She started to shake as she stood there holding the cast, her whole body trembling so badly that she dropped it back to the floor with a thump. Margaret pulled her hand up into the sleeve of the hoodie and hoped no one would notice as long as she wore the sling. Careful to keep her hand tucked up inside her sleeve, Margaret made her way down the stairs to the kitchen table.

"...doesn't come down in five minutes, it's mine!" Brian Junior was shouting, wrestling Paul off his chair.

"Nuh-uh!" Little Paul screamed, flailing his arms frantically. "I called it first!"

"Well I'm older!"

"Quiet, the both of you," her mother said, not looking up from the dishes. "Mara's come to eat it herself. Good morning, honey."

"Morning, Mom." She flinched inwardly. To her own ears, at least, she sounded like she wanted to kill herself. Lillian Dunn didn't seem to notice.

"Did you hear anything strange last night, honey?" her mother asked absently as she began fluttering around the kitchen. There was something strange about the way she moved and talked, like she was half asleep.

"No," she said, pushing her brothers back from her breakfast. "Why?"

73

"Mr. Richter called this morning to ask. Something killed one of his heifers last night. He found the half-eaten carcass this morning."

Margaret had to choke back another wave of nausea as images from her dream flashed back through her mind. The taste of blood, the rush of joy, the howling wolves.

"That's horrible," she said after a moment.

"I know. I hope we don't have another pack of coyotes."

When her breakfast was done, Margaret moved robotically into the study she shared with her father to collect her book bag, trying to remember to hold her left arm limp and not use it while she double-checked her books and homework. She went to kiss her mother goodbye, but she stopped short when she saw the strange, glassy look to her mother's eyes. Lillian Dunn didn't seem to notice that anything was amiss, simply waving her daughter out the door with a vapid, "Have a nice day, dear!"

Something was terribly wrong, and her impossibly unbroken arm was only the beginning of it. The memory of her grandfather's voice finally managed to shout its way past her shock and denial: *'Ye cain't fix a problem 'till ye've stopped t'look at et! Use yer brain, girlie.'* Still, her mind recoiled from the morning's events: the nightmares, Mr. Richter's cow dead and eaten, her mother's stupor. Her arm. A rational world as she understood it simply couldn't contain these events.

The bus came and she got on, doing her very best not to think.

At school, no one asked about her arm. Not how it was doing, or if it hurt. Not even if her pain meds were up for sale.

Her friends smiled and waved, but walked by without talking to her. Acquaintances passed her by almost as if they couldn't see her. Teachers didn't notice when she raised her hand to answer questions; some almost missed her when she tried to hand in her homework. It was so unnerving that, by the end of third hour, her hands were trembling, her heart raced constantly, and her breath caught every time she tried to talk. No one noticed that, either, not even her closest friends.

She sat by herself at lunch and finally, reluctantly, set her mind to figuring out what was going on.

The problem was that none of it made any sense at all. Waking up naked and sweaty could be explained by the nightmares she'd been having. Her arm healing overnight was simply impossible, so she'd leave that alone for the moment. The blood must have come from somewhere, though. Something about the Richter's heifer itched at the back of her mind, but she refused to acknowledge that level of insanity. She was five-foot-eight and a hundred thirty pounds... she was strong, sure, but that was just silly.

The only part that made any sense at all was the way she seemed to be turning invisible, and that only if the fairy tales her grandfather had liked to tell her were true. But there were no such things as witches and curses!

Except... there were rumors of a coven in the school. Anthony wasn't the only one she'd heard it from.

Margaret looked around for her friends, saw them sitting at the usual table. They glanced around the room from time to time, like they were looking for something, but whenever their eyes passed her table they glazed over for a moment then passed on. People walked by with laden trays, glancing at her otherwise empty table before making room for themselves elsewhere, as if she and her table didn't even exist.

She knew who was supposed to be a part of the coven. Dominic Richardson, from her English class. Amber Lee, the girl who always looked at you in the locker room. Aaron Pohl, that everyone said was gay and that Anthony Domiano thought was their leader. And she knew they met Monday afternoons in the library.

Jennifer Hobb hung out with them, too, she knew, even since the rumors had started. Jennifer said it was all superstitious ignorance and that they were just trying to find peace after being driven out of the Church by assholes like Anthony Domiano. Anthony and everyone else thought that they were creepy and Satanic, but Jennifer went to her church and she knew that Hobb was a good Christian and wouldn't be friends with people who were really evil. If they were really witches, though... if she really were cursed...

Madness.

But the more she thought about it, the more a curse was the only explanation that made any sense at all.

"You have been blinded by the modern world," Father Masters had said. "You cannot read the signs of the times or even the writing on the wall."

She believed in miracles of God... why not curses of the Devil? If she was cursed, maybe witches could help her. If they weren't the ones who'd cursed her in the first place. But she'd never done anything to any of them, had she? She didn't even know any of them at all, except Dominic. Hopefully, Jennifer had something else going on today. With a little luck, no one would ever know she had talked to them at all.

What would they want in exchange? Witches in fairy tales never did anything for free.

That thought haunted her through the second half of the day, as one terrible price after another floated up from the stories her grandfather had told her as a child. An unnamed favor. An impossible task. Her firstborn. An ounce of blood. A finger. Her virginity. Her immortal soul.

During fifth hour English, Dominic kept glancing at her out of the corner of his eye. He was the only person who seemed to see that she was there. Mrs. Crebbley didn't take her essay until Margaret had waved it in front of her face twice, after which she didn't bother to raise her hand to answer questions. She was too afraid that she wouldn't be seen. Her fears were borne out by sixth hour, during which no one acknowledged her existence at all. The bell rang and she went to her locker in a stupor. She tried to talk to her friends, even tried grabbing strangers for their attention, but only her closest friends would acknowledge her existence more than to step out of her way. "Hey, Mara! See you tomorrow!" was the strongest response she could get from anyone, and that from Elissa Reed, her best friend since elementary school.

Margaret half-ran, half-walked to the library, torn between a growing urgency and an ingrained habit of not drawing attention to herself. Still, she hesitated for a few moments outside of the door. By walking in, she would be admitting not only that this was really happening to her, but that she didn't think anyone except a witch could help her. Why didn't she think the Church could help?

Because she didn't want anyone, not even Pastor Mary, to know. She just wanted this, whatever it was, to go away so she could get back to her life.

Taking a deep breath, she pushed open the door. The library was empty, lacking even the librarian at her circular desk console that sat in front of the door. She almost panicked and ran back out to the hall, before she realized that there were voices coming from the back room. Almost sneaking around the checkout desk, she peeked in the door first. There were four boys and two girls: Dominic was talking to an equally tall, well-dressed boy who was probably Aaron; Anthony's nemesis, Alexander, was sitting quietly with Amber almost in his lap, listening while the others talked; Jennifer was sitting near the back, talking to someone Margaret couldn't see. She almost ran, afraid of even Jennifer knowing.

Margaret gathered her courage and stepped into the room.

They didn't turn as one, but she had the strangest impression that they had somehow sensed her enter. They knew, she was certain, that there was something wrong with her, although they might not know what it was. Most of them didn't quite stare, just Amber – whose attention was disturbingly like Anthony's – and the small, familiar-looking boy at the back.

Dominic was the first to speak. "Can we help you?"

"You guys," she hesitated, stumbling over herself. "You... you're witches, right?"

There was a long pause while they shared a long-suffering look and the boy at the back slowly sank into his chair, like he was trying to hide.

"Would you like the long answer or the short?" Dominic said at last.

"Short?"

"Probably not the way you mean that word. We're Pagans. Some of us are Wiccan, some animist, some agnostic."

Well, so much for Anthony's coven. What was she going to do, now? She couldn't go to that weird place downtown, someone might see her go in. "Oh... so you can't help me."

"You don't know that until you actually ask us for help, now do you?" One of the other boys pointed out, the well-dressed one Dominic had been talking to when she came in. He was tall and skinny, his wavy brown hair brushing his shoulders and almost hiding the thick silver ring hanging from his right ear. "Hi. I'm Aaron, and this is Dominic."

"Hi," she said. She wondered why he didn't introduce the others. There was really no way to do this that wasn't going to make her feel like a moron. She shouldn't have come, but it was too late now. As long as nobody else saw her... "I'm Mara. I... I think somebody put a curse on me?"

They didn't laugh at her, which was nice. She couldn't have handled being laughed at by people everyone made fun of. They just sat expectantly, waiting, except for Alexander, who was watching the others as much as her, and Amber, who was blushing, now, and staring at her hands.

"What makes you say that?"

She should have known they would make her try to explain. Distantly, she heard the library door open and close.

"Well, I..." she began, trying to find a place to start the story that didn't involve blood or her nightmares, which were too disturbing to tell anyone. They waited patiently.

"Hey, babe, whatcha doing with these losers?"

Oh, no. Not Anthony. This was the last thing she needed now. Why, of all the people she knew, was he the only one who really noticed her today?

"What do you want, Anthony?"

"Just to talk," he said, shrugging his shoulders.

"Not now, Anthony."

"Oh, come on," he insisted, waving her out of the room. "You don't need anything from these faggots, do you?"

"They're going to help me with my history report," she lied. It even sounded lame to her. Involuntarily, she took a step away from him.

"Oh, I'll get Rosenberg to do it for you."

He grabbed her by the arm and she heard chairs move.

"Let go of me, Anthony," she said, pushing him away with her other hand, the one that was supposed to still be broken. Although she couldn't possibly have pushed him that hard, especially with the sling in the way, he stumbled back.

"Hey, babe," he said weakly, "I'm not into the rough stuff."

He came back toward her anyway, though, but Dixon was already in his way. The shorter boy had vaulted over the table to land neatly between them.

"Girl doesn't want you, Domiano."

"Fuck off, faggot."

"It's all about faggots with you, isn't it?" Dixon mocked. "Projecting much?"

It took a moment for that to sink in but when it did, Anthony swung his fist at Dixon with a snarl. Dixon didn't even flinch; he just stepped inside the reach of the wide swing and, before it would have had the chance to connect, smashed his forehead against the taller boy's nose. Anthony yelped and fell backwards, landing on his butt this time and holding his face in both hands.

"Someone tells you to back off, Domiano," Dixon growled, "you do it. Or I'll pull you off and put you down, just like I've done since we were kids."

He pulled a box of tissues from the desk by the door and threw it into Anthony's lap.

"Now fuck off."

Anthony Domiano scrambled out the door.

"Mara, are you okay?" Jennifer asked, having come up behind her at some point during the confrontation.

"No," she said, leaning into Jennifer's offered embrace. "No, I'm not."

Alexander and Jennifer led Margaret to a nearby table and tried to make her comfortable. Amber was looking anywhere but at them, her face flushed. In the back corner, Dominic and Aaron were helping a small boy Margaret only half-recognized to his feet — his eyes were wild and his breathing was ragged — but they settled him quickly and returned their attention to her.

"So," Dominic said, "you think someone put a curse on you?"

"Yeah," she said. "I've been having nightmares for almost two weeks. I'm running through the forest, hunting deer or something, and... I'm full of this terrible hunger and... at the same time, joy. Then, when I... catch it, it's like an ... like ... it feels..."

She paused, swallowing and looking away. She couldn't bring herself to say how good it had felt. Could barely stand to think of it.

"Then," she went on, "last night... I had the dream again, except... this time it was my parent's woods, around our house, and my neighbor's fields, and... I woke up with blood under my fingernails and in my mouth and..." She choked, holding her head in her hands. "People have been ignoring me all day. I can talk to them or wave at them... even grab them by the arm, and almost no one will even acknowledge that I'm there... except you guys and Domiano."

"My parents' friends," Alexander said, "the Richter family, found one of their heifers half-eaten this morning."

She sobbed, nodding. "They live next door to me."

Silence fell over the room, stretching for long moments before Jennifer gasped: "Mara, your arm!"

When she had pushed Anthony, the sling had mostly fallen off, and now, when she'd cradled her head in her hands, the sleeve of her hoodie had pulled up to reveal an uninjured arm.

"It was better when I woke up this morning." She said. Or tried to. It came out more as a squeak, but nothing came out when she tried to repeat herself.

They didn't say anything. They just stared at her. Silently.

"Please," Margaret said into the silence, "tell me there's something you can do to help me."

"I don't know," said the boy in the back corner. "But anyone who's not gonna try is a shithead."

On the one hand, it was good to hear Jacob speak out. He didn't stick up for himself much, and never for anyone else. On the other hand, Margaret Dunn was obviously deranged. She hadn't been a week ago, but did that mean anything? Dominic had heard that being attacked could really fuck with people, sometimes. He had seen the invisibility effect, though: her friends had pointedly left her out of their conversations, but not like he'd seen girls do to each other before. There were no coy looks, no sarcastic remarks about the wind blowing. It really had looked like they couldn't see her. Mrs. Crebbley certainly hadn't been able to, and Margaret had drawn his attention the way every Don't Look at Me spell he'd ever met had.

'And I just can't say no to a beautiful girl,' he thought to himself. 'Particularly not one who's crying.'

"Well," Dominic said, "let's take a look at you. Aaron?"

Aaron gave him an odd look, but nodded.

"Come here, let's make a circle." With hand motions and short commands, Dominic directed everyone into a circle around Margaret, Aaron, and himself.

Then Dominic carved a Circle around them all. Lacking his athame, he focused his will through his right hand as he circumambulated the group. It wasn't his best work, but it was a firm enough boundary to form the clear space needed for this kind of thing. He sat Aaron behind Margaret, placed himself atop the desk in front of her and entered his trance with a few deep breaths, each slower than the last. He tried to draw her into the trance by her eyes, but after a long, fidgety minute, he decided that he couldn't: she was just too scared, and the slippery 'invisibility' kept him from getting a good grasp on her aura. It was a cheap trick, on the one hand, the sort of thing he'd seen little kids pull in games of hide-and-seek at festivals; but had been done with enough power that it seemed to be sticking, and there were other layers to it that he couldn't quite grasp.

Dominic shook his head. Taking a deep breath, he re-centered himself, and looked again. There was Margaret. There was her aura. There was the Don't Look At Me, and the thread that led back to its maker. There was ... something else that tied into the Don't Look At Me. And there, low in Margaret's belly, worming through her aura, was a third thing, tied into the first two in ways he didn't understand, that smelled of copper and scorched earth and squirmed away from his gaze.

Something serious was definitely going on here. He hesitated to say what, but he knew where Jacob's mind had already gone. Dominic couldn't deny that it fit the mythology, but he wasn't going to be the first one to say it out loud. She had thrown Anthony several feet, though, apparently by accident, and her arm should have been in a cast for weeks. And there was no denying that he'd felt something when she'd come in, and again, stronger, when she'd pushed Anthony. And the timing ...

"Well...?" Margaret asked at last, after he'd been feeling her out for a good five minutes.

"I... don't know," he said. "Someone's done something to you, I'll go that far, but..."

She shuddered. "Can you do anything?"

"Again, I don't know. If you were one of us, I'd suggest you do some cleansing rituals, but since you're not... Well, something like that is hard to do for someone else."

Aaron was nodding along with each of his points, and Amber was listening raptly. Alexander and Jennifer both looked skeptical, but Jacob was staring at him like he was missing something painfully obvious. Dominic just raised his eyebrow at him and waited for Jacob to suggest it, himself.

"But I am cursed?"

"Something like that."

Margaret didn't look particularly relieved or comforted.

"Dude," Jacob said, "I think the evidence is pretty clear."

"What do you think then, Jak?"

"The blood, the nightmares, the miraculous healing... last night being the full moon? Hello?"

Alex laughed, and Aaron glared at Jacob. Amber stared wide-eyed, back and forth between the three of them, and Jennifer looked like she'd been hit upside the head. Dominic just waited, watching Margaret and Jacob carefully.

"Last night was the full moon?" Margaret asked in the smallest voice yet.

The circle gave a chorus of assent. Margaret started crying again.

"Jennifer," she choked out between sobs, "you were there that Sunday, weren't you? You remember? You saw?"

Margaret's question caught her off guard. Of course she remembered.

"Yeah," Jennifer said, very reluctantly.

"Will... will you tell them?"

All eyes turned to her, and she squirmed nervously under the attention, but slowly told them about the guest preacher, his sermon, and the attack. She didn't tell them about the rest, though: how Masters had somehow moved too fast for her to see and kicked a giant dog hard enough to lift it into the air. She certainly wasn't going to tell them how the hound had leaped over the six-foot fence without so much as a limp from that kick. She was not going to give any of this insanity more credence than it deserved. Particularly not since almost everyone got that look that said they were starting to take Jacob's implication seriously.

Being attacked and having her arm broken had clearly unhinged Margaret's mind, that's all there was to it. It must not have been broken as badly as they'd all thought. That was the only sane and logical explanation for her arm being healed already. The nightmares were just that, the blood was a delusion, and so was her assertion that no one would talk to her. Anthony had followed her in, after all, and no one here had trouble acknowledging her existence.

Jennifer told the story like it had been drug out of her by whips and chains. Her very reluctance made Dominic suspicious of what she might be leaving out; he knew her well enough to be sure there was exactly no chance that she was playing anything up. He'd never heard how exactly Margaret had broken her arm. Yeah, he'd heard it was an animal attack at church, but... the witness account was more disturbing. Not that he was an expert on the subject, but that really wasn't the way any other dog attack he'd heard of had gone down. As the story wound to a close, Margaret settled from sobbing to shaking.

He was going to take the bait, he realized: *'Whatever is really going on here, I'm going to buy into Jacob's werewolf theory because Margaret Dunn is just too attractive for me to let her keep crying like that.'* However shallow and two-faced it might be, however it might just feed her insanity, he was going to do his best to help because he couldn't stand to see a pretty girl cry.

Why everyone else decided to play along, though, was a mystery to him.

"So," Alexander asked in an amused voice, "Don't take this wrong, but ... what do we know about werewolves that we didn't learn from American Werewolf in London?"

There was another silence before Jacob asked him: "Dom?"

"I'm on it," he said, shrugging. "I'll hit up my dad's store, but someone should raid the library, too."

"Me," Aaron volunteered, very much to Dominic's surprise. He couldn't remember the last time Aaron had gone out of his way for anyone but Jacob or himself.

"Y'all have until moonrise," Alexander pointed out. "I'll hit the hardware store in case you don't come up with anything in time."

84

"Hardware store?" Margaret asked, confused.

"The power of the full moon lasts one, two, or three nights depending on the month and who you ask," he explained. "Do you want to be running loose if it's three and we can't fix you in the next five hours?"

Dominic narrowed his eyes, examining Dixon's face carefully. Alexander didn't believe a word of it: he was going to tie up the crazy girl. Not necessarily a bad plan. Margaret's face was aghast and everyone else's so shocked that he almost didn't stop himself from laughing. It was impossible to say who actually thought she might be a lycanthrope and who was just playing along because they were afraid to jump off the crazy train, but no matter what, this was going to be the most interesting night of his life so far.

"You know what you'll need," Dominic asked Alexander.

"Yeah. The internet is a wonderful thing."

Amber went with Alexander.

As Aaron left for the library, Jacob went over to Margaret and offered her his hand.

"You wanna help us research?" He asked her.

"Yeah," Margaret said, taking his hand up. "Sure."

She looked dazed as Jacob led her out the door.

Jennifer sat, stunned and staring after them for a long minute before turning to Dominic.

"Is she on drugs? Are all of you on drugs?"

"I don't think so," he shook his head, pawing through his pockets for rolling papers. "But I can't always tell. I just didn't want to tell Jake 'no'."

"Should we really be playing along? I mean, shouldn't we be calling her parents or the school counselors or something?"

Dominic shrugged, sifting tobacco from his pouch into the Zig and rolling it deftly between his palms. "I don't know. But I'm gonna do my research. They'll call the shop before moonrise looking for me."

He stood, tucking the cigarette behind his ear and pulled on his coat and hat. He checked his bag and pockets and was

MARK OF THE WOLF

turning to the door when Jennifer asked in a small voice: "Do you think it's possible?"

"Anything's possible. I know a woman who lives up in Chicago, I see her at the big festivals. She lights her cigarettes with the tip of her finger." And the campfire with a mild glare, but he wasn't sure Jen was ready for that yet. "Why don't you go with them?"

She shook her head. "I have to get home."

He nodded. It wasn't like he believed it, either. Not quite, anyway.

"So... how do you know what we'll need?" Amber asked nervously.

"Like I said, the internet is a wonderful thing," Alexander told her seriously, then added with a sly glance. "And I dated this crazy Goth girl back in junior high. It sounded like a whole lot of fun until I realized that she wanted to tie me up, not the other way around."

"Are you serious?"

"Dude, this girl had a serious thing for razors. No way was I gonna be tied down naked with her around."

"You're pulling my leg."

"Would I do that?" He asked innocently as he measured out a few lengths of heavy steel chain. She wasn't sure, that was part of the problem. She could see that he didn't believe Margaret, which made her a little nervous. Did he just want a set of chains for some other reason? Silk rope sounded fun and kinky, maybe, but chains?

"So... what do you think is going to happen tonight?"

Alexander stopped wrapping the chain around his hands and looked up at the ceiling. He didn't answer at first. For a moment, she thought he wouldn't.

"I don't know," he said. "Hell, I don't even know what I want to happen."

Dominic finally found what he was looking for in the darkest corner of his father's private collection. The Grimoire of Therianthropy. He'd first seen it about three years ago, when his father had bought it from an old collector desperate to pay for his cancer treatments. The woodcut prints of the werewolf and the rakshasa had fascinated him before his father had hidden it. It couldn't have been right here the whole time – he'd looked! – but there it was, bound in leather with brass fittings and the title etched fancifully on the front and the spine. It was a collection of essays and lesser books: "Concerning the Rakshasa of the Indus (1894)"; "Book of the Fox Women (Japanese)(1733)"; "The Werewolf Lore of Northwestern Europe (1827)"; and, what he really wanted, "Book of the Wolf (German)(1579)", among a dozen others concerning the Celtic and Russian bearmen, and the various shapeshifters of Africa, some in English and some in other tongues. But the Book of the Wolf wasn't in the German he knew.

It bothered him a little to find the Grimoire on this particular shelf, though. Purely historical pieces were kept on another wall. This book shared shelf space with Shadows of the House of Lore, Mirrors and Veils, and Elder Book of Rites ... all books he'd been told contained knowledge they'd "trust him with later". The Grimoire of Therianthropy tingled with echoes of long-forgotten magics. It had been present for some serious magical work, and it might even have participated.

"Is this shit for real?" The book shook a little bit in Dominic's hands.

His father was upstairs, manning the store. All he had to do was ask. In this house, it was permission that was easier to come by: forgiveness only came for legitimate mistakes. A downside to theology focused on personal responsibility rather than redemption.

Dominic had seen Margaret throw Anthony down, had felt her aura flare. Alexander had verified that there had been a mutilated cow. Jennifer had confirmed the time and place of the attack that broke Margaret's arm; and he'd seen the cast himself. Last night was the first full moon since. If he asked his father, the one thing he'd be sure of was that he wouldn't be laughed at.

Still, he decided he'd get more evidence first. Robert Richardson had been very certain his son's magical training included critical thinking skills. "Werewolf" was just too crazy not to get the full brunt of them.

Dominic checked his watch: four hours to moonrise. If Margaret wasn't crazy, time was running out. *'Unless, of course,'* he thought, *'she only changes on the one night of the moon, instead of all three.'* The mythology did conflict, somewhat, on that point, and still other stories made it something that the werewolf could control. *'Was there any wild werewolf action Saturday night, the first night of the moon?'* They were really out of their depth, here.

He'd been studying older versions of English since he was ten, so he decided to read those three werewolf essays from the Grimoire first, since he couldn't read the Book.

Werewolf Lore of Northwestern Europe described a plague-like curse of lycanthropy that decimated the outlying settlements of the Holy Roman Empire. The manuscript claimed that the outbreak began when a "gypsy witch" cursed a woodsman to "bear the Mark of the Wolf and ravish the fruits of [his] people" until he came willingly to her bed. For unknown reasons, this curse was more prolific than previously known forms of lycanthropy, and by 1460 there were a dozen distinct packs roaming northern Europe between Bohemia and the Ukraine. An unknown number migrated east and south before the Pope sent in "a hundred most expert monster-hunters from Rome," trained and tested in the Caucasus Mountains and the Crusades. According to this piece, werewolves became true monsters upon receiving the Mark, able to transform at will and always choosing to do so under the light of the full moon, ravaging mankind as savage predators.

The second piece, On Diagnosing the Curse of Lycanthropy, was short and to the point. It began: "The most reliable way to see who in your village is a werewolf is to stand all your people under the light of the full moon and kill him who changes. Failing that, dose all your people with an infusion of wolfsbane. Him who dies was the Wolf." Of course, wolfsbane (known to modern science as *aconitum napellus*) was deadly poison to anyone who ingested it, so that was a little suspect. It also described a number of divinations to perform should it become impossible to gather the whole village in one place, or if you were afraid the werewolf would run or attack when confronted, and an assortment of ways to achieve the stated goal of killing the werewolf. He bookmarked the divinations.

The final manuscript, Concerning the Man Who is Wolf, turned out to be useless: thick with allegory and references to books he'd never read and most of which he hadn't even heard of. It was from much later than the others, according to the Grimoire, and it almost felt like the summary of another, larger work. It made repeated reference to two particular tomes, and he'd look into those when he could. The first, Mirrors and Veils, which his father owned, was far too cryptic and disorganized to try to open tonight. The other was the Liber Caecissima, Krypsomachos' great Book of Secrets, which he'd heard of and had wanted to get his hands on for some time... assuming it actually existed. Like Satan's Bible and the Lazarite Codex, there were many scholars who considered it a myth.

The other books, from the store upstairs, were less helpful. Nothing more than crudely generalized histories of the myth in film and literature, and accounts of historical werewolf trials.

He checked his watch again: an hour and a half. He hoped the others were having better luck.

———————

Jacob wondered, as he often had before, how to tell myth, legend, and outright lie from fact in matters magical. In this line of inquiry, he felt particularly lost. Despite the evidence, he wanted to reject the very possibility of werewolves. Werewolf stories almost always ended badly for everyone, especially the wolf.

He, Aaron, and Margaret were camped out in the most secluded corner of the public library, in the northwest end of the non-fiction, claiming the window and desk near the one and two hundreds. Aaron read slowly, glancing often toward Jacob and occasionally toward Margaret, who alternated between frantic page-turning and staring blankly into space. Between the three of them, it didn't take long to exhaust the non-fiction available on werewolves, nor did it take any time at all to rule out most of the fiction as useless.

In the end, surrounded by a disastrous pile of discarded volumes, they came up with very little. A half-dozen encyclopedia entries, each of which at least partially contradicted at least one other. A towering pile of fancifully illustrated but factually spare novelty editions that included UFOs, Bigfoot, and sightings of the Loch Ness monster. Ancient aliens.

One good book.

Out of all of it, they were able to draw some very rough conclusions. Lycanthropy – it wasn't always called that, but it would work – seemed to happen one of three ways: a curse, a ritual, or an attack. The last was not actually the most common until the late Middle Ages, but the unsuspecting werewolf could recognize what was happening to him by several signs: the taste of blood in the mouth, blood under the fingernails at the full moon, and dreams of violence.

Hopefully Dominic was having better luck.

―――――――

Dominic pulled his Oldsmobile into Margaret's driveway at 8:10 – about twenty minutes after sunset and exactly thirty-two minutes before moonrise. Alexander's Buick and Jacob's Taurus were already parked near the door of the barn. He pulled up beside them.

He could see Margaret on the porch, talking to an older man that he assumed was her father, but decided against introducing himself. Instead, he pulled the duffel bag of supplies from his trunk and moved into the barn, where he could see the others waiting. Alexander and Amber were sitting on a hay bale, waiting patiently by their own duffel bag; Aaron lounged against one of the walls while Jacob paced the floor.

"Any luck?" Jacob asked him.

"Some," Dominic hedged. "I have a divination to see if she really is a ... werewolf, and I've cobbled together a binding on the off chance..."

Jacob made his grumpy face, lips pursed as he frowned and his brows pulled tightly together, but Dominic ignored it. He set the duffel down near Alexander and Amber and fished out a stack of photocopies and bundles of herbs and candles.

"Here," Dominic said, handing the candles to Alex and passing the papers around. "Give the candles to Aaron, then go over the notes. Jacob, Amber, the two of you can help me set up the rest of the circle. I'll do the divination myself, but I'll need a circle of five to do the binding."

By the time Margaret made her way to the barn, Aaron had finished marking the circle and laying out the candles. Dominic and Jacob, following along behind him while Amber got the censer lit, were almost done laying out the other physical components of the circle. Alexander was puzzling over the photocopies.

"I told my dad we were doing a photo project," Margaret said. Her voice was high and frightened, and she clutched a camera bag to her chest. "He didn't care. At all."

"So we won't be disturbed?" Dominic asked, aware that there was more to what she meant than exactly what she had said, but unsure what it was or what to do to make it better.

"No," now she sounded downtrodden. "You could probably kill me out here and they wouldn't notice. It's like someone's turned my whole family into zombies."

He'd never even heard of a Don't Look at Me being so potent. Was that one of the *something elses* he'd seen in her aura? He had even less idea what to do about that than this werewolf business. Cleansing someone else's aura was tricky at best, particularly if that someone couldn't help with the process.

The last of the light was fading fast and, by the time he finished sprinkling the inner circle with wolfsbane and Jacob had set the last of the quartz crystals beside the candles, it was full dark.

"Alright," he said, standing up and dusting off his hands. "First things first. Mara, stand here in the center of the circle. Be very careful to step over the line and not to break it. Excellent. Now, the rest of you, light the candles on the ground, and by the time you're done I should be ready."

The steady wind out of the north made lighting the candles more difficult than it might otherwise have been. Meanwhile, Dominic dug back into his bag to pull out a fist-sized sachet. Taking three deep, slow breaths to center himself, he prayed quietly: "Goddess Mother, Keeper of the Night, be with us now."

Finally lit, the circle of candles danced madly, casting a flickering, surreal kaleidoscope of orange and yellow and red. The eerie lighting made Margaret look alien and terrible. Dominic set himself up at the edge of the circle nearest to the barn door, looking her in the eye

"Are you ready, madam?" he asked.

"I ..." she hesitated. "I'm as ready as I'll ever be."

Dominic took a candle from Aaron and the censer from Amber. He uttered a few words in Old English as he lit the taper candle. He chanted as he sprinkled on the herbs from the sachet onto the coals. He lifted the smoking censer to chest level and walked a circle around Margaret. She managed to face forward for the whole process but could not keep her hands still and shifted her weight from one foot to the other and back.

The smoke coiled around her, in utter and unnatural defiance of the wind that so excited the candles, and settled at her feet like a fog.

––––––––––––

His part in the preparations complete, Jacob settled himself against a stack of hay bales, as far from Alexander as he could get without seeming to abandon Margaret.

He saw the fear in her eyes. More than that: he felt it. He felt it swirling and twitching, receding and returning in waves. At the ebb, her fear was an endless winter wind, sucking away at her will to live; at the flood, it was like a howling storm.

His own fear, by contrast, was a dull ache, warm and familiar.

Aaron took a place by Jacob's side: tall, silent, looming. Aaron was not afraid. He was angry, his belly churning with the cold fire that always accompanied Alexander's presence. But, Jacob sensed, he was also curious – dispassionate, but curious – and watched Dominic closely as he performed the spell. Jacob joined him in that.

Dominic walked around the candle-and-crystal circle with his arms extended in front of him, candle in his right hand and censer in his left. His chanting carried a weight beyond the words, each falling into the candle-and-crystal circle like a stone, making ripples in the rising energy.

The magic wound Jacob's senses tight and sharp, and his own fear, discomfort, even his thoughts began to recede in the face of Margaret's hurricane of fear, Aaron's icy sharp anger, and Dominic's focus. He became aware of Amber's confusion, of Alexander's fascination, emanating steadily from where they stood on the other side of the circle.

And something else. Outside the barn.

Thick smoke poured off the censer in Dominic's hands. At first, the smoke dissipated in the steady wind. As Dominic chanted, the energy in the circle rose and the smoke began to pour off the coals in a thick rope.

The *something else* was coming closer, becoming clearer. Angry. Hungry. It made his skin itch.

The rope of smoke curled clockwise around Margaret, moving against the wind like a living thing. Around and around it went until it settled as an impossible fog at Margaret's feet. To Jacob's eyes, the cloud of smoke looked like a reclining hound. A wolf.

Moment by moment, the sense of ravenous rage grew stronger and stronger. It was coming from Margaret, too, as well as from outside the barn. Jacob began to fidget, scratching his arms and shaking his head from side to side. Amber looked uncomfortable, too, shifting her weight from one foot to the other and back.

The image of the wolf vanished from the pool of smoke at Margaret's feet. The smoke boiled briefly as the sense of something outside resolved itself into a half-dozen distinct *presences*, each bearing the same sliver of darkness that he'd sensed in Margaret the moment he'd first seen her.

"Someone's here," Jacob blurted.

The smoke rushed out of the circle, against the wind, toward the far door of the barn, before dissipating as the spell broke under the pressure.

"Well, well," came the voice, low and menacing. "Look what we've got here."

Seven figures stood under the high arch of the barn door. Five men and two women, all dressed in bikers' leathers and chains. Three of the men stepped forward while the others stayed to block the door. One, gone gray but still muscular, was flanked by the other two – one much younger, brown-skinned with cruel-looking and uncanny eyes; the other, older and bearded, just looked hard. Malice rolled off of all of them in waves, churning Jacob's stomach. The three men at front were worse than the others, and of them the young one radiated something worse, still, that Jacob couldn't name.

"I don't know what you think you're going to do for your friend, here, but she's ours, now." The man's tone was mocking. "Why don't you just leave her to us?"

The bikers advanced slowly and Margaret shuddered, taking a careful step away from them.

"No!" Jacob barked, surprising himself. "You leave her alone!"

The bikers all laughed when Jacob shouted. Step by menacing step, the three men kept advancing. The barn felt smaller, now, than it had before they arrived.

Alexander flinched. This could only end in disaster.

94

Margaret moaned. Out of the corner of his eye, Alexander watched her fall to her knees, shaking her head. Why didn't she run? Why didn't any of them run? Not that there was anywhere to run to, besides the fields: the bikers were all between them and the house.

Alexander readied himself, drawing a deep breath and shifting his feet. For all the good it would do, the leader would be in punching distance in half a step.

The older man's fist took him in the side of his head before he even knew it was coming. The world exploded into a million stars. Someone screamed, but a boot landed in his ribs before he could begin to wonder who it was.

"Boy, I don't ask for nothin' very often, and I expect to get it when I do."

The next blow was a stomp to his side, forcing the last of the air from his lungs.

Aaron watched, stunned, as Margaret fell to the ground, landing on her knees, and began to moan. It started low, and slowly rose to a high, wailing sound.

Aaron stared in horror as she tossed her head, kicked her feet and scratched at her arms, keening all the while. Sweat poured from her body, soaking through her tee-shirt until, panting like she was fevered, she began to tear off her clothes. He was so shocked that he didn't notice Alexander go down, let alone that he wasn't getting back up.

"There, girl," the older man said, "don't fight it. It hurts more if you fight it, the first few times." He clearly thought that was funny, but Aaron did not. "Caleb, make 'em forget."

He and Dominic had time to share a glance – *'What the fuck?'* – before the wave of power washed over them. The energy was sick, twisted. Its touch made Aaron want to vomit.

For this, at least, Aaron was prepared. He and Dominic had played games like this for years: forming psychic shields and testing one another's boundaries. Here, at last, was a need for those skills in earnest. In his mind's eye, Aaron turned and

95

attenuated himself, a knife edge against which the warlock's brute psychic attack could gain no purchase.

He reached deep into himself, felt Dominic do the same. They locked eyes briefly. There was only one plan possible. Together they struck back: gathering their will and forcing the biker's energy back into himself. The warlock flinched. He didn't try again.

"Well?" The leader asked after a long pause.

"I can't." The warlock admitted grudgingly, earning a murderous glance from the bearded man.

"What?" asked the leader again, still not turning away from Margaret, who had stripped off her shirt and bra, and lay in the dirt, panting. Reddish-brown hair had grown down her spine and in a tuft between her breasts. Her arms had grown more muscular and her hands were now claws.

"These kids are witches. I can't put the spin on 'em."

That earned them and the biker-witch a hard, dark glance.

"You worthless shit," the old man spat, kicking Alexander again. "Well, it's not like these punks are going to tell anybody anything, now is it?"

Amber and Jacob cried out. Margaret's head snapped up and around. Her eyes were wild and wide, nothing human left in them. Her attention landed on the leader – burly, laughing over Alexander's prone form, the closest thing in front of her.

Before Aaron knew what was happening, Margaret leaped up at the lead biker.

She finished her transformation from young woman to wolf in mid-air. Outstretched arms became canine paws. Her mouth, open in a silent scream, became a wolf's maw, full of glistening fangs. A fit athlete's torso became a furred barrel body, rippling with animal muscle and sinew. Her feet vanished into her jeans.

She hit his chest with a meaty thud, knocking him to the floor, but he only laughed.

"Loyal little bitch, aren'cha?" He said, grabbing her by the muzzle. Between his grip and the jeans entangling limbs no longer suited to them, she was effectively pinned. "Come on,"

96

he said, pulling the pants off her now wolf-shaped legs. "It's time to hunt!"

Aaron's eyes followed them out the door. He couldn't bring himself to move.

'Holy shit,' he thought to himself. 'Werewolves.'

Dominic watched them depart, stunned. He wanted to chase after, or help Alexander up, to say something funny to make it less real... anything. He couldn't. He actually thought he might faint. Was this what shock – real, medical shock – felt like?

He hadn't believed until he'd seen Margaret start to change. He sure believed now. The pack had come to claim her.

Dominic shook his head, tried to steady his breath.

The werewolf had spoken to them with such casual contempt. It was infuriating. But seven adult bikers versus four high school kids... well, at least Jacob had the stones to talk back. Alexander had been about to do something, for all the good that had done anyone.

Somehow, Amber and Jacob were still able to move. They were rolling Alexander onto his back, making sure he was breathing. Making sure he wasn't bleeding. His face was a mess. Had the werewolf broken his ribs?

Desperately, painfully, he wished he'd asked his father for help. He was certain that if werewolves were real, his father knew about it. Dad always liked to hint that his youth had been more interesting than Mom's, and Grandpa had always promised that there were secrets waiting for him after his Third Degree. Too bad Grandpa Henry's lung cancer had had other ideas.

"What next, D?" Aaron asked, sounding as hollow as Dominic felt.

"My place. Dad'll sort this out."

"Always running home to Daddy." It was a rote response. It didn't have the usual bite.

"You got any better ideas?"

97

"No."

Fallout

Bit by bit, Alexander drifted back to consciousness. First came the slow realization that he wasn't dead, followed quickly by the pain. Every breath was fire. His head pulsed with white agony. Slowly he became aware that only his face and his ribs hurt and, a little later, that probably nothing was broken. He hadn't had his ass handed to him like that since eighth grade.

A voice called to him from what seemed like a great distance, and he tried to open his eyes. The world was bleary, but it was coming back. He was laying on something soft, possibly even a bed, with arched beams crisscrossing the ceiling above him to create the sense of a dome.

"Alex," the voice came again, familiar and male, from just outside his view and somewhere to the right. Another presence hovered at his left, clutching his hand with delicate fingers. Amber. "Good, you're waking up. Gave us a bit of a scare, young man."

He groaned and tried to sit up, but his inner balance was so twisted that he couldn't. His vision swam until he gave it up.

"Am I gonna be all right?" Alexander managed to ask.

"I think so," the man answered. He recognized the voice, now. It was Mr. Richardson, Dom's pops. This must be the Midnight Candle. "Your ribs and cheek aren't broken, miraculously, but you'll have a hell of a shiner in the morning."

Alexander grunted but it came out as a groan. Mr. Richardson chuckled a little.

"Try not to sleep any more tonight, you probably have a concussion."

"Noted," he groaned. A concussion, huh? That might explain the way it felt when he tried to move. Hadn't had one of those in a while.

Mr. Richardson gave Alexander a comforting pat on the shoulder then left them alone. Alexander just stared at the ceiling. He hurt too much to do anything else, even turn his head to look at Amber. He tried to focus, to find his One Point and start the healing process. Even that hurt, so he just waited.

After a few minutes, Amber said quietly: "I was so worried. You just laid there, so still... so long..."

Worried didn't begin to cover the tone of her voice. Distraught might. "How long was I out?"

"It's been an hour since we got back from Mara's, so almost two."

"Fuck." Why hadn't they taken him to the hospital? "What happened after that guy stomped the shit out of me?"

He still couldn't turn to watch her face, but it probably meant something that she squeezed his hand until it hurt.

"I saw most of it. Mara started moaning and pulling her clothes off. The ... others just stood there while the one who hit you made fun of us for a while. He told one of the others to 'make us forget'. That one tried to do ... something, but Aaron and Dom stopped him somehow while Mara ... changed." Amber squeezed his hand as hard as she could. "He kicked you again and ... Mara ... the ... wolf ... jumped him, but he just kept laughing. Then they left."

So Margaret wasn't crazy. Well, hell. That made the world a much nastier place.

What else was real?

"Help me up?" He asked, hoping it wasn't going to be a disaster. Amber pulled him into a sitting position and, as he directed, helped him fold his legs into a half-lotus. It made his head spin and his stomach wrench, but he knew that he was just going to have to work through it if he wanted to spend tonight in his own bed. Thank god his parents were still out of town.

He took deep, slow breaths, gathering himself into his One Point, the chakra just below his belly button, like he'd been taught in Ki Aikido. The world swam, but he held on to his concentration and his guts with all the willpower he could muster. After what felt like forever, he had gathered himself together enough that he could stand.

"Are my keys around here anywhere?"

"I have them," Amber said firmly.

"We've got to get us home. What time is it, anyway?"

"Late. Don't worry, I'll get you there safe."

That didn't seem quite right.

"You have to go home too, and you can't keep my car overnight."

"I know. Your parents are still out of town, right? I'll stay with you."

"It's a school night. Won't you get in trouble?"

"It's okay. I won't get caught."

They had barely abandoned Alexander to Dominic's father's care before they began tearing at each other's clothes. The shock and the adrenaline had long since faded, leaving only exhaustion, cold fear, and a powerful gratitude to still be alive. Their coupling had been a desperate, frantic: trembling hands and demanding mouths, tangled hair and throbbing cocks.

At last, hours later, they lay in Dominic's bed, holding one another quietly. Their sweat cooled, their hearts finally began to slow, and Aaron slowly went limp inside of him. Sandalwood incense wafted through the room, almost masking the potent odors of sweat and sex. Dominic basked in the afterglow, languished in that long moment of peace where neither past nor future existed, just warmth. Aaron's body pressed close, spooning against his back, head pressed between his shoulder blades. Aaron was the taller of them of them by a little more than an inch, but the anatomical reality of sex – contrary to pornographic literature – was that two bodies of such similar height did not line up conveniently. Part of him wanted a cigarette or a joint. Most of him, including the parts that remembered all too clearly how Aaron usually stormed out when they were done, didn't want to move.

"We could have died tonight," he said quietly.

Aaron just squeezed him tighter, expressing his understanding far more eloquently than words ever could.

"Why didn't the werewolves kill us, Aaron?"

"I don't know," the taller boy mumbled into his back, squeezing Dominic's shoulder hard. "Shut up."

There was the boy he loved and hated: an ambivalent relationship in the Freudian sense of the word.

Dominic tried to relax, to shut up and forget it all, but it wouldn't go away. The night's events played themselves over and over in his head, and that question kept coming back. Why weren't they dead? Every scrap of information they had warned of death and destruction in the wake of the wolves. The reality didn't fit the data; therefore their data must be incomplete. Damn his father and his instructions in logic. Damn the werewolves and whatever it was they wanted.

'*I could have lived my whole life,*' Dominic thought, '*and never learned that that monsters are real.*'

He shook his head.

'*I hate that that sounds nice.*'

TUESDAY, SEPTEMBER 8TH

By the time the pack made it back, just after dawn, Jacob had come to doubt his decision to come back and wait for Margaret. Would she want to see him – anyone? – after her ordeal? Would it even be safe? Like Aaron had said, Margaret attacking the pack leader could be interpreted any number of ways. They still didn't know if she was the kind of werewolf that killed indiscriminately, or if she would even remember what she'd done when she woke.

The pack did not announce themselves with howls, but Jacob felt them coming, their palpable hunger slaked by the night's hunt. He didn't know what he expected, but he was surprised how much like normal wolves they looked. Wolves the size of Great Danes, yes, but mortal creatures nonetheless... except for their graying leader, who stood naked and uncanny among the pack, a mauled carcass thrown casually over one shoulder, and the red-eyed, barely wolf-like creature that Jacob knew was their warlock, just as he somehow knew the smaller wolf with a hold on one of the carcass's dangling legs was Margaret. The leader met Jacob's eyes, surprised and impressed that he'd waited. Nothing in his face said so; Jacob just knew, the same way he knew the rest.

The alpha werewolf threw down the carcass and pointed to Margaret.

"Stay," the pack leader commanded, his voice backed with a power Jacob could feel but not understand. She growled but obeyed.

"Keep 'er safe for us," he told Jacob with a mocking laugh.

The pack turned as one and ran back into the woods. Margaret-the-wolf sat beside her prize, eying him warily as she chewed the haunch. It wasn't long, though, before she gave a huge canine yawn, licking her chops and lying down in the bloody hay and mud to guard her snack while she slept.

The transformation came: a ripple of receding fur and reforming flesh as she stretched her limbs unconsciously, paws becoming delicate hands and feet, digitigrade legs lengthening into shapely thighs and calves, before settling into a more comfortable position on her side.

He did his best to play the gentleman, to keep his gaze meticulously elsewhere, but the soft curves of her body were more temptation than he could resist. The swell of her breasts and her pale nipples, barely a shade darker than the rest of her, drew his eyes. Her skin was pale; her sex hidden behind a thick, wild bush. The hair on her arms was darker than it had been yesterday, and it came to him suddenly that he had never seen hair on a girl's legs before. She lay stretched out, unconsciously showing off almost everything she had, but the gore that painted her breasts, matted in her hair, dribbled down her chin and splattered up her arms ... Lying there, hirsute, peacefully drenched in blood, she looked nothing short of monstrous.

He felt lust, disgust, and sympathy by turns.

A few minutes later, a muffled whisper started in his head, accompanied by flashes of movement and a sense of violence. 'She's waking up,' he realized when she started shifting uncomfortably. A sense of disorientation washed over him, but for once he knew exactly where it came from and kept his head.

Oh, God, her thought came to him as true dawn broke the horizon, heralded by a cock's cry. *I have to go to school.*

He'd brought a beach towel from his car to sit on, but it occurred to him belatedly that Margaret would probably like to cover herself.

Margaret woke to the smell of blood, earth, and hay. There were a thousand other scents, so many that it made her head spin, but if she focused on just those three, then things seemed to stay where they belonged. The metallic taste of blood lingered in her mouth and she had to try very hard not to think about the sticky substance that covered her face, arms, and chest. The pale light of dawn pushed against her eyelids and a rooster crowed somewhere in the distance.

'Oh, God,' she thought, groaning. 'I have to go to school.'

"Are you alright?" The voice came from several yards away, hesitant. 'Afraid,' something inside of her growled, eager. She knew she should recognize the voice, but right now she felt accomplished just knowing who she was.

"I don't think so," she managed to say, trying to sit up. Images and distant sensations, like someone else's memories, flashed through her head. Trees flying by at impossible speeds, the feel of the wind rushing through her fur. The death-scream of a rabbit and the taste of hot blood and sweet marrow. The face of a deer and the orgasmic rush of joy as she tore out its throat, the blood spraying over her muzzle and pouring down her body.

Finally, she was sitting up enough to see who was talking to her and where, exactly, she was. In the barn, lying not three feet from the half-eaten carcass of a deer, the ground even more wet with blood than she. Jacob was standing over her, pointedly looking away, his face hot with embarrassment as he held a ratty beach towel in her general direction.

It was then that Margaret realized she was wearing nothing but blood.

She tried to scream, but that didn't work very well because she was trying to vomit at the same time. The world was spinning again and she couldn't breathe. Then everything faded away.

"Are you alright?" He asked, trying not to look as he came close enough to offer the towel. A hungry voice growled in his head, but Margaret fought it down as she struggled to sit up.

"I don't think so," she answered in a shaky voice. Images and sensations flashed though him, too fast and muddled to decipher.

After a few moments of struggle, she worked herself into a half-sitting position and tried to look around. Looking anywhere but at her temptingly nude, horrifically splattered body, he held the towel as far towards her as he could without further invading her space. He felt her recognize him, felt her acknowledge the towel... and suddenly the world was lost in a wave of nausea. He was naked and covered in gore, fighting to breathe and scream and vomit all at once and it was all-just-waytoomuch.

Margaret fainted and the world came back to Jacob as he was falling to the ground, himself. He landed on his hands and knees, panting and trying to find himself in the lingering storm of images and sensations. After a long minute, he was able to collect enough of himself to throw the towel over Margaret's shoulders and stumbled back to his seat on the hay bales near the wall.

She regained consciousness quickly, sitting up a little more gracefully and drawing the towel around herself slowly.

"What time is it?"

"Six fifty-eight," he told her, checking his watch.

"Did I..." she hesitated. "Hurt anyone?"

"No, I don't think so." He wanted to be more reassuring, but he didn't really know. "How do you feel?"

There was a long pause. For a moment, he thought she wouldn't answer.

"I don't know. Dirty. Naked." *Violated.* "I can't be a werewolf... there's no such thing!" *There was no magic circle, it's all just pretend. Violated!* She shuddered. *...Powerful...*

He shuddered, too. He wanted out of her head. He wanted out of everyone's head. He could feel her disgust, her horror. It was his own. He had no idea what to do, and he knew that she didn't either.

This time Amber recognized the strange blue light. She was in her boyfriend's bed, wearing only her panties, and alone. Today was Tuesday. A school day. Why was she here?

Yesterday's events returned to her in a wave: Margaret going insane at pagan group; the world going insane when Margaret Dunn turned out to actually be a werewolf; herself going insane with... weird thoughts she couldn't control. She could hear Alex breathing heavily just a few feet away. He'd been so potent last night, so powerful. He was so grounded, she hadn't even suspected it until yesterday afternoon, when he'd stared down Anthony Domiano. It had made her even hotter than the werewolves' auras had... than Margaret's aura had. He'd had the shit beaten out of him last night and he was still doing his calisthenics. She couldn't help herself, she rolled over to watch. His back had been unmarked, but when he lay down to do his sit-ups, he wasn't as bad off as she remembered. The swelling on his face had already gone down and the two huge bruises on his chest were starting to fade.

"How?" She gasped.

"How what?" He grunted in between sit-ups.

"Your face! Your ribs!"

He sighed.

"You know how I told you I never get hurt at tournaments?" He asked, staying on his back for a moment to look at her. "I fibbed."

"What?"

"Between my metabolism and my meditations, I heal really fast."

"Since when? Why didn't you...?"

"What, say something? Tell you?" Alexander waved his hands, eyes wide. "And why?"

He met her eyes, shrugged, and looked away.

"Since, eighth grade, or so?" He shook his head. "Before the werewolf, I felt crazy just thinking about it. I was afraid if I said something, tried to prove it to anyone, it'd stop."

He didn't resume his exercise, he just stared up at her. His eyes were the most perfect peridot green, his hair so glossy black, his skin so rich and warm and brown. She smiled down at him and lay her head on her arm to watch. Eventually, he began his sit-ups. She watched for another half-dozen reps before it was more than she could resist. Amber climbed off the bed carefully, sitting so Alexander's head landed at her knees and caught him as he came down. He had enough time to make a quizzical noise before she bent over to kiss his lips.

The tops of her bare breasts brushed against his soft hair and she moaned into his mouth as his hands came up into her own hair. She bit his lip. He thrust his tongue into her mouth. He kissed her desperately, like he realized, as she did, how close to dying they had all been last night. As his hands pulled gently through the locks of her hair, she made a decision somewhere in the back of her head, and moved her hands from his hair to slide across his chest. It was his turn to moan as he arched his back into her touch and ran his own hands over her back and down her shoulders.

Finally, Amber came up for air, leaving Alexander gasping on the carpet.

"Amber?"

"I want this. I want you."

"Are you sure?"

"Do you ... not want to do this? I mean, I'm not your first. Am I? Don't you want me?"

"Amber, I ... Yes. No. Yes. I don't know?"

"What do you mean you don't know?"

"Amber, I ... Come here. I just need to know... is it me you want, or is it just because we could have died?"

"You, Alex. I want you."

"Then you can have me."

———

Margaret tried to sneak inside, wrapped in the towel, but she was caught at the door.

"Good morning, honey," her mother said in that pleasantly vapid tone she'd never used before yesterday morning. "Did you have a nice jog?"

Margaret just stared, mouth agape.

"That's nice. Why don't you go wash up? You're a little ripe."

Ripe? Probably. And not just a little. It terrified her that somehow her mother could mistake the gore she was soaked in for the sweat of a morning jog. She stumbled up the stairs to her room, desperately grateful that she didn't encounter anyone else before she could lock herself in her bathroom. She turned water on scalding hot, just as she'd done yesterday morning. She scrubbed until she thought she would rub off her skin. No matter how hard she tried to flay herself, though, the wounds closed before her eyes. Eventually, she managed to wash away all the blood she could see, standing under the water until she was beyond certain that nothing remained in her hair.

She was a werewolf. There was no denying it. She couldn't remember much of what had happened last night, but what she could recall added up to only one conclusion, insane or otherwise. She didn't want to think about it too hard, though. If she was lucky, there was a cure. Margaret grabbed her biggest, fluffiest towel to dry herself off then put it to the mirror so she could try to look herself in the eye.

She looked the same, Margaret thought. No taller or more muscular. Her eyes hadn't turned funny colors. She couldn't see anything different, except that it looked like small woodland creatures had affixed themselves under her arms and between her thighs, and her legs looked as if they had never been shaved. She didn't wax her privates, but she'd never let them get that unruly!

'*I didn't look like a feminazi yesterday, did I,*' she wondered to herself. Had she just not noticed or did it take time for all the changes to settle in?

She shaved and dressed, putting on twice as much makeup as usual just to feel almost human again.

Would anyone notice, today, that her arm wasn't broken?

Her mother had breakfast waiting for her when she went back down. She ate it mechanically. She had no idea how she was going to make it through the day.

How did you face the world when you were a werewolf?

When would the pack come for her again?

Jacob was waiting for her by his car, parked just inside the gate. Did he know this was where she usually waited for the bus, or was he trying not to be noticed?

"Did you make it in," he asked.

"Yeah," Margaret said, not wanting to talk about it.

"That's good."

The silence hung about them like the morning fog. Several times Jacob looked like he was about to say something then thought better of it. Eventually, just when it looked like he was going to work up the courage to ask whatever horrifying question had been occupying him all morning, she cut him off with a question of her own.

"Why did you stay?"

His jaw worked silently for a moment. She's spoken just in time.

"I came back, actually, just a little before dawn. Someone had to," he said with a little shrug. "Besides, I know what it's like to be on the uncomfortable side of magic."

"You're cursed, too?"

He didn't look at her, staring across the fields instead. He wasn't as beautiful as his friends Aaron and Dominic – few, if any, straight boys were – or as classically handsome as Dixon or Domiano. He was neither muscular nor soft, and he spent enough time in the sun to tan his skin and bleach his blond hair. The 'boy's uniform' of tee-shirt, jeans, and sneakers flattered him as little as it did anyone else, and he had an unassuming way of talking and moving that made him easy to overlook.

"In a sense," he said. "Some people call it a gift, and maybe it would be if it weren't so strong. If there were someone who could teach me to control it... maybe then. But it hurts."

Before she could ask 'what hurts', he turned to look at her. His eyes were startlingly blue, the color of the tropical water in her mother's travel magazines, and filled with pain.

"People's emotions, their feelings, their thoughts... all pour off of them like heat from a stove. I know, a little bit, what you're going through because I can feel you going through it." He met her eyes only briefly, turning away again before he continued. "When you came into the library yesterday, you were so confused. This morning you were scared, disoriented and dizzy. You couldn't remember what you did last night, except in little flashes that were more confusing and frightening than actual memories."

"So, you can read people's minds?" Margaret asked, dubious but glad to be talking about something other than her own troubles.

"Not really... or, not usually. Sometimes, when it's really bad, I can hear what people are thinking... but the thoughts, the voices, are so clouded with emotions that I can almost never pick out what goes with who," he explained, fidgeting with his hands. "It was so bad yesterday, when Tony and Alex fought, that I almost passed out. Usually, though, I just feel what people are feeling and know things I shouldn't be able to know."

"Like what?" She was genuinely curious, now. If she could be a werewolf, maybe he could be a mind reader.

"Like..." he hesitated, waving his hand while he fished for an example. "I know that Jen was lying about the guest preacher when she told us about the attack – there's something very important about him that she knows and isn't telling. I know that Dom knows she left something out, but not what. I know that Mrs. Crebbley had an affair with Coach Holland last

110

year. When I walk down the halls, sometimes, I catch random bits of people's lives – who's really in love, who's just together for looks, who's cheating on who."

"Sounds like you have an unhealthy interest in other people's sex lives."

"Maybe. I always figured it was because that's what people our age spend the most time thinking about."

"Do I think about sex that much? What am I thinking now?"

Jacob frowned at her.

"I don't know. I can't feel much of anything, right now... I've gotten myself back behind my walls. And I haven't known you long enough to say how much you think about anything." A large plume of dust appeared down the road and Jacob checked his watch. "That'll be the bus. Are you gonna be alright?"

She nodded, lying reflexively. No one ever really wanted any other answer to that question. *'I guess if he really can read minds,'* she thought, *'he already knows I'm lying.'*

"I'll see you at school, then."

⸻

The school bus smelled worse than usual: stale sweat, dog poop, mud, and weak antiseptics. Body odor, bad cologne, too-strong perfume, and detergent. A half-dozen strong odors that she couldn't quite identify, but which she instinctively recognized as people smells.

The first free seat she found was beside an unwashed punk girl who stank of cigarettes, cheap beer, pot, and sex. She scooted over to make room for Margaret, glancing at her nervously. Margaret tried to smile, but she must have failed because the girl crammed herself as close to the window as she could, hiding behind her greasy hair. It was a victim's reaction, Margaret realized – she'd seen it enough in Raechel to recognize it – and it hurt her to provoke that sort of feeling in anyone. At the back of her mind, though, something growled eagerly: the same voice that had reveled in Jacob's fear when he had handed her the towel.

111

It took nearly an hour for the bus to make its stop-and-go way to Lawrence High. Margaret spent the whole time trying very hard not to think about what was happening to her. It did her little good: whenever she really succeeded in blanking her mind, images of blood and wolves would flash before her eyes. She was almost grateful to arrive at school.

That gratitude was short lived, though. Had the halls always been this loud, this foul-smelling? The whole building teemed with people-smells: skin and sweat, lotions and body wash, shampoos and perfumes.

Gym class was the worst.

The locker room had always been rank: the sharp, acrid odor of hairspray; the cacophony of conflicting perfumes; the reek of sweat soaked into the very tiles, of mildew growing in the lockers. If the boy's locker was worse, it must be a portal to Hell.

Today she could pick out each of the individual stenches more clearly. She could tell who hadn't taken her gym clothes home recently enough. She could detect the underlying malaise of urine, menstrual products and bleach, almost overpowered by that strange, acidic people-smell she'd first noticed on the bus. It had been strong in the halls and was stronger still here. It lingered in some corners more than others, but it was everywhere.

People slipped by her like a mere obstacle – certainly not fully human, and perhaps not even really there. Most girls slid by without acknowledging her at all. Boys' eyes fell on her with naked lust, but they glazed over as they approached and moved on without so much as a whistle. Her closest friends would smile and nod as if they'd already spoken, before their eyes glazed over, too, and they moved on, laughing among themselves.

A few people, though – the quiet ones, the shy and the unpopular – seemed to notice her in ways they never had before. They stared at her with wide, wild eyes; some looked down as they scurried by; all gave her wider berth than strictly necessary. All roused a strange desire to pursue. All of them were surrounded by that same acid scent. Like the punk girl on the bus. Victim's reactions. Suddenly sick, Margaret realized what the smell was, what it meant.

It was the smell of fear.

She shuddered as she moved to her locker, her mind suddenly and blissfully blank. She changed in a haze, barely remembering to maintain the illusion of her broken arm.

Jennifer was surprised to not find Dominic waiting for her doing his yoga outside the weights room. She couldn't remember the last time she'd beaten him to class. The usual crowd gathered slowly, seemingly oblivious to the glaring absence, until Coach Holland came and let them in.

She pushed through her workout mechanically, waiting for him to scramble in late. Each minute that passed, Jennifer forced down another anxious scenario, each more implausible than the last.

'*Dominic never misses class!*'

And, yet, when the bell rang, Dominic Richardson had yet to appear.

Jennifer showered and dressed as quickly as possible, haunted by possibilities she refused to name. Hair still wet, she sprinted around the outside of the building, hoping to catch some of the others still at breakfast.

She was in luck.

Amber and Aaron were still sitting in their usual corner near the fire exits, lingering over empty plates. Just seeing them was a reassurance. If something awful had happened, they wouldn't be here, would they?

Amber's face was pale, but she smiled as Jennifer approached. Aaron gave her a solemn nod.

"Hey, guys," she said. "Dominic didn't come to weights this morning. What happened last night?"

The smile melted off Amber's face and she shuddered.

Aaron's eye twitched, and the corners of his mouth turned down hard.

"You're lucky you didn't come," Amber said.

"Poor Margaret," said Jennifer. "It's so sad that the attack fucked up her head."

Aaron barked an ugly laugh, his eyes wild, and Amber shook her head violently.

"No," Amber said. "Jen ... No. Mara's not crazy. She's ... she... she changed. We all watched it happen. It was horrible, Jen. Please, can we talk about it later?"

"Amber..." Had they all done acid or something? There was no way Amber had actually seen Margaret Dunn transform into a werewolf. It simply wasn't possible.

But the idea haunted her for the rest of the day.

'*Wolves stalk outside walls of this very house,*' a treacherous part of her mind recalled the strange line from Father Masters' sermon. '*...But you cannot see them because you are blinded by the modern world.*' The same treacherous part of her mind called up other events from that day, reviewing the attack almost endlessly. The massive dog, the impossible way Masters had crossed the courtyard and the incredible way the dog had leaped the fence. The miraculous speed with which Margaret's arm had healed.

The rational part of her mind refused to accept the connection. The preacher could not have moved that fast, so she must have imagined it. A broken arm could not have healed that fast, so it must not have been broken. Magic did not exist, therefore there could not be werewolves and Margaret could not have been attacked by one. As all of the above were true, Father Masters' sermon must have been metaphorical and an uncomfortable coincidence.

'*What about miracles,*' that treacherous part of her mind demanded. '*Aren't miracles magic? And if you believe in saints and angels, why are monsters and demons so hard to accept?*'

Each of them managed to make it through the school day, catching glances of each other in the halls and in class. By almost unspoken conspiracy, they gathered in the circular atrium at the front doors, where the hallway past the library met the end of the lunch hall and door to the administrators' offices under a huge circular skylight.

Dominic was the first to arrive. Shortly before the final bell, he wandered out of the library to stand in the exact center of the circular tiled floor and stared out the skylight, letting the crowd of students – first a trickle, one or two at a time, but quickly growing into a deluge – wash by him.

Given a whole day to think about the last night's events, he had only become more disturbed by them. He'd always known the world was bigger and more occult than almost anyone, including his friends, wanted to believe. He thought he'd seen it all, really: 'dragons', for lack of a better word, of the astral plane; spirits dancing in the fire; creatures of love and beauty he could only describe as angels; possessions and hauntings; countless physical manifestations of magic as well as psychic ones. Werewolf blew it all out of the water. Literally overnight, his entire world had been shifted on its foundations: he was now as clueless as everyone else; he had no idea what was real and what wasn't.

He opened himself to the rushing traffic of students, let their lives blend briefly with his, taking impressions as they went by but holding onto only the smallest traces. Love, hate, jealousy and desire. Angst and pain, arrogance and pride. All the joys and agonies of adolescence and humanity jammed together within these concrete walls, trapped and resonating. He let it all fill him, let it expand his awareness like his parents had done with LSD. Lives were his real drug. Pot was just something he did on the weekends.

One by one, they gathered under the skylight, staring uneasily at each other until most of the crowd passed and it was just the seven of them and a handful of slow-moving stragglers. Dominic came back to himself slowly, trying to remain as aware of his friends as possible. They were nervous, he could read it in their faces, but he could almost feel it radiating off of Jacob and the girls. Alexander had a strange, subtle, air of anticipation about him. Aaron was as tightly shielded as ever. Jacob, always trying to keep the world out, squeezed himself so tight that it almost hurt to be around him, but his fear was palpable too. None of them spoke until the last of the students had left.

"So..." Alexander said at last. "My house? The coffee shop? The bar?"

Jacob and Amber chuckled bleakly.

"My place is closest," Dominic pointed out, "and we'll have my Dad and his library."

Margaret and Jennifer looked nervous, but the others nodded. The Midnight Candle was the best place for this conversation: private, but with access to expertise and lore.

"Don't worry," Amber reassured the other girls. "Dom's parents are cool."

"I've never actually been into the magic shop," Jennifer admitted sheepishly.

"But..." Margaret said, "what if someone sees me and tells my parents?"

Alexander choked on a laugh and Aaron gave her a dark look, but Dominic's raised eyebrow had the greatest effect. She blushed and ducked her head. "I'm sorry, I didn't mean it like that. It's just that they'll flip if they find out. Hanging out with you is one thing, but going in there..."

"It's cool," Dominic said before Aaron could go off at the mouth. It did annoy him, too, though: she'd come to them for help, but didn't want to be seen going into a 'witch store'. "I was going to go in the back, anyway, so we could hit the kitchen."

"Isn't it a little early to be muchin' out, Dom?" Amber teased.

"Girl, you know I've always got the munchies."

Aaron snorted and rolled his eyes while Jennifer, Jacob and Margaret laughed. They adjusted their book bags on their shoulders, steeled themselves with deep breaths, and moved toward the door. Dominic took the lead, flanked by Aaron and Jacob. Amber took Margaret's hand, following a little behind. Jennifer hovered toward the back, near Amber and Margaret, watching them all with a wary eye. Alexander brought up the rear. They had little sense of true camaraderie, yet, but a strong sense of mutual unease: each lost in his or her own thoughts about how the world had changed last night. While none of them owed any loyalty to Margaret at all, and there was no small tension between Aaron, Jacob, and Alexander, their shared experience had formed the beginnings of a bond.

Dominic pushed the door open and let the others file past him, still trying to get a sense of each and all of them, to guess where things would go from here. Instinctively, he felt for that bond, the threads of psychic energy between them all. He wanted to feed that energy, make it stronger. He had the sneaking suspicion that something could go horribly wrong if he tried, but his intuition also told him that something was coming, that some great event loomed on the horizon and that they would need strong ties to survive the coming storm.

Anthony Domiano intercepted them just outside the school. He had been waiting, leaning against the bronze lion that overlooked the parking lot with his bag thrown over one shoulder, scratching nervously at his short brown hair.

"Hey, Margaret," he said, using her name for the first time since he had asked her out. "You got a minute?"

"Yes, Anthony?" she asked as the others stepped away from her, giving them a sort of symbolic privacy, but remaining well within earshot.

"I just wanted to say I'm sorry about yesterday," he said, looking at her feet. "I came on a little too strong."

A little? He had tried to man-handle her!

"Thank you," she said, grudgingly.

"And," Anthony went on, his gaze rising as high as her chin but drifting periodically downwards. "I wanted to ask if you'd like to go out with me again."

"No."

"Why not? Because you're hanging out with these losers now?" Anthony finally looked her straight in the face as he made a sweeping gesture toward Dominic and the others.

"No," she snapped. "Because you spent the whole night staring at my chest and talking about how you like to pick on people smaller and weaker than you."

117

"Oh, come on, babe!" he protested, taking a step closer to her. "It's all in good fun. Everybody gets picked on sometimes."

Domiano took another step closer and reached out for her hand. She pushed his hand aside and stood her ground.

"Hey," he said, reaching for the other hand. "Your arm's better already!"

She growled at him. It was a low, bestial, grating sound that carried clearly across the walkway. Dominic never would have imagined that any human being could make such a sound. People fifty feet away stiffened their spines, looking around for the source of the noise. Anthony jumped back, his eyes wide and his face white.

"Hey, babe," he gasped. "What's up with your eyes?"

"It's called 'anger', Anthony Domiano," she snarled, her voice dropping in pitch without losing a bit of volume. "Or have you never looked up from a girl's breasts long enough to see it? Now leave me alone!"

"Yeah... sure... I'll see you around..."

Margaret trembled as she watched Domiano leave, her breathing deep and ragged. Her hands opened and closed, and she even took a step in the direction he'd fled before standing straight and turning back to them.

"That," said Jacob, "was the coolest thing I've ever seen."

"Absolutely," agreed Alexander. "I've been beating the shit out of Tony for years and never seen that look on his face. Not even the first time I took him, Martinez, and Richards all at once."

Dominic was intrigued by how differently each of them responded to Margaret's violence than to Alexander's. They were clearly impressed, even awed. Jacob's face shone like she was his new hero. Even Jennifer, who also looked a little afraid, was nodding her approval. The attention made Margaret blush.

"Well," said Dominic with a sweeping gesture. "Shall we?"

He led them onward, down 19th street to Massachusetts, turning left and leading them another few blocks north, before cutting through the parking lot of the apartment complex

118

across from Central Junior High and leading them behind the Phill Zone to the back door of the Midnight Candle. The back of the building was unimpressive: a small parking lot butting right up against a Civil War-era stoneface with a short stair leading to the store and a pair of fire escapes leading to the apartments above. Dominic led them up the shorter escape and into a well-appointed kitchen.

"Any of you guys hungry?"

Alexander and Jennifer raised their hands.

"Pizza rolls sound good? And garlic bread?" They made agreeable noises, so he turned on the oven and laid some foil over a pair of cookie sheets. "Hey, Aaron, why don't you lead everyone down to the office in the basement and I'll be down in a minute."

Not two minutes after everyone had been led out the door, Dominic's father appeared in the doorway.

"So," he asked, arms crossed over his chest. "Which one's the Wolf?"

"The shorter brunette, with the really long hair. Her name's Margaret. The other girl you don't know is Jennifer; she who ditched out on us last night."

Robert Richardson nodded, his eyes turning introspective for a few moments.

"I've been making headway in the Book of the Wolf, but it's slow. I'm a little rusty on my Old German. Are you ready to be my research buddy again?"

"Yeah, I just want to try to get everyone on the same page, first. I don't know yet what we're going to do, but I want everyone agreed that we're going to do something."

Dominic's father nodded approvingly.

"You'll do well when you take my place as High Priest of the coven. You have all the right herding instincts, and as much raw power as your mother and I combined."

"You know Mom doesn't like it when we talk about power."

"Yeah, well, your mother's one of those 'we're all equal' idealists. You and I both know better."

Dominic didn't answer, but he did know. He or Aaron, alone, were almost as powerful as the entire Inner Circle combined, but if he even hinted at that idea around his mother, he'd be bound to the Outer Circle until he was senile. *'We're all equals in the eyes of the Goddess.'* He'd heard the lecture before. *'Pretending that our gifts are of greater value than another's is the most dangerous form of hubris and elitism.'* Somehow she failed to see the hypocrisy of that assertion beside her belief that women were closer to the Goddess and that men could not truly create anything, only shape what women had made. Besides: 'equal in the eyes of the Goddess' didn't really address strength, skill, or talent here in the mortal world.

"Where is Mom, anyway," he asked. "I haven't seen her in a couple days."

"She's been coaching the Deans, trying to prevent a divorce. She actually didn't come home last night... although perhaps that was for the best."

Dominic tried and failed to suppress a surge of resentment. His parents had been High Priestess and Priest of the coven for longer than he could remember, ever since Grandpa Henry had abdicated in his son's favor. Somehow it seemed that there was always some other emergency just when he really needed their help.

Marvin and Leanne Dean were very senior members, initiated before he'd been born. If they divorced, it would cause a lot of trouble with the Inner Circle, maybe even force someone to leave the coven.

At least Dad was here this time. Otherwise he'd be completely lost.

Crossing the threshold, the first thing that struck Margaret was the smell. The rich and pungent aroma rising off the complimentary coffee bar hit her immediately, cloyingly accompanied by the bowls of sugar and creamer.

Another step inside brought a riot of other smells. Frankincense and myrrh, familiar and yet surprising in this context. Sulfur and patchouli, more expected. Bay and sage and a variety of kitchen-smells. Lavender and eucalyptus and jasmine. Dozens of smells she could not name: sweet and sour, musky and acrid; subtle and strong.

She sneezed and coughed and tried to focus on her other senses.

Gentle, almost hypnotic music filled the store. Airy women's voices with Renaissance Festival accents. Meandering harps and flighty woodwinds and soft piano.

Racks of incenses and herbs filled half of one long wall. A display rack of crystals made up the balance. The opposite wall was filled with books, punctuated by heathen statuary and more crystals. At the far back was a pair of doors – one with a keypad and one with a padlock – and a bulletin board.

Margaret was surprised how mundane the place looked. The Midnight Candle was clean and well-lit, with an overall atmosphere of professionalism that surprised her.

If the titles or and the statuary had been a little different, she wouldn't have known that she wasn't in a Christian bookstore. The comparison embarrassed her more than a little bit. Did Christianity look as crazy to outsiders as this looked to her? Jen looked as uncomfortable as she felt, but Amber was picking gently through the New Arrivals section and Aaron was taking a moment to grab a few packets of herbs off a pegboard display before leading them down to the basement through the code-locked door. Who'd have figured the witch-store had high tech security?

The stairs were well-lit, as well, and carpeted. In fact, the whole basement was more upscale than the store itself. The staircase led into a wide lounge area, with a door at either end, and a large white table in the middle. Piles of books occupied the table, around which sat four chairs. A pair of plush recliners sat under the stairs, an end table between them and to either side. The room was lit by a line of track lights along the far wall, and a golden chandelier provided a little bit of mood. Three of the walls were painted with window-scenes of a fantastic garden, full of flowers and orchards – greens and golds and reds and purples and blues and whites. Margaret took a moment to examine them while the others settled themselves at the table. Nestled in among the branches and flower beds were frolicking faeries and dragons, and the paintings were so well done that she almost had to touch the wall to see that there were not, in fact, actual window frames.

"Wow," she heard Aaron say. "Dominic's been holding back on us. Look at all this stuff!" Looking over her shoulder she saw that he was leafing through an antique-looking tome bound in leather and brass. Amber and Jacob were examining the book collection, as well, while Jennifer was settling herself in one of the easy chairs, looking more and more uncomfortable. Jennifer kept looking at her with a strange mixture of doubt and fear that Margaret didn't understand.

It was only a few minutes before Dominic followed them down the stairs.

"Dad'll bring the snacks down," he said, pulling a twisted white paper from behind his ear. "Anyone mind if I smoke?"

"That's not ... weed, is it?" Margaret asked nervously. She'd heard from a few sources that Dominic Richardson sold pot, and that sure looked like the joint that had been passed around her class during the DARE program.

"Hell no! I want my wits about me right now. Oblivion later."

"I mind," Jen said with a hint of anger. Dominic raised an eyebrow at her, but tucked the cigarette back behind his ear.

"Alright," he said. "I guess the place to begin is to ask: Mara, what do you remember?"

She jumped a little. Honestly, she'd been trying so hard not to think about it that she wasn't sure.

"I remember the ritual... you guys chanting and burning that stuff that made me choke. When the moon rose, I started to itch all over. Then those ... bikers showed up and..." The bikers. Suddenly she remembered. "Oh, God, I've seen them before."

"You have?" She wasn't sure who asked, maybe several of them.

"Yeah... I saw them at the bar where Tony took me out a last week, the night before the ... the night before I was

122

attacked. They were staring at me, and there was this other creepy guy with them... but he wasn't there last night."

"You actually went out with Anthony Domiano?" blurted Amber.

"Well, I, uh," Margaret stammered. "It seemed like a good idea at the time?"

They all waited for a few moments, and when she didn't continue Jennifer asked: "Is that all you remember?"

"Almost," Margaret admitted with a shrug. The rest had seen it, so there wasn't any point in holding it back, even if it did make her uncomfortable just thinking about it. "The... bikers came, and I started getting really hot, like I had a fever or something and I couldn't breathe... I was just so hot, I started..." She blushed. She remembered very clearly pulling off her clothes in front of everyone, but she couldn't bring herself to say it. "After that I don't really remember much, just flashes of running and hunting, then waking up naked and ... bloody."

She shuddered. It wasn't something she wanted to dwell on at all. She couldn't bring herself to look up.

"That's it?" spat Jennifer, skeptical. Margaret couldn't blame her. She didn't want to believe it either.

Jennifer was disgusted with her friends. If that was the best they could come up with, she might just have to take her mother's advice and write them all off as crazy. Dominic must have seen it in her face, though, because his expression went cold, even a little angry. She'd gotten that look from Aaron so often that it was funny, but somehow Dominic's endless patience with her skepticism made it different on him.

"We remember the rest," he said firmly, his voice almost hard.

He started the story with their arrival at Margaret's parents' farm and her father's pointed refusal to acknowledge her guests moving toward the barn or even listen to her weak explanations for their presence. He told her how they did a ritual to test their insane theory. He described Margaret's increasing anxiety as the sun set and moonrise neared, how she scratched at her arms and seemed to develop a fever, how Jacob had sensed the werewolf pack before any of the others. He told her how the leader had pummeled the hell out of Alexander – not that she could see much sign of it, that bruise on his cheek looked several days old (*'But was it there yesterday?'* came the unwelcome thought) – and how Margaret had changed.

"This is all bullshit," she told them, although the memory of the day Margaret had been attacked danced through her mind. The monstrous canine – wolf or dog, a treacherous part of her wondered – and how fast Father Masters had moved and how the dog had jumped the six-foot wall. "All of you need to go see a shrink, get on some meds or something."

"Mara," Dominic said, his blue eyes turning from icy to arctic. His gaze held Jennifer in the chair even as her heart hammered in her chest. "Please come over here."

Margaret did as she was asked, hesitantly at first, but stalking purposefully within two steps. Dominic had pulled one of the pouches from his wallet chain and was measuring it into a rolling paper by touch.

"I asked you not to smoke," Jeniffer protested weakly.

"I'm not," he said. "Mara, it's going to suck to be you for a moment, but please bear with me."

He didn't bother rolling the herb into a cigarette, he just squeezed most of it to the front of the paper and flicked his lighter under it. A pungent odor that wasn't tobacco or anything she'd ever smelled before filled the room. It choked her a little, like any smoke did, but Margaret's eyes went wide and she fell to the floor coughing and clutching at her chest like an asthmatic. The small pile of herb burned itself out quickly after Dominic dropped it in the ash tray, but Margaret continued to hack and wheeze as he helped her to her feet.

"What color are Margaret's eyes, Jennifer," he asked calmly.

"What?" she started. "Hazel. What kind of crazy test is this?"

"Look again."

She did, reflexively, and gasped. Margaret Dunn was glaring at Dominic with eyes the color of butter amber, glowing softly like an animal's eyes in the dark. Her lips were pulled back in the beginnings of a snarl and a hot, curling menace poured off of her like sweat. '*Hey, babe,*' Anthony's startled question came back to her. '*What's up with your eyes?*' No one's eyes were that color, and Margaret's definitely hadn't been a minute ago. A part of her wanted to accuse them of playing her. To say that Margaret had faked a coughing fit to put in crazy colored contacts. To deny their insane assertion and walk out. But Margaret wouldn't be part of a joke that over the top, and frankly they sounded like pretty weak denials even inside her own head.

'*Wolves stalk outside walls of this very house...*'

She shuddered.

—————

Dominic helped Margaret to a chair while Jennifer stood stunned. Hopefully that would do the trick. He would hate to have put Margaret through that for nothing. And thank the Goddess it had worked. He hadn't been certain her eyes would change without the ritual. He couldn't add wolfsbane to his standard mix, being so damn toxic, but it was definitely going to have a permanent place with the other herbs on his wallet chain from here out.

"Sorry about that," he told Margaret as she started breathing regularly again. "I couldn't think of anything else to do to convince her."

"Did it work?"

"I don't know," he said, still looking at Margaret. "Jennifer, do you still think we're bullshitting you?"

"This is crazy."

"Yes. Yes, it really is," he replied with a sick laugh. "You gonna stick around and help us do something about it?"

There was a long pause during which Dominic didn't let himself turn to face the room. He wasn't really certain what his face looked like right now and he didn't want to push Jennifer

125

over the edge from 'scared and believing' to 'scared and running'.

"I..." he heard her stutter. "I need time to think."

"You know where to find us."

Book of the Wolf

SATURDAY, SEPTEMBER 12TH

Aaron sat on his back porch, looking out into the yard. The motion-sensitive light had winked out some time ago, leaving him in that dim twilight of a city at night. He itched for a cigarette, but as permissive as his parents had become since they'd left their Twelve Step program early last year, they could not tolerate anything that smacked of addiction. It reminded them of their own "former" addiction. It was almost impossible to watch television when they were home, although they hadn't ever gone so far as canceling the cable. Well, he could smoke soon enough: he was meeting everyone downtown in an hour.

For now he waited, trying to focus on the various problems at hand. Dominic's reticence, for all that he'd set it aside the night of the ... encounter. That encounter, itself, and all the implications thereof. Amber dating Alexander, dragging him back into Aaron's life. Any one of them alone would have been upsetting enough, but taken together? He found it difficult to think, almost impossible to concentrate on anything in particular.

The screen door creaked open and slammed closed behind him and the light came on, blinding him. The old porch creaked under a heavy, even tread.

"How are you doing, son," his father asked.

"Fine."

"Are you sure? You seem upset about something."

"It's nothing."

"Really? Nothing doesn't usually have you staring out into the yard every night for a week."

There were times when he almost missed the sullen obliviousness of those last few months, or even the bitter rages from when they'd first joined when he was in seventh grade. It had been easier to keep to himself, then. Easier to evade their attention, and easier to evade their questions when they had noticed things.

"Is it Dominic? You haven't been spending as much time with him lately."

"He's mad at me." Aaron didn't mean to answer, it just slipped out.

"Mad at you? Why?"

"I don't know."

He could feel his father's eyes on him, knew the lie had been seen through. Dominic was the only one he could ever fool, really. Dominic and Jacob.

"Well," his father said, resigned. "If you decide you want to talk about it, you know where to find me."

He did, but he wouldn't. He couldn't. He'd spent too many years afraid of the vitriol that could be unleashed by the smallest request. Even now, four years and Twelve Steps later, his parents could be vicious if they were in the wrong mood. Back then... They had never abused him, not physically. They had always found it more satisfying to use words to reduce him to tears.

Amber found Dominic in the back room of the coffeehouse with a cigarette in one hand, a cup of coffee in the other, and his head bent low over a book that was older than everyone they knew put together. His hair was tied back in a braid and wrapped around the back of his head with the aid of a pair of hair sticks. It wasn't sexy, but Amber wasn't sure there was any other man on the face of the earth – straight or gay – who could manage the look with the dignity Dom did. He even made it masculine, somehow. His sleeves were rolled up almost to his elbows, and a notebook sat under his right arm.

"How's it going, D?" she asked, walking up to put a hand on his shoulder. He didn't jump, but his coffee lurched in his hand.

"Slow and steady," he said, sitting up straight and turning to face her. "You?"

"Pretty good. Your dad lets you out of the shop with that thing?"

128

"It's our compromise. His office isn't big enough for the both of us, and this isn't the only translation project he's got going right now." Dominic leaned back in his seat and took a huge drag off his cigarette. "Some friend of his – one of the guys who's helping us out with this project, in fact – needs some paleographic back-up with an old copy of the Lazarite Codex."

"The what?"

"Lazarite Codex. Also known as the Lazarus Bible," Dominic lowered his voice dramatically. "One of the most pernicious heresies to plague the Catholic Church. No matter how hard they stomp on it, no matter how many heretics they burn, it just keeps coming back."

"Oh," said Amber. "So... what's the heresy?"

Dominic sighed, rolled his eyes, and gestured widely with his cigarette.

"The New Testament is almost entirely a lie. The Pauline Church is worshiping the wrong god. Judas betraying Jesus to the Elders was part of the plan. But, then, while Jesus was dying on the cross, Judas hanged himself and stole the stairway to heaven. God wandered off in disgust, and when Jesus rose from the dead there was no Ascension waiting for him. Now Jesus wanders the earth, trying to protect Mankind from Judas, who has to devour the souls of the faithful in order to maintain his godhead." Dominic shrugged. "That's the short version, anyway. I'm a little sketchy on the more intimate details. It's in the big pile of research projects labeled 'I'll Get to That Some Day', ya know?"

Amber shrugged, too. She did know, but Dominic read more in a week than she did in a month. Or sometimes two.

"Now sit down, kid" he admonished. "Ya makin' me nervous. Where's Alex?"

"He's coming eventually," she said with a shrug, pulling up the seat opposite him. "He's been going to the dojo every day since ... it happened. He takes as many classes a day as they'll let him."

Dominic closed the book and raised an eyebrow at her.

"So how much time does this leave for you?"

129

"Enough," she sighed. "Barely. But I've gotten more homework done this week than usual."

"Ah, the silver lining."

"So, where's everybody else?"

"They assure me they're coming," he said, fishing his grinder out of its pouch and measuring herbs into it carefully. "I talked to Aaron and Jake this afternoon at the store. I got Mara's phone number from Jak-o-Man. Her folks are still out of it, and it's starting to freak her out worse than the werewolf thing. You ever hear from Jen?"

Amber sighed again, shaking her head. Jennifer was freaked out by the whole situation, even worse than the rest of them: '*Just... leave me alone for a while, Amber, please,*' she'd begged on Wednesday. They hadn't spoken since.

Amber wasn't doing great, herself: nearly every night's sleep after the first had been interrupted by nightmares. Margaret changing in the basement of the Candle and killing them all. The pack coming for them at school or even here. She'd started searching the internet for anything she could find on the subject of werewolves in particular and shapeshifters in general, but so far she wasn't finding anything that fit with what they'd already seen and learned from Dominic's sources.

"Wait, you got Margaret's number from Jacob?"

"Indeedie-do," he said, pouring the ground herbs into a waiting paper and rolling it deftly between his fingers.

"Now, that's interesting."

"I thought so, myself."

Dominic lit his cigarette, took a deep drag, and exhaled a beautiful smoke ring. The familiar tingle of his energy washed over her as his circle of protection fell into place.

"That's so easy for you," she complained.

"I've had a lot of practice," he pointed out. "You could practice more."

No amount of practice would change the fact that he'd been born stronger than Amber. Dominic and Aaron, both. She could tell when they cast the circle that what she and Jacob contributed together didn't match what either of them put out alone. A lot of books insisted that women were more powerful

Wiccans, but her own experiences didn't bear that out at all. At least she was stronger than Jacob. That was some small comfort.

Amber pulled out her English homework, squirming in her chair to get comfortable.

Aaron appeared soon enough, just as she and Dominic were settling into a companionable silence. He swept into the room with long, graceful strides, giving them a half-bow as he approached the table. Amber smiled and waved; Dominic nodded, his face carefully neutral where last month he would have worn a broad smile. They tried, sometimes, to pretend that it was a secret, but Amber knew that something was going on between the two of them. Or had been, at least, until recently.

"Ladies," he said.

"Aaron," they replied. Dominic gestured for the taller boy to take a seat. Aaron did so.

"Where is everyone?"

"Coming," Dominic said.

Aaron nodded, pulling out a book of his own.

Alexander parked his Buick almost literally within spitting distance of the coffeehouse, but he spent half an hour walking around the block before going in. This new world – full of werewolf biker gangs and magic you could see working – was still settling into place, and there was a part of him that just wanted to go home and get high until things made sense again. Or until nothing made sense, whichever came first.

Eventually he went inside, ordering a coffee on his way to the back room. Only half the Crew had beaten him there. Aaron glared at him, as usual, but he didn't get up and leave. That was a nice change. Alexander pulled up a seat between Amber and Dominic, casually placing a hand in her lap, and sipped his drink.

"'Sup?"

"Waiting on everybody," Amber said, kissing him on the cheek. "How are you?"

"Good," he decided after a moment's pause, glancing toward Dominic and Aaron. Aaron shrugged. Dominic gestured vaguely at the tome in front of them.

"I've been fighting with this all day. It's slow going, but it is going," he waved a notebook at them. "So far I've got descriptions of three different kinds of werewolves. But I thought I'd wait until everyone got here to get into it, so I wouldn't have to repeat myself too much."

Alexander shrugged. "Fair enough."

He glanced around the room, noting the book-covered walls and the comfortable chairs that his friends had ignored in favor of this, the largest table. He didn't come here often: the cigarette smoke was thicker than he cared for, and, by their unspoken mutual avoidance treaty, it was Aaron's territory.

The music that murmured from the mediocre speakers in the corner wasn't bad – the college station was pretty hit-and-miss, depending on who was behind the mike and how high they were – but he wasn't a big fan of rock this cutting edge. In his experience, 'cutting edge' and 'independent' generally meant 'amateur' and 'under produced'. The clientele was an interesting blend of people their own age and college students and actual adults. Almost a third of the patrons were bent over what looked to be textbooks, despite the fact that it was Saturday, another third seemed to be reading for pleasure. Fun times.

Amber, Dominic, and Aaron already had their noses stuffed back in their own books. Great.

Alexander sipped at his coffee and gathered his patience, wishing he'd brought a book of his own.

The simple fact of the attack still shook her, never mind the occult elements. The suddenness of it, the fear and the pain. The lingering fears and doubts.

Was it some punishment for her sins?

Some test of her faith?

Such thoughts were a sign of weak faith or arrogance, she realized that. Who was she to be so singled out by God?

On the other hand, she had trouble believing that such events were truly random. If God had not singled her out, then someone had. Who? Why?

What had made her so appealing to the werewolves, to people she had never even seen before in her life? Her darkest thoughts pointed to the pale man in the fine black clothes, the one who had sat among but aloof from the pack when she had seen them at the restaurant. A monster among monsters, a cut above – below? – the rest.

The plume of dust preceded Jacob by a few minutes, so she waited, watching from her bedroom window.

If she was lucky, she could slip by her parents unnoticed. The unnatural way they ignored her changing behavior terrified her. At the same time, she was terrified that they would slip the curse and notice something was wrong. How in the world could she explain to them what she didn't, herself, understand?

In less than an hour Dominic Richardson – a boy some of her friends had warned her to fear as a homosexual, a witch, and a drug user, even a dealer – would reveal to her, explain to them all, exactly what she had become. Part of her knew already: she was a monster. Only a monster felt that sort of rush at the sight and scent of fear. Only a monster felt like *that* at the sight and scent of blood. But one question haunted her above all others: would knowing be worse than not?

Jacob's Taurus pulled into the drive. She grabbed her bookbag from the bed, slipped it over her shoulder, and took the stairs as quietly as she could. A lifetime of habit forced her to shout as she crossed the threshold – "I'm going out to study!" – but she ran to Jacob's car, desperate to avoid speaking to her family in a way she'd never been before. He was just opening his door as she dashed past, settling into the passenger side while Jacob blinked at her in surprise.

Wisely, thankfully, he didn't question. He just closed his door again and said, "Hey. Ready?"

She nodded, not quite trusting herself to speak. Jacob buckled his seat belt, pulled into the barn to turn around, and took off at a sedate pace.

The sound of the engine made her head hurt. The only other vehicle she'd ridden in since the full moon had been the school bus, and while that had been louder the engine had also been farther away. Jacob's car was clean, so there were thankfully few odors. A touch of oil and gasoline, which she figured were inevitable, air freshener and cleaners, but mostly it smelled of him. Jacob used the same brand of soap as her father, but no aftershave. She couldn't name his laundry detergent, but she liked it. The small space, already thick with his scent, served to amplify it, and she was surprised to realize that she could tell the lingering scent from that of him, now. He was nervous, she thought, but not afraid – not the way he had been that first morning after the moon, or the way those few who noticed her in the halls were.

"Do you know what he's going to tell us?"

"No," he told her. "I don't think even Aaron does."

"Does that mean something?"

Jacob frowned.

"I don't know."

They made the rest of the trip in silence.

"Well," Jacob said as he pulled into a space in the lot south of New Hampshire. "There it is."

"Yeah."

Margaret took a deep breath as she got out of the car, steeling herself with a heartfelt prayer. *'Please, God, let him have good news.'*

Jacob led her in. They each ordered a hot chocolate before he led her to the back. Everyone was waiting for them. Everyone but Jennifer; that familiar face was denied her. She had a moment of desperate fear and resentment: *'What have I become, how far have I fallen, that the only people who will talk to me are outcasts – literal witches?'* She shook herself, trying to push away that uncharitable thought, and took the seat Jacob pulled out for her.

They greeted her with varying degrees of warmth. Dominic and Amber were the most welcoming, despite their reputations – the former as a condescending and cross-dressing queer, the latter as an iron-hearted and leering lesbian. Aaron greeted her politely but impersonally, although his tone warmed considerably when he spoke to Jacob. Dixon's nod was wary, like he wasn't sure which of them was the dominant predator. They all welcomed Jacob like a long-lost brother, although he shied back physically from Alexander's outstretched hand.

"Well?" was all Jacob said when they had settled in.

Dominic looked around, getting nods of readiness from everyone before answering the unspoken but inevitable question.

"Okay, gang, here's the skinny. I've dug up the specs on three kinds of werewolves. There's a curse that's put on a person by certain circumstances – a couple of cursed thrones and valleys, a couple of gods and sorcerers who thought it was funny, that sort of thing. The curse usually has some built-in getaway clause, and, if the victim knows it, they can get free relatively easily. There are references to this in a couple Greek sources, namely a throne to which the victim had to return on the same night of the next year. There's another kind that's self-inflicted – make yourself a charm, take off your clothes, piss a circle around them, and *bamf!* you're a wolf. Piss around your clothes again in the morning and you're a man. First sources I can find on this one are Roman. And last, what I think we're dealing with, a thing called the Mark of the Wolf that seems to be the inspiration for modern werewolf mythology."

Dominic sipped his coffee and pulled another notebook out of his bag, consulting it before continuing.

"We haven't finished translating the relevant passages from our primary source, The Book of the Wolf. Even when we do, it's going to be pretty murky because... well, it's a premodern language, and the text is obscure and obtuse by turns. What we've got so far is mostly just confirmation of details from other sections of the Grimoire: the gypsy curse I told you about Tuesday, after Jenn left; the transformation into a full-time monster; the vulnerability to wolfsbane. What I've learned that's new, so far, is an even shorter list: werewolves can be hurt or killed by anything if you're a badass, but they are – as legend has it – particularly vulnerable to silver. One pamphlet -" he added this last with amusement "- even suggests silver-tipped arrows."

Everyone else laughed, but Margaret and Jacob were not amused. The darkness she had felt under the moon and when she had argued with Anthony stirred in her belly, suddenly aware of the conversation.

"You're not suggesting –" Jacob began.

"That we arm ourselves against the bastards who Marked her," Dominic interrupted. "Hell yes I am."

"But not ..." Margaret asked slowly. "Not against me."

"You haven't turned evil on us yet," Alexander pointed out. "Despite what the book says."

"But I might," she asked. Her voice was sad, but her back was stiffening and her hands were curling into claws.

"There might be some element of socialization involved," Aaron suggested, "dictating how far you go. But you have been more aggressive, haven't you?"

"No, of course, not! I –" She cut herself off, realizing that she was clutching the edge of the table in a white-knuckled death grip, as if she were preparing to throw it across the room, and that she was leaning forward in a way that could only be described as aggressive. Her feet were planted firmly on the floor, not tucked over to one side of the chair, as was her habit. The small hairs on her arms and the back of her neck were rising. Her heart was beating faster. *'Fight or flight?'* whispered the little voice she was coming to associate with the Mark. *'Four of them, one of us. If we run, will Jacob keep up?'* That last thought made her pause, brought her back to herself a little. Why had she left Jacob out of the tallies? Why had she assumed he would he would follow – not chase – if she ran?

"I..." She floundered, looking back up from her hands to see that they had all moved their chairs back. They eyed her warily. Dominic hand his hands on the Grimoire like he was

136

ready to pick it up and run. The rest looked ready to abandon their belongings. "I guess I have. I'm sorry."

She sat back down and they all relaxed. Dominic took a deep drag off his cigarette and Aaron lit one of his own. Amber was hanging tightly to Alexander, but her eyes – wide, hungry – were all for Margaret. When Margaret met Amber's gaze, the other girl turned away, blushing furiously. Jacob put a tentative hand on her shoulder. She wasn't sure if it were meant to be comforting or calming, but it managed a little of both.

"I'm sorry," she said again. "Is there anything else? A cure or a ..." – she tried to remember the fairytales her grandfather had told her, the fantasies she'd read before her girlfriends had warned her that it wasn't cool – "... a counter spell?"

"Not so far." Dominic shrugged, thumbing the corners of his notebooks absently. "The essays and pamphlets collected in the Grimoire are mostly historical and/or scholarly in nature. There's the divination we used at Harvest Moon, a few others, and a bit of advice on how to destroy, distract, or escape a rampaging werewolf, but... no. There are references to a couple other volumes, one of which I can get my hands on, but those haven't panned out yet. I'm sorry."

Margaret's shoulders slumped. "That's all right, I guess. Thank you for trying."

Dominic shrugged. "Don't thank me yet. I haven't done anything. But I also haven't given up."

He had to leave them early, as usual. Even though he'd called before curfew and gotten Dom's parents to cover for him, he was still in trouble for staying out late Monday night, and his early-morning departure had become suspect after the fact. His father didn't call it punishment, of course, but when he'd left the house at noon he'd been warned that he had to pick his younger sister up from dance practice at six. That was usually Stephanie's job, but Jacob knew better than to ask what had happened to her car. There would be an explanation – his mom had needed it to run some errand or another, or it was 'running funny' – and maybe it would even be the truth, but he'd be in trouble for questioning his father's authority. Family Dinner would take until past eight, of course, and there would be something to keep him from going back out.

"You don't spend enough time at home," his mother would say. Or: "You're spending too much time with those creepy friends of yours. Why don't you get some nice friends?"

If he argued with her, it would be real trouble. His father would join the fray.

"Don't talk back to your mother," he'd snarl. "Just who do think you are?" Or, maybe: "Do you want to go to a military academy?"

It always came back to the military academy, eventually. His father thought that would cure him of most anything. His attitude problem. His love of books. His lack of faith. His supposed homosexual tendencies. His father was convinced that spending time with Aaron and Dominic would make him gay. Somehow that didn't conflict with how angry he'd been when he caught Jacob downloading pictures of naked women off the internet.

He left Margaret with the rest of the Crew – Alexander promised to drive her home, even though she lived outside of town, too, and on the opposite side from him – and just went down to his room after he'd brought Ricki back in time to help Mom with dinner.

The basement of the Mathews' household was divided into two halves: the laundry room and his bedroom. When he'd turned twelve his father had offered him what had sounded like a good deal at the time. Help remodel the basement, take over the house laundry duties from his mother, and he could have a room of his own. It had taken him a couple months to realize that he would have been given the basement under any circumstances – his parents had decided that he was too old to share a room with his sister – and that he'd just been sold to the idea and extra chores to make everyone else more comfortable. He did appreciate the privacy, though, however little it was.

138

There were random inspections to make sure he kept his room clean enough, and if his father were upset about anything else, he became a real hard-ass about staying on top of the laundry. Some weeks he was running the washer every goddamn day.

It wasn't as nice as Dominic's place, or Alexander's, but it was better than Aaron's room and after seeing where Amber lived, once, he felt bad about complaining. He had a nice bed, a comfortable second-hand chair, a coffee table, and plenty of book shelves. Although they disapproved, his parents didn't actually bar him from buying science fiction novels, and they'd even given him his own stereo for Christmas one year. They wouldn't let him buy books on witchcraft, though, or even check them out from the library. He'd been grounded for a month the last time he'd tried.

Jacob sat himself down in his favorite chair and tried to decide what he was going to do with himself. This werewolf shit was fucking with his head. A month ago, he'd thought that he had a handle on his own problems. He had almost convinced himself that if he just prayed hard enough it would all go away. The deeper he meditated, the closer to the Goddess he felt when he prayed or when he Drew Down the Moon, the easier it was to sort out what *he* was feeling from what *everyone around him* was feeling.

But, when he did slip – when he stopped pretending it wasn't possible to hear what people were thinking and see their auras – it hurt more. Everyone else's feelings were just so intense, so overwhelming. It was getting harder to come back to himself, too.

Then Margaret had shown up last week and it had gotten really, really hard. Just being in the same room as her hurt, sometimes; she glowed so brightly. When it didn't hurt, though, it scared him worse because it felt good. Like Dominic, and Aaron to a lesser degree, she seemed to have enough energy to share with him: that if he just knew how to ask, she'd prop him up and lend him the strength he didn't have. He could feel the monster inside her, the Mark, coiled and waiting. Especially today, when he'd touched her. It was a darkness hiding at the back of her mind, in the center of her body. He'd never felt anything so clearly, before, and that was what scared him the most.

Sighing, he drew his legs up under him and leaned back in the chair. He tried to let his mind go, to slip into the meditative trance Dominic and his books had instructed. The peace and emptiness they described still eluded him, but he was getting closer. He could relax his entire body at will now, open himself up until he could see everything in the room without his eyes. Working down from the crown of his head, he relaxed each of his muscles, one by one. He slowed his breathing and his heart, and let his senses spread out as far as he could without stretching. He wasn't as strong as the others, not even Amber, but he was getting better. He could feel the far edge of the basement, beyond the washer and dryer, and to the top of the stairs. He could feel his mother and sister pattering back and forth in the kitchen. Like he'd felt the werewolves coming that first night, he felt his father open the door at the top of the stairs.

"Dinner's almost ready," his father said, just loud enough to be heard. "Come up and set the table."

It was nearly midnight by the time Dominic made it home, but his father was still working in his office. To Dominic's surprise, his mother was there as well, standing at her husband's shoulder with a steaming mug of coffee in her hands.

Mindy and Bob Richardson didn't look like the heads of the oldest coven in the Midwest, not in their street clothes at any rate. They were both tall and thin, light-eyed and dark haired – although most of his was gone. They didn't have visible tattoos or wear an overabundance of jewelry.

"Your father tells me you've gotten into something of a mess." There was no accusation in her voice and only a little bit of it in her eyes. Dominic shrugged uncomfortably.

"That's an understatement."

"I'm sorry I wasn't here to help you sooner." There were times his mother could make an apology into a guilt trip. This might or might not have been one of them: Dominic was upset enough with himself over not asking for help from the start that it was hard to tell.

"Me, too." He hated feeling guilty. That was natural, of course: everyone hated feeling guilty. But it was worse, somehow, because as a witch the only thing you were expected to feel guilty about was a genuine screw-up. Yeah, he'd made a bad call about asking his parents – who doubled as his clergy – for advice about the Margaret situation; but given the information he'd had, that had been the only logical choice. So he tried to turn the guilt around. "Did... did y'all know about this shit?"

They exchanged a guarded look, and when they turned back to him, their faces were posed in the soft serenity he associated with their roles as High Priestess and Priest.

"Yes," said the High Priestess. "You would have been told upon receiving your Third Degree."

A secret of the Inner Circle, meant only for the wisest and most experienced members of the coven. That made sense, of course. He wouldn't trust the Outer Circle with that sort of thing: half would run screaming, half of what remained would want to examine the darkness under a microscope, and the rest would try to preach peace, love, and brotherhood to the werewolves. He, himself, had gone more than a little bit out of his way to conceal truths far less terrifying from Aaron, Jake, and Amber. If it was a matter for the Inner Circle, though, he might be in a whole other kind of trouble.

"So... being of the Outer Circle, myself, what's to be done about my having found out about all this?"

This time there was no significant glance. The matter had already been decided.

"Nothing, as long as it can be kept from the coven. You're to be raised to the Inner Circle as soon as a place opens for you, anyway." The High Priestess – now wearing her Mom face again – sighed, hanging her head a little. "Which will be soon. I don't think the Deans can be reconciled. At least one of them will be leaving the coven... I don't know how many they'll take with them."

Bob put a consoling hand on his wife's arm.

"It was going to happen sooner or later. We're too large as it is, and it's not the first time the Crystal Dream has split."

"No, but it's the first time on our watch." She shook herself physically. "But that's in the hands of the Goddess, now. Pull up a chair, honey, we have research to do."

———————————

SUNDAY, SEPTEMBER 13TH

When Jennifer was younger, back before their Baptist congregation had become the Rapture Baptists, she'd gone to the same church as her family. Then, when she was twelve, Reverend Baker had come. The angry, charismatic preacher had frightened her almost from the day they'd met. By fourteen she had convinced her parents to let her attend a church of her own choice. They had reserved veto rights, but never invoked them.

More than anything else, it was the gentle tone of Lutheran sermons that had appealed to her. That and the emphasis on Grace. The way this church and Pastor Mary had filled her with the sense of God and goodness from the first time she'd crossed the threshold.

She didn't listen to the sermon today, not really. She bowed her head in silent, meditative prayer and let the words wash over her while she searched her soul for answers. What was wrong with Margaret? How could the others believe what they claimed to believe? But, on the other hand, if she did not believe them, how could she claim to be a woman of faith? Whether they were delusional or not, the most important thing was, what should she do? Tell her parents? Tell the school? The authorities? Try to undermine the delusion by making them give her real proof?

'Weren't Mara's eyes enough?'

By the end, though, she still hadn't reached any conclusions. There was only one course of action that seemed to make any sense at all.

"Pastor Mary," Jennifer said hesitantly, coming up behind the woman as the majority of the congregation filed out. "Can I talk to you for a moment? Privately?"

The Pastor nodded, her expression solemn. "Of course, Jennifer. May it wait a few minutes, though?"

Jennifer nodded and waited her turn while a few parishioners came to compliment Mary on her sermon or ask for an interpretation of some piece of Scripture. Eventually the sanctuary had all but cleared and the woman's attention was hers.

"Please, come to my office," she said, leading the way. "What would you like to talk about?"

Jennifer followed, not saying anything until she'd sat and Pastor Mary had closed the door behind them. She glanced around the room only briefly. The stained-glass windows or the massive bookshelf behind the desk might have held her attention under other circumstances, but today they seemed inconsequential.

"I have something really ... strange to ask you," she began while the woman sat herself companionably in the other chair this side of the impressive oak desk.

"Go on."

"I have a ... friend. She thinks she's a werewolf. It's so stupid, but ... Most of my friends believe her and I don't know what to do."

"Your friends don't do drugs, do they?"

Jennifer shifted uncomfortably, but she didn't evade the question: "A couple of them smoke weed, and I think one of them might do mushrooms sometimes, but ... "

Pastor Mary nodded.

"It's Margaret Dunn, isn't it?" she asked.

"What? No! Well ... yes. How did you know?"

The woman sighed.

"I suspected that the incident was more than it seemed," she said, "but I thought Father Owen would have told me if that were the case."

For a moment, Jennifer forgot to breathe.

143

"You... you don't believe..." she stuttered. "But that's crazy!"

"I'm sorry to tell you that it's not. Werewolves are quite real, and if Miss Dunn thinks she has become one, it's very likely that she has. Especially if she has managed to convince others of the case. Are they good friends of yours?"

"Some of them."

"Are they fools?"

"Only sometimes."

"Well," Pastor Mary sighed, rubbing her arms with her hands. "I suppose there is only one thing to be done. Go home, Jennifer. Come back tomorrow afternoon and I'll tell you what I've been able to find out."

Mary led the young woman from her office almost absently, her mind already on her quarry. Father Owen Masters. Her mentor, her friend, the father she'd never had.

Again, as so many times before, she wished that she possessed some of the psychic gifts she had seen in others. The lack had ultimately convinced her to abandon the life she'd briefly shared with Father Owen: roaming the world, hunting down and undermining evil, spreading the Word by example.

She had been glad of his company, these last weeks, delighted to spend time with him again after so many years. But, she had also wondered why he was still in town so long after his sermon. Even as they sipped their coffee or tea and reminisced about her youth or debated dogmatic law, he carried a familiar air of waiting. She'd seen him like this before, of course. He always knew when a hunt was coming.

Margaret Dunn, Marked as a Wolf. A sad fate for such a sweet girl.

She found him at the Jazzhaus, hunched over the bar with a glass of whiskey and a cigarette. A local band played on the stage and the club was dotted with their followers, but even the other barflies gave Owen Masters a wide berth. He was still dressed in his clerical robes – she'd never seen him out of them,

144

in fact, or without his embroidered black gloves and yarmulke – and he wore a scowl that spoke quite eloquently of God's wrath. He held his own gaze in the mirror behind the bar, staring so intently that she was surprised he noticed her approach.

"Well, well, if it isn't my dear Mary." His speech wasn't slurred, but it held a familiar bitter tone. "Get 'er a drink, barkeep. You're a gin and tonic girl, as I recall?"

She hated seeing him like this.

"Well, don't you cut a fine figure of the cloth?"

"Don't presume to preach to me, Mary. There's exactly nothing in the Bible against a good stiff drink to fortify yourself against the hard times to come, so long as you face them with faith."

"That's not the point and you know it."

He threw back his drink and scowled at her.

"Another Glenlivet?" asked the bartender. Masters nodded.

"And what is the point, Mary?"

He always used her name too much when he was drunk, ever since they'd met back in 1965. It disturbed her a little that he looked almost exactly the same today as he had then, not even a little grayer in the beard. Maybe, just maybe, he was a little harder about the eyes... more likely she'd just grown up enough to read it. She had seen stranger things, though, than unnatural longevity.

"One of my flock is a werewolf."

"I know."

"Why aren't you doing anything about it? You've worked greater miracles, I've seen you! For the love of all that's holy, Father, why didn't you even tell me?"

"She hasn't asked," he said, downing half his glass in one gulp. "You didn't ask."

"Why do we have to ask? How could she even know that you could help her if you don't at least try?"

"If her faith were strong enough, she would seek me out."

"Why, Owen? Tell me, please."

"Those are the Rules, Mary. I've explained it to you before."

Mary took a deep breath.

"Then explain again," she said, "because I still don't get it."

"Your faith isn't strong enough. The Rules are the Rules, and they bind us all by degrees in accordance with our power." He finished the whiskey and took a long drag off his cigarette. "Don't lose hope, though. The girl who followed you here has the potential. She might yet save your lost sheep."

"What?" Mary gasped, looking over her shoulder. Jennifer Hobb was, indeed, watching them from a few tables away. There was no way she could have overheard their conversation – as loud as bands in this town liked to play, there was little chance the men to either side of them could hear – but she was surprised and embarrassed that she hadn't noticed her tail. "I see. Well, do I call her over?"

"She knows you've seen her. She'll come over when she works up the nerve." He ordered another drink and lit a new cigarette, his eyes never leaving those of his reflection. "Calm down, Mary. Have a drink."

Startled and unnerved, she accepted both the offer and the unclaimed bar stool immediately to his left.

Jennifer was surprised by how easy it was to follow Pastor Mary. It helped that the roads were all but empty on a Sunday night, but that also made her nervous, thinking that all her pastor need do to notice her was to look backwards.

A little to her surprise, they went straight downtown, where Pastor Mary began ducking into dive bars. Louise's, the Replay Lounge, the Red Lion. The woman would duck in momentarily, always coming back out before Jennifer could figure out how to get in. When she did not come out of the Jazzhaus so immediately, Jennifer didn't wait for her flagging courage to fail.

The door on the ground opened into a steep, narrow stair, ill-lit and lined with thick layers of illegible fliers. At the top was a landing with an ATM and a chair for the bouncer, who was too busy flirting with a girl at the corner of the bar to notice as Jennifer slipped by.

The place was mostly empty: the few Sunday night patrons congregating either by the bar or by the stage at the far end of the room. It was dark, the air blurry with smoke from cigarettes and the candles that lit the tables. The chairs were battered and duct-taped office rejects, tilting wildly and rolling only reluctantly.

Pastor Mary and – as Jen had hoped and suspected – the mysterious Father Owen were easy to spot: two figures of the cloth at the bar. The old man stared into the mirror behind the bar, smoking a cigarette and throwing back tumblers of pale yellow liquor with gusto while the woman scowled at him. Jennifer didn't have the nerve to get close enough to listen in, but she picked out a table from which she could watch them. They didn't talk for long: Masters' sharp gestures said clearly that he was already displeased with the world before Mary began to rail at him. Mary's pleading ended abruptly with a glance over her shoulder and a startled expression when her eyes met Jennifer's, and the pastor joined her elder at the bar.

Jennifer's heart skipped a beat. She was caught.

'Well,' she thought, '*better to face the music now.*' The decision made, however, it still took her a few minutes of slow, deep breaths to wind up her courage.

"Good evening, Miss," the old priest said when she came up behind him. He glanced at her only briefly before returning his attention to the mirror behind the bar. He patted the bar stool beside him. "Have a seat."

He ordered another drink for himself and Pastor Mary with a gesture, but warded the bartender away from Jennifer with another.

"Thank you, sir."

"Call me Owen."

"Of course, Father Owen."

"You seem troubled, Miss." His voice had not been smooth at the pulpit; commanding, powerful, yes, but not smooth. Now it was harsh, almost gravelly with smoke and drink. Still, his unplaceable accent was precise, his cadence metered.

"Some strange things have been happening lately, sir. Pastor Mary seems to think you know something about them."

"It's fairly likely."

He made the admission with a shrug, bringing his cigarette to his lips. His eyes never left his reflection, forcing Jennifer to either meet his eyes in the mirror – a simultaneously awkward and uncanny exchange – or stare at his inexpressive profile.

He wasn't going to make this easy for her, it seemed. Jennifer floundered for a place to begin.

"Are there such things as werewolves?"

He nodded. Jennifer watched the reflection of his eyes slowly close and open as he did so.

"Since men first named the poor wolf as the incarnation of all that is wild and monstrous, there have been men who've donned the mantle of that myth to become greater monsters than they could be on their own."

Jennifer paused, running through that twice.

"Is that what werewolves are? Men trying to be monsters?"

Owen Masters nodded.

"Most of them. Some are harmless shamans. For a long time it was something you had to do to yourself. Then someone made it into a curse that works something like a disease." He took a sip of his liquor. "The movies got that much right."

He hadn't quite come out and said it, but that was close enough. She shivered despite the warmth of the air.

"But you knew that already, deep down, or you wouldn't be here. Why don't you go ahead and tell me what's really bothering you."

He did have the truth of that, she knew. So she told him everything, beginning with her long-standing friendship with the witches of Lawrence High to provide a little bit of context for the day Margaret walked in to beg their assistance.

"I'm scared, Father," she finished. "Most of my friends are heathens, one of the few who isn't has been cursed, and everything I thought I knew is wrong!"

"God has a plan for everyone, Miss Jennifer," Masters chided, stubbing out his cigarette and gesturing for another whiskey. He still refused to look her directly in the face, but she could feel her skin crawl with the intensity of his reflected gaze. "I know that it sounds like a terrible platitude, but don't forget that. Their fates are their own. The best you can do for them is to teach by example. They're doing the right thing already, aren't they? Have they asked anything in return for their help, even the cost of supplies?"

The question startled her. They hadn't, of course. It hadn't occurred to her that they might.

"No, never," she was forced to answer.

He nodded, smiling a little.

"Then just keep the faith, girl. They'll see the Light eventually."

Mary and Masters watched the young woman walk off in a daze before turning back to each other.

"I like her," said the old man.

"So do I," admitted Mary. "And she's talked to me about some of these friends before. She understands that they were driven away by well-meaning fools, but she's very distressed that they've fallen off the Path. Do you think you might recruit her?"

Masters turned his eyes back to the mirror for a few minutes before answering.

"Yes," he said at last. "I think I will, in a year or five. She has certain potentials that are best developed on one's own, at first."

Mary looked at him expectantly.

"What, you think I'll actually tell you what I see in the future?"

"There's a first time for everything," she said with a shrug.

"True," he laughed. "But the time for that first is not now."

Dominic was sitting at his desk, finishing off his homework so he could get back to the research when his phone rang. He answered with a drawl: "Y'ello."

"It's Jen."

"Good to hear from you. How're you doing?"

"Better," she said. He could hear her draw a deep breath. "I'm in."

"Glad to hear it."

"How can I help?"

"We're meeting tomorrow after school, at the coffeehouse. We're gonna try to figure out what to do next, then."

"I'll be there."

"Glad to hear it. See you Monday."

"See you."

As he hung up the telephone, Dominic had the feeling that things were getting on track.

Lady of the Black Roses I

The caretaker – who never asked her name nor provided his own – was a wiry, fey old man with wild white hair and sparkling black eyes, whose tanned, leathery hide was rarely covered by more than a colorful sarong. He had set her to work, first, at cleaning up the various scattered camp sites around the property. It was, of course, a task that he didn't care for, but she didn't mind it. Although he was spry for his age, the caretaker was getting on in years, and Caitlyn was happy to start with the most remote parts of the ground and work her way in. Her other duties included cutting firewood, felling dead trees marked by the land's other caretakers, and helping the land's patrons find their way around on those extremely rare occasions that anyone asked. It was a small price to pay for his overlooking her semi-permanent encampment and the fine meals he cooked up for them both in the trailer the Sanctuary provided for him near the front gate.

He was an old pothead, of course, but he wasn't a lecher. He made no effort to get her drunk or high, and never even tried to talk her out of her clothes, much less into his bed. Most of the time he didn't talk at all, actually, but he was very clever when he did. When her duties were done with on any given day, and they'd finished their dinner, they would sit together on the lake shore in companionable silence while he sucked down a joint and she smoked her cigarettes. Sometimes they'd split a beer.

"So, how long you plannin' on stayin' here," he asked at last, one night after she'd been hauling wood for him for nearly two weeks. "Not that I mind the help."

"Well," she said carefully, pulling the cork from a bottle of mead that one camper had been kind enough to leave for them, "I suppose I should leave before it gets too cold."

"A lot of folks would say it's been getting pretty cold already," the caretaker pointed out with a wry smile.

"I'm warm-blooded," she said with a smile of her own. "But probably not enough to stay out here all winter. I guess I should find a place in town."

"As to that, I've been talking to the owners and, well, they've agreed to let you stay here in my stead for the winter, if you'll let them interview you and run a background check."

She shook her head slowly.

"Sorry, friend, but that won't work. I really appreciate the offer, but... "

He nodded. "I imagined you'd say as much, but I thought I'd offer since you've been such a big help to me."

It was past time to move on if the owners were asking about her. It was time she found more permanent lodgings, anyway. Lawrence would do. It was a little pricey, but it was close enough that she could come back to the camp on a whim. There were a few such places in the United States, known to the Groves but not affiliated with any Order. She'd picked this one because it was within the domain of the Wolf King of Kansas City – all her sources had told her that he kept an even tighter lid on things than his counterparts in Berlin and Moscow, and so far the evidence of her eyes had borne that out. This much open land around population centers like Kansas City and Topeka should have been rife with monsters, but the populace went blissfully unmolested.

She'd thought about St. Louis or Columbia, near the Ozark "Avalon", but the caves and valleys of the Ozarks were infamously lousy with werewolves and worse. People blamed all the disappearances on alcohol-related accidents, runaways, and internet perverts, but the hunters knew. The Orders had offered her a half-million pounds annually to police the region, plus whatever she could get for bounties on the local market, but she'd turned them down flat. She was out, by god.

MONDAY, SEPTEMBER 14TH

There was a new face at the coffee shop that night. Tall, thin, and muscular, with a long rectangular face. A tangle of red hair fell down to her shoulders, constrained by a pale blue kerchief. Her most notable feature was the sleeve of roses tattooed on her left arm, climbing up from under the wide leather cuff of her wristwatch to somewhere under her tee-shirt, which read 'Dragons Do It Best' above an illustration of a serpentine dragon coiled around a surprised-looking woman. She was curled in the plush chair that sat in the corner, reading a thick paperback whose title was hidden in her lap. She glanced up at him as he entered, out of the corner of her eye, but returned her attention to the book almost immediately. Dominic could tell that she was a practitioner by the way her presence brushed subtly against his own as he crossed the room, but she didn't push at his shields, so he didn't push back.

Any other time he would have gone up and said 'hello', but with Margaret's lycanthropy hanging over his head, he had to keep his priorities in line. Insanity now, new friends later.

Dominic claimed the usual spot, the big circular glass table at the back corner of the library room – coincidentally across from the redhead – taking the corner seat that was the furthest point from the entryway and from which he could see everything and everyone in the room. He rolled himself a cigarette, took a sip of his coffee, and pulled both the Grimoire and his notes from his bag. He and his father were nearly done with the translation: they had a rough-hewn draft that they were now refining and double-checking with a few of his father's scholarly colleagues, and the time was coming to have some uncomfortable discussions with his New Age friends about Old World magic. When a recipe this old called for pigeon's blood, the only substitutions were further up the food chain.

Jacob was the first to arrive, still dressed in the clothes that he'd worn to school. Not that his parents would let him wear anything more interesting, of course. Hell, Jacob's father was so crazy he'd have probably seen changing into something nicer as another sign of 'homosexual tendencies'.

There were three or four other people in the room, but it was interesting to Dominic that the only one who drew Jacob's eye was the same woman who had caught his own. He caught her attention, as well, and they stared at each other for a few moments before Jacob simply walked up to her and extended his hand.

"Hi," he said, "I'm Jacob. Do I know you from somewhere?"

"Cait," she said, extending her own hand. "Yes, but I don't know where."

Seeing the bonds between people was Dominic's own, personal gift, and there was definitely a bond between them. It sprang to life the instant they touched, apparently new-formed but thicker and more tangled than any newly-formed relationship should be. He always did love a puzzle. Subtly, furtively even, he unfolded his psychic shields to look at them more closely. The woman was a powerhouse: in or beyond his league and Aaron's. Like Margaret or Alexander, there was something coiled tightly within her that he couldn't sense with any clarity through her straightforward but highly effective shields. She didn't hide behind a complex web like he did, or by twisting herself sideways like Aaron, or squeeze herself closed like Jacob, or drown herself in white light like Amber; instead she had built a wall around herself. It was almost amateurish in construction, but it was backed up with enough raw talent that it didn't make a difference. The bond with Jacob didn't come through her shields; it slipped around them instead on a different psychic plane. Usually, someone who could keep her shields from interfering with her relationships wouldn't use such a blunt technique. Jacob's shield of denial was cleanly punctured, but for the moment the woman's energy was keeping him stable and grounded sympathetically.

The others filtered in while Jacob and his new friend chattered happily. Dominic greeted each of them in turn. A wary smile softened by a gentle touch for Aaron. A warm smile and nod for Amber, spread to Alexander with a manly thrust of the chin, returned in kind. A nod, bordering on a bow for Jennifer and Margaret. A short joke, a few words ... each time

154

his gaze went back to Jacob and the redhead, and the rest of the Crew's attention followed his.

It was horribly rude, of course, but they just couldn't help themselves. Jacob Mathews never talked to strangers. His reaction to Margaret had been uncharacteristic enough. To have him warm so quickly to this woman, too, was mind-boggling.

––––––––––––

Caitlyn could tell that the people piling up at the back table were Jacob's friends by the way they watched and whispered. They were an interesting bunch: the tall gay boys in black, the muscular power-sink and his clinging ladyfriend, and the two odd-girls-out who came in last. Some of these, she knew, were among the powers she'd sensed out at the Sanctuary last moon. She wondered if they knew that the shorter brunette was a werewolf – her Mark wasn't the strongest Caitlyn had ever seen, but it still stood out in a room full of humans. Eventually, as Jacob's enthusiastic rambling began to flounder, the (slightly) shorter of the gay boys walked over to them with a warm smile. He met her eyes and held them for a little longer than was really polite before introducing himself.

"I'm Dominic Richardson." He extended his hand. "This is my crew: Amber and Alexander, Jen, Margaret, and Aaron. You already know Jak, it seems."

"Caitlyn Hannah." She took the proffered hand with a wry smile. His grip was strong without being hard, his palm dry and a little chapped from too much time fondling papers. "Your crew?"

"Well, they're all my friends, but not always each other's friends. So they're mine."

She peered at him closely before smiling.

"You're very protective of your friends, aren't you?"

"Honey," he said, breaking out his best lisp, "you have no idea."

Out of the corner of her eye, she could see the other tall boy's eyes darken with jealousy. *'So that's how it is, eh?'*

Binding

Dominic watched his crew settle in after Caitlyn's departure. She had not warmed to the rest of the group as quickly as she had to Jacob – she had been almost wary of Alexander, Aaron, and Margaret in particular – but she'd seemed nice enough. Each of them had ultimately received a casual psychic probe, but he couldn't begin to imagine what she'd learned from it. Their reactions might have been similarly lukewarm, had it not been for Jacob's enthusiasm. Margaret in particular seemed perturbed by the woman: tracking Caitlyn's movements with her eyes. Had the older woman acknowledged it in any way, he might have thought it was a predator thing. Instead he wrote it off as a more ladylike sort of territorial behavior.

"So, ladies and gents: werewolves."

That got them back on track a little more quickly, all eyes turning to him.

"I've been going over everything we've read. I've talked about everything with my High Priestess and High Priest. As far as we can tell, there's just no cure for the Mark of the Wolf. It's a curse, not a disease, so what we would need is, in fact, a counter-spell. Problem is, if the sorceress who first made the curse built in a counter-spell, no one's ever found it. If anyone's come up with one since, I haven't found it yet. So, from what we can see, the next best thing is a binding."

Amber, Aaron, and Jacob nodded slowly, each making their "thinking face". Alexander raised an eyebrow, however, while Margaret and Jen exchanged a confused look.

"What, exactly, is a binding," Jennifer asked, her face carefully neutral.

Margaret's face, on the other hand, showed that she had a very clear mental image of what a binding might be. Dominic wondered if this was the influence of the Mark, or if she was remembering Dixon's trip to the hardware store.

Dominic rubbed at his jaw, trying to determine the best way to describe the theory to a pair of Christians with little or no background in magical thought.

"I'll save the macro-level theory for another night," he decided after a moment. "In short, a binding is a way to restrain someone or something without causing harm. For example, one might use a binding to keep a stalker away, or to help a friend give up a bad habit. In this case, we're going to try to bind the Mark of the Wolf in order to limit its ability to influence Mara's thoughts and behavior."

Margaret nodded slowly. "That makes sense, I guess."

"This is ritual magic?" Alexander asked.

"Usually," Aaron told him.

"Absolutely, in this case," Dominic agreed. "We'll get everyone together, cast a circle, and call upon the powers that be to help us bind the Mark. What we need to do tonight is hammer out what, exactly, sort of ritual everyone's comfortable with."

Again, Aaron, Amber, and Jacob were nodding right along. One by one, Alexander, Jennifer, and finally Margaret began to nod as well. Dominic smiled. Consensus was key to any magical operation, even at the planning stage.

TUESDAY, SEPTEMBER 15TH

"Sorry I'm late," Jacob said, following Dominic up the stairs to his flat. "I got handed more chores every time I was about to run out the door."

"It's cool. I just wish you'd called."

"You know how my folks are, Dom."

"Yeah. Yeah, I do."

Dominic poured them each a tall glass of water. Jacob took his with a nod of gratitude, downing half of it in a long gulp before sipping the rest. He took long, deep breaths between drinks, and was visibly more collected by the time he emptied the glass.

"I have to do this, don't I?"

"If you want any control over your gifts, yes. If you want to help Mara, yes."

"Okay." A deep breath, let out in a resigned sigh. "Where do we start?"

Dominic patted his friend on the back.

"The first thing we do is cast a circle. You have done that by yourself?"

"Yes."

"Good. Show me."

Jacob nodded, sitting down in the middle of the room with his legs crossed. He put his hands on his knees and imagined himself within a circle of white light. Breathing in and out, each breath slower than the last, the familiar sensation of peace settled over him. It was harder with Dominic watching him than it was when he was alone, the other boy was like a beacon of heat and light that kept drawing his attention from what he was supposed to be doing. Slowly, the circle of light settled into place around him.

"No props," Dominic asked, a little surprised. "No salt or incense? No invocations?"

"I can't keep anything like that in the house," Jacob said. His voice sounded dreamy even to his own ears. "I read that you can use visualization instead of ritual. Is that wrong?"

"No, not at all. Visualization even works better sometimes; it's just harder. Good job. Keep going."

He did, sinking deeper into himself and pushing the Circle outward until it ran into Dominic. It felt like turning a corner and catching his shoulder on the door frame. The shock brought him back out of the trance.

"What was that?"

"Those were my shields," Dominic smiled and sat down facing Jacob, folding himself into a lotus position. "Now, you just showed me that you do already know how to ground and center. The thing I need to teach you, I guess, is how to hold onto that when you don't have perfect peace and quiet."

The taller boy composed himself.

"Now, do it again."

Once more Jacob called up the image of the circle. Dominic's shields didn't surprise him this time, but they still stopped Jacob from pushing the white light far beyond the tops of his own knees. Dominic watched him intently for a few moments, making Jacob self-conscious. The peaceful feeling contracted and he almost lost the image. It took him several more deep breaths to really reclaim his focus.

"There you are. Now, reach out and touch the shield with your mind."

He did. The circle slipped. He grimaced, taking another deep breath, and began visualizing another circle. It happened again.

"What am I doing wrong?"

"I'm not sure, but let me back up and see if that's any better for you."

It was. Jacob could push his white light out far enough for it to stabilize. This time when he reached out, it didn't break. He wasn't sure what to expect when he touched Dominic's aura – maybe nothing – but what he found surprised him nonetheless. The mental hand he had reached out stopped dead about an arm's length from Dominic. The shield was as solid as anything Jacob had ever sensed and, although he couldn't see it in a literal sense, the image of an intricate, tangled Celtic knot flashed in his mind. He concentrated on that image and it grew more complex the closer he looked at it. It was knots, plural, not singular: layered one within the other like those hollow Russian dolls.

"Very good." Dominic's voice came to him as if from a great distance. "Now watch closely."

The knots opened, threads of thought sliding across one another to let Jacob in. They twisted, grew, and expanded until Jacob's own circle was contained within them, leaving Dominic bare to Jacob's examination.

Jacob did his best not to look. It was too intimate, and too likely to trigger the painful surge of knowing he was trying to avoid.

"No," Jacob said, holding his hand up between them. "That's too much."

Dominic's shields slammed closed so hard and fast, it almost made a noise. Dominic gasped, clutching one hand to his chest and another to his head.

"Fuck!" Dominic gasped. "What the fuck did you just do?"

THURSDAY, SEPTEMBER 17

Alexander looked at her, a single brow raised. "That's grounding and centering?"

"Well, yeah." Amber frowned at him. "What did you expect?"

Alexander shrugged. "I don't know. Something more ... involved than that."

She sighed.

"I should have known. You're always so grounded... I thought it was natural."

"Nope. They taught me that in aikido. So, what's next?"

"Have I told you about the tools?"

"A refresher course wouldn't hurt." In English: he hadn't been listening the last time.

They shifted to the side so that he could better see the altar. It had begun life as a foot locker, now painted with runes and spirals, and draped with a similarly embroidered violet-on-white cloth. The Goddess and God symbols were fairly self-explanatory: simple and idealized images of a man and a woman, they were idols and they looked the part. A tall pillar candle stood behind each of the statues. The pentagram representing the element of Earth placed solidly in the middle. A bowl of Water and one of salt sat to each side of it, and a cauldron in which to burn incense just behind. The black-lacquered willow-wand representing Fire. And, last but not least, the athame: a dull, black-handled, double-edged knife representing the element of Air and used only to direct energy during magical Workings.

"Now let's cast a Circle."

Alexander nodded. The research he'd done on his own made that seem like a good next step. He wondered if she'd

160

employ any of the half-dozen techniques he'd seen on the internet. She didn't.

She pulled the altar out from the wall and into the center of the room. Solemnly, one by one, she took four pieces from the altar and placed them on the floor. The bowl of salt to the north; the cauldron and a few sticks of burning incense to the east; a burning candle to the south; the bowl of water to the west. She didn't say anything aloud except to name the directions for him, but the way she knelt at each quarter before moving on to the next spoke of deep communion even to Alexander's atheist eye. She completed the circle by walking its perimeter, athame extended, her expression bordering on ecstasy.

He was startled to feel each of the elements swell in response to Amber's call. It was hard to say which surprised him more: that she actually had the power, or that he could feel it. He had always suspected that magic and ki weren't terribly different, and on the one hand that seemed to be the case: he felt them in the same way, a vague knowing at the edge of his physical senses like a footnote at the edge of the page. On the other hand, the things he felt were fundamentally different: at first the circle seemed to be an extension of Amber's aura, but the energy changed as she moved from one quarter to the next. The barrier she left behind was tangible, and discernible ... presences rose to her call, simultaneously watching within and without the Circle.

Then it snapped into place and Alexander Dixon had to adjust his definition of the word "awe". The whole of the Circle was definitely greater than the sum of its parts. The last of the presences answered Amber's invitation and she quietly called upon the Goddess. The Circle closed and the world ... shifted. He almost swooned. He tried to ground, but there was nowhere to ground to. Opening up his One Point only made him One with the Circle and the massive presences at the edges. For a moment he was falling into infinity. Then something – massive and eternal beyond even the elements – caught him. Consciousness faded into oblivion.

He came back to himself some minutes after Amber had banished the Circle. The look on her face was somewhere between worried and proud.

"You felt something?"

"Yeah. Yeah, I felt something."

Now, if he could only feel his arms and legs. That would be fantastic.

"I can't wait to show you the Great Rite."

SUNDAY, SEPTEMBER 20TH

"Kyle Beal Sanctuary? Some kind of State Park?"

Jacob shook his head.

"Cybele Sanctuary. It's like our church. I don't know how to explain it to you so that it doesn't sound stupid. But you'll see. Trust us. Please."

If he and his friends hadn't been so open and helpful, Margaret might have been less comfortable with the prospect. The most she'd gotten out of any of them had been Jennifer's reassurance that she'd been there before and that everything was on the up-and-up: just a semi-private camp ground between Tonganoxie and McLouth. A haven to hippies, Pagans, and nudists. She couldn't decide if she was intrigued or horrified at the idea. Maybe she could have decided if she'd had a clearer image to work with; her imagination had failed her.

Jennifer was riding with Amber in Dixon's four-door. Dominic was driving Aaron and the two large duffel bags of supplies. She was riding with Jacob, who also had to be back in town on a curfew.

Not that she minded. Quite the opposite. He was the only one who seemed to really understand the horror she felt, and he was pleasant company on his own merits. Quiet, companionable, and although she was fairly certain that he thought she was pretty, there was none of the leering she got from most men. He was a good listener, and when she wasn't in the mood to talk he always seemed to know whether she needed him to do the talking himself, or just share the silence.

The forty-minute drive was a silent one except for Jacob's hard rock radio. The loud, discordant, thrashing sounds soothed her. A week ago, she couldn't have told any two songs apart; today, she caught herself singing along.

She hoped, prayed, that with the Mark bound she'd be herself again. She prayed that people would stop cowering away from her at school – Friday she'd terrified one girl into a corner with an unhappy glance. She prayed that she could finally get the Crew to help her with whatever curse made her parents and so many other people ignore her.

They had been off the paved roads for nearly twenty minutes when the caravan finally turned into a drive at the bottom of a hill. There was no sign, no monolith, no marking at all except a plain black mailbox small white numbers painted on the side. The drive wound through a tunnel of trees that opened up at a faded red farm gate. Just past the gate was an unmanned booth with a pair of hand-made signs. "Welcome to Cybele Sanctuary." "No Guns."

Jacob rolled down his window, dropped his car into first gear, and followed close behind Dominic and Alexander's cars. The woods opened up, briefly – a field to the left and a ridge to the right – then closed back together as the road wound up the hill and around behind the next stand of trees.

The scenery was a little lost on her, though, because the Mark welled up in her throat as soon as they crossed that threshold. Something about this place scared her – scared it.

She felt stifled, constrained, like the car had gotten suddenly smaller. She wanted to run as far and as fast as she could. There was something here ... something large, more powerful than anything she had ever imagined.

"Are you alright?"

"No, I'm scared."

"It'll be okay. You're safe here. Everybody's safe here."

A glance at his face told her that he really believed it. This was where he came to feel safe. This was his temple, his church. Jacob had faith in his Goddess the way had faith in Christ. Somehow, she hadn't understood that before.

They parked just before the road sloped up the hill, everyone piling out of the cars to stretch. Jacob jogged on ahead, ducking into a green building with bright red birds painted on the sides. Without being asked, Alexander shouldered both bags while the others began visibly composing themselves. The road split halfway up the hill, the left branch curving around and up to what Jacob — who caught up to them before they reached the fork — called the Ridge, the right branch skirting between a steep slope and a row of buildings. Jacob named each of them for her: the dining hall, the bath house, the south cabins. The road ended outside of south cabin six, where a short footbridge led into the woods. The main path twisted and turned farther than she could see, but they took a side path down the hill shortly after the bridge.

The path opened up on an honest-to-God stone circle. The grass was cut here, and the path more carefully maintained. Flat yellow stones had been arranged in a circle nine feet across, with taller stones — albeit only calf high — standing upright in the center and at the four compass points. A clear opening was marked on the downhill side, near a limestone bench and a path that led farther down the hill. Reddening leaves rustled on the branches overhead.

Their faces composed and solemn, Dominic and Aaron worked with a casual efficiency that spoke of practice: placing candles atop the standing stones and at the cross-quarters, laying out everything else they would need precisely where it would be needed. Dixon sat himself on the bench, his hands in his lap, breathing slowly. Amber hovered, hands fluttering, at the edge of the circle where Dominic and Aaron worked; Jacob looked torn between doing the same and hovering at her own shoulder.

Too soon, Dominic seemed to think everything was in order.

"Are you ready, Margaret?"

She shook her head, too scared to speak, but she entered the circle anyway. She took the hand Dominic offered and let him lead her to the center. He knelt to one side of the knee-high stone and indicated for her to do the same across from him. A black rope lay coiled to her right, a pair of knives lay to her left, while two shallow dishes and a candle balanced precariously atop the stone between them.

"Do you remember what you need to do?"

Again she shook her head.

"That's all right, I'll walk you through it." Dominic took a deep breath, releasing it slowly. "Everyone else?"

"Yes."

"I'm ready."

"When you are, chief."

"Yes."

Dominic left her briefly to walk the circle, taking the black-handled knife with him. He traced the air over the stones with the point of the knife, his expression fading into serenity. The circle complete, he returned to face her across the stone altar. The Mark had given over its protests by now, retreating instead to a dark corner of her mind.

"Guardians of the Watchtowers of the East," Alexander began, standing downslope where they had entered the circle. "Masters of the Element of Air, hail and be welcome in our circle."

"Breathe deeply," Dominic told her as each of the others called out to one of the directions. "Slowly. In and out. Just focus on your breathing."

She did. In. Out. In. Out.

"Relax," he guided her. "Feel your body fill up with light as you breathe in. As you breathe out, let a little bit of tension go with it. Start with the top of your head. Relax."

Perhaps it was the soothing quality of his voice, some trick of his eyes, or the simple nature of the breathing, but she found that she could relax. He spoke to her slowly, patiently, encouragingly, while the others performed the ritual around them. They cast another circle, each silently tracing the sign of the pentagram in the air at their quarter.

"Breathe in slowly... one ... two ... three ... Breathe out," the slow, steady rhythm of Dominic's voice never wavered as he released first one of her hands to dip his fingers in one of the bowls, anointing her brow, eyes, and lips with water, then the other hand to anoint her again with oil, this time tracing signs upon the centers of her palms as well.

"Now, repeat after me," he said. "I, Dominic Richardson, do bind the Mark of the Wolf in the name of the Goddess."

"I, Margaret Dunn, do bind the Mark of the Wolf in the name of Jesus Christ." She made the changes without thinking, almost without noticing. He guided her hands together, binding them gently with the cord. She almost panicked, but his eyes and his voice held her. The whole world seemed to be vanishing into the particular blue of his eyes.

He bound her hands together between her breasts, an image of prayer, winding the cord around her ribs and around her neck before tying the final knot and letting the ends hang loose to the ground. Somehow, his eyes never left hers.

"I, Dominic Richardson, do bind the Mark of the Wolf in the name of the Goddess."

"I, Margaret Dunn, do bind the Mark of the Wolf in the name of Jesus Christ."

He raised the white-handled knife to cut off a lock of her hair and folded it carefully in thirds. From the bowl of water, he pulled three lengths of yarn – white, red, and black – winding each delicately around the lock of her hair.

His voice fell so low that she could barely hear him.

"I, Tiresias, do bind the Mark of the Wolf in the name of Lilith, Dark Goddess of the Crystal Dream."

"I, Margaret Dunn, do bind the Mark in the name of Jesus Christ, my Lord and Savior.

"So mote it be!"

He lit the candle between them and the world vanished into his eyes. Blue faded into black, and then there was nothing.

The fullness of the moon was coming quickly. The werewolves were getting bored. There was tension between them, dissent within the ranks, and without prey to unify them it was beginning to show. The leader was restless, impatient to be rid of the warlock. He was terrified of not having one, though, and unwilling to simply throw him out. The lieutenant bore no such fear: he simply wished Caleb gone. Somehow, they thought the warlock unaware of their animosity. Fools. The lesser wolves – weaker than any of their leaders, individually, and terrified of them as a whole – stepped lightly, striving to avoid the wrath of their temperamental masters.

The Monster found it all incredibly amusing.

"So, what next," the warlock asked again, pausing a fraction of a second too long before adding: "Boss."

He asked the question nearly every night, likely hoping for some opening that would allow him to usurp his master's position. It was a fool's quest. The warlock was strong, but he would not best the leader in a fair fight and he was apparently unwilling to simply strike from behind. Instead, the warlock was developing some intricate plot that he was unlikely to execute.

"We wait," the leader growled. "I've been haunting the bitch's dreams. The moon is almost full, and I will drag her into the fold when it is."

It was more information than he had given up on previous nights. Perhaps he grew weary of the demands, or perhaps he was only now formulating a plan. The warlock almost protested, demanded more, when he realized that he bore the weight of the Monster's attention and wilted, staring back in fear.

This also amused the Monster greatly.

"What do we do until then," the second asked, coming as close to agreeing with the warlock as the Monster had ever seen. "I don't know about you, Michael, but I'm starting to itch."

The leader nodded, slowly. The Monster was not surprised. It had expected the pack to grow bored long before this; it would have, at their age. Only centuries of practice had provided it with the patience it now possessed. What trouble would they get themselves into in the name of fun? It smiled to

167

itself, looking forward to finding out. It had been cautioned against pointing out that they had been instructed only to Mark her and wait. Events would unfold as its master had foreseen. Its task was to watch and wait, acting only if the girl's life were in danger.

The leader drew breath to answer, but he staggered before he could push the words past his lips. The pack moved as one, ready to take advantage of even a moment's weakness. They were not fast enough, though: the leader's eyes turned and his snarl bared wolf's fangs.

This was a sign of something larger, the Monster knew, because in that instant its own master was watching the pack through its eyes. With its master's Sight, the Monster could see the cord of power that bound the leader's Mark to the girl's. Something on the far side of that cord had changed, something the Monster's master had been waiting for.

"Boss?" The lieutenant asked a thousand questions with that one careful word.

"The girl's witches, they've done something to the Mark." The leader's voice was marked with equal parts rage and bafflement. He rose, pulling on his jacket, checking his knife and gun.

"Don't be hasty, now." The Monster spoke, but it was the master's voice that spilled from its lips. The pack froze. The Monster remained seated. The leader stalked past it, the pack following, though they gave the Monster wide berth.

Alone, the Monster smiled to itself. It did not stand or walk through the door. It flowed like water, slipping under the door as a shadow.

At first there was nothing, and she fled from that nothingness without knowing why. It wasn't dark. It wasn't light. Just nothing.

"We must find the Mark," Dominic's voice came to her. "We must find it and bind it here or the work will be unfinished."

Still she ran. Fear gripped her heart and faith deserted her. She knew this void. She dreamed of it often enough. The Mark was here, yes, but so was the pack: she could hear them howling in the distance. So she ran.

"Mara! Mara!"

'*Run!*' she tried to tell him. '*Run!*' The howls of the pack echoed in the void.

"Mara, focus!"

Dominic's voice was thunder, and he stood before her, arms outstretched in the middle of oblivion. She crashed into him, a tangle of arms and legs – human arms and legs, she was astonished to find – both naked as the day they were born.

He helped her to her feet and the nothing rolled back from them, a circle of solid ground floating through space.

'*Thank God he's gay,*' she thought desperately. He smiled and they were dressed, she in the clothes she'd worn that day and he in a white robe. The pack howled again. They both shivered, but Dominic held her hands too tightly for her to run.

"We have to hurry, but we have to stay focused, too."

Margaret nodded slowly. It was easier to not panic if she looked at him instead of the black nothingness that surrounded them.

"What do we need to do?"

"The Mark is in you somewhere. You need to lead me to it."

"How?"

"Concentrate on it. Picture it in your head."

Picture it? She'd never really pictured it, had she? What would the Mark look like? It was just this ... thing within her. A pulsing, coiling darkness. Red-tinted, maybe, and waiting. Whispering. A darkness that meant to tempt her into evil, violence, and predation. She thought of it and she felt it move.

"Concentrate," Dominic said again, his eyes unfocused.

She did, and the image became more concrete. A shadowy mist, highlighted with waves of blood-red. It watched her, but it had no eyes. It whispered to her, but it had no mouth. It squeezed at the edges of her mind, but it had no hands or body. Truly, it had no shape: it molded itself into the dark corners of her mind, hiding among her own worst impulses and inspiring them to grander sins and depravities.

The image in her mind came slowly into focus, and a red mist rose at the edges of the circle Dominic had made for them. The pack howled, drawing ever closer, and the Mark grew stronger and nearer still.

The ground upon which they stood grew wider, more real, and the Mark now flowed in a circle around them, no longer hovering at the edges of their false reality. They stood in a field, she realized, the field that surrounded her family farm. The pack had brought her here, too, in her dreams. Or had she brought them here?

The Mark swirled around them faster and faster, a tendril of black-and-blood mist spiraling into the space between their arms. Dominic's eyes snapped into focus once more, his hands tensing in hers. Was it hours? Minutes? Days? However long it took for them to gather up every last tendril of the Mark, it was too long: she could see the pack on the horizon. They charged.

"Focus, Mara."

"But they're here!"

"Focus!"

The pack was upon them, howling and snapping. Three wolves ran ahead of the pack: the warlock, black, red-eyed and monstrous; the leader, huge and grizzled; the lieutenant, smoky and black-footed. Margaret pulled her hands from Dominic's and ran, or tried to. Michael and his lieutenant were on her in two steps, tearing at her with their fangs. It wasn't her clothes they tore away, or even her flesh: it was humanity. Where they bit, they uncovered fur.

Dominic's focus never wavered. He screamed, struggling to hold onto the Mark with his bare hands even as the monstrous black wolf barreled into him.

There was a blinding light. Her family's fields vanished. Once more they drifted through that terrible nothing: she and Dominic and the pack.

Dominic screamed again, echoed by the howls of the massive wolf he wrestled with, and this time there was truly nothing.

INTERLUDE

Room with a View

The apartment was Spartan, the central room furnished only by a tall stool, a high-backed chair and a battered mattress lying on the floor with neither frame nor box springs. Although meticulously clean, the place gave the impression of being long used and abused, then abandoned. The white paint on the plaster walls had dulled to gray and begun to peel, and the glass in the window was scratched and cracked. A rusting radiator had been built into one wall, and there were no electric outlets to be seen. The small kitchen held a gas stove, once-white like the walls, a sink and an empty pantry, and the minuscule bath held only a claw-foot tub and a chamber pot.

A woman sat on the stool, naked, her eyes downcast as she basked in wan sunlight filtering through the cloudy sky that lay outside the window. A silver chain graced her slender umber neck, and her dark hair was piled atop her head in a tangle of chocolate curls and dreadlocks and braids. She might have been in her twenties, but it was hard to tell. Her face had an ageless quality that hinted at more years than her youthful body might imply, and her presence bathed the otherwise lifeless room in a warm serenity. Looking up, as if she had heard some sound, she turned her violet eyes to the window.

She blinked, and the overcast sky was suddenly the view from a porch, looking out over quiet street. It was autumn; red and gold leaves piled in drifts at the base of half-bare trees who danced slowly in the wind. A man walked up the porch to the door, dressed in the black robes and Roman collar of a priest. A black skullcap was pinned atop his long, graying hair, and he paused momentarily outside the door. His face was tired, the weight of his years and labors pulling heavily on his wide shoulders. With a gloved hand he pulled a massive, antique key from his robes and inserted it into the door. The door to the apartment, opposite the window and somewhat to the left, opened to reveal the same porch and weary, aging priest.

He closed the door behind him and she turned, the window shifting to a third view: the sun setting over a storm-wracked beach of fine, white sand.

"Welcome home, Owen," she said, her lips turning up in humor at the name. "How is the world, today? How is our granddaughter?"

"All things proceed, but slowly," he told her, running a finger around the delicately embroidered circles and glyphs on the back of each glove before carefully removing them. Each of his hands was pierced by a silver rivet with more arcane symbols engraved on each side. "And she is well, although very worried. As I have told you, things are troubled among her flock. There is hope, though. Her wayward sheep is aided by a heathen, a girl of great faith, and several of yours – one a necromancer."

"But she still cannot, herself, help them?"

"No. Her faith is still too weak."

"Poor girl."

The woman's deep, amethyst eyes turned sad, and she turned them back toward the window. In minutes, night had fallen, and the lightning now cracked white against the black, moonless sky. In the distance, the lights of a building could be seen at the far end of the shore. Out to sea, a ship's lights blinked into existence then vanished.

"Come here," she said to him softly. "We are home, at last, and would not be if our plots and schemes required our direct attention. Let us leave them out there in the world."

He came, taking off his skullcap and the silver clasp that held his hair. He brushed his fingers down her cheek and she leaned into his caress, sighing as it drifted down her shoulder and across her back, settling into an embrace that put the cold

175

metal binding in his hand against the edge of her lowest rib. She caressed him through his robes, nails tracing an intricate and meaningless pattern against his side. His other hand stroked her hair, undoing the loose knot of dreads that held her wild curls in check. Unrestrained, her hair tumbled down to the tops of her breasts and even farther down her back. Again, she sighed happily.

"Who would have imagined," she whispered, "that our bargain would bear such fruit? That such love would spring from our pact?"

"No one could. No one did." His hand moved from her hair to caress her face, again. "And it makes our work harder for both of us."

"It does," she conceded, "but the world will be better still for the effort when we are done and restored to our rightful places."

"It will."

PART II – SACRIFICE

Call of the Mark

MONDAY, SEPTEMBER 21ST

Margaret woke in her bed, uncertain of how she'd gotten there. She could remember the ritual clearly, but the aftermath … not so much.

Jacob had gotten her home, that much was clear. Had he helped her to her room? Even the way her parents were now, surely they'd have noticed that. Wouldn't they? She was in her nightgown, which meant she'd had more help than just making it up the stairs. Jennifer, maybe? Amber?

She held her head in her hands, trying to gather up the images and impressions of what had happened after those final words – so mote it be! – like the pieces of a shattered bowl. Had she transformed? No, there was no blood in her mouth, like there had been the first times. Had she really seen visions of the pack? No, that was impossible … But wasn't everything that had happened to her in the last month impossible? Margaret wracked her brain as she went through the motions of her morning routine, but nothing was any clearer by the time she'd bathed and dressed.

Was the Mark truly bound? Was she herself again? It was hard to say. She didn't feel different this morning, but she hadn't noticed feeling different when she'd first been Marked, either. Only the most radical changes had really stood out, and many of those only in retrospect.

She faced breakfast with her family with as much courage as she could muster. They were exactly as she feared they'd be: so absorbed with themselves that it was almost like she wasn't even there. Her mother handed her father a last cup of coffee as he dashed out the door toward work, running just a little late. Her brothers fought each other over who had – and who deserved – the larger portions of cereal and sausage. They hardly acknowledged her when she left to catch the bus.

Standing beside the road, she realized that she had heard the bus before she could see its plume of dust. It had been the other way around, before. When she climbed on board, she was assailed by the stenches as she had only been since being Marked. Bound or not, her senses were still sharper than they had ever been. But no one slammed themselves against the side of the bus to get away from her; she even had to ask for a seat. Maybe something was different. She tried to ignore the smells of the bus – greasy, acrid, and sharp – and the impression of something twitching in response somewhere in the back of her mind. She almost managed.

When she got to school, she found it was harder to make it through the halls. The people who had ignored her since she'd been Marked continued to do so; those who had thrown themselves out of her way as they would have dodged a large truck now only watched her from the corners of their eyes, careful to avoid her direct notice but no longer concerned with clearing a path for her. Her friends, though, now ignored her completely where once they had at least acknowledged her briefly, the way her parents did.

Now that the tide of students no longer parted for her, the halls were a hell of scent and sounds that she had to fight to escape. Laughter and curses reverberated off the walls, punctuated by the tinny clash of slamming of lockers and meaty slaps of flesh. The air was a miasma of colognes, perfumes, and unwashed bodies; soaps, shampoos, and detergents. Other scents, too, she realized: more subtle but more meaningful. *Lust*, a little voice whispered from the back of her mind. *Fear*. Other things that neither she nor the voice could identify. Superhuman senses were not as much fun as television led you to believe. And, even with the Mark bound, she was stuck with them.

'*For the rest of my life*.' She had held a wall in place against that thought for a month now, but it slipped through. '*I'm stuck with this … cacophony for the rest of my life*.' The thought almost staggered her.

Dominic woke with difficulty, clawing his way back to consciousness. This was not his bed, he realized slowly, and he had not slept alone: Aaron's familiar, half-unwelcome warmth pressed against his back. The air was cold, clean, sharp. He knew before he managed to open his eyes that he was still out at the Sanctuary. The dim light filtering through the cabin window told him that it was early dawn. Soft grunts and cries from the other room of the divided cabin told him that they were not alone.

Trying to gather his wits, Dominic slid out of the bed. He resisted the urge to push Aaron's hands aside even more forcefully for his presumption. What had happened last night? Who else was in the cabin? The boots at the door gave him the second answer: Alexander and Amber. Well, they'd had their suspicions, anyway, but why did Aaron need to blow their cover now? He was the one who kept ending things! Was this another bid at starting back up? *'Fuck that!'* Even if his mind hadn't already been made up, outing them like this would have been the last straw.

A rhythmic grinding of mattress and springs joined the other noises the two were making. Dominic fled the cabin.

He stopped briefly to shower in the bath house, but his goal was the dining hall and the communal coffee maker. He and his family had donated enough coffee to the cabinet over the years that he didn't feel bad raiding it, and by the time the brew had finished perking he had found himself just a little focus. He borrowed a cup from the kitchen and sat down on one of the benches looking down the hill to the lake.

He could remember the ritual clearly. The feel of power rising, filling their circle like water filling a bowl, and condensing toward the center as everyone else had focused themselves on him, on Margaret, and on the binding. He could remember falling into her eyes, her falling into his, and then ... nothing. Had they finished? Had she led him to where the Mark hid inside of her, or had they left the work undone? All that power had gone somewhere; he'd felt it rush through them, into them.

Dominic had done deep trance work before. The impressions it left were often surreal, but he could remember it clearly for all that. This ... absence, this blackout, made him doubt their success.

It took him until the end of his first cup of coffee to remember that it was Monday. He had been expected home about six hours ago. He was still expected at school in less than an hour.

"Fuck," he said, letting out a shuddering breath.

He refilled his mug and made a collect call from the pay phone in the dining hall.

"Dominic?" His mother's voice held more worry than he expected. Aaron must not have thought to call in.

"It's me."

"Is everything okay?"

"I think so."

"But you're not sure?"

"I ..." He wanted to paint a good face on it, but lying to his mother was almost as bad an idea as lying to his High Priestess. Theoretically it was his mother on the phone, but it was the High Priestess who had helped him and Aaron design the ritual, and they were really the same woman. "I don't know what happened after the ritual. We finished the rite, I think Mara and I made it to the astral part of the binding, but ... I blacked out and she's not here to tell me if she remembers what happened."

"Will you see her at school today?"

"Assuming I make it in time."

"You're already going to be late for your zero-hour."

"Yes."

"I'll call you in, but be there for the rest of the day." Her voice got a little hard. This was the High Priestess speaking. "We'll talk when you get home."

"Okay," he paused. "I love you, Mom."

"I love you, too, honey."

Dominic slugged back the second cup of coffee, poured another, and gathered himself as he stalked back to south cabin six. He pounded on the door before sticking his head in

"Up and at 'em, peeps," he said loudly. "It's a school day and we're in enough trouble as it is. Whose dumb idea was it to stay here last night?"

Standing the doorway, he could see into both sections of the cabin. Aaron was dressed, smoking a desultory cigarette from the edge of the bed. Amber and Alexander were struggling into their clothes

"His." Aaron thumbed toward Alexander in the other half of the cabin.

"Ours," Alexander corrected, giving Aaron a dour look.

Amber nodded vigorously, holding her pants up with one hand and pointing at the boys with the other. '*Both of them,*' she mouthed, but Dominic doubted she'd argued too strenuously.

"Get our gear," he told Aaron. To the others: "I'm going to try to get everyone together at the coffee shop tonight. I'll call you with details after school."

Aaron grimaced; Alexander and Amber nodded. Dominic stalked back to the dining hall to slug down another cup of coffee and clean up after himself. By the time he was done, Aaron was waiting with bags in hand.

"Let's go."

"You're mad at me."

"Yeah, I'm mad at you."

"Why?"

"You know why."

"Tell me anyway."

Dominic ground his teeth.

"Because you took advantage of me and outed us to our friends."

"It's not like they didn't know we're gay."

"Correction the first: it's not like they didn't suspect. Correction the second: you're gay; I'm bisexual."

"Whatever."

"Also, let us return to point one."

"I didn't ... take advantage of you. I just kept us warm."

"But I was unconscious, wasn't I, so I don't really know that. But I accused you of taking advantage, not rape, so let's not start splitting hairs!"

"We've slept together before! Hell, just last week!"

"First, that was different. Second, I was awake and consenting! And, third, it's never going to happen again!"

"Nothing happened last night, Dom!"

"I don't know that, but even saying I believe you, you still outed us, and you still took advantage!"

They climbed into the car together, both sullen and silent.

Adrenaline and fresh country air got them back into town, but those had given out by the time Dominic made it to his first hour class. His eyes were grainy, despite the shower, and his throat was dry. However much sleep he had gotten last night, it seemed to have done him little good. Somehow he stayed conscious, but when he walked out of AP US History he could not recall anything that they'd covered. A stop at the soda machine helped some, but not enough. He fell asleep twice before lunch.

The teacher pulled him aside after his second class.

"Are you alright, Dominic? You're usually so attentive."

"No sleep," he lied, mumbling an apology.

That almost earned a smile. "Learn your lesson?"

"Yeah." And he had: no more big voodoo on a school night. Why had they chosen Sunday? Right: the New Moon.

Jennifer was similarly concerned, when he saw her in their third-hour Latin class.

"Aaron said it was over, but neither you or Mara would wake up. What happened?"

"I'm still trying to figure that out. I need to talk to her, see what she remembers."

"You guys do know what you're doing, don't you?"

"This is kinda uncharted territory, Jen."

Lunch helped. School food was notoriously bland – even bad – but it was nutritious, and it provided him with some protein energy to jump-start his body. By the time he caught up with Margaret in their fifth-hour English class, he almost felt like a person. Battered and abused, but a person, and glad that he had only one class left for the day. Mrs. Crebbly sat, scowling as usual, like a fat gargoyle scribbling on papers behind her desk. He was still moving slow: most of the class had already arrived.

He scanned the room for Margaret, finding her huddling alone in the back. He sat near her, grateful that Crebbly was not a teacher who bothered with assigned seating. She looked tired, too, and a little harried, but no worse than usual since being attacked. And a good deal better than he felt.

"Madam."

"Hello, Dominic." She managed a genuine smile. "You don't look so good."

"That's all right," he managed to smile back. "I feel like Death warmed over."

"Did it work," she asked, almost whispering. "Is it bound?"

Dominic sighed, trying to open himself enough to examine her aura. He was too tired.

"Does it feel bound?"

"It feels ... distant."

He nodded. That made a certain sense.

"And how do you feel?"

She thought for a moment. "Calmer."

"Then it's bound," he told her, with more conviction than he felt. "Do you remember what happened?"

"No."

The bell rang, class started, and they were forced to sit silently while Mrs. Crebbly rambled garrulously about Voltaire's Candide and its "revolutionary" themes. Dominic had not been impressed by the book, but maybe once he got around to learning French the original would live up to the legend. The bell rang again, and they only had a moment before Margaret had to dash to her sixth hour class.

"I want to get everyone together tonight," he told her. "Talk about what happened, see how everyone's feeling. Can you make it?"

184

"After six or seven. I need to try to catch up on my homework."

"Alright."

He watched her go, rubbing his chin. The hall didn't part for her like it had, she almost had to fight her way through now. Once they were certain the Mark was under control, they could do something about the strange obfuscation spell the pack's warlock had put on her.

He took a deep breath and shook his head.

"Time to face the music."

He took the walk home more slowly than usual, trying to compose his thoughts so that he could make a coherent report.

"At least there's coffee waiting for me."

His parents were both working the book store when he got home, waiting for the invasion of light-fingered kids from Central Jr. High, across the street. They didn't have it as bad as the Phil Zone, next door – even a New Age book store didn't have as many temptingly pocketable items as the head shop – but they still talked about banning everyone under the age of sixteen the way Phil had. They also talked about moving farther down Massachusetts Street, maybe expanding to a full-scale espresso bar. He doubted they'd do any of it.

They greeted him warmly before grilling him about the ritual. They were just worried, he realized, not angry. He told them everything he could remember and promised to keep Margaret away from the store – and a possible encounter with the coven – during business hours until they were absolutely certain the Mark was under control.

"You're doing well, son," his mother said. "Your father and I are proud of you."

"Thank you."

"Be careful with this," his father admonished. "We know it's your burden to bear, but don't be afraid to come to us whenever you need help."

The after-school munchkin rush came and went, and Miranda Haydon-Richardson left her boys to make dinner. Robert watched her ascend the stairs, remembering when he had been Dominic's age and they had just been initiates under his father's tutelage. In a lot of ways, things had been simpler then. More fun, too. He poured another cup of coffee for himself and for his son, enduring a little bit of friendly abuse as he poured cream and sugar into his, topping it with a dash of nutmeg.

"You've been great about helping me translate," he said.

"Thanks," Dominic laughed. "I could just about speak in Old German, now."

"Useless though that may be."

"Yeah."

"There's a lot of refining left to be done with the translation, but I think we both know that if your binding doesn't work, there's nothing else in there that will be any use to you."

"Yeah." Dominic looked away. Robert could tell by the boy's tone that he had thought about it.

"What next?"

Dominic didn't answer right away.

"I don't know."

"You should look into Mirrors and Veils."

The boy grimaced, fingers tightening convulsively on his mug. Bob sipped at his coffee, waiting. Again, Dominic didn't answer right away.

"I've looked at it, some," he said at last. "It doesn't make sense. It skips around and it's so metaphorical and ... and it scares me just a little."

Robert nodded.

"It should. But if what you need is in any book I own, it's in there."

Dominic didn't turn to look at him, but the boy glanced out of the corner of his eye. His face went still, calculating. Such a sharp kid. Hopefully he hadn't tipped his hand too far.

"You've read it," it wasn't a question. "Any passages in particular I should look for?"

Robert shrugged and shook his head.

186

"It's been a decade or more, and the book scared me too. Like you said, it doesn't make sense. I just know I don't have any answers for you anywhere else in my library."

Dominic nodded. He was still suspicious – a father can tell – but he accepted the statements as they stood. Mirrors and Veils had not come to him in any of the usual ways. It was no gift from a friend, no estate sale find, no black market antiquities deal.

In the late seventies, the senior members of the Crystal Dream had been invited to attend a meeting of covens with well-documented histories. They were not as old as some, but Heinrich Rikardzon – Americanized to Henry Richardson when he emigrated in 1951 – had held a certain notoriety. The meeting had been in Britain, of course, at the covenstead from which Gerald Gardner had brought his particular witchcraft to the light of public scrutiny. Henry had brought his wife, his son, and his daughter-in-law-to-be to participate in both the rites – which had been beautiful, powerful, and had even included a Samhain rite at Stonehenge – and in the politics. The latter had included meetings with representatives of the Orders of Odysseus and Herakles, a number of seers, and the ignominious Rasputin.

One of the seers had pushed past the formidable Heinrich to speak to his son.

"I brought this for you," she had said, forcing the book into Robert's hands. "Let your son read this, and he may survive the road to greatness."

Her eyes had been wild, mantic. It had no more occurred to Robert to refuse her, then, than it had occurred to anyone else to bar her way.

Jacob couldn't pick her up this evening. It surprised Margaret how much that disappointed her. Borrowing the family car wasn't difficult – just a matter of asking – but being chauffeured was pleasant, and dealing with her family...

"Hey, Mom, can I borrow the car?"

"Sure, honey."

Her mother used to ask where she was going, who she'd be with, when she'd be back. Did she need to eat before she left? The questions a reasonable mother would ask. This strange, enchanted woman didn't even look up from the television. Some people prayed for this sort of inattentiveness, but it cut Margaret to the quick.

By the time she reached the coffee house, they were already waiting for her. Anyone and everyone Dominic had named his Crew had come out. They were sitting comfortably on the stone steps that faced the old post office, those who didn't smoke sitting upwind from those who did.

Jacob sat on the lowest of the steps, his back against the stone buttress framing the stairs, looking up at the others. Amber sat curled in Alexander's lap while he lounged on the other side. Dominic stood at the top of the buttress next to Jacob, posing dramatically with a cigarette in one hand and one of his cigarette-shaped sticks of incense in the other. She had heard that he sometimes wore women's clothes, but she hadn't seen it herself before; the wide skirt he wore fell to his ankles in heavy folds; it was covered in pockets and shockingly unfeminine. Aaron sat at his feet in his usual tailored finery, the line of his shoulders and the set of his jaw speaking clearly of tension. Jennifer hovered at the edge of the group; a grateful, welcoming smile spread across her face as Margaret walked up. Each of them had a cup within easy reach, fragrant and potent to her nose.

The Mark stirred within her, struggling within the binding, but still picking up on the strange social currents within the group. It respected Dominic, almost approved of the way he managed his pack, although it felt that she could do a better job – rule with a firmer hand. Aaron and Alexander, the Mark watched carefully: competing betas who might someday decide it was their place to lead. She was certain that she could handle Aaron, should she decide to make that bid herself; his desire was not so much to be the leader as to supplant Dominic. Dixon posed a greater challenge, but one the Mark felt she could probably overcome.

188

Caitlyn, the older woman they had met last week, was there as well. She stood atop the other buttress with her hands in her pockets and her cigarette dangling from her lips. In ragged jeans and a stained tee-shirt, she was like a twisted reflection of Dominic: possibly handsome but certainly not pretty. Her presence made Margaret uncomfortable: *'We're not going to talk about any of this in front of her, are we?'* The Mark, though, was outright hostile toward Caitlyn. The Mark warned that she was a threat: because she was new, because she was female, and because it was absolutely certain that she was a monster, too.

That last part hadn't been quite as clear before the Mark had been bound. Well, none of it had, actually. It had taken her most of the day to figure out exactly what had changed: she didn't feel the Mark's urges anymore, or think its thoughts as if they were her own, but at the same time she was more aware of it. The rest she had been able to sort out, in part because she had been able to pick up on a great deal of it with her human senses. Caitlyn's secret, though ... If nothing else, it explained the way the older woman looked at her. One predator sizing up another, wondering what it would do if pressed.

Margaret looked around for somewhere to sit, but she didn't see anywhere that wouldn't be crowding someone.

"How are you doing tonight, Mara," Jennifer asked.

"Alright." She really didn't want to talk about any of it in front of Caitlyn. Had Dominic invited her or had she just happened to be here? "How about you guys?"

Caitlyn blew a smoke ring. "A fine evening," she said. A little bit of a brogue came through, but Margaret couldn't place it exactly. It wasn't the sort of accent you heard on Monty Python, or her grandfather's Irish, but it was definitely from the British Isles.

Other members offered a chorus of assents, some more enthusiastic, others less.

Dominic raised the incense-cigarette to his lips with a subtle glance at Caitlyn, blowing a smoke ring of his own. "Fan-fucking-tastic."

Jacob shivered, and some the others gave Dominic looks that made no sense. Caitlyn appraising. Aaron ... jealous? Amber wistful and Alexander carefully blank. She exchanged a confused look with Jennifer. What were they missing?

Caitlyn chuckled, breaking up the tension.

"I think we're exceeding the capacity of the stoop," she said.

"Then let's walk," Dominic suggested.

Everyone shrugged, nodded, and stood – Amber almost pitching herself down the stairs as she attempted to escape Alexander's lap. Margaret started to move to catch her, which – strangely – made Amber's face turn a startling shade of red.

Jacob, smiling and blushing a little, offered her his arm. She only had to think for a moment before taking it. Somewhere in the back of her mind, the Mark twitched disdainfully. Jennifer walked on her other side.

The others formed a circle around them. Aaron and Dominic took point, Alexander positioned himself in back. Almost at random, they chose to wander south, following the Mass. Street Strip as far down as the courthouse before turning around and following the sidewalk up the other side.

They made small talk. She and Jennifer talked about track; there had been practice, today, although the official season would not start until spring. Alexander talked about his martial arts. She wished that any of them shared her interest in photography. This was in no way what they had met up to achieve, but Margaret found that she didn't mind. *'When was the last time I actually socialized like this,'* she thought. *'Not quite a month, but it feels like so much longer.'*

It was Monday night, and downtown was mostly empty. It only took one circuit to see most of what there was to see.

"Why don't we walk along the river," suggested Amber.

No one objected, so they followed 8th street to the Riverfront Mall parking lot, skipped across the train tracks, and followed the river downstream. Fine sand shifted under their shoes, and Margaret found herself slipping and bumping into Jacob quite often.

'*So this is what long walks on the beach are really about,*' she decided, half cynical and half amused. The Mark grumbled its dissatisfaction. It had definite ideas about Jacob's place, she knew that, but she didn't understand what that place was exactly or why it became ... antsy in his presence.

'*He is weak,*' it told her, as loud and clear as anything it had ever communicated. '*He is ours, so use him as you will, but do not treasure him.*' The Mark did not communicate in words, not exactly, so there was little doubt what it meant by *use* – or, for that matter, by *ours* and *weak*. It did not call Jacob 'ours', exactly, for it did not distinguish itself from her or vice versa. Weak things existed to be shamed and abused until they broke or grew strong, and when it suggested that she use him as she would, it drew graphic images from her own unguarded thoughts as well as from its own twisted nature.

Jacob's arm tensed under her hand and a look at his face reminded her abruptly that he could read minds. It was so hard to believe, and he worked hard to hide it, but he had proven it to her the morning of her second change. Was he reading her mind now? He said he couldn't help it, any more than she could stop the changes that were overcoming her. Could he tell her thoughts from the Mark? She tried to smile reassuringly, but she wasn't sure she succeeded.

"Hey, look," said Dominic. "Hippie beach party."

He waved expansively at the three large sitting logs gathered around the remains of a fire.

"Hippies?" Alexander asked, skeptical.

"No broken bottles. Hippies clean up after themselves." Everyone laughed. "Let's sit." No one argued, so he sat, rolling a cigarette that was entirely tobacco. The warding herbs got a little hard on the lungs.

He watched Jacob and Margaret from the corner of his eye, smiling to himself. Dinner, a nap, and some help from his mother had restored his second sight, so Dominic was able to get a look at her aura at last. The darkness that had floated through and around it was weaker now, a haze where it had been deep shadow, a mere thread where it had been a rope. He also took the opportunity to look at Jacob's. His shields were down again, probably since last night, but he seemed to be staying grounded – he wasn't panicking, at least, although the looks he occasionally sent Margaret made Dominic wonder what sort of impressions Jacob was picking up from her. He had not, however, let go of her arm at any point.

'*Good for him.*'

It was a beautiful September night: sharp and clean. The stars were bright points with no more than a hair-sliver of moon to distract the eye.

Jennifer sat with Margaret and Jacob. Amber sat beside her, joined to Alexander at the hip. Caitlyn and Aaron took the remaining seats: Caitlyn on his left, Aaron on his right. An ... interesting ... configuration.

Those who smoked did their best to position themselves downwind of those who did not, but the cold air coming off the river was erratic. If any woodpile had remained, Dominic would have rebuilt the fire.

Caitlyn was doing a remarkable job of appearing interested in everyone's drama. She was older than them – he guessed by four or five years, although she hadn't said – so maybe her own high school bullshit was far enough behind her for it all to be funny again.

They avoided speaking of their families for everyone's sake. He tried to herd the conversation away from Anthony Domiano stories, as well; they made Margaret uncomfortable for some reason. The boy had made such a nuisance of himself, though, that it was hard to avoid him entirely, and the rivalry between Alexander and Anthony was the stuff of legends. Dominic could feel Aaron tensing when those stories came up, and he glared death at Alexander if he seemed about to point out that Aaron was one of the people he had rescued from Anthony's ministry of the fist.

The conversation had lapsed for a while, though, when Jacob's face suddenly went white. Margaret tensed beside him. Still arm-in-arm, their hands came together in a desperate

192

clasp. Dominic sensed it a moment later: hunger and hatred emanating from the woods.

"What's up?" Caitlyn demanded when the Crew, as one, turned their heads toward the darkness between the trees.

Jacob said, "I'm sorry Caitlyn."

"Sorry?" she demanded. "Sorry for what?"

The werewolf pack stepped out of the woods behind Margaret and Jacob, scowling and snarling, radiating menace in their spike-and-chain laden leather.

"Well, well, well," the leader laughed. "It looks like you kiddies have found some new friends. Too bad it's just a couple more bitches, or we might be worried."

Alexander stood and it surprised Dominic to realize that he was on his feet as well. Everyone was standing, even Caitlyn. There wasn't anything they could do, though. The werewolves spread out in a semi-circle, blocking them in against the river.

Dominic drew a deep breath, trying to keep his center. He felt Alexander and Aaron doing the same, drawing in as much magic as they could. Alexander went from powersink to supernova, like he had when he'd thrown Domiano off of Margaret; he even took a step forward.

"Oh, look," mocked the warlock. "Isn't that cute? They think they can take us."

The warlock didn't bother with shielding his aura: purple, black, brown, and red, his soul looked like a blood-spattered bruise. Except for the shadow of the Mark curling through their auras, the rest just looked like people. Brighter than most, with the grim marks of a life on both ends of violence and cruelty, but nothing like the warlock's.

"Shut up Caleb," growled the second.

Dominic suddenly wondered if Caitlyn could see auras. Did she already know what Margaret was? If not, she'd know soon enough.

"Come here, girl," the leader commanded Margaret, reaching out his hand. "You're one of us now. You're mine."

"No," she said, her voice high and tight. "Please no."

"Come here," he repeated.

"Come to us," the other werewolves chanted in chorus.

193

Margaret felt them coming at the same time as Jacob, but she didn't recognize the itching sensation in time. Not that it would have mattered; they had already been surrounded. Now she strained her neck, watching them over her shoulder because she was too scared to even stand or turn around.

She shouldn't have been able to see so clearly on a moonless night, but she could see the lead wolf's scowl clearly, read the evil in warlock's grin and the patient obedience in the lieutenant's face. Their chains rattled like thunder, but not so loud as to drown out the hammering of everyone's hearts. The pack's hearts pounded with anticipation, the Crew's with fear. The Mark was happy to point out the difference.

"Come to us," Michael said a third time. She hated that she knew his name, but the Mark had provided it the first time she'd laid eyes on him. 'Michael' and 'master' were synonyms to the Mark, and it screamed at her from deep in its cage: '*Obey him! Obey!*' The Mark was bound, though, and she refused because she could... and felt it grow stronger, fed by her own resistance.

Michael growled and reached his hand out to grab her.

She had been too scared to move, now she was too scared not to. She lunged away from him, dragging Jacob with her effortlessly.

"No!"

The Mark howled at her for obedience and Michael was doing ... something. The pack began to chant – "Come to us. You are ours. Come to us." – and Margaret's blood began to burn. So she prayed.

"Our Father in heaven, hallowed be your name..."

It didn't help. Her blood boiled, her bones turned to fire, and her insides began to move. She hurt so bad she couldn't think except to know that she was overheating. Sweat poured off of her body, soaking her clothes, which chafed painfully at her suddenly hypersensitive skin. She could hear shouts and

194

her eyes were still open, but her body had hijacked her brain. Everything else was just static.

Dominic watched in horror as the werewolf invoked Margaret's Mark, forcing her transformation, even as the coldly analytical part of his mind noted how it was done. It terrified him further that he could probably return the favor if he had the balls. If it would actually gain them anything. The poor girl writhed in the sand, crying softly and tearing futilely at her clothes.

"All right, pillock," Caitlyn snapped, stepping to the front. "That's enough."

The pack leader's head whipped up. "What did you call me?"

"I called you a pillock, you Wolf-Marked cunt."

Dominic wished he could see her face, because her energy had changed. Her shields were still up, blocking most of his senses, but he could feel that she'd opened herself like a bulls-eye lantern and he could see that whatever she'd shown the pack had made all but the three strongest take an involuntary step backwards.

"You fucking bitch," the leader stepped forward with an inhuman snarl. "I'm gonna gut you for that."

She took her own step forward to meet him with her own inhuman noise: something more like a hiss. The entire pack – the leader, his second, and the warlock included this time – took a step back.

"Bugger off," she told them in a low, dangerous voice. "These kids are mine."

The pack fled.

"You haven't seen the last of us," the leader warned before he followed his people.

"I know," Caitlyn said to their retreating backs.

A profound silence followed, broken only by the noise of the river. Even the nighttime insects seemed to have been frightened into silence by that strange display. Dominic just stared at Caitlyn's back, equally terrified, confused, and aroused. He wanted to ask what had just happened, but the speech centers of his brain seemed to have shut down. No one else was forming words, either. He had almost found his tongue when a chorus of howls split the night, drawing a last cry of pain from Margaret.

Dominic looked down just in time to see the transformation begin. Margaret lay on her back, legs akimbo and her arms outstretched, mouth open to admit a thin wail. She had gotten her shirt off and her pants down to her knees. The change came suddenly, shredding her remaining clothes, as she rippled and flowed into a brindle wolf-like creature.

The transformation happened almost right on top of him. His arm hurt like hell after the way Margaret had used it to throw him to the ground and his head spun from the impact. Sand, it turned out, was not as soft as advertised. Her fear, which had held him stone-still as much as his own, now gave way to horrendous pain. It bored into his mind the way her fear had, even as it poured through his skin wherever they touched. His stomach churned with it, but it was sympathetic pain. She screamed, he screamed, and he thought it might just kill him ... but somehow he managed to remember that it was her pain, not his own. She was literally tearing her clothes off, and when her skin brushed his, the world became nothing but searing, flashing agony.

Then the pain was gone. Instead of a girl on top of him, there was an oversized wolf. Light-colored, though he couldn't see it clearly in the moonlight. It scraped him with its claws as it stood, tearing him carelessly open – sharp, hot pain in his own body standing out starkly against the fear and pain he felt pouring off the others. Margaret was gone; this was the Mark. Fear remained, but rage rose quickly to overwhelm it. People were screaming, he couldn't say who, and panic filled the air like a siren.

Margaret the wolf snarled, set to lunge – *Challenger!* * the thought ripped through his mind – but something knocked

196

her over, first. Someone knocked her over: Caitlyn, who somehow managed to pin Margaret to the sand, half sitting on her.

"Stay back," she said, calm.

Someone else, Aaron, helped Jacob to his feet. The rest of the crew lined up beside them, all dripping with confusion and fear, touching one another for reassurance. Jennifer was panting and sobbing, hanging onto Amber while Alexander held them both up.

"Where are they? What happened?"

No one answered right away. Caitlyn looked at them. They looked at her.

"Cait scared them off," Dominic said, his back straight and his face serenely blank, the way it was when he led a particularly potent ritual.

"You weren't very surprised when they showed up," Caitlyn said back, deflecting his passive-aggressive accusation with one of her own. Margaret writhed beneath her, a hundred fifty pounds or more of supernatural muscle; Caitlyn's arm twisted, flexed, and bulged, but she didn't budge an inch. Her eyes flashed down to Margaret the wolf. "Or by this."

The Crew exchanged a complex series of glances.

Dominic spoke for them again: "We should talk."

"We should. But first I need to know if your friend is going to try to eat us if I let her up."

"She hasn't yet."

"That's not a strong vote of confidence."

"We're kind of new at this," Jacob said, gently shaking Aaron off. For the first time that he could remember, Jacob deliberately opened himself and looked at someone. *Frustration, determination, calm: 'How do I deal with (these kids; this wolf; the pack; my cover)?'* Not the barest fragment of fear about her.

"But you're not." Her shields were a massive wall, but he could see right through them. In her own mind, Caitlyn's face and hands were splattered with blood. Bruised darkness coiled around her – a life of pain and violence, like the werewolves' auras – and a serpent of fire coiled below her belly. "You've been doing this for years!"

She murmured something he couldn't quite hear, but the thought came through clearly: *'*Your Sight is far too clear, little brother.*'*

Her power flexed as she tried to squeeze her shields tighter. Aaron and Dominic, to either side of him, flexed their own in response. That was too much for him. He fell to his knees, hands digging into the sand as he tried to ground and center himself, to get his walls back up. His head swam, his stomach heaved. He couldn't see or hear anything, and the things he could feel blended together into a senseless cacophony.

When he came to, everyone was shouting. Margaret the wolf stood over him, growling. Jennifer and Amber were taking turns crying and screaming. Alexander tried to approach; Margaret snapped at him.

"Well, hell," Caitlyn said from somewhere to his right.

"That about covers it," agreed Dominic.

Jacob tried not to move, but Margaret the wolf already knew that he was awake. She stepped off of him, keeping herself between him and as many of the Crew as she could. She growled again, and the Crew backed up.

Jacob shifted to his knees slowly. Margaret the wolf backed up to stand at his side. Slowly, so slowly, he reached up to lay his hand on her hip. He was afraid she would growl and snap at him, maybe even bite. Instead, his touch seemed to calm her. The growling stopped, and didn't resume when Caitlyn and Dominic stepped forward. Her fur was coarse and thick between his fingers. Cautious, he moved his hand forward to her shoulder. She didn't flinch or growl. She turned her head to look at him, a bit of humanity peeking through those yellow animal eyes.

"We're safe," he said. "She remembers who she is, now. She knows who we are."

"How do you know?" demanded Caitlyn.

"You're sure," Dominic didn't quite make it a question.

"I'm sure." Jacob scratched carefully between Margaret's ears, hoping she wouldn't take it wrong. He couldn't help himself. She leaned into his touch, giving her tail a single wag. "Yeah, I'm sure."

Caitlyn frowned at them, suspicious, but didn't ask again.

"How long?" she asked instead.

The Crew turned first to Jacob, then Dominic, and said nothing.

"Not even a month," Dominic told her.

"Bollocks. You don't even know how much she'll change yet, do you?"

"We've an idea."

"I doubt that." Caitlyn shook her head. "But she hasn't bit any of you yet? None of you have the Mark?"

They shook their heads, echoing each other in a chorus of negatives.

Jacob stared at her, his arm now over Margaret the wolf's shoulder.

"You already know we don't. You knew Mara did when you met her."

"Lad, you are far too sharp for your own good. Keep your insight to yourself."

Jacob flinched and Margaret growled.

"Easy lass," Caitlyn backed up a step. She gave the crew a sour look. "You kids seem to have this under control, so I'm gonna leave before I antagonize her any further. Are you sure you're safe?"

"As sure as we can be," Alexander hedged.

"Well, at least you're not complete fools."

Teenage Werewolf

Caitlyn Hannah left the children on the river bank, using every hunter's trick she knew to vanish quickly and silently. The wolf could probably track her; hopefully it wasn't so inclined.

Gods help her, she was supposed to be retiring!

It was safe to assume that the werewolves she'd seen tonight were the ones who had attacked the girl; to think otherwise stretched coincidence and credulity. This was the Wolf King's territory; if the pack were rogue they would have been snuffed out as soon as Margaret had been Marked. So they had sanction, which meant that she couldn't just shoot them. They probably wouldn't kill anyone, but they would be allowed to take Margaret whenever they wanted. Why hadn't they taken her already? Were they waiting for her second moon? How were these things done in America?

The Knights of Herakles had an ambassador at the Wolf King's court, of course, but her knighthood had been honorary. She had been a Sister of the Holcombe Brotherhood and a Left Hand of the Grove and an Agent of the Faerie Queen. She was still a Sister, but any authority or privileges that she'd had had gone with the other two. It would be unseemly to go to the ambassador over such an incident. Maybe when – and it was when, not if – the pack attacked the other children, then she could approach the court. Of course, if she went to the court on their behalf, she'd have to tell them about it. And be there to see them attacked. And explain to them both why she had the authority to petition the court and why she hadn't done so sooner.

And the entire mad line of reasoning seemed to assume that she would stay in Lawrence and continue to associate with a bunch of dumb kids sheltering a werewolf. Which was insane. It could only end in her being outed as a monster who hunted other monsters.

Her old handler's words came back to haunt her: '*You have an unfortunate track record of vigilantism,*' he had told her, mockingly, at her final debriefing. '*However nobly you desire to resume your old life, we realize – even if you do not –*

that you will not be able to help yourself. If you see a problem, you will try to fix it.'

This ... this ... thing she was doing right now: this was the "vigilantism" Sir Ashley had mocked. This was the reason he had cited for the Queen's reluctance to let her go, although she knew perfectly well that the Queen simply resented letting anything escape her grasp.

The smart thing to do would be to cut town right now. Kansas City or Topeka were close enough to enjoy the all benefits she'd moved here for, if not quite so scenic. Maybe take the big plunge and buy some little piece of land in between.

Of course, when was the last time she did the smart thing?

FRIDAY, SEPTEMBER 25TH

The Mark didn't rattle at its cage so much as pace the edges of it, watching and waiting. Her inhumanly acute senses of hearing and smell were impossible to ignore, as the Mark kept a running commentary on the input they provided. Sweat. Lust. Rage. Fear. Despair. The halls swam with them. Weren't there any happy people in the whole school?

There were other smells, as well: less visceral but only slightly less personal. Perfume and cologne. Body wash and shampoo. The spearmint of toothpaste, and sweet tang of lip gloss. A near endless variety of laundry detergents and other soaps and cleansers.

And, she was just beginning to sense, under it all was another layer. A panoply of other odors, indescribable in words, each unique to an individual.

The din of conversation and stomping feet, punctuated by slammed lockers, cries, and slamming doors, made her head ache. Raised voices, many in laughter, some mocking. Here and there, words made it through to her ears, meaningless without context.

'How much worse would it be to hear, see, feel their thoughts,' she wondered. *'No wonder Jacob keeps to himself. No wonder people think he's strange.'*

She forced her way through the halls. It was easier today than yesterday: people didn't really acknowledge her, but the slightest touch, a firm word, was all it took to clear most out of her way. She was careful not to use either on those who still tried to avoid her, who mistook whatever they perceived the Mark as to be a threat to themselves.

Jacob was fortunate in that he also seemed to inspire people to protect him. Dominic and Aaron; Alexander, if Jacob would have him. Caitlyn seemed to be volunteering, too, and Margaret couldn't deny that she was drawn to him. The Mark was baffled, frustrated, and infuriated that such a weak creature held such sway over his betters.

'I'm grateful Jacob's people are so willing to help me, too,' she thought. *'I wonder if it's for my sake or for his?'*

Between classes, she caught Anthony watching her from down the hall. The Mark watched him back, even when she turned away. So very strange that, out of everyone in the school, he was the only one besides Dominic's Crew who could really see her. That they were unaffected by the pack's curse made a certain sense: they were witches, after all. Anthony was a Christian, though, if not a particularly good one. But so was Jennifer, and still a skeptic despite everything.

What was it that made them different from everyone else?

SATURDAY, SEPTEMBER 26

"You know," said Amber, "I really think she would have hurt us."

Alexander nodded, staring across the fields that adjoined his back yard. Music blared at them from inside, loud enough to be heard through the double-paned glass patio door. Chandra Dixon did love his operas.

"Do you think," she hesitated, a little bit ashamed to even think the question, let alone speak it. She stared out over the grass, too, unwilling to look him in the eye. "Do you think it's safe to help her?"

They sat just past the edge of the concrete, as close to the fire pit as they could get without putting their toes in the flames. It was cold, one of the first genuinely cold nights of the year, and her coat smelled like the back of the closet.

"No," he said. "But... No pain, no gain, right?"

"I don't want to be a werewolf, Alex. And I really don't want to die."

He shifted, leaning forward and looking into the fire. Winter meant coats and sweaters, an end to watching his muscles dance under tight tee-shirts. He sat with his palms together and his elbows on his knees.

"I don't want to die, either." Alexander's jaw clenched briefly, and he stared straight ahead the way he did when he was absolutely focused on something. She loved that focus about him, admired and respected it; doubly so when it was trained on her. "I want to live. Especially now. There's a whole world out there I never knew about, and magic like I didn't believe existed. Mara ... the things you and Dom have shown me."

He held his hands a few inches apart, and he made his shift from perfectly grounded to roaring with energy. Only his hands moved, but he was suddenly full of tension and potential. The air between his hands shimmered and danced like the fire. Not even Dominic, the most experienced among them by far, could conjure elemental energies so strongly that she could see a visible manifestation. And here Alex was doing it just weeks after she had taught him to cast a circle.

"You can't refuse the call to adventure, Amber," he said, staring at the power he held in his hands.

"What? Adventure? Alex, what are you talking about?"

"The hero's journey. Joseph Campbell wrote about it. He was a student of Jung. He wrote about the patterns in myths and what they meant." Alexander let the ball of energy dissipate without effect, grounded himself again. He moved his chair around to face her. "The hero's journey starts with an unmistakable call to adventure, and to refuse the call leads to fates worse than death."

Amber shook her head, clenched her hands on her knees. Ran his words back and forth in her head. She stared at him, trying to decide if he was having a joke at her expense.

"That's insane," she said, at last.

"So's a teenage werewolf," he said, leaning back in his chair again and looking her in the eye. His expression was earnest, utterly sincere. "A teenage Christian werewolf. Who somehow knew what was up right from the jump. From the word 'go'. She's attacked at church, goes to the hospital, goes back to her shockingly normal life ... Then she wakes up a week later covered in blood, and comes straight to us for help. I'm still trying to figure that one out. Does Dunn know more about what's going on than she says?"

Amber's head was spinning. What did any of that have to do with his adventure theory? Was he accusing Margaret of something?

"I don't understand. What are you trying to say?"

Alex sat up again, his hands moving restlessly up and down his thighs, opening and closing spastically.

"I'm saying that Margaret is our call to adventure," he said, taking a deep breath and turning back toward the fire. The tension left his body again as he exhaled. "She is our call to greatness."

Amber licked her lips, watching his face carefully.

"And to refuse the call leads to a fate worse than death?"

He nodded.

"That's the Rules according to Campbell."

"Running away from the werewolf leads to a fate worse than death." Amber shook her head. She threw her hands up in the air. "I don't get it. Like what?"

"We could die in obscurity." He said it like it was the most obvious thing in the world. "Unsung. Forgotten forever."

'*What?*' she thought.

"Is... is that so bad?" She asked. "Living quietly?"

His pause was not one of hesitation, but rather of emphasis. His shoulders were set, his back straight even as he leaned forward in his chair, staring out past the cornfield, past the tree line, past the horizon into a future only he could see. Perfectly still, completely loose, he vibrated with potential action. He seemed capable of *anything*. In that moment, Amber had her first glimpse of the person that Jacob and Aaron feared, the person that Domiano saw as his chief rival. He put the whole of his being into the single word:

"Yes."

It wasn't that Aaron was heartless. Deep down, Dominic believed that Aaron truly loved him. It was just that, growing up the way he had, Aaron was so much more experienced in expressing his darker feelings, to the point where even the lighter ones were expressed in a negative way.

"We need to get the fuck out of Dodge."

Like right now, for instance.

"We've come this far, Aaron. Why not take it all the way?"

"Because she's going to turn on us," he said. "Sooner rather than later."

Dominic knew that Aaron was worried about everyone. Himself included, of course, but it would break Aaron's heart if anything happened to Dominic or Jacob, Amber or Jennifer. Even Alexander. But he expressed it all as fear and hatred of Margaret: who she had been, what she had stood for, and what she had become.

"How can we know that?"

"You're the one who read the books. You're the one who taught us everything we really know about werewolves. She's a predator! Hell, she's one of the Popular Girls, she's always been a predator! Even if she wasn't a monster before, the Mark will make her into one."

Dominic scrubbed his face with his hands. That was what the Grimoire assured them. Every article and pamphlet he could find on the subject stated emphatically that, once Marked, there was no salvation. But they also stated that the transformation from mortal to monster was instantaneous, which was clearly not the case.

Their observations seemed to contradict all the available data. Clearly, then, the data was incomplete. Only further observation could explain the discrepancy. His father's voice echoed in his head: *'The scientific method is the key to great magics, Dominic. Observe, hypothesize, experiment, repeat.'*

Dominic had tried to explain all this to Aaron before. He decided to try again, but Aaron cut him off.

"I don't care, Dom," he hissed, his eyes narrow and his teeth bared. "It's not worth the risk. We could die! We could be Marked ourselves! I don't want to be a monster! I don't want to die! It's not worth the risk!"

Try as he might – and, honestly, he didn't try very hard – Dominic couldn't pretend that there wasn't a risk. The key was convincing everyone that it was worth it. Knowledge alone wasn't enough for Aaron. It had to be personal. Alexander and Amber had to be thinking the same thing, so did Jennifer. What would it take to convince them?

By Dominic's best math, Jacob was the key. Aaron would do nearly anything Jacob asked, when it came right down to it. Alexander might just do anything to win Jacob's friendship back. Amber would follow Alexander, either way. Jacob and Margaret clearly had something going on, but who knew which way he'd jump if Aaron pushed him hard enough. So the trick would be to give them all reasons to be *on board*, not just *along for the ride*.

Jennifer would be the hardest. For all she was sworn to the Shepherd, she was no sheep. She wouldn't follow any of them anywhere without a damn good reason. And for all that she didn't quite fit, she was actually more important to most of the Crew than Alexander was.

"You're plotting something, Dominic. I can feel it."

"Aren't I always? Spiders to the end, the both of us."

"True enough."

The decision to meet for coffee anywhere but the Crew's usual dive was as deliberate as it was unspoken. As was more and more often the case, Jacob's availability was limited by the demands of his family, so they had agreed to meet downtown and save Jacob the time and gasoline needed to pick Margaret up from her family's house.

Her father had always taught her that "early is on time and on time is late", so she had meandered into La Prima Taza at quarter of six. It was forty-five minutes and three refills later when Jacob finally appeared.

"There you are," she said, standing. "I was starting to worry."

"I'm so sorry." His eyes were wide and a little moist, and his hands were trembling. She could smell the peculiar sweat of stress on him, and a lingering whiff of anger. "My parents wouldn't let me out of the house."

"Oh, dear. Was something wrong? I wouldn't want to keep you ... "

"No. No, it's ... That's just how they are."

"I'm sorry. I don't understand."

"It's okay. I'll... I'll go into it some other time. Is that okay?"

"Sure." Margaret was confused, but she decided to let it go. Family could be a touchy subject. Jennifer and Dominic had both hinted more than once that Jacob's family was particularly difficult.

"Thanks," he said, relaxing visibly. He gestured for her to wait while he went to the counter to get himself a drink. He had mostly shaken the fear-and-anger-scent by the time he returned. "So ... how are you doing?"

"I'm okay, I guess. Coping. I wish we could do something about my parents, but ..." That was an understatement. She was starting to have nightmares where her entire family were dead-and-rotting zombies, not just zombie-like.

"Do we have to wait until we have the Mark under wraps? Helping them might be easier."

It was something she'd considered, of course. "Maybe, but ... I don't want them to see me as a monster. I don't want to risk them being hurt."

Jacob nodded. "I see."

"How about you? Are you doing alright? Jen told me about the things you said to Caitlyn." Things that only confirmed and expanded what the Mark had already told her about the older woman. What kind of monster was she?

"I'm as good as ever. And Cait ... the things I said ... the things I saw ..." He trailed off, staring into the depths of his Italian soda. "She's lived a hard life, Mara. She has a monster inside her, too. She can help if we don't scare her off."

"If we don't scare her off?" Margaret's voice skipped up half a register. "Jacob, she's strong enough to hold me down with one hand! I remember that much!"

Jacob shrugged uncomfortably. Margaret looked away.

"I know it sounds backwards, but ... I know what I know. I saw so much that night. Everything was so clear."

Margaret sipped at her coffee, her brow furrowed with thought.

"I don't mean to doubt you, Jacob. You've been so supportive, and I really appreciate it. But ... really, how can you be sure?"

He shrugged again, looking away.

"I just am."

"I'm sorry. Let's talk about something else."

"Sure. How's track practice going?"

"It's ... interesting. The running feels good, better than ever. But the Mark loves the competition. It wants me to run like I've never run before, and I ... I think I could break just about every record in the school if I let it loose."

"Really? Wow. Are you stronger, then? Not just when you change, but now?"

"Yes. Much stronger. I haven't really pushed myself, since ... but I don't want to arouse suspicion. Everyone may be ignoring me, but ... if I'm suddenly lifting a whole lot more than

208

I used to be, Coach may want to check me for steroids or something."

"Seriously?"

"Three girls got checked last year. Domiano and Dixon have both had to drop this year and last, and a few other boys as well. They take doping pretty seriously."

"I had no idea. And you're that much stronger?"

"Weights I was struggling with six weeks ago are too easy, now. I think I could arm wrestle Dixon." Honestly, she would have thought that was clear by the way she'd man-handled him on the beach, or by the way she'd pushed Anthony around.

"Wow."

"Yeah."

"So ... it's not all bad, then."

"I guess not. I do like being strong, and not just strong for a girl. But now, I ... I guess I'm worried about my femininity as well as my humanity." She blushed, looking down. Jacob blushed too.

"You don't have anything to worry about," he said, just a hair too emphatically.

"Thank you," she said. Her face felt hot as she looked away. He smelled peculiar. It took her a little while to find her voice back.

"We seem to have finished our drinks," she said at last. "Would you like to walk?"

"Yeah," Jacob said, smiling. "I'd like that."

They bussed their table, dropped another dollar in the tip jar, and set out south along Massachusetts Street. It was a little past sunset, the evening air cool, the breeze just strong enough to flutter the edges of their coats and toss Margaret's hair.

Jacob let his hand hover close to hers, and he smiled when she took it.

They meandered back and forth across Massachusetts Street, peering in the windows of shops that had closed hours ago. Goldmakers, the Creation Station, the Sunflower Gallery. The Phoenix Gallery was a mutual favorite, with their eclectic collection of fanciful glass and exotic wood. It was dinner time, so the streets and sidewalks were packed with people leaving the closing stores for the distinctive local bars and restaurants that the city was so proud of. There were mostly families and couples this time of day; later the college kids would come out. Margaret hadn't spent a lot of time downtown, until recently. Most of her friends and their families had favored the Plaza, in Kansas City. But this was where Dominic's Crew came to meet.

This was the first chance they'd had to just hang out without the Crew. Yes, they'd been alone in the car together, but it had always been about her curse. This time it was just ... them.

Was there a "them"? Did she want a "them"? Did he?

Was she a part of the Crew? Could she be a part of the Crew, or was she their project ... their problem? Which did she want?

Eventually they found themselves walking beneath the trees of South Park, which were beginning to turn red. They disdained the gazebo and the benches and sat themselves down beside a tree on the back side of the park. She had to loose his hand so they could sit, so she took the opportunity to slip his arm behind her back. He flinched from surprise, but he didn't try to escape.

Was it the Mark's influence, or could she be this bold without it? Did she want to be?

She was relieved when he pulled her closer. Had he read her mind for what she wanted? She knew it would hurt him if she asked. The Mark's response didn't comfort her – *if he knows what we want he can better serve* – but its unconcern did.

They seemed to have run out of things to say, but the silence that fell was more companionable than awkward. It was quiet on this end of downtown. The parks didn't see as much traffic at night after summer ended. The air still reeked of exhaust, and she could hear traffic two blocks away, but without so much humanity pressing immediately around her, the Mark was calmer than she could remember it ever being in the company another human. Without the distractions that usually surrounded them, she could really pick up on Jacob's scent.

He turned his head, probably to say something, but it came out a gurgle when she kissed the inside of his neck. His heart raced, and his scent changed subtly. She did it again, getting a full gasp this time. The arm he had around her tightened and she could smell the lust begin to pour off him. A little voice in the back of her head thought that was gross, but it wasn't loud enough to keep her from turning into Jacob's body and kissing him below his ear.

His face turned to hers and he caught her mouth. He still tasted like his cherry soda. She put her hand on his chest; he reached up to touch her face. He was so timid. Was this his first kiss? It wasn't hers, though there hadn't been many before him. She coaxed him gently, running her fingers up his arm to where his hand cupped her cheek.

His heart rate jumped, and it drowned out the traffic. The smell of him drowned out the smell of the city. The arm she was leaning on clutched her tightly to him.

She climbed onto his lap, on her knees with his legs stretched out behind her. His frantic heart beat was like a symphony thundering in her ears. She sucked on his tongue like candy, nibbled his ear, clutched him to her breast. She could feel him getting hard through their jeans. She kissed her way across his face, back to his ear and down his jaw. His head lolled back, and she pressed her face into the curve of his neck.

The hollow of his throat loomed large in her vision.

Her vision went red.

The world vansished.

There was a white flash in her mind: *Stop!*

The world came back.

Jacob was still beneath her and but now he stank of fear. He wasn't hard anymore. His neck was in her teeth. She hadn't really been going to tear it out ... had she? Just ... she shuddered. She'd been going to hold on real tight.

She climbed off of him, shaking even harder than he was.

She was going to leave, but he caught her hip as she tried to stand.

"You don't have to."
"But I…"
"We can take it slow."
She sat back down and tried very, very hard not to think.

Monsters Versus Monsters

SATURDAY, OCTOBER 3RD

The night was oddly warm, the way October gets sometimes in eastern Kansas: a soft breeze hinting at a chill to come but not yet delivering. The sky was mostly clear, wispy clouds doing more to emphasize the moon and stars than to cover them. It was till two days before the height of the moon, a full day before she should have felt the call, and by the time Margaret realized that late-night photography was not the real reason she was wandering around the wooded edge of her parents' land, it was too late to phone the Crew for help.

The moonlight, although colorless, was almost as bright to her eyes as the sun. She could pick out stalks of grass and individual leaves in the trees. She could smell car exhaust and hot asphalt from the far-off road upwind, and the musky, meaty odor of her neighbor's horses. In the quiet of the night she could hear the gentle rustle and cries of livestock for miles around. She could the hunting cry of a fox and the whisper of bats' wings.

Margaret looked up at the moon and felt the Mark flare, and the last of the binding fray. She knew she was lost. She prayed that she wouldn't hurt anyone. She almost prayed that the other werewolves wouldn't come for her, but stopped – the first was the important one. Whatever the pack wanted from her, it required her alive. *'Please my Lord Jesus,'* she repeated with all her heart as she turned her eyes to the moon. *'Don't let me hurt anyone.'*

The first times the change had come, her conscious mind had been unable to handle the shock – shutting down and letting the magic of the Mark take over, refusing to recall in detail anything that had happened between moonrise and dawn. It came to her in flashes, sometimes, and in her dreams, but never when she tried. Later, when the werewolf had called the change, when Michael had forced her to transform at the quarter-moon, her mind hand been driven under by the pain. She had come back some minutes later, Dominic's friend Cait holding her down with improbable strength while everyone else stood as far from them as they could without fleeing the scene.

This time she, she decided, she was going to experience the change. Michael had told her to relax into it. It galled her to do anything he said, but she didn't have any other sources to go by. But she would do it her own way, too.

She had her camera, timer, and tripod. They were already mostly set up for night photography. All she had to do was switch lenses, adjust the focus, and set the timers with trembling hands. She peeled off her clothes as her skin began to itch, folding them with trembling hands and standing bare to the moonlight.

It started in her blood and in her bones, burning like it had in her dreams. She shivered slightly; warm for October was still not weather in which to be naked. A howl echoed in the distance as the change brought her to her hands and knees. Her muscles were moving under her skin in ways she had no words to describe and her skin was stretching to accommodate them. Soon her whole body burned, drowning out all other sensations, even sight and sound and scent. Then the fire cooled in her veins, and the world had changed.

Margaret had read that dogs do not see in color. Something about rods and cones that she could not recall or comprehend at the moment. Was that true of wolves, as well?

It did not seem to be true of her, but neither were the colors she saw now anything like the colors she had known before. The land and trees were cast in earthy hues of gray and brown, small animals scurried through the grass in faint shades of blood-red. The moon was a huge opal, shining every shade imaginable, and the stars were pinpricks of gold fire.

The howl came again, closer this time. It was the voice of Caleb, the witch-wolf, and to her dismay she could not sense her maker nearby. Caleb should not be here without Michael. The rest of the pack would not harm her, but that one might. He might hurt her just for fun or even kill her to spite their master.

She ran but she knew that she could not run far without feeding. The Mark needed fuel, needed blood. Where did the pack feed? She shouldn't keep robbing her neighbors, it was wrong, but the wind brought the smell of horse back to her and, although her human mind recoiled, she turned and ran toward the Heffernan farm. She would not escape the witch-wolf running that direction, but she would not escape at all without food.

The guard dog barked at her once. She tore out its throat. She looked no further for sustenance: swallowing what she had already taken and devouring as much of the rest as she could before the howl came again. Too close. Run. One last morsel – the heart – and she fled. The Mark flared again and the fire burned in her veins and she ran like the wind.

She had no idea what she would do when he caught her – and he would, eventually, his Mark was stronger – but she would not just wait for him. Her mind raced. Her heart pounded. Her legs pumped like pistons. She spied a rabbit in the underbrush, the blood-red life of it pulsing in time with its hammering little heart. She all but swallowed it whole, adding its life to her own. She could not face the wolf-witch on her own. She needed help. Then it came to her: Caitlyn Hannah. The older woman had stared down the whole pack, she could manage the witch-wolf by himself. Margaret didn't know exactly where Caitlyn lived, but she knew which apartment complex to search: they'd talked about it the last night the pack came for her. She was running in the wrong direction.

Margaret turned on a dime, running back toward town. Not exactly the direction the witch-wolf was chasing her from, but too close for comfort. She gobbled up everything she came across as she ran: mice, rabbits, a feral cat, and even an owl snatched out of the air as it dove for prey of its own. That she could consume them all in two or three bites shocked her. That she had room for them all was astounding. Still the Mark craved blood. It demanded bigger lives. That urge she would not satisfy, but still the Mark grew stronger as she fed it with blood and her refusal to give in.

Caitlyn was sitting alone in her apartment, smoking a cigarette and sucking down a stout when the unmistakable howl of a werewolf split the night.

'*There goes my evening,*' she thought, setting down the beer and reaching under the couch for the lacquered lock-box that held her gun. She set it on the table and popped it open with practiced ease, dialing the combination and working the complex latch in seconds. Inside was the gleaming beauty she had, in a moment of dark humor, named Conflict: a custom piece, hand-forged and machined by the master Joseph van Helsing IV, himself. Three and a half kilos of meteoric iron, twenty-one centimeters long, five 13 mm rounds in the spindle, and nearly every square centimeter of it engraved with glyphs and runes. A rune-marked silver knife, a box of alchemical rounds, and three full round-catchers shared the case. The shoulder holster, a custom rig that held the gun under her left arm and held the large knife and the spare ammo under the other, lived in the coat closet. She pulled the holster on one-handed, listening intently for the next howl. It came soon enough: much closer and in a different voice. Caitlyn grabbed her coat and dashed out the door as the first wolf's cry came again, this time from just outside.

There was a brindle wolf on her doorstep. It cowered when she pointed the gun at it, whimpering and looking up at her with pleading golden eyes. A presence of evil brushed against Caitlyn's senses, coming up fast.

"Margaret?"

The werewolf yipped and whined again, looking over its shoulder. Caitlyn's aim didn't waver, but her eyes flickered in that direction. The howl came again, and a monstrous red-eyed werewolf came careening around the corner. The werewolf at her feet whined again. Caitlyn didn't hesitate, but she didn't hurry either. She raised her gun, took her aim as the creature rushed them, and fired. The unmistakable thunder of a large-caliber handgun echoed up and down the street. The witch-wolf's flank erupted with blue flame and the force of the bullet spun it almost halfway around. Caitlyn waited to see if it would come back or run, sighting carefully down the barrel. It ran. Caitlyn holstered her gun.

She couldn't see any neighbors peeking out of their windows, but they might have been looking a second ago and they might come look at any moment.

"Come on, girl," she said to the creature at her feet. "Let's get you home safe, then I need to make some phone calls."

She ducked inside for her keys.

She had informed the appropriate authorities when she had settled in town, and her reputation was such that there had been no difficulty arranging to be unmolested on the issue of her nonexistent green card. The Wolf King had agents among the various local police agencies, as did the Church of St. Lazarus, so it would be easy to get herself off the hook as long as she didn't get arrested before the appropriate people could be assigned to the case. Still, it irritated her that she was having to deal with these issues so early in her retirement. It was her own fault, she supposed, for letting herself get involved with these unlucky kids.

SUNDAY, OCTOBER 4TH

Dominic was already sitting at his desk when the phone rang. Despite the early hour, he was hip deep in a research paper. The full moon was tomorrow, and he had to be sure to have everything for Tuesday taken care of as well.

"Madam Omar's House of Iniquity." Never let it be said that he was not completely without humor in the mornings, as long as he'd had his first cup of coffee.

The voice on the other end wasn't as amused as he'd hoped they'd be: "The binding failed."

"Oh," he said.

"The wolf-witch made me change and it snapped. I felt it."

"So you've had a rough night," he said slowly. "Do you remember what happened?"

"A rough night?" The voice – Margaret's voice – voice cracked, and there was a strangled noise that might have been a laugh or a sob. Maybe he'd been a little too flippant. Maybe too much humor this morning. "Yeah. Yeah, I have. I changed. I ran. I had to eat some of my neighbor's animals. The Heffernans are going to be really upset, I feel so bad. I was afraid the werewolf would hurt me, and I remembered that woman, Caitlyn, scared them off and where she said she lived, and ... She scared him off. Brought me home, but then she left. I woke up outside, by my clothes."

"So," he drawled, trying to jam the information into context. "Even without the binding, you're still not one of the pack. You're still not hunting people."

"Oh, God, Dominic! I shouldn't be hunting anything!"

An idea occurred to him. It was a bullshit theory, made up on the spot, but it seemed plausible.

"Your wolf body probably weighs quite a bit more than what your human body does. I bet it's literally starving on what a girl your size eats. If we load you up on some dinner tonight, before you change, and have food ready for after ... I bet we could get a lot of that hunger under control."

"Assuming the pack doesn't come for me. But it won't work. The Mark needs lives."

"Lives? Are you sure? And how do you know?"

"Of course I'm sure. It's inside of me, Dominic. It talks to me. I know what the Mark needs."

He sipped his coffee and chewed on his tongue.

"Alright," he said. "Let me talk to everyone, let me see what we can put together for tonight."

"Dominic." There was a long pause on the other end; he waited. "It took you and Aaron weeks to put together the first ritual. It didn't work. They're going to come for me no matter what you do. I don't want them to hurt any of you again."

Now it was his turn to pause. Had she really just told him to back the fuck off? Was this going to turn into that kind of Greek tragedy?

218

"Are you sure?"

"Yeah. Yeah, I am."

"Okay," he said. "Just ..." He drew that word out for a while, trying to pull his wits into working order. "We're still here for you if you need us. Do you want to meet up tomorrow, touch base? I have learned a couple things since we talked last."

The line was briefly silent. Dominic waited.

"Yes," she said, finally. "Yeah."

"I'll catch you in class. We'll work out the details."

"Yeah," she said again. "Thanks.

The line went dead.

Dominic stared briefly at the phone, shaking his head as he hung it back up.

"Well," he said. "That just happened."

Two creatures hovered at the edges of the physical world, the white mists of the astral at their backs as they watched over their prey. The moon was rising, and the pack was eager. Still in their motel room, the werewolves huddled around a table that groaned with the litter of take-out barbecue and somewhat more than a case of beer. They jostled with each other for the scraps.

Hiding in the astral plane, the creatures were invisible to the wolves, but there was one who could see them: another monster, far older and much more terrible than the Wolf-Marked. That one lounged in a corner, his long, too-white fingers interlaced and his left boot resting on his right knee. He, too, watched the pack with condescending amusement, and he gave no warning to the pack that they were being spied upon. This was the Monster, the one of whom they had been warned: a creature of many faces and none, like themselves.

The pack was raucous, half drunk. Crammed into the motel room like sardines in a can. The leader, a gray haired and bearded creature whom they immediately dubbed Grouchy, sat by the window smoking a cigarette. To his right sat an older, even more grizzled wolf they would call Gramps, who seemed to be his second. To Grouchy's right sat a younger monster, who reeked of magics, and watched his companions with hate, suspicion, and contempt; they would call him Chuckles. There were two women: the older one, with skin like tanned leather, they dubbed Betty; the younger, darker one, they named Sasha. The two boys, so boring as to be distinguishable only by their height, would be Sam and Joe. All easy prey in such tight quarters. They would be even easier prey in an hour when, fully loaded, they would climb upon their motorcycles and ride out to terrorize the girl-child.

The creatures in the mists saw nothing wrong with this, themselves, but they understood the need to interfere. The pack had stepped out of place last night, drawing the attention of a Knight of the Old Orders. The Wolf King had no desire for such attention, and the Fifth Street Devil's Club must be punished for their foolishness. So they two, the Wolf King's claws, would strike now, while the pack was still sober enough to put up some fight – enough to be amusing, at least.

Acting as one, the two creatures donned human faces and stepped into the physical world once more.

"Oh, look," said the first of the pair. It took on a high, lilting, woman's voice. "Here's the bad doggies, still at home. Don't y'all know the moon's halfway risen?" It took on a woman's flesh as well, voluptuous and half-naked. Her hair fell to her shoulders in platinum waves, a man's dress shirt, cut-off and tied-off to bare her midriff, barely contained her swollen breasts. Jean shorts cut indecently high revealed more than they hid, while red snakeskin cowboy boots reached halfway to her knees.

The pack turned, teeth bared and their eyes already changed.

"Maybe they knew they were in trouble," said the second, appearing identical to the first except with smaller breasts and wider hips. "Maybe they thought they could get outta their whoopin'."

The gray-haired leader stood, and the pack followed his cue.

"Who the fuck are you?" Grouchy snarled, pulling a chain off his shoulder.

"Anna," the first told them.

"Uma," said the second.

Their voices were saccharine, their smiles vapid.

"And y'all're in trouble," they concluded in sing-song chorus.

Grouchy yelled and lunged down the narrow opening between the TV-topped dresser on one side, the bed on the other. The pack followed, shoulder to shoulder and cheek to jowl in the close confines.

Anna and Uma's smiles changed from vapid to cruel and eager: battle was almost as sweet as the flesh of children.

Grouchy reached them first and they worked in tandem, grabbing him by the arms and throwing him back into the chair, knocking Sam and Joe down in the process. Next came the lieutenants: Anna took the old one, Uma took the warlock. Gramps took a boot to the ribs and stumbled back a step, barely dodging the left hook that followed. Chuckles transformed mid-air into something as much man as wolf, but that offered him little protection from the brass-bound club Uma pulled from the air and used to smash him into the far wall.

The remainder of the pack, scrambling around their fallen leaders – clumsily vaulting the bed on one side, knocking over the television on the other – was felled with deft, brutal blows of fist, foot, and club. The three strongest were already finding their feet, but the other four were down. One, the youngest male, lay broken in a quickly growing pool of his own blood.

"What are you," the leader demanded. "What do you want?"

"We are a message from the Wolf King," Uma told him tartly.

"You drew attention to yourself. Your idiot warlock tangled with a Knight of Herakles, in the middle of town, no less. She hasn't reported to the Orders' ambassador yet, but she will."

"That bitch ain't no knight."

The Monster, who had not moved a hair through the course of the brief battle, spoke up: "What would you know of such things, mongrel? The Old Orders have long employed monsters such as she: half-bloods and Shadows of Man." Grouchy snarled, but the Monster's attention had moved on. "Manusha-rakshasi. It has been a long time since I have seen any of your people so far from the Indus. The Wolf King has risen in power since last we met."

They smiled at the Monster, flattered to be so recognized here in the West, and posed in lurid fashion for his pleasure. Then they turned to the pack: "This is the only warning you get, dogs. Do your business and get out. Don't fuck up again."

"You killed my boy."

"We did. Next time, we will kill you all."

They took the body with them. The Mark was bitter, but the flavor could be covered, even complimented, with the correct blend garlic and ginger, peppers and vinegar.

Blood Moon

Margaret waited in her family's barn for the moon to rise. Between her parents' eerie, distant behavior, the discomfort of her supernatural senses – the din of three televisions and two arguing brothers, the reek of the chemicals the family used around the house – and the Mark's growing need for open air, it was getting harder and harder to keep herself inside. The hay-smell of the barn mostly covered the exhaust of the far-off highway, and there were few enough cars on the road that passed her drive that she was actually getting to know them by the sounds of their engines alone. Her homework was done, she'd started a new journal, and she'd shot through her last roll of film last night. There was nothing left to do but wait and pray.

The journal had been an impulse buy. She had tested the limits of her parent's distraction this afternoon, riding along to Hastings with them. They had not refused her, although they had essentially ignored her when not directly addressed. Nor had they abandoned her in the store. They had refused to buy her an expensive leather-bound journal, but they had spotted a smaller one bound in a blue-and-white paisley print that suited her as well or better. Margaret hadn't kept a diary since junior high, when she had picked up her first camera, but she couldn't think of any better way to sort through the experiences of the last months.

Just after sunset a car came rattling down the road, pulling to a stop at the far side of her drive. Not much later came the crunch of boots on gravel, then on grass, and Caitlyn Hannah appeared at the back door of the barn, where she could not be seen from the house. She was dressed all in black, a man's suit with a red tie and a gold tack, her hair gelled back from her face in a pompadour.

"Good evening, Mara," she said,

"Caitlyn? What are you doing here?"

"I thought I'd come keep an eye on you. The pack came for you last night; they're sure to come tonight."

"Did Dominic send you? I asked them to leave me alone tonight. I don't want anyone getting hurt."

"No one sent me," Caitlyn said with a firm shake of her head. "No one sends me anywhere, not these days. And I'm not going to get hurt, not unless that pack forgets the rules. Powerful people own this part of the world, and they don't like trouble. But I can go if you'd like."

Margaret hesitated, which Caitlyn seemed to take as acquiescence. The taller woman sat herself down on a hay bale and lit a cigarette. The odor of the tobacco was pungent and thick, but not quite as sour or acrid as most of the cigarettes she'd smelled. It was more like a cigar.

"What are you?" Margaret asked, after a while, winning a bark of startled laughter from the other woman.

"Well, that's right to the point, isn't it? You Americans!" Caitlyn shook her head. "Don't rightly know, to tell the truth. Wyrm-kin, some seers have called me, but no one's sure what they meant, since there's really no such thing as dragons. I was born what I am, not cursed or Marked, and never met anything else quite like me, so I've had to figure most things out as I go."

"Are you just strong, or do you have ... powers? Senses?"

"I'm a Sister of the Groves, if that's what you're asking. A druid, though not NROOD or ADF. I can see the unseen, weave webs, and cast circles and spells as well as any of your witchy friends."

"But you don't ... change?"

Caitlyn shook her head.

"I am what I am, as you see me. No more, no less."

Margaret looked away.

The sun was setting, and she could begin to feel the call of the Mark rising. Still the pack was nowhere to be seen. The moon rose, and by midnight Margaret could no longer resist the Mark's need to change. She stood naked, covering herself against Caitlyn's bland scrutiny, and did her best to let it wash over her the way it had last night. This time, though, the pain was more than she could stand, and her conscious mind fled. Her last thought was a prayer that she would find prey that did not belong to anyone.

224

Dawn came, and Caitlyn was still there, waiting with a cigarette in hand. Half a coyote lay nearby as she struggled to her knees.

"They never came?"

"Never," the older woman confirmed, her brow wrinkled in thought.

"I wonder what ..." Margaret wasn't even certain how to end that thought. Kept them?

"Who knows? Maybe they're just trying to confuse you."

Margaret shuddered at that thought.

"Well enough, though. Now there's even less reason to tell any of the boys I was even here."

"What?"

"Let's keep this between us girls, shall we?"

Margaret nodded, though she was uncertain what Caitlyn wanted to hide.

MONDAY, OCTOBER 5TH

The sign on the door to the Midnight Candle read "CLOSED", but the door still opened for them. Jacob and Margaret slipped through, feeling strangely guilty. Dominic's father stood behind the register, counting down the drawer.

"Go on down," Mr. Richardson said with a smile. "The door's open. Coffee's still hot if you want some."

Jacob snagged coffees for both of them.

"Thank you," Margaret said to Mr. Richardson, then again to Jacob when he handed her the coffee.

Together, they slipped through the store and down the stairs.

Dominic was waiting for them at the table in the basement. Usually, Jacob and Margaret could make it half down the stairs, even sit down at the table, before they drew his attention. Today, his eyes were focused on them before they even entered the room. Margaret's hand tightened on his arm; she knew that he'd felt them come into the building. He didn't want to, but Jacob could see Dominic's aura dancing through the webs and knots of his shields.

"Where's everyone else?" Margaret asked.

"On their way," Dominic said. His posture was stiff, the notebook at his elbow closed, his hands clasped before him as if in prayer. His hair was down, framing his face. No cigarette hung from his mouth or fingers, no ash tray interrupted the pattern of Tarot cards laid out across his end of the table. An air pot of coffee sat in the middle of the table, with mugs, pizza rolls, cookies, and a couple of two-liters of soda taking most of the space that wasn't filled with his cards.

"You said to be here at seven," said Jacob. "It's almost eight o'clock."

"I wanted to be sure you were the first ones here."

Jacob gave Dominic a strong frown.

"Why," Margaret asked.

"There's a lot to talk about, and I wanted you two to be settled and focused. And I didn't want to have to go through the thing where everyone stares at you coming down the stairs."

Jacob and Margaret exchanged a glance, but sat down without further complaint, sipping their drinks.

"Just you staring, then?" Margaret quipped.

Dominic chuckled. "Just me."

One by one the rest of the Crew filtered in. Aaron, with a cautious nod for Margaret and a friendly hand for Jacob's shoulder. Amber and Alexander with smiles, albeit some reserved, for them all. Last came Jennifer, sober and focused, but with a smile and a word for everyone. They had worked out their seating arrangements weeks ago, keeping Alexander on the far side of the table from Aaron and Jacob, with Amber and Jennifer sitting between them to keep the peace.

"Okay, everyone," Dominic said, sitting back in his chair and folding his hands in his lap. "Get your drinks. We've got bad news, good news, and more bad news."

He had everyone's attention. Jacob envied him – not for the attention itself, but for his comfort in that position.

"So, the first bad news is that the binding didn't hold. Maybe we didn't actually pull it off in the first place, maybe it would have held if the pack weren't here to call Mara out. We can't really know for sure, and we can't really afford to do much in the way of further testing. We have no idea what kind of time table we're on, or what the werewolf pack is going to do — with Mara or the rest of us."

A grim sort of silence shrouded the table for a moment. Dominic cast his gaze over them all. Aaron and Alexander met his eye. The rest stared at their hands in their laps.

Margaret spoke first. "What's the good news?"

"There may be another solution. I've been looking into other sources, there are references to a book that may have a ritual to remove the Mark."

"I thought you said there wasn't any?"

"I said that I couldn't find any. The sources I had then said there wasn't any. On the other hand, I've only found the one source saying otherwise, and it could be wrong."

"What's the other bad news," Margaret asked.

"The ritual may not actually exist. I may not be able to find the text my source refers to. The references were vague allusions. The ritual may be to *move* the Mark, not *remove* it."

Amidst a sea of confused faces, Alexander saw where that was going, sitting up so straight and sudden that it made Jacob jump.

"So you're looking for volunteers," Alexander said.

Dominic shrugged and grimaced, something in his eyes that made Jacob uncomfortable.

"We're not at the volunteer stage yet. I don't even know if I can find the Liber Caecissimus. And if I do find it, well ... it's going to be old-school magic. 'Eye of Newt' may or may not be code for the center of any eye-like flower, as Cunningham claims, but 'blood of bat' is serious. No substitutions. Life's blood." The eyes he met this time were shocked, a few accusing. He couldn't lie to them about this, though. "When it comes down to brass tacks, the ritual might well call for something higher up the food chain than 'bat'."

Jacob shuddered a little at the thought. Beside him, Margaret flinched hard. He was more grateful than usual that he couldn't hear her thoughts right now. What price was she willing to pay not to be a monster?

She had already changed, long before the pack arrived. Clothes folded neatly and clean for the morning, human flesh giving way to monstrous fur under the light of the setting sun. Thought gave way to feeling, plan to impulse. The moon called and she ran to answer, snatching up prey as she went.

At first she found shelter in the wilderness – such as it was. The clean wind in her face was a fine thing. She reveled in the crunch of dead grass under her padded feet, the cold, hard loam tilling under her claws. She took pleasure the easy prey of feral dogs and a half-tame deer. But the tame fields and barely feral woodlands could only hold her attention for so long.

The scent of the city came to her every time the wind changed, and that called to her as strongly as the moon, itself. Humanity called to her. The availability of prey changed radically: no feral animals, but strays, and pets let run outdoors. Rats and mice were plentiful, even though their woodland cousins were settling into hibernation. In the trash bins just outside of the city limits she found her first raccoon: plump, juicy, succulent, and surprisingly salty.

When the pack finally came, they found her in the middle of town, stalking between houses and looking in windows.

Come with us, they called. *Run with us. Hunt with us.*

And she did.

They ran through the streets. The three leaders ran at the front: large black wolves with varying degrees of gray in their fur. Michael ran point, grizzled with age at the muzzle and along his back. Michael's closest ally ran to his right, a shaggy beast whose patchy gray and black pelt had probably been darker, once, but never uniform. The wolf-witch ran to Michael's left: deformed and monstrous, with man-like hands and limbs that looked like something from a horror movie. The

228

oldest female ran behind the second in command, and the next strongest male ran behind the witch. She followed them, while the smallest male and female ran behind her.

There had been another male when last she had run with the pack, but she spared his absence little thought.

Where she had only looked through windows, the pack yipped and howled at them: stirring fear in the houses and working tame dogs to a frenzy. She joined them, at first, but drew back. These people, these dogs, were no threat or challenge to their strength: there was no sport here. A human thought intruded past the power of the Mark: 'These wolves are like Anthony Domiano. Bullies. This posturing proves nothing.'

The pack found a dog in a large yard, and circled it as they howled. She pulled away, watching, trying to fathom the reason for this ritual. A man finally came to the door to address the commotion. 'Will they enter the house,' she wondered, 'a more savage show of strength?' But they only tore the dog to shreds before its horrified human's eyes: fur and limbs thrown to the corners of the yards, entrails in an artful pile where they had circled. She watched disdainfully, but followed when they ran on, jumping the fence and charging down the alley.

Michael led them to the river, where he raised his head and sniffed the air carefully.

The others were watching her, now. By refusing to participate she had drawn attention to herself. The youngest female circled her first: a plain, gray wolf with slender limbs and a high, dark ruff. Margaret-the-wolf whuffed in contempt, sat, and simply stared the challenge down. The youngest male came next. He was a little larger, tawny, with large paws and a long, narrow muzzle. He charged her, but flinched when she did not even rise to face his challenge. He charged again, but she slid out of the way gracefully, rising to her full height and smacking him in the face with a paw. The blow was more startling than powerful, but the young male fell to the ground. She growled when he started to rise, and he stayed down.

Now even the leaders were watching her closely. The other, less junior, male and the last remaining female had begun to circle her slowly. She stood her ground carefully. Would they fight with her singly, and risk their positions, or would they attack her together for the sake of cowing her?

The female was larger, stronger, and more senior, but the male's body language was more aggressive. She struggled to keep her eyes on both of them, but she watched him more closely and did her best to keep her body language defensive without being passive, implacable without being aggressive. She could not defeat them all, not in one night, maybe not at all.

The female sat, apparently content that Margaret was sufficiently cowed.

The male approached her head-on, but slowly. He was about her mass, taller but leaner, his coat a smoky gray color. They locked eyes and she bristled. He bristled back but did not attack. He growled. She growled, taking a step forward. The distance between them could be covered by a single strong lunge. He neither advanced nor backed down. He made an appeasing huffing noise but did not break eye contact.

She exhaled slowly, relaxed slightly. He relaxed as well, his mane settling against his back. He whuffed again, tilting his head and relaxing eye contact.

Margaret was uncertain how to read this. He seemed to be acknowledging her as equal, or at least saving the challenge for later. The other werewolves were growing restless, and she could hear movement – possibly threatening movement – behind her. She whuffed back and he sat without retreating.

She turned to make sure there were no more threats behind her.

The impact on her back caught her completely off guard and drove her to the ground. The male she had thought had backed down had seen his opportunity and made his move with a fox-like leap. If he had been trying to kill her, she would already be dead. Instead, however, he was trying to mount her.

Her only advantage was that he had the angles all wrong, his wolf-dong flapping against her hindquarters rather than penetrating her. He tried to back off for a better angle, but in doing so lost his hold on her.

She surged forward, out from under him. He chased, expecting her to run. Instead, she turned on a dime: charging in, back under his long legs and biting down on his back left hamstring, savaging it between her jaws while he tried to clamber off of her and away from her fangs.

The other werewolves charged in, tried to pull her out from under him, but she used his body as a shield while she broke his leg and tore his ligaments. Finally, she was done, and ran out from under him again – making certain to catch his testicles with her claws as she moved.

As soon as they were separated, the pack backed away, leaving the youngest female to lick the male's wounds. The pack leaders approached her, hackles raised. She took a single step back and sat, neither submitting further nor offering challenge. They sat down as well. Michael and the lead bitch snarled at her, but the monstrous wolf-witch nodded once, subtly, and his tongue lolled out in a canine smile.

Challenge

TUESDAY 6 OCTOBER
"You're weak, Michael."

For a moment Michael thought that Big Hugh had finally turned on him. Hugh was the only one strong enough to challenge him. But it was Caleb's sneer that brought the funeral to a halt.

"What did you say?"

Michael turned. Caleb was barely an arm's reach away.

"I said you're weak," the warlock stepped up into Michael's face, still man-shaped, but his eyes glowing red. "You gave Heidi to that Wolf King. You let that hunter bitch on the river back you down. You let the Wolf King's monster bitches kill Ralph. You let that cunt thrall of yours hamstring Craig – who knows when he'll walk again? And all for what? Some Chicago seer told you to? So you can get rid of me? You're weak, Michael. Go fuck off and die in a corner somewhere."

That shit sure as hell had the gang's attention. They watched, silently forming a ring around the two feuding men. None raised a hand to interfere: Michael hadn't enjoyed that level of support in years.

Michael didn't even answer the challenge except to snarl, and lash forward with a head-butt that drove Caleb to his knees. Or should have. The warlock was stronger than he looked. It did drive him back, though, making room for Michael to unleash a wide-swung haymaker.

That blow landed solidly, and sent Caleb to the ground. He came back up swinging, a body blow that would have done Michael serious harm if he'd had any follow-through. Instead, Michael threw his whole body weight and all the strength his lycanthropy gave him into a downward blow that took Caleb square in the face.

Caleb's neck crunched and he crumpled to the ground, where Michael kicked him savagely in the ribs several times. He felt ribs give under his boot, heard bones break, saw blood splash on the pavement. Finally, he backed off, and the gang stepped back, too, forming a wider circle.

Michael was surprised to discover that he was panting. The fight hadn't been long, hadn't taken that much out of him. It maddened him to be challenged. The boy owed him everything: he'd been giving hand jobs for heroin when the pack had found him, painting back-alley walls with whatever occult gibberish he saw while chasing the dragon. Ruger had saved him, given him a gift of power, all at Michael's order. Now the punk had the nerve to defy him.

He thrust his chin out at Lonna, and his old lady slid in to check Caleb's pulse.

"Not dead," she pronounced.

Michael grunted.

"Lee can keep an eye on him, then."

Lonna grunted. Lee said, "Yes, boss."

Lee stood over Caleb's broken body, looking scared and confused. The rest of the pack followed Michael to their bikes. The Monster, their ever-present shadow, stood aloof some feet away. He had not raised a hand to help Michael, either.

"You coming?" Michael demanded loudly.

"I will join you later."

The Monster watched the pack roar away, swerving back and forth across lanes of traffic for no reason except the terror it caused the other drivers. When they were past its vision, the Monster followed them with its other senses, finally turning his attention away when it was clear that they were not going to further torment their thrall.

The wolf-girl Michael had left stood nervously over the warlock, small and dark in a world made pale by the strange light of the late autumn sky. The thick black ringlets of her tightly curled hair bobbed as she looked back and forth between her charge and the Monster, itself. She seemed uncertain how or if to aid Caleb. As the Monster approached, she took a long step back, the blood draining from her warm brown face. The Monster shook its head, long hair billowing as if there were a strong wind.

"You need not fear me, little sister," it said, holding its hands out in a gesture of placation. "Even if your master were to cross mine, which he will not, you would have nothing to fear from me. I am here to observe and report."

It continued forward as it spoke, kneeling when it reached the wolves so that it could more closely examine the warlock. Its long coat and hair pooled carelessly in the wolf-witch's blood. Caleb's eyes were bright and aware, and his Mark undiminished by the beating he had taken. The monster reached out a pale, slender hand and took the wolf's outstretched limb carefully. Thick dark fur sprouted in among the curling human hair, and broken nails showed hints of protruding claw. This close, the Monster could hear bones and muscle grinding and shifting, popping slowly back into their proper places as the wolf-witch put his Mark to good use.

"I have underestimated you," the Monster said to the wolf. "I will not do so again."

The wolf barked a bitter laugh.

"So good of you to say."

"Speak to me, later, when you are recovered."

The Monster stood slowly and found the wolf-girl staring at him with dark brown eyes more curious than they had been a moment ago. It reached out a hand to delicately brush first her cheek and then her hair.

"You have all feared me. You need not have, save your master. The task is almost done, and then I shall leave you. And you, Lee, or your friend Heidi, so abruptly thrust into the Wolf King's care, will serve by my side. One more waning and waxing of the moon, and then we shall see what comes of your master's ambition."

Liber Caecissima

"Liber Caecissima."

Every time Aaron said the words aloud it sent a shiver up his spine. He'd taken Latin, too. He knew what it meant. Literally, it translated as "book most secret", or maybe "book of most secret things". Dominic had also called it the Book of Secrets; admittedly a more natural translation despite the very ... gamey feel of it.

He ought to be thinking about college applications, right now. Or at the very least tomorrow's homework. These were critical months of his life. The work he did or didn't do would determine the whole of his adult future. Margaret's ... little problem had already taken up two months of his life. He couldn't afford to give her Gordian knot any more of his time and energy.

And yet ...

"Liber Caecissima."

The shiver had a familiarity to it, a particular flavor of cold. It was the cold he felt in the graveyard, or standing over that slab out at the Cybele Sanctuary. It was the cold he felt in his dreams of death and the dead.

"Liber Caecissima."

It was the cold he felt when uttered the words that had come to him in a dream, the ritual he believed to be a memory from a life before this one. In the dream he had gone to the dead for information. He could remember neither question nor answer, but he remembered the ritual, and the tools he had made afterward.

He should be focusing on this life, and the future he wanted to make with it. But all he could think of was that now, at last, he had a question. And that the dark of the moon was tomorrow.

———

Alexander ran a search for "Book of Secrets", just to say he did, but Yahoo! brought him back so many hits that he didn't bother looking at any of them. "Krypsomachos" – and three different spellings thereof – was more productive. A little. A thousand conspiracy pages. A blues bar in Chicago. Myths and legends about a book containing every secret and scrap of lost knowledge produced by human history. An occult tome dating back to Pharaonic Egypt. Nothing relevant that Dominic hadn't already told them.

Once more, he concluded, the internet proved to be completely useless.

Amber was more optimistic of course, blaming her failure to find anything useful on censorship perpetrated by filter programs employed by the Lawrence Public Library. Alexander had used those computers, though. He couldn't believe that they would censor occult wisdom and still allow him unrestricted access to Japanese cartoon pornography.

Even if they did find this great Book of Secrets, what then? It might or might not have the ritual Dominic's book alluded to. Dominic had shown him the text: it was far from clear. Nothing in the book was clear, according to Dominic. The dedication said it all: "I have plumbed the depths of Mystery and come back less than whole. These things I have done with mirrors. These things I have seen beyond the Veils." The book had no proper title, either. Mirrors and Veils was just a moniker attached to it by some swooning Victorian medium.

All this danced through Dixon's mind as he waited outside the public library. Amber was inside, struggling with her homework. His was long done, of course. He never struggled with it the way she did, at least in part because he wasn't as emotionally wound up in it. Nothing less than perfection would suit Amber, and her 3.9 GPA failed to convince her that not everything she did was garbage. Alexander's own grades weren't as good, but he only put forth a third of the effort she did. Part of the reason for that, of course, was that he couldn't sit still that long. He'd only been sitting here for a quarter of an hour, but his legs itched and throbbed with the stillness. He began to pace, stalking between the great square columns and around the bike racks.

What if the infamous grimoire (and Dominic assured him it was as well known a mystery as Satan's Bible) was real? What if it did contain the ritual Dominic thought that it did? He'd already volunteered himself half-jokingly.

Only half? The thought gave him pause, almost made him fall off the bike rack he was balancing on. He covered by jumping down with a flourish, tried to clear his head by running up a column. Had he really been joking at all?

Margaret Dunn was an athlete, but not a body builder. Anthony Domiano was a big, strong man, and Margaret had pushed him around without really trying. He'd heard rumors about her track performance this year; there was talk of steroid testing. And, now that he was paying attention, she felt strong – like the little old Japanese men who visited the dojo and juggled the biggest American black belts. All that could be his.

"Heavy thoughts?" Amber's question startled him out of a hand-stand. She did know him well. His acrobatics were more extreme when his mind was somewhere else entirely.

"Mara," he told her. "The Grimoire. The pack."

He hadn't been thinking about the werewolf pack, but he should have been. They hadn't been seen since the height of the moon, though Jacob told Dominic that Margaret dreamed about them almost every night. Dominic's books promised pillaging, screaming, and dying in the wake of a single werewolf. They didn't mention packs at all, but one would assume that the carnage would only increase. Yet Margaret fought the impulses of the Mark and the pack managed a low profile. They were predators, but not a ravaging horde. They were working an angle, and the Crew needed to figure out what it was.

Dominic had to be working on it already. He and Aaron were the uncontested brains of the operation.

"Me, too," said Amber, hugging herself tightly. "Made it hard to think about school."

Alexander wrapped his arm around her shoulders and they set off together. There was a little place he knew a few blocks away, off the road, and hidden in the woods between the river and the train tracks.

"I just don't understand why this is happening to us."
There was a little petulance and a lot of whine in Amber's tone.

"Shit happens. Doesn't need a reason."

"Yes it does. Everything happens for a reason. And you wonder about it, too. I see it in your face. What does the pack want? Why Mara? She couldn't have been the only pretty girl at the restaurant that night, but they stalked her all the way back to Lawrence and got her the next day. At church."

Alexander nodded. She was right on all counts.

"Why didn't they just take her then," he said. "Why don't they just *take her* take her, now? Why bother hexing her family? Why not hurt or kill us for trying to help her? Are they waiting for something? Are they working for someone? The well-dressed monster Mara saw at the bar that night before? Why aren't any of them acting like the werewolves we've read about?"

"All of that," Amber agreed. "More. Why?"

"I don't know. We need to find out. We need a Sybil."

"A what?"

"An oracle. A seer. Someone who can answer questions. See the past and future. Guide us on our Hero's Journey."

"The Hero's Journey again?" The look on Amber's face told him what she thought of that idea. He had to get her to read Joseph Campbell. He doubted that the myths were true in the details... but the pattern was there, and it rang true as a whole.

"We do have the Tarot," Amber said after a moment.

He hadn't thought of that.

"That works?"

"Sometimes. If you know what you're doing."

"Why didn't we try before?" He hated not knowing as much as anyone else. He was just starting, and they'd been studying witchcraft for years. If he was going to be a part of this, he had to be a peer. He couldn't be the new guy.

"Dominic probably did," Amber shrugged. "I mean, haven't you noticed he always has his cards out when we're meeting? I'm sure that's one of the things he's reading about."

"Oh. Yeah. I guess I didn't think about it." Alexander furrowed his brow. "Why hasn't he said anything?"

"Probably because he hasn't learned anything useful, or that he can explain. But that's no reason for us not to try."

"It isn't?"

"It doesn't work that way. I don't know how to explain."

Amber took his hand, letting him help her down the short, rocky slope to the half-hidden path into the woods. They followed a trace of a stream until they came to a set of four-by-fours laid down as a bridge. Another such bridge led them to a path of grass that had been mowed before the cold killed it. In one direction, the path led to a rectangular clearing, well hidden from almost every angle; in the other direction, the path led to a small hill, a pond, and a waterfall that fed down to the river. They took the latter, passing a crude wooden sundial, and settling on a bench sheltered by the winter skeletons of weeping willows.

"This is where Jacob, Aaron, and I did our rituals before Dominic started taking us out to the Sanctuary. I still come here sometimes to do things by myself."

Alexander nodded, looking around. It would be good for that, he supposed. He'd been coming here for a few years, himself, before he'd ever met Amber. How strange that they'd never run into each other.

"I'll call Jacob about doing a Tarot ritual tomorrow, and I'll do one myself tonight."

"Can I help? Can I watch?"

"Am I allowed to say no? This is something I've only done with Jacob and you're ... distracting."

"And still on Jake and Ron's shit list. It's cool." The lie rolled off his lips with practiced ease. It wouldn't be cool until they forgave him and Anthony magically became a real person again and they all went and partied together in a rainbow fucking wonderland of joy and happiness.

"What happened between you three that you're still mad ten years later?"

"Ask them. Hell, ask Tony. I'm not gonna make things worse by being the one who blabs."

"Don't you trust me?"

"It's not about trust. It's about keeping a promise." Even that was more than he wanted to say, but ... he owed her at least that much. She was sleeping with him after all, and wasn't that how things worked? And he was getting more ... invested in her than he'd thought he would. He owed her an answer, really, but he owed Jacob and Aaron his silence.

"Come on," Amber stood, reaching out to him. "I'm getting cold. Let's go back to my place. Mom will be at work by the time we get there."

WEDNESDAY, OCTOBER 7TH

Aaron parked his car on the side of the road less than half a block from the cemetery. He could have parked closer, probably, without drawing attention to himself, but he wanted at least a little bit of plausible deniability on the off chance he ran into the police. It had never happened to him, of course, but he knew people who'd been caught breaking into the cemetery at night.

To call it "breaking in" made it sound more dramatic than it was. The northwest corner, right off the street, didn't even have a fence. You just walked up, hopped over the half-buried stone wall, and cut across a short field of unmarked graves. He could feel them stir as he wove between them, cold death stirred by the presence of warm life. He reached the footpath with a dozen long strides, followed the pavement to the far side of the grounds, where he could be least seen from the caretaker's house.

The ritual was simple, requiring only two tools: a bone wand and a circle of string. The wand, balanced lightly in his left hand, was one of his few real secrets from Dominic: eighteen inches of black-lacquered ash dowel, with the bones of small animals tied carefully along its length and a weasel's skull tied to the head. The image had come to him in a dream last summer, and he had purchased what he needed at the

Renaissance Faire the following September. The slender silk rope was white, and he had used it in the self-initiation rite Dominic had helped him perform at about the same time.

He found the place he wanted, off the path and behind one of the half-dozen small mausoleums the cemetery boasted, where the moonlight struck the ground this time of night. There was very little moon tonight, however: he had chosen the last night of the waning moon for this. A large, flat tombstone lay in the grass, satisfying that requirement of the spell.

His mind a serene blank, he tied twelve knots in the cord so that the last joined the two ends into a circle that was just big enough for him to kneel within it, his ankles crossed over the stone center. The rite had come to him in the dream as well, but he had never had a cause or the courage to perform it before tonight.

Three times he knocked on the earth with his wand. Although he did it gently, as not to crack the brittle skull, he felt the earth tremble beneath him and heard the world toll like a great bass bell.

"SAPHPHAIOR BAELKOTA KIKATOUTARA EKENNK LIX. O you spirits of death, I call upon you. Rise Rise Rise, I call upon you. DÖOU SHAMAI ARABENNAK ANTRAPHEU. BALE SITENGI ARTEN. She who moves below has given me the words you must answer to. She has given me your names. ACHNOUI ACHAM ABRA ABRA SABAOTH! Come forth. Come forth. Show your true face and speak true words."

The shadows deepened, and the light of the stars grew somehow brittle. Something cold and comforting welled up within him, spilling out of his skin to fill the circle. Something outside the circle welled up in response.

Shadowy figures rose from the earth, one by one, circling him slowly. Their whispers, so familiar, so haunting, filled the air. More came, and more. Soon they came by twos and threes. A hundred, maybe several hundred, wispy shadows of every shape and size flickered and danced in waves around his circle, whispering among themselves and uttering hoots and wails that Aaron imagined would have brought Amber to tears. Faces appeared and vanished among the writhing shadows: sad, hungry, dead.

Strangely, he was unafraid.

For long minutes they gathered, and he made not a sound. He watched his breathing, held the circle with a thought, and carefully kept the ends of his wand within its confines, across his knees. His legs hurt, but he knew better than to stretch them and risk breaking the circle.

At last, a figure emerged from the crowd, less ephemeral than the rest. It stood as tall as he, thin and only generally man-shaped, a void against which the night sky seemed a beacon.

What truth do you seek, o summoner of the dead? The shadow's voice was the rustling of dry leaves, the rattle of old bones.

"I seek the Liber Caecissima." Aaron pitched his voice carefully: warm, reasonable, friendly. The dreams had warned him: speak gently to avoid the wrath of the grave.

The dead stilled, became almost invisible. They would have been utterly invisible, were it not for the shimmer of silver where their outlines met and crossed. Only the great shadow remained clear while their whispers became a mad rustle, as if to make up for their stillness.

That which you seek lies outside the knowledge of the dead. Seek then the realms of dream, which are known only to the living. This much is known among the dead: a serpent guards the gate.

Aaron considered for a moment, then nodded. His mind was strangely blank. Was this how Dominic felt in the middle of his most potent rituals? Like a cup, full of knowledge and power far beyond that which was truly his own? He bowed to the dead, as low as the confines of his silk circle would allow. He raised his wand and completed the ritual, knocking three more times upon the earth.

The swelling power broke, began to recede. The dead retreated, whispering among themselves, but the shadow remained a moment.

The Book of Secrets will not serve you. Seek the Rites of Blood, o necromancer.
Then it vanished.

FRIDAY, OCTOBER 9

Jacob closed his eyes and let the gentle strains of his Celtic harp compilation carry him into the trance. He swelled past the edges of his carefully cast Circle, filled the basement until he could see every inch, every knick-knack, every hanging shirt and pile of laundry; he could feel the soft nap of the carpet, feel the weight of the earth pushing in against the walls, the tread of his family walking around upstairs.

Breathe in, breathe out. Center, expand.

His awareness spread slowly upward, the sensations crystallizing as he walked through the house in his mind's eye. The basement stairs led directly into the kitchen, which opened into the dining room on his right. The dining room flowed into the living room on the right; to the left was his father's office. Past the living room was the hall, with the front door and the coat closet and the stairs leading up to his parent's room and his sisters'.

Ricki and their mother moved around the kitchen in a complex dance. He couldn't see their auras as much as feel them, but whatever gift he possessed translated the psychic sensation of them into a synesthetic panorama. The two women were a peculiar blend of contrasts and similarities: where his sister was muted, gray, their mother was bright and clear. Both women lived within a rigid matrix of light and shadow, crowned with grace, but one withered while the other flourished. There was more to them than what he could sense, but another figure cast a shadow over them that he could not see through: Mr. Lucas Mathews. Little Stephanie was outside or upstairs, somewhere on the edges of his perception, a bright spark of hope and innocence.

The family patriarch owned the living room. Jacob could hear the television through the floor, but he knew it was just background noise to drown out the sounds of the kitchen while Lucas pawed through the paper. His father was thick, layered, and teeming. The outermost layer was dark and calm—the shadow that spread throughout the house. He, too, had the inflexible matrix of light and shadow, but Jacob thought he could see through it to a seething core of fear, rage, and – beneath it all – a deeply suppressed need.

The phone rang and his trance shattered. Margaret's face flashed in his mind.

Another ring, a pause during which Jacob tried to catch his breath and re-find his center. A few light footsteps and the creak of the door at the top of the stairs.

"Jacob," his mother called. "Telephone."

His mother was waiting for him at the top of the stairs with the handset, bound to the wall by a nine-foot curly cord. They had a cordless phone, too, but that lived in his father's breast pocket.

They couldn't talk long; dinner would be on the table soon, but they had long enough.

"Girls calling?" his father's voice came from behind him. He hated how his father liked to listen in on everyone's calls.

"Yes, sir. We're meeting for coffee."

"Just the two of you?" Did he want to know if they were meeting alone or did he want to know if Aaron and Dominic would be there?

"Yes, sir."

"How long has this been going on?"

"For a week or two." Well, longer, but just them hadn't been going on for very long.

"Are you dating?"

"I think so. We haven't really talked about it."

"What kind of girl is she?" Asked amiably enough, but a loaded question none the less.

"Athletic. Quiet. Runs track. She goes to Holy Cross. She's a friend of Jennifer Hobb." They knew Jenn's family through the church.

244

His father nodded approvingly.

"You remember what I taught you about being a gentleman."

"Yes, sir," he said, though he remembered no such thing. It was the answer Lucas wanted; that was all that mattered.

The entrance to the Coffee Break was subterranean, a glass door at the bottom of a set of concrete stairs that descended from the sidewalk. Between the stairs and the building, itself, was a concrete retaining wall that had probably once held a planter, but now held a small table in between a pair of precariously perched patio chairs. Dominic sat in the more precarious of those two chairs, other customers all but walking under his feet as they descended past him and into the building. He watched each of them as they went by, noting their gait and their dress, trying to gauge their moods and personalities. Despite that regular, and occasionally boisterous traffic, he found this placement to be more peaceful than the crowded interior, and somehow, paradoxically, more private.

His perch also gave him the perfect vantage to watch as Caitlyn rounded the corner from the parking lot. She was dressed more flamboyantly than usual: tight jeans and leather boots that came almost up to her knee, a turtleneck under a light blazer; it was all black except for the emerald sweater that set off her red hair. Her back was straight, her step jaunty, and her eyes clear. She looked like she was in a damn fine mood, and it was instantaneously infectious.

"Good evening, madam," he said. "Would you like a cigarette?"

If he startled her, she gave no sign. She sat down in the chair beside him, and took the offered clove.

"Thank you, my good man. How is your evening?" Perhaps it was his imagination, or maybe just the word choice, but her usually subtle accent seemed thicker. Ye Gods, he loved that accent.

"Quite well, thank you. Yourself?"

"Very well," she admitted.

"Good to hear it," he said. "And I must say, you look lovely tonight."

"Thank you."

"Have fun and exciting plans for the evening?" Dominic asked. As Caitlyn settled herself, he did some adjusting of his own – sitting up straighter and squaring himself to the chair – and watched her surreptitiously from the corner of his eye.

"I will admit that I was going to move from here to the pub somewhat later in the evening, but nothing specific. Yourself?"

"Not particularly. Most of my friends are ... otherwise occupied, so I just thought I'd come out tonight and see who I found. And, behold! Caitlyn Hannah."

Caitlyn laughed, and leaned back in her chair as far as the cold plastic and narrow perch would permit.

"Indeed, here I am, in all my ... glory, for want of a better word. Otherwise occupied, you say?"

"Dating each other," he said, waving his hand and rolling his eyes. "Doing homework. Sulking. I'll leave you to guess who is who."

She laughed again, louder this time, her chair shaking precariously under her.

"I think I can guess," she said, wiping a tear from her eye.

Dominic grinned widely, and waggled his eyebrows at her.

Caitlyn laughed again, this time until she coughed.

"I need coffee," she said at last. "Need a refill?"

"Yes, please."

THURSDAY, OCTOBER 15

Amber and Jacob sat in her room, facing each other across her bed. Sticks of sage and mugwort incense burned on her altar, filling the room with a thick smoke. They chanted, passing the tarot deck back and forth between them, taking turns shuffling it.

When the incantation was complete, Amber took the lead, laying out the basic ten-card spread. She laid them face-down: two cards in the center, one above, one below, one to the left, one to the right, and a column of four cards rising from bottom to top. Jacob turned them over one by one, announcing their names while Amber wrote them down.

"The Fool crossed by Judgment; the Hanged Man above, the Devil below; the Six of Cups to the left, the Ten of Swords to the right; the Page of Disks; the Wheel of Fortune; the Moon; the Tower."

Together, they stared at the cards for several minutes, entranced.

"The Fool," Amber intoned. "Beginnings and initiations. Moving forward blindly, blissfully unaware of the pitfalls ahead. An innocent. A new soul. Jacob – what do you see?"

"I see us," he said. His eyes were half closed, his voice strangely faded – as if he were speaking to her from across the school cafeteria instead of within arm's reach. "Fumbling blindly. This is only the beginning. We have no idea how far this will go, how dark the path will get."

She jotted down everything he said faithfully. So far, this was obvious. Was he faking the trance this time?

"Judgment crosses the Fool," she said. "Transformation, rebirth. Letting go of the previous life. Death and resurrection. A challenge; a decision. Absolute change. Jacob – what do you see?"

"I see the wolf-pack," he said, a little stronger but at the same time as if from farther away. "I see them coming, and going. I see figures watching us – shadowed, ephemeral – a wolf lounging on a throne; two old men, one in robes who bleeds from the hands, the other in rags with salt-blinded eyes; a bare-breasted woman with serpents coiling in her hair and clawed feet."

He wasn't faking. His words conjured images in her own mind. She could see what he saw, see the things he described – were they men? Monsters? Gods?

"Above, the Hanged Man — that which we must pursue, the ideal, the goal. A punishment. A change in perspective. Suffering for the sake of growth. What do you see?"

"I see a sacrifice. Death traded for life. Blood for madness. The werewolves. One wolf. A noose and a knife."

These images, her mind recoiled from. The wolf-pack, circling. Dominic standing over her lover, knife in hand. Alexander falling, only to rise again a wolf. Jacob, hanging from the ceiling. Aaron, a shadow wielding a bloody knife.

She could not bear the knowledge. She tried to thrust the images from her vision. She hated herself for her cowardice even as she begged the Goddess for the forgetting.

The pen shook in her hand. She wrote nothing.

"Below," she choked on human speech, "the Devil — that which helps us, that which hinders us, root causes and shadowed influences. Temptation. Corruption. Addiction. The shadow repressed. What do you see?"

The first word past her lips, the others came in sequence, pulled against her will by the weight of those that came before them.

"I see monsters," he said, breathless, and — at last! — sounding afraid. Once more the serpent-haired woman flashed in Amber's mind, and the two old men. "I see a seven-headed shadow. Gods of the old world. We are pawns at the hands of powers we can't understand, immortal and otherwise."

These things, too, appeared in her vision. The shadow with seven heads stood behind the old man with salt-blinded eyes, a thing of endless and terrible motion. The man with the bleeding hands was painfully familiar, but she could not bring herself to name him. Faces and shapes spread out behind them, innumerable, awe-inspiring, ranging from beautiful to terrible.

"To the left," she sobbed, "the Six of Cups — that which is passing away. Childhood. Happiness and nostalgia. What do you see?"

Tears streamed down her face as she resumed her record, desperate for anything to focus on besides the visions Jacob shared with her.

"I see us all. I see Jacob, Alexander, Ron, and Tony – each one's hand upon another's throat." Jacob was referring to himself in the third person now. They'd only been this deep once before. "I see Dominic standing outside a circle, waiting to be let in. I see Jenn and Mara, kneeling before an empty cross. I see Amber, fumbling in the dark. I see joy and comfort. I see certainty."

'*Alone*,' she thought, tears dripping on the page as she wrote. '*I'm always alone*.'

"To the right the Ten of Swords," she choked. '*Of course the fucking Ten of Swords*.' "That which is new-come and that which is coming. Ruin. Agony. Betrayal. Death. What do you see?"

"I see death," Jacob said, his voice losing some essential element of humanity. "Terror is coming. Agony and bloodshed. Secrets and betrayal."

No images in Amber's mind accompanied these statements. She could still feel him, some, but Jacob had gone farther, now, than she could follow.

Without warning, Jacob reached out and pulled another card from the deck – the Lovers: "We will each of us be forced to choose: between love and lust, death and life, and we will all choose wrongly."

Amber's whole body shook as she moved on to the next card. It took her three tries to speak.

"At the base of the pillar, the Page of Disks – the Querent. A youth, a student, new to the world and learning its ways. What do you see?"

"It is we," Jacob's eyes were open, now, but it was clear he saw nothing of the room. "Untutored and ignorant, fumbling through mazes of corn. The paths are guarded, but we can see neither those who watch over us nor those whom we pursue."

'*Pursue? Aren't we the ones being chased?*'

Tears continued to run down her face, pouring off her chin and nose and eyelashes onto the page. Her hand shook so hard that she could barely read her own handwriting.

"Next, the Wheel of Fortune – influences from without; hopes and fears. ... What do you see?"

Her hand still shook, but somehow the letters had grown clear again: a sharp, neat script that looked nothing like her own. That same alien hand had filled in the portions above, which she had deliberately left blank.

"We are the pawns of greater powers, whose faces we have already glimpsed too closely. The hands of Fate grip our threads tightly, and the moon will wax and wane and wax again before She is done with us."

Amber's mouth was dry, her lips parched. The voice that rang in her ears as she turned her attention to the next card did not feel like her own.

"Next the Moon – influences within. Facing fear. A trial or journey. Lies and delusions. What do you see?"

Jacob's eyes were glowing now, violet light emanating from behind the mortal blue. A figure moved inside him, a young woman occupying the same space but not quite the same time.

"Each of us will be changed forever." His voice was utterly alien, now. "We shall die and be reborn, and none shall escape unscarred. The Moon is the palace of dreams, but we must pass through the nightmare lands to reach her.

Amber's right hand recorded Jacob's words of its own accord, independent of her actual thoughts, which circled themselves without end or purpose. The words that flowed from her lips were equally without her volition.

"Finally the Tower – the Conclusion. Ruin. Collapse. Destruction. Ego death. Madness and suffering. What do you see?"

"All these things – all these things and more. One of us shall swallow Doom so that another may live quietly. He shall be betrayed in his heart through lust. One of us shall swallow Death for fear of Life, and lead three more to their Dooms. Three Fools shall walk the night, two from our number, and the third already sealed to his fate. Greatness and ignominy alike begin during these days."

Jacob's eyes fluttered and the trance ended. The circle collapsed around them and the presence of the Goddess departed. For a moment, she seemed to brush through Amber – good luck, she seemed to say.

He was crying, too, she realized, his face tear-streaked and his eyes puffy.

Amber tried to hand Jacob the pad where she had recorded it all, but he pushed it back.

"No," he said, his voice cracking. "This time I remember."

"That was ... what the hell, Jacob?"

He laughed, a wild and broken sound.

"I don't know," he said. "It hurt. But it felt incredible at the same time."

"I could see what you saw at first, even when I didn't want to, but then you went somewhere I couldn't reach."

"I know. I tried not to leave you behind, but I couldn't hold on."

"We need to call Dominic now. He has to know about this. We have to stop now. Someone's going to get hurt. You ..." Amber choked on the words. She didn't want to say it, didn't want to remember it. "You're going to die! And maybe worse!"

"We can't stop. It's too late. And we can't tell them."

"What are you talking about?"

"We can't tell them anything, Amber," he said, wiping his face dry with his shirt then looking her in the eye. "This is our burden. We have to Keep Silent."

The weight of his words fell on her like a blow. For a moment, her blood ran cold.

"Keep Silent," she said. The fourth side of the Witch's Pyramid: To Know, To Will, To Dare, and To Keep Silent.

"Keep Silent," he repeated, putting his hand over hers. "We can't tell anyone. We have to pretend we don't know."

Again, her blood ran cold. The weight of his words seemed to grow heavier.

"Keep Silent," she said again. "Pretend we don't know."

THURSDAY, OCTOBER 29

Every day this week had been a greater challenge for Dominic than the last. School had never bored him, before – at least, not like this. He had sought out every challenge the system had presented, and made up his own when he found them inadequate. AP classes, scholarships, contests. He had forced his education to live up to his standards, even as he had driven himself to the top of his cohort within the coven.

Until Margaret had come to them, begging for their help.

Having discovered kinds of magic and mystery that he had previously believed mythical, he had thrown himself into the search for her cure, and the search for whatever other secrets might yet have been hidden from him.

Mirrors and Veils had offered him a challenge he could not resist, the opportunity to undermine his own reality all over again, to take everything he had learned in the last two months and blow it out of the water.

School had waned further and further in his attention. In the first week after their attempt to bind Margaret's Mark had failed, he had scoured every book in his father's library, bombing two tests and forgetting to do his homework. The following week he had combed through every newsgroup and website and gopher archive he could find, forgoing sleep on three separate nights. This past week, he had been cold calling the few rare book collectors and private libraries that were not his father's friends, begging for clues about where he could find the Book of Secrets.

His research options and patience exhausted, it was time to turn to magic.

He had been preparing for this contingency, of course. There were rituals in Mirrors and Veils that he had high hopes for. But there were also things in his own coven's repertoire that he had not yet tried, and that was where he would go first.

Having made the decision in the morning, though, it was almost impossible to sit through the school day. Only fear of his mother's glower kept him from going home at lunch. His hands trembled with anticipation, and he could barely hear anything his teachers said. He was poor company to his friends, begging them to repeat everything they said at least once.

Finally, somehow, he was home and the sun was beginning to set.

Dominic took every care he could think of in preparation for the ritual. He performed both the standard Lesser Banishing of the Pentagram and the less common banishing of the Hexagram: elemental then planetary cleansing. He cast the circle with elaborate formality in the purest tradition of his coven: first with a censer of myrrh and dragon's blood resin, then with a bowl of blessed and salt-laced water – air and fire, water and earth – and finally with his athame. He wished that he could have begged his mother for the coven's sword, but that required both the agreement and the participation of the whole coven, neither of which were possible. He called each of the elements in turn, invoked the Goddess, begging them all for their assistance and protection.

The circle cast, the Nameless and the quarters invoked to guide and to guard him, Dominic knelt at the foot of the altar and called upon the Goddess and the God once more.

"Hecate, you who bear a torch in each hand, who guided Demeter through the underworld to seek her daughter, guide me, too, through the underworld to the answers I seek. Apollo, patron of prophets and seers, show me a vision of the Liber Caecissima."

He lay down at the foot of the altar, his head pointing west, and let his mind go blank before conjuring the image of a spiral, down which he sank.

Down, down. Down until a second sky opened up around him. Down and down until, at last, his feet touched green, grassy earth – soft and loamy between his toes.

A tree rose from a hill not far ahead, its branches dressed in every season and laden with every fruit imaginable, stretching up into the infinite sky from which he had come. He approached the tree and embraced it, an old and familiar friend. Three times he circled the tree, and on the last he found an opening in its roots. It should have been too small, but he managed to crawl inside.

Down, down, and down he spiraled once more, crawling his way through the roots of the World Tree. Creatures watched him from among the roots, too subtle to be seen. They did not guide him so much as shape his path, but he knew he was where he must be when he emerged from the roots to find himself under a scorching sun.

Bleak desert stretched out behind him, but before him lay a bright blue-green ribbon of life. Great palaces of stone rose above a sprawl of mud-brick houses. A goddess arched over the world, forming the sky, and a falcon-headed god shone as the sun. Reed boats traversed the river, dodging between hippopotami and crocodiles.

He looked around for the great pyramids or the Sphinx. There were none to be seen, but there, near a complex half-familiar from a thousand photographs, a small flat-topped temple drew his attention. A single stride brought him to the foot of the structure, another stood him atop the roof. A man stood beside him, tall and regal, clutching a golden wand 'round which coiled two living serpents, his helm and sandals marked with wings.

"It began here," Dominic said, half asking and half already certain.

"Yes. Long ago, while your ancestors still worshiped their dead and goddesses they could hold in their hands. Wotan was not yet even a dream and Ishtar still walked among the Hebrews, who had not yet made their journey into Egypt."

A shadow fled from the temple, priests and priestesses in Kemetic garb gave futile chase. The shadow escaped into the desert and the temple crumbled beneath Dominic's feet. Mountains thrust up in the place of sand, brick, and stone. The river overflowed, and the desert disappeared. The man with the staff was gone and Dominic stood alone on a green cliff, with the waves crashing below him.

A woman stood before him, facing away, with a gun in her hand and a sword at her hip. A serpent coiled in her belly and a wolf lay dead at her feet. In his dead hand, the wolf clutched the shadow that had fled the temple. The woman took it gingerly, more afraid of the shadow than she had ever been of the wolf.

Another shadow appeared, this one in the shape of a man, dressed in an elegant waistcoat and a long coat that fell to the ground.

"The burden is yours now," the shadow man told her.

The shadow in her hands shimmered and coalesced, taking the form of a leather-bound book. The cover held a single glyph of sweeping lines that terminated in circles.

The woman and the shadow man, never quite distinct, faded. They took the cliff and the sea with them, leaving only the book and the glyph, which seared itself into his memory before it, too, faded from sight, leaving Dominic adrift in a deeper Void than he had ever explored before.

He was lost, alone, and without anchor.

He tried to conjure an image of his body in his room. He couldn't. He tried to remember his mortal name. There was only Tiresias. He tried to scream for help, but he couldn't remember how to speak. The Void shrank and expanded by turns. The world was reduced to darkness and fear, and began to contract at an alarming rate. There was only fear.

Breathe. He had to breathe.

A name burst from his lips.

"Hecate."

Breathing. Breathing was happening.

A point of light appeared in the distance. He called into the darkness again.

"Oh Goddess, beloved."

The point of light drew nearer. Divided into two. A face appeared between the lights. A woman.

"Tiresias." Her voice was warm, welcoming. "Chosen of Lilith."

She was young, pretty, but unremarkable except for her dress: a garment that fell in graceful folds from shoulder to knee, tied at the waist by a simple rope, and sandals whose laces wound almost as high. The torches she bore in each hand cast strange shadows through her hair, hiding the details of her face. A hound stood at her left and a pole-cat at her right.

"Hecate," he whispered, prostrating himself. "Mistress of the crossroads. She who guided Demeter and so many others."

"Rise, Tiresias. Your humility does you honor, but your allegiances are well known. Have no fear. I shall guide you back to the mortal realm."

She turned, and a path appeared before them. He followed without question or hesitation. He was a child of the Goddess. He could do no less.

Dream Rites

FRIDAY, OCTOBER 30

Alexander met Dominic and Aaron outside the school like they
had asked: later than usual, by the pool instead of out front
with the bronze lion. They were waiting for him with grim
faces, holding their arms across their chests. They almost
avoided looking at on another.

"Where's the Crew?"

Dominic grimaced.

"We should probably leave them out of this."

"Huh? Leave them out of what? Why?"

"Come with us," Aaron said. "We'll explain on the way."

"You're talking to me now?"

"Don't antagonize him," said Dominic. "Now come on."

They loaded up into Dominic's car instead of walking
back to the magic shop, and turned the wrong direction out of
the parking lot. Alexander waited, silent, in the back seat for
them to begin explaining.

It was Dominic who started: "If we tell the others, they'll
want to be involved. I think that will be the opposite of help."

Aaron picked up from there: "We don't need a full circle,
it would be too noisy, too chaotic. Our synchronicity isn't good
enough with all four of us. Dominic and I would just do it
ourselves, but ... we need an anchor. A ground."

"You ground better than anyone we know," Dominic
finished. "You can keep us from getting lost."

"Lost? I don't understand. Start at the beginning."

The two boys in the front exchanged an angry look.

"Dominic and I have both been looking for clues as to the
location of the Book of Secrets. He in his way, and I in mine.
We think we know how to find it, but it involves a spirit-
journey. We will need someone to watch over our bodies and
guide us back to them."

"Dom?"

"That's the gist of it."

"I know you're holding out on me, guys. What's really going on here? Your father said the book was a myth. Now you're saying you've found it?"

"We've found the path that leads to it."

"Well, where is it, then?"

"It is hidden in the realm of dreams."

"What? Dreams aren't a place. Dreams are something your brain does while it's defragging. Dreams are illusions made of misfiring neurons ... TV your brain makes for itself."

"Sometimes," Dominic conceded. "But the human mind projects those illusions into the astral plane – a region of the ether we like to call 'the collective unconscious' – where they all come to a boil and overflow back into our sleeping minds. Sometimes dreams are defrag errors, yeah. Sometimes they're dramas we make up to help us sort through our lives. And sometimes they're reflections, fragments of a larger universe echoing back to us from elsewhere."

"That's some serious gobbledygook, D."

"That doesn't change the fact that it's true."

"Dudes, I think you've flipped your fucking lids."

That earned him an angry eyeball from Aaron. Alexander sat back in his seat for a moment: there was a strength in Aaron that hadn't been there a week before.

The drive had by now taken them, by meandering means, at last to Dominic's home.

"You're insane," Alexander repeated as they climbed out of the car. "How can this book – this legendary book, according to your father – possibly be hidden in a dream? That aside, how the fuck are we going to get it back out?"

"For the latter," answered Dominic, "we've consulted Mirrors and Veils. The former... well, I'm a little curious about that one, myself, but at this point I'm pretty reluctant to nay-say anything."

Alexander conceded that point with a grunt and a shrug, following the taller boys up the fire escape to Dominic's apartment.

"So ... what's the plan, then?"

"You get to read the ritual while Aaron and I perform our purification. Then we'll do some breathing and chakra meditation in order to achieve the synchronicity we're going to need. Then you'll perform the ritual."

"I'll perform the ritual?"

Dominic pulled a sheaf of paper off of his desk and foisted it into Alexander's hands.

"Read. Questions when you're done."

Alexander read while Dom and Aaron performed their own preliminaries. The ritual was straightforward: it followed the same internal logic as all of the other Wiccan rituals he had read, the few he had seen. He didn't exactly understand all the symbolic elements, but that wasn't necessary. His role was theatrical, window dressing, as far as he could tell. Whatever heavy lifting was going to take place, it was all going on inside Aaron and Dominic's heads.

Dominic's altar was set up in the middle of a sun room. The antique hardwood flooring had been laid over with custom tile, into which a circle had been formed as a guide. A cabinet took up one wall, holding – Alexander snooped inside it without hesitation – all the tools, herbs, oils, and materials Dominic might possibly need for any occasion. The altar was prepared: the tools and materials he would need were already set out. The other boys had finished purifying themselves and were now anointing each other. Alexander skimmed the ritual once more – broken down into simple steps and bullet points for his convenience – and began double-checking what he was going to need. By the time they were ready, so was he.

"This is completely insane," Alexander said again as he placed the last of the thirteen candles around the outermost circle.

Together, they invoked the Goddess and God in the form of Hecate and Hermes Cthonius, traced their magic circle first in salt-laden holy water, then in burning incense, and finally with Dominic's athame. Dominic drew a symbol in salt on the center of the altar table, between his idols, and called out an invocation in some foreign language. He and Aaron laid down on the floor so that their heads almost touched and their feet threatened to break the circle. Alexander sat in line with their feet at the edge of the altar, forming the last side of the triangle.

He counted out their breathing with a pair of wooden blocks, the way he had been taught in Akido. In – two, three, four, five. Hold – two, three, four, five. Out – two, three, four, five. Hold ...

It was harder than he'd thought at first, in part because Aaron and Dominic simply could not hold their breath as long as he could. Their training had been different. But almost as hard was the memory of falling into the void when he had tried to ground inside the circle Amber had cast. It needed to be done, though, and he refused to be a coward. This was doomed to fail, but it would not be his fault.

Slowly, carefully, he found a rhythm Aaron and Dominic could hold, and matched himself to it. Their heartbeats pounded in his ears, and ever so slowly he brought their bodies into time with his. They were slipping into their trance, he could feel it, and it was time to slip into his.

In – two, three, four. Hold – two, three, four. Out – two, three, four. Hold- two, three, fourr.

He grounded into the circle, and the world slipped away. No, wait: he slipped away. There was nothing but the world, his breath, and the breath of the two young men beside him.

The world slipped slowly into the void. Together, he and Aaron worked to fill that void with a single thought: the glyph that Dominic had found in his vision. Bit by bit it came into being: first a dim glow, then an impression that grew more and more clear, until the bright lines of the glyph seared through the darkness of the void.

They walked around it in circles, examined it from every angle. The answer was here, they just had to find it.

Then they did.

Almost at the same time, they realized how the lines intersected. They reached out, grabbed hold, and pulled it open with an act of will. A doorway appeared. They stepped through without even looking.

The emptiness of the void was replaced by rolling hills covered in soft green grass. A steel gray sky boiled with clouds and cracks of sunlight as a light rain trickled down their collars. The ground fell off in a sheer cliff at their heels, and a path wound out before them, disappearing into the heath. The sound and smell of the choppy sea covered almost everything else.

They looked to one another, to the path, and back. Aaron gestured grandly for Dominic to proceed first. He did, breathing deeply of the salt air and letting it out slowly. A wind blew off the plains, beating his street clothes against his body until they shredded themselves from the force. He breathed in deeply and exhaled, letting his street clothes go and replacing them in his mind's eye with his ceremonial robes flapping gently behind him. Looking over his shoulder, he saw that Aaron had done something much the same and now wore a long black coat covered in buckles and pockets with a high collar that completely covered his neck.

A thick fog rose as they walked, obscuring everything but the path. The two witches proceeded without pause or hesitation, keeping foot to the path without fail. It was thick, a cloud come down to the earth that pushed back as they walked through it. Alien silhouettes moved just beyond the path, somehow backlit in the swirling whiteness. Just as Dominic was considering conjuring a torch, the wind rose again and drove off the fog.

They were in a forest, now, thick with underbrush and spider webs. He conjured a staff to clear the way as he walked, but the webs that crossed the path seemed to reform in his wake, and Aaron cursed behind him as he was forced to push through the webs as well. Small rustling noises came from the trees, and furtive things followed them from just out of sight, shaking branches and cracking small sticks. Dominic kept his attention on the path.

The rustling increased, though, the farther into the woods they went, and the path became ever more narrow. The movements in the underbrush became harder and harder to ignore. Clicking and chittering sounds joined the rustling of plants and earth.

Fear poured out of the forest first: a cold wind that forced its way into their lungs and pushed them back toward the mortal world. Then the spiders came.

The first ones were small: hundreds of thousands of them packed so tightly together that they could hardly be differentiated from one another. The spiders swarmed out over their feet, crawling up their legs and their fluttering clothes.

Dominic shuddered a little, but stopped to let the spiders pass.

Aaron made a strangled sound, high and wild.

Dominic took a deep, calming breath. He exhaled slowly. "Give us some space, please, little brothers."

The spiders spilled off of him as quickly as they had crawled on. Turning, he saw that the spiders had covered Aaron up to his neck, wave after wave ascending toward his face. Aaron was making increasingly awful noises, unable to move except for his trembling.

Taking another deep breath, Dominic stepped forward and exhaled. The spiders moved back. Two steps toward Aaron and the spiders began to spill off of him, as well. Close enough to touch, Aaron was finally free of his crawling cocoon.

Cupping one hand on Aaron's cheek, Dominic turned and held the other hand out over the road.

"We are brothers," he said in a low, calm voice. "Let us pass."

The waves of tiny spiders drew back in undulating waves, until they had finally retreated back to the edges of the path.

Then the big ones came. First the size of rats, then the size of terriers, they inched out of the underbrush one by one.

"Dominic," Aaron's voice trembled. "I don't like this."

The spiders moved slowly toward them, one long limb at a time. Larger and stranger noises began to emanate from the woods.

"Then ask them to go."

"They won't listen to me."

"They will," Dominic said, his voice slow and steady. "Ask them nicely. They are our brothers."

"Let us through," Aaron's voice trembled.

"Like you mean it," Dominic said. "But nicely."

"Clear the path. Let us through."

The spiders backed away, forming a line to either side of the path.

Dominic patted Aaron's cheek and turned around. Three paces down the path, though, another spider blocked the way: big and brown, hairy as a bear and large as four door sedan.

Dominic froze in his tracks. Aaron made a garbled squeaking noise.

"Grandmother Spider," Dominic said, slow and diffident. "Please let us pass."

The spider stepped forward. It made strange, alien chattering noises with its mandibles. That made Dominic pause. In his previous visionary work, Grandmother Spider had never once made noises at him.

"You are not Grandmother Spider."

More chattering.

"Go back, sister. Do not bar our way."

More chattering.

"Let us pass, in the names of the gods we both serve.

More chattering, and the spider began advancing on them.

"Back the fuck off!"

Aaron's shout came while Dominic was still attempting to formulate a strategy. The giant spider froze in its tracks. Aaron stepped around Dominic and took the lead, his right hand extended.

"Clear the road, creature, as your brothers and sisters have done. We have tasks which must be accomplished!"

The enormous spider took another step forward, but it was slower than it had been before. Dominic shrugged, and backed Aaron's play. He thrust his own right hand forward in a gesture of warding, and stepped up to Aaron's side.

"Back," he said, loudly and firmly. "In the name of Grandmother Spider, I adjure you. In the name of the Great Goddess I command you. Clear the road that we may pass!"

The spider took a single step back.

"Back," yelled Aaron, advancing. A skull-capped wand of bone had appeared in his hand. "Be gone!"

"Leave us be, O Spider," Dominic commanded, keeping pace with Aaron. He performed a banishing pentagram as he moved – his right hand slashing up from his left hip to its full rightward extension, then straight across to the left, back down to his right hip, up above his head, and finally down to his left hip where he had begun – and a bright blue star formed in the air before him as he did so.

The spider moved back a single leg at a time, at first, but faster and faster as they approached. The spiders on the sides of the road scrambled over one another to get back into the underbrush. The big spider chittered and chattered at them incessantly, and began to make terrible, high, keening noises as they advanced on it.

Finally, as they crossed some line they could not identify, the spider vanished before their eyes, and took the woodland path with it.

For a long moment, Dominic and Aaron walked alone in the void. In the distance, they saw the glyph that had brought them to this place glittering in the darkness. They dove for it, but the void gave way and deposited them, again, in a world.

Hard stone rose up to meet them, bruising their hands and knees. It was darker here than in the void: there they had been able to see themselves and each other, despite the absence of anything but the glowing glyph; here, they were blind.

"Aaron?"

"Here. Can you see anything?"

"Not a damn thing."

"Hell."

"Where are you?"

"Over here. Grab my hand, and we'll try to find the way out."

It took a few long minutes of calling back and forth, but they found one another eventually.

"Where now?"

"Uh... this way?"

"Fine."

'This way' led them first to a wall, but that gave them direction: a confusion of unlimited options gave way to simple binary choice.

"Right hand on the wall," Dominic asked, "or left?"

"Left," Aaron said, "in case you feel the need to punch something."

"Okay," Dominic drug the word out to six or eight syllables. But he put the wall on his left, and began to advance.

The world was absolutely dark, and completely silent save for their own breathing and occasional curses as one or the other of them tripped over a stone or ran into a low-hanging stalactite. The cave – that's what it seemed to be, at least – was dead and dry.

"So ..." Aaron asked. "What next?"

"No clue. Probably at least one more challenge. A total of three is pretty traditional. It really depends on who or what made this place, and when."

"Who or *what*?"

"Are you ready to discount any possibilities?"

"No."

They continued in slow, careful silence. The walking, itself, was not hard: the floor was level except for the occasional trip hazard – cracks and crevasses, fallen rocks and stalagmites. The stalactites were surprisingly few and far between, but that just made the anticipation worse: when would the next blow to the head come?

It had probably not been that long, but it felt like they had been stumbling in the dark for hours when Aaron finally said, "Are you sure we're going the right way?"

"You picked, man. But yes. To the best of my ability to determine, this works like any other spirit journey: which way you go isn't as important as the fact that you keep going."

"How do you always know what's going on? I don't believe you've ever done this before."

Dominic resisted the urge to sigh.

"Who says I know what's going on," he said. "I've gone on a lot of spirit journeys, man, but this booby-trapped dream shit is brand fucking new. I'm making this up as I go, and you are welcome to make suggestions at any point."

Silence reigned for a long time, punctuated only by escalating obscenities as one or the other of them tripped over something or cracked their head on a low hanging rock.

"Did you hear that," Aaron demanded abruptly.

"No."

"There it is again."

They stopped and Dominic strained to hear whatever had gotten Aaron's attention.

"I don't hear anything, man."

"Then breathe quieter!"

Dominic slowed his breath and focused.

"All I can hear is you, man. You're hallucinating. Sensory deprivation does that."

He was starting to hallucinate, too: the darkness was starting to come alive with slowly undulating masses.

"The fucking hissing, man. You're telling me you can't hear it?"

"No," Dominic said. But he could hear something, now: a dry sound, like sand pouring down a hillside, but too quiet to be certain of. "Come on. This can't go on forever."

"Can't it? This is a dream, after all."

"Right. And dreams are finite. Things only feel like forever. Come on."

The sound got more persistent, more clear, and the illusion of writhing darkness got stronger.

Then something brushed against Dominic's leg: a small touch, but firm and somehow suggestive of a much larger mass.

"Fuck!"

"What," Aaron demanded. "Do you hear it, now?"

"No. Something touched me."

But then he did hear it: a sharp, distinct hissing noise that rose over the pouring-sand-sound he had already been ignoring.

And the touch came again: cool, undulating, firm. His first atavistic instinct was to jump back, press himself against the wall. Instead, he leaned into it. He only offered the slightest resistance, but whatever it was pushed back harder. It was bigger than he'd realized: the slight pressure against his ankle became an implacable force that pushed his entire leg back, nearly bowling him over.

He yelled, high and sharp. Aaron's scream came like an echo.

The darkness shouted back: hissing and rattling.

One or both of them stumbled, and the comfort of physical contact was lost.

The pressure against Dominic's leg increased suddenly, and he was thrown to the ground, pinned between the thick, smooth, sinuous force that dragged against him even as it pushed him hard against the wall. He tried to call for Aaron but his voice didn't seem to be working. The darkness pressed against his eyes, the hissing rattled his bones.

Something else touched him.

It was cool, smooth, and softly textured against the back of his neck. Slender and long. It brushed up against his nape and slid around his neck and down inside his collar, warming as it lingered on his skin.

"Snake." The word trembled, hushed, past his lips.

Something else brushed past his ear and into his hair. Another slid over his shoulder and down his chest.

"Aaron, they're snakes."

Was that Aaron spitting obscenities under his breath, or just more hissing, slithering snakes? Had Aaron heard him? Was Aaron still even there?

More and more of the long, wriggling forms poured over him. Some were tiny, maybe not even as big around as one of his fingers. Some were as big as his wrist. One was as big as his thigh. Some moved slowly over him. Others squirmed across his body with lightning speed. They were in his hair and inside his clothes.

Dominic's heart raced. He began to sweat profusely, and the dry reptilian bodies moving over his skin seemed suddenly cold. His hands were trembling so hard that he couldn't even brush them off of him.

"Aaron!"

"I'm kinda fucking occupied!" The shout came back at last.

Aaron wasn't dead or gone. He wasn't alone.

That knowledge brought him back to himself. He was still trapped in absolute darkness. He was still covered in snakes. But he wasn't alone.

He tried to put his left hand back on the wall. He was so completely buried in snakes that he couldn't find the wall, at first. When he did, it was only by pushing through the thick layer of writhing, scaly flesh. He had to shuffle his feet along the ground, unable to bear the thought of crushing any of them under his heavy boots.

First spiders. Now snakes. Aaron shuddered, and swore under his breath.

"Obstacles mean we're going in the right direction," he muttered to himself.

Spiders and snakes. Common fears. They were in a labyrinth, a puzzle. The task was to identify the moving parts. Would rats be next? Clowns?

Aaron strained his senses against the darkness. The susurrus of writhing reptiles was as distracting as it was soothing, but at least it largely overwhelmed the distressed noises Dominic was making. Specks of light swam before his eyes, striving to resolve themselves into shapes. That, too, was a distraction.

The waking world loomed above them, impossibly far beyond the spider woods through which they had just crossed. Something else waited below, something long dead and

268

wrathful that watched their every step. Both those things were problems for later.

Here was what mattered now. Serpentine bodies writhing against one another. Vast and small, slow and swift. Dominic, ahead of him, clawing at the cold stone walls, disoriented without sight to provide context to sound and texture.

The biggest spider had been the key to the first test. The biggest snake would almost certainly be the key to this one.

Aaron inhaled deeply, gathered his power about himself, and prayed.

"Horned One, be with me. Dark Goddess, be with me."

He stepped forward boldly.

The snakes swarmed up his legs, like they had been waiting for him, but he moved forward without pause or hesitation. There was no light in this place – how could there be? – but the shapes of things began to reveal themselves to him. There were snakes everywhere, of every size and description. Garden snakes the size of a pencil; vipers as big as his bicep and as long as his leg; constrictors as big as his thigh and longer than he was tall. And, finally, over there, a gargantuan serpent pressed Dominic up against the wall of the cavern – an act of casual, perhaps even accidental, hindrance, as the creature's head was somewhere deeper down, past a bend in the tunnel.

They crawled over every inch of his body and their weight dragged at him, but the snakes failed to hinder Aaron's steps, and he moved over to Dominic's side with relative ease. Even straddling over the leviathan was more a challenge of his flexibility than his footwork.

"Come on, Dom," he said, touching the other boy's shoulder. "We have to keep moving."

His touch did not drive the snakes off of Dominic's body, but – strangely – it did drive them away from his feet.

"You got a plan?" Dominic asked, more collected than Aaron would have given him credit for. The way he swiveled his head ear-first made it abundantly clear that he had not yet figured out how to see in this place, and Aaron could feel the tremors of fear going through Dominic's body.

"Working on one. First step: will the snakes out from under our feet. I've got that covered for now, like our trick with bugs, but I don't know how long that'll hold. Next up: follow the big one."

Dominic grunted, barely audible over the hisses and whispers and sand-like sound of slithering, and stretched his own hand out around Aaron's arm to touch his shoulder.

"Lead on."

Dominic kept his left hand on the wall and Aaron kept his right hand on the biggest serpent, and together they marched into the shadows. Their combined power kept the snakes out from underfoot, even though it did not drive them off of their bodies or out of their clothes. The writhing, somehow both slick and dry at the same time, was unnerving and uncanny – no physical hindrance, but a constant distraction.

The hindrance came from the snakes that had not yet clambered over them. The deeper down the tunnel they travelled, the more snakes there were. They piled in knotty masses as high as the tunnel permitted, and the two witches had to push their way through. The snakes parted only reluctantly, threatening to crawl into Aaron's and Dominic's noses and mouths, and clung to them, heavy, when they managed to find a pocket of air.

Still they persisted. Step after step. Silent, dogged. They kept the serpents out from under their steps and out of their lungs by sheer force of will.

They marched for what felt like hours. Days. Months. One hand to the wall. One hand on the monster. Snakes everywhere but their noses and mouths. They even had to close their eyes, lest the serpents press in through their pupils.

An eternity passed, measured only by their footfalls and the varying pressures of serpentine flesh.

Then the pressure vanished. The wall dropped off to the one side and the leviathan curved off to the other. No snakes pressed against them as they advanced, and even the ones that had clung to them most tenaciously fell off. They stumbled into a world too big to comprehend, and Aaron's eyes flew reflexively open as he fell to his knees.

Light. There was light here.

The cavern they had discovered was immense, easily twice the size of a football field, with a domed roof as high as it was wide. A little to the far side of center, a hole in the ceiling permitted a surprising amount of sunlight which in turn illuminated a huge tree atop a hill in the precise center of the cavern. Only about half the branches bore leaves, but the lowest branches seemed to bear some sort of fruit.

The body of the gargantuan snake wound past them to the far side of the cavern and half of the way back so that its head rested by the roots of the tree. Its scales glistened, glossy black with undertones of green and red and gold. Nothing on the scale of the beast had ever, truly, lived. Surely not even the dinosaurs had possessed such colossal mass.

Aaron glanced over at Dominic, who nodded. As one, they moved slowly toward the hill and tree in the middle. The serpent did not seem to notice them. Its long body writhed back and forth restlessly – small movements, on the scale of the creature, but enough to crush them if they were too close at the wrong moment.

As they drew closer to the tree, it became clear that only one of the branches bore fruit, per se, or even leaves. The rest bore snakes, which seemed to seep from within the tree, itself: what looked like leaves were emergent serpent heads reaching up for the light, and what looked like fruit were half-grown snakes dripping from the branches like macabre sap. The one branch bearing true fruit and leaves hung with two apples – one gleaming, metallic gold, and one blood-red – and a treasure: a golden sheepskin draped haphazardly, just within reach from the ground.

"Well, isn't this just a mish-mash of stories," Dominic grumbled. "I bet you anything the golden apple reads Kalliste."

"No bet," Aaron grunted. "And that is not a hell I care to unleash. The fleece, maybe?"

"We don't have a Medea to drug the dragon. That leaves the other apple. But what the fucking hell *do* we do with it?"

"We don't repeat Eve's mistake, for one."

"Oh! Serpent and apple. Good call. Question still stands, though."

"Feed it to the serpent, I think."

"Oooh," Domimic said. "I like it."

"Good. Now you take point."

"Fuck."

Still, Dominic went first, clambering up the slick, unstable hill ahead of Aaron and making the good footholds clear for him while Aaron kept his eyes on the leviathan as much as on the path. In the physical world, the climb would have been at the outermost edge of Aaron's physical capacity. In this place, it was a matter of long minutes and careful attention. At the top, all three treasures were in easy reach for a tall man. The serpent's head was only a little farther away than the treasures, but it gave no sign that it knew or cared that they were there. After the struggle through the serpent tunnel, the whole process was anticlimactic.

Aaron plucked the red apple from its branch, and the ground shifted beneath their feet. The hill, more a pile of fallen stalactites than anything else, gave way in a slide that flattened them both.

They never found their feet. By the time they had made it to their knees, the leviathan had roused itself and was hissing violently high above them.

"Aaron! The goddamned apple!"

It had fallen from his hand. Aaron scrambled over the loose rocks to reclaim it.

"Where's Alex when you fucking need him," he grumbled, trying to find sure footing. The serpent's head swung back and forth, searching for the source of the disturbance. It honed in on them just as Aaron reclaimed the apple, and its head shot toward them with terrifying speed.

Aaron threw the apple as hard and straight as he could, but it was luck more than anything that put the apple down the snake's gullet rather than in its eye or across the far side of the

272

cavern. The creature froze mid-strike, shaking its head back and forth as it retreated.

"What next," Aaron demanded, faint.

The monster's distraction, however, proved only momentary. Its gaze fixated on them again.

"Wrong apple, I guess," said Aaron as the great head pulled back to strike again. "My bad."

"Well, hell," Dominic muttered as the head rushed toward them. "Exit stage tripe."

Standing beside it, the snake's head had been as tall as they were. Now it was the size of a monster truck. Mouth gaping wide, it struck the hillside like the wrath of a god, and it swallowed them whole along with at least their combined weight in broken rock.

And, once more, they found themselves in the that black, empty void between worlds. The waking world glimmered above, even farther than it had been before. Below them, and not nearly so far, a sucking abyss. The glowing symbol that had brought them here in the first place hung, bright and silent, between everything and nothing.

Instead of floating in the void, though, they were hurtling through it with explosive force. The glyph drew ever closer by the moment. There! Aaron reached out with both hands and all his will, but fell short.

The void vanished.

They landed in a tangled heap on a deep plush carpet, skidding almost hard enough to give themselves rug burn. Rolling apart, they scrambled to their feet, once more dressed in the clothes they had worn to school.

Aaron took his time collecting his wits and getting his bearings. They stood in the middle of a wide circle of carpet. Bookshelves lined the circle, with pathways radiating out in six directions. A casual glance revealed that each of those paths was likewise lined with books. The titles were in English, Spanish, French, German, Latin, Chinese, Japanese, and an assortment of characters that he couldn't even identify.

"This place looks huge," Dominic said. "We should split up and look. Focus on the glyph."

"Yeah," Aaron said, his head still ringing from the impact. "Sure."

A fucking polyglot library in a booby-trapped pocket dimension lodged between the astral plane and the realm of dreams. It was probably Dominic's notion of paradise.

He massaged his temples slowly. This place made his brain itch. He couldn't get his shields up properly, couldn't isolate himself from it. He had to concentrate. Whispers came at him from every direction – was this what it felt like to be Jacob?

Drawing a ragged breath, he reached out to the shelves to steady himself. His hand skidded past the wooden shelf and landed directly against the leather spines of the books.

It was like touching a live wire. The force of it hurled him across the circle, where he crashed into the opposite book shelf. A half-dozen volumes fell from their resting places, and each one that hit him was another jolt, like the time he'd run afoul of the science lab's Van de Graaff generator. Laying on the floor, trembling with the shock of the power that had run through him, the whispers seemed even louder.

Aaron began to giggle.

The whispers didn't seem louder. They were louder. The books were whispering to him. They were – at least some of them – the memories of the dead he had sensed below him in the serpent tunnels. The dead were everywhere, here.

Spiders and gods and elementals were Dominic's domain.

The dead were his area of expertise. This victory was going to be his.

Carefully, whispering soothing sounds to each of them, he returned the books to their rightful places. Then he opened himself up, touching as many of the spirits as he could as he did so.

The whispering escalated – for a moment, it was almost a true sound, audible to mortal ears – then subsided.

There, in the direction Dominic had gone, were two presences that were not dead. One was Dominic, himself: golden, blue, and vibrantly alive. The other was neither living

274

nor dead; if it had ever been alive, it was so long ago that the distinction between life and death had become irrelevant. The book.

Aaron wound his way through the shelves, following the sense of Dominic's life and the subtle guidance of the many dead. Each separate presence he detected, he acknowledged and thanked. In gratitude, some of them offered him secrets, or power, which he accepted with gratitude. Things inside him began to move and shift. Something appeared at the back of his mind – an echo of sorts that he could neither quite hear nor forget – but he dismissed it for the moment.

The bookshelves were a labyrinth, twisting and turning senselessly, but he had been given a thread and the distance between himself and Dominic closed steadily. At last, he made a final turn and found Dominic seated in a plush chair before a fire. A woman – short, plump, with freckled white skin and ink-black hair – knelt before him, a suppliant hand on his knee.

"You must," she was telling him. "Before it's too late, you must." She seemed to sense Aaron as he approached, and turned to include him, as well. "Both of you must flee this place while you can."

Aaron looked Dominic in the eye and raised an eyebrow.

"She says she, too, came looking for the Liber Caecissima," Dominic explained. "She has been trapped here for years, that her body was slain by the book's guardian."

"Is that so," said Aaron, stepping forward.

"You must believe me," the woman said. She stood and glided toward him, clutching closed a silk robe that had probably had greater effect on Dominic. "The book's guardian is deadly. They will not let you live long, even if you retrieve it."

She pressed herself against him, as if that would sway him. He let her do it, let her touch confirm his suspicions: the cold touch of her skin igniting the cold fire of his aura, ice calling to ice. He permitted himself a small, sharp smile when her eyes widened.

"Much of what you say is true, sister," he said to her, running his hands back through his hair and willing his garments to change back to his ritual robes. "But you did not die after coming here. You died so that this place could exist. Your spirit is woven throughout the substance of this labyrinth, and the layers above."

She stumbled back, face ashen.

"Why would you say such a thing," she demanded.

"Aaron?" Dominic's voice was measured. Aaron knew that tone well: Dominic always used it when he thought they were about to fight.

"Because it is true, sister. I had some sense of it above, but your touch confirmed it. And your comrades, your sisters who were similarly sacrificed, are reassuring me that it is true even now."

Dominic was standing, now, but he had moved around the chair so that he was no closer to the ghost than to Aaron. Good. He might not be comfortable with how Aaron was handling the situation, but he was following his lead.

"Is this true," Dominic demanded. "In the name of the Dark Goddess, I beg you speak truly."

"Yes," the spirit conceded, half grudgingly and half defeated.

"So there is no guardian, then," Dominic pressed. Aaron nodded approvingly.

"There is a guardian, but it is she who gave us purpose, not she who slew us."

"Please, sister," Aaron said in gentler tones. "Tell us what was done to you, to all of you. How did this come to be?"

"There was a man. A sorcerer. Very handsome. Very persuasive. He promised to teach us the secrets of the book. I don't really know what made us special, but he found and stalked and seduced us one by one... all across Europe and Asia. Thirty-six of us, with me the last. I didn't know about the others until after, of course. The guardian came while he was half done with me, killed him. She let us hide the book he had used to turn us from people into a place."

"And where is the book, now?"

"You have been kind to my sisters, sir, but you strike me as cold. I will not tell you. You cannot have the book."

Aaron shrugged. "I don't want it for myself. I'm actually doing this mostly for him." He indicated Dominic with a thrust of his chin.

"We cannot let the book back into the world."

Aaron shook his head.

"Please, sister. I beg you. Do not make me force you."

"You must force me, sir."

Aaron nodded, and conjured his bone wand to his hand.

"The fuck is that morbid shit," Dominic demanded.

Aaron ignored him.

"By rite of bone and blood, I reign over the dead," the words came to him from nowhere. "By Hecate and Hermes I command you, sister, give up the Book of Secrets."

The lights flickered, but she shook her head.

"I refuse."

"By Hades and Proserpine I command you, sister, give up the Liber Caecissima."

All the lights vanished save for the flames in the fireplace. The walls trembled, and Dominic looked ill.

"I refuse," she repeated.

"By the bones of Tartaros and the icy waters of the Styx, I compel you, sister, give up your charge that you may rest in peace!"

There was a sound like breaking glass, and the entire library shook like a snow globe. Books flew from their shelves. Shelves toppled. The fire extinguished itself and Dominic was thrown against a wall. Only Aaron and the spirit of the woman appeared untouched ... until the woman fell to her knees.

"Call the book by the seal that brought you here," she said.

Aaron nodded, and called the glyph to his mind's eye. He gestured for Dominic to do the same.

"Thank you, sister," he said. "I pray to all the powers I have just called that you and your sisters find peace and release."

The library vanished, and Aaron and Dominic were once more left in the void. The glyph hovered between them, at last, and they reached out together to take it.

In their hands, the glyph became first an urn, then a clay tablet, then a papyrus scroll, and finally a leather-and-brass bound codex.

Together they clung to the book. The void stretched out around them, empty and infinite.

One ... two ... three ... four. One ... two ... three ... four.

The ritual had gone on for longer than he ever would have imagined.

Alexander Dixon's entire body ached with the rhythm of their breathing. His lungs strained as if he were literally breathing for all three of them. His hands and arms ached from clapping for so long. His hands burned from the thousands of tiny impacts. His hips were attempting to eject his legs from their sockets.

One ... two ... three ... four. One ... two ... three ... four.

For long minutes, it had felt like a farce. The three of them had struggled to find their synchronicity. Each of them had fallen out of the rhythm at some point, and a few dangerous moments, none of them had been in sync and the circle had threatened to fall apart. Only the fact that he could feel the circle at all had given him the will to continue.

Then it had happened: even as the circle trembled and threatened to collapse, they had found their rhythm all at once, and the ground had dropped out from under them, just as it had when he'd tried to ground into Amber's circle. But only Dominic and Aaron had fallen: Alexander, the anchor, had held his place in the mortal world, floating above the great void he could feel below them.

He had felt them find the door. He had felt them pass through, watched as they confronted shuddering shapes in a writhing void, first with diplomacy then with force, and then vanished through a trap door into a deeper place he could not see. He had felt it when they overcame the second challenge, though, and had known the moment when they overcame the third and final challenge.

278

He saw them, then, as clearly as if they stood before him, grab hold of a glowing power. Then the labyrinth threw its final trick at them: it vanished, leaving them alone in the void between dream and death, falling into that void from which there would be no return.

But they had planned for this. Somehow, they had known. They had brought him. Alexander was still anchored here at the top of the world, and he could catch them.

As quickly as he could think it, the two began to fade into the shadows, clutching their prize. Alexander reached out to them, his arms growing impossibly thin as they crossed distances as vast as the galaxy, itself, and caught them by their collars.

He had stopped clapping. Their breathing began to waver. The circle began to tremble.

Alexander inhaled deeply, and settled himself into the very walls of the circle, the way he settled his body into his One Point at the beginning of a match.

Exhaling with a wild kiyai, he pulled.

Then the world exploded.

Lady of the Black Roses II

The fire was born at the base of her spine, crawling through each of the seven sigils hard-wired into her nervous system, then back down. It woke her from a dead drunk sleep, spread out from her core to her furthest extremities. The alcohol burned from her blood, replaced by an uncanny knowing: someone was after the book.

Caitlyn Hannah turned to her altar at once. There, in glowing shards, lay the crystal that the Monster had given her when the book had first come into her hands. This was the first sign.

Caitlyn rolled from her bed. She dashed to her closet, dressing and arming herself. Someone wanted the Book of Secrets, had found it hidden in the world of dreams. The book had been a burden, almost as terrible as the blood, but she couldn't give it up unless the other signs appeared. She shoved rounds into Conflict's chambers with practiced haste. The gun woke with hungry anticipation.

Among the glowing shards of the guard crystal lay an antique skeleton key. Caitlyn took it gingerly – the magic inside it was delicate, and a wayward thought might break it – and brought it across the room to her door. She placed her forehead against the cool wood, pictured the binding-glyph in her mind, and thrust the key into the door. It slid home, and a room appeared in her mind's eye.

Caitlyn Hannah opened her eyes, took a deep breath, and kicked down the door.

The apartment was long instead of wide, with few walls or doors dividing one part from another. She'd come in the kitchen, beyond which lay an empty bedroom to the right, the bathroom to the left, and a living area with two closed doors. Candle light and curls of incense smoke escaped from the transom of the far door. She could hear a rhythmic wooden clacking coming from beyond it.

Caitlyn stalked across the living room, reaching beyond the door with her mind. The rhythm continued uninterrupted. Her entrance had gone unnoticed. She felt a circle, powerful and well contained in the next room, but the door didn't feel like a part of it.

She eased the door open.

If it had opened in instead of out, she'd have broken their circle. The chamber was professionally appointed: tile floor cut with a permanent set of circles, tool cabinets on the walls, and a richly dressed circular altar in the center. There were three young men sitting arranged around the altar, two lying with their heads together, one sitting at their feet and clapping wooden blocks together.

She drew a bead on Alexander, the most physically fit of the three. He was staring right at her, though he didn't seem to see her. He started trembling and stopped clapping the blocks. They were almost done.

Caitlyn stepped forward and pointedly broke the circle with her foot.

Power surged through her, a painful backlash. The boys twitched and gasped. Light flashed and the smell of ozone filled the air. The book materialized in the center of the altar atop of it. Sign two of three.

Their eyes were on her as they struggled to rise. Alexander Dixon's eyes were bright, eager for conflict; Aaron and Dominic's eyes were dark with rage and confusion.

"Well, kids, looks like a bit of a mess to me."

"Who are you?" Aaron was the first to speak. White mist coiled around him, dry like bones.

"Caitlyn Hannah, Left Hand of the Druid groves. Caretaker of that book you've just stolen."

"And you'll shoot us to get it back?" Alexander looked her in the eye, waiting for an opportunity. He'd been dumb enough to stare down the wolves by the river. He might be dumb enough to make a move on her.

"That depends on what you lads say next."

"What did the sorcerer say?" Dominic's voice was cold, even though it trembled. "The one you killed to get the book."

Her head snapped toward him. How did he know that? Only she and the Monster had walked away from that scene alive.

Alexander made his move. Even distracted, she saw it coming. She put her knee in his face when he lunged, sending him back across the room to land in a heap.

"You've got balls, lad, I'll give you that. Use your brain first next time, would you?" Then, to Dominic: "To what end would you put the book?"

"To cure Mara."

Sign three of three, as set by the old seer who had stowed the book away for her. The crystal might have shattered under two instances: either the trials had been engaged, or they had been circumvented. The book's physical appearance meant that it had not been intercepted by an immortal Power. The third sign, the life-or-death, was the purpose to which the grimoire would be put. The one appointed to hold it after her would use the book to aid another.

Caitlyn holstered her gun.

"There's no cure, lad." She said it reflexively.

"Mirrors and Veils says otherwise." Dominic put his hand on the book. "The ritual is in here somewhere."

If there were a way to unbind the Mark of the Wolf, it would be in that book. How many people had she killed that she might have saved, had she had the nerve to open the book? How many secrets might be hers? She might even know who and what she was. Or her mind might have been broken by some antediluvian riddle. There was no way to know.

She reached down a hand to Alexander, who took it without any apparent sign of resentment. If she read his expression aright, it was one of grudging respect. Just a little strange, that one.

"Keep it, then," she told them.

"What?"

"It was my burden, now it's yours. You might want to be careful, though. When word leaks out that the Book of Secrets is back in play, you're going to be in a lot of trouble."

They all talked at once:

"What kind of trouble?"

"What do you mean? How do you know?"

"Who are you, really?"

282

Caitlyn sighed.

"You kids got a smoke? Or a drink? This is going to take a bit."

Samhain

SATURDAY, OCTOBER 31ST

The night was cold and damp. The easterly wind had brought a steady, drizzling rain, made surreal by the diffuse light of the nearly-full moon behind the ever-shifting clouds. Margaret sat at the top of a small hill, sharing a picnic blanket with Jennifer and Alexander, huddled close under a cluster of umbrellas. Below, Jacob, Dominic, Amber, and Aaron were setting up for their ritual. Also at the bottom of the hill, off to the side of where the ritual preparations were taking place, lay a low-burning camp fire, sizzling and steaming in the rain.

The Mark of the Wolf stirred in Margaret's belly, restless, but not panicked the way it had been the first time she had come here. It whispered to her, but she ignored it. Instead, her attention drifted back and forth between the two scenes.

To her left, Jennifer had asked Alexander about his black eye – a wound which, though he'd received it only the night before, already looked a week old. The question, reasonably, had prompting a retelling the story of how he, Dominic, and Aaron had acquired the massive leather and brass tome sitting between them.

"... then," Alexander was saying, waving his left hand wildly, "after what turned out to be almost three hours of impossibly synchronized breathwork, me clapping those damn blocks, and what I can only describe as a shared hallucinatory experience, the pain and exhaustion hits all three of us really, really hard – I almost stopped breathing – and we wake up. The Book is sitting on the altar like it's been there the whole time, and there's Jak's British friend Cait looming in the doorway with a gun pointed at us."

Dominic had already relayed the broad strokes of the tale to her and Jacob this morning. While Alexander talked, Margaret listened with only half an ear. Another day, Margaret might have been interested in the subtle differences between the two tellings. Tonight she was ... adrift. Calm, but unfocused.

"I'm not saying I don't believe you," hedged Jennifer. "God knows I'm prepared to believe anything at this point. But … what? How? And what does that have to do with why you have a black eye?"

Below, the others were preparing for their ritual. She had seen them do magic before – the binding, of course, and a few smaller things – but this would be the first time she witnessed their religious rites. As with their magic, they wore no ceremonial robes or any of the accoutrements she had would have assumed went with witchcraft. Dominic and Amber wore skirts; Jacob and Aaron wore jeans. They all wore hoodies and jackets against the rain.

"I honestly have no idea how she or the book got there. I mean, she explained, but it didn't make any sense to me. My eye happened when I tried to jump her while she and Dom were yelling at each other and she kicked me in the face."

"You what? Didn't you just say she had a gun?"

The altar props were just as simple: a small table in the center, holding a tiny iron cauldron in which a fire was being lit, a knife ("athame," Jacob called it), a clay goblet ("chalice"), an assortment of herbs in small jars, a pair of shallow bowls for water and oil, and a colored candle for each direction. Arranging it all involved a bit of ceremony, followed by a few moments of silence.

"It seemed like the thing to do at the time," Alexander said, shrugging and raising the hand he wasn't leaning on. "I'm probably lucky she didn't shoot me."

Jennifer barked a shrill laugh.

"What else did she tell you?"

Even after all the time she'd spent with Dominic and Jacob and the Crew over the last months, Margaret still expected Dominic and Aaron to don black hooded robes and lay Amber naked on an altar. She wasn't sure what Jacob would be doing in that scenario, or that Amber wouldn't be into it, but she could hear them all laughing at the thought. '*Hell,*' Margaret thought to herself, '*the Midnight Candle doesn't even sell robes like I'm imagining. Everything they have is white or pink or purple.*'

"A bunch of stuff I didn't understand," Alexander said. "Possibly because I'm almost as new to this magic shit as you two are. Possibly because I had just taken the hardest headshot of my life. That woman is seriously strong."

Jacob, Dominic, Amber, and Aaron each took a turn walking around the altar, shifting things to make room for other things, arranging everything to their mutual satisfaction.

"Cait told us a bunch of stuff about how she, apparently, used to be a professional monster hunter," Alexander shook his head, "and how she was made official caretaker of the book after she hunted down some serial killer werewolf sorcerer who had stolen it, but she was afraid to keep it on her person and bullied her Druidic order into helping her build a magic box to hide it in. Except Dom and Ron didn't believe that last part at all – they didn't call her on it, and they sure didn't tell me anything, but I know them both well enough to say when they think someone's lying."

Now the conversation began to claim more of Margaret's attention. The Mark stirred a little, rising up in her belly.

"You know that's insane, right?" Jennifer's voice rose. "She has to be making all of that up. A retired monster hunter? A serial killer werewolf sorcerer? Her Druidic order?"

"I mean, the book wasn't there. Dom, Ron, and I cast a magic circle, we all went into a trance, and they went on a magic quest. We woke up, the book was there, and a figurative guardian monster appeared to make us prove our worth."

"Literal guardian monster," Margaret interjected, "actually. We don't know what she is, but I can smell that she isn't human. Jacob says he can see it in her aura."

"Oh," said Alexander, sitting up a little straighter.

"She what," said Jennifer, staring at Margaret with wide eyes. "He what? You what? Just ... what?"

"Do you remember," Margaret asked, "how she held me down by the river, when I changed, right after she scared off the pack? That ... that wasn't human."

"Oh," said Jennifer. Even in the dim stormy night, Margaret could see Jennifer's face pale. "So."

"Yeah," said Alexander. "Damn."

There was a long, awkward silence. Margaret turned her eyes back to the ritual preparations.

"So," said Jennifer, making a noise like she'd swallowed something large and unpleasant. "You guys performed a magic ritual. And went on a magic quest. To find a magic book. Which is sitting right here in front of us."

"Yeah."

Jennifer scuttled as far from the book as she could without leaving the blanket and the shelter of the umbrellas.

Below them, Dominic anointed Aaron and Amber with oil – upon the brow, the breast, and right above their waistbands – then handed Amber the oil so that she might do the same for Jacob and himself. So anointed, Dominic took the knife from the altar and walked a circle around the others, blade extended, the gesture somehow including everything his eye could see. To either side of Margaret, Alexander and Jennifer shivered. For her own part, Margaret felt something inside her relax. The Mark grew still. The Circle drawn, Dominic took his place at the north. Aaron spoke first, his voice low and reverent as he lit his candle.

"Powers and spirits of the West; guardians of the primal Water from which flows the river Styx; keepers of the dead, guides of the path between this life and the next. We call you to our Circle to be honored on this night of Samhain."

Margaret could hear the speakers clearly in the quiet of the woods, though she and the other non-participants sat some yards away. While they almost certainly could not make out their words, Alexander and Jennifer grew quiet out of respect. Dominic spoke next, lighting his own candle.

"Powers and spirits of the North; creatures of Air, intellect, and the upper realms. We call to you to join our circle on this night of Samhain."

It was Amber's turn to light her candle, invoking her element with reverence and awe.

"Powers and spirits of the East; keepers of the primal Fire and the light of knowledge and the secrets of rebirth. We call you to join our circle this night of Samhain."

Jacob lit his candle and spoke slowly, his voice deepening.

"Powers and spirits of the South; creatures of vast Earth, of fecund life and deep time. We call you to join our circle this night of Samhain."

They held together in a long moment of silence, then incanted in unison.

"So the circle is cast. So mote it be."

Amber and Dominic stepped forward into the center of the circle, and Dominic knelt at Amber's feet. Both bowed their heads for a long moment, then both raised their hands to the sky. Dominic drew breath as if to speak, but all that emerged from his mouth was a long, loud tone that he maintained as he drew his hands down from the sky and toward Amber.

The scene was surreal: hooded figures standing at and around an altar, shadows in the silvery night, silhouettes barely visible against and the orange glow from the altar. Margaret wished she had her camera with her, with film and a lens up to the task of capturing the image at this distance by moonlight.

A shudder ran through Amber's body, and she reached up farther toward the sky, her head tilted back in ecstasy. She lowered her hands, stood up straighter, and seemed to grow by inches.

Amber brought a hand down to touch Dominic's face in a regal gesture, then reached for the ground with both hands open.

"Come, O God," she evoked, raising her hands slowly as she spoke. "Rise from your earthly slumber of death. Rise and join this circle. Rise and dwell in the body of your priest."

Then she laid her hands on his shoulders, and a shudder ran through his body. He stood, slowly, and they faced away from one another, back to back so that Amber faced Aaron in the West and Dominic looked out to where Margaret sat with the others.

"Aaron," Amber called, gesturing for him to step forward. "It is you who serve the Crone. Invite the beloved dead into the circle."

Aaron stepped forward at her command, and nodded at her words. He turned and faced the West again, speaking loudly but gently.

"We call upon you who have passed beyond the Gates of Life, you who have loved us and have watched over us from beyond, be welcome in our circle. We call upon you Mighty Dead, honored of the Craft, be welcome in our circle. We call upon you still imprisoned in the trap whence we have lately escaped, felled before your time, be welcome in our circle." Aaron pulled a small bottle from the pocket of his jeans and poured it out at his feet. "Accept this offering, and those we shall lay before you."

While Aaron was speaking Dominic had unobtrusively knelt and retrieved the chalice and athame from the altar. When Aaron was done speaking, both he and Amber turned back toward the center of the circle, and Dominic handed the chalice to her. Amber raised the chalice for all to see, then filled it with wine from the altar and held it out toward Dominic. Dominic, in turn, raised the athame high, then touched it to his forehead before reversing the blade and lowering it slowly into the chalice. They stood there, posed, his wand in her cup, then separated.

She raised the cup to his lips and he drank. He took the cup from her and she drank from his hand in turn before reclaiming the chalice and offering wine to Aaron and Jacob as well.

"Speak, Aaron," Amber said, "of my descent to the dark realms."

Aaron bowed his head, then stood tall and spoke.

"In the early days of the world, there was only life and death, creation and destruction. The Goddess walked the earth, making mortal things, and when they died they were claimed by the God and taken to the realms of death. The Goddess lived in the light and the God lived in shadow, never taking the last breath of a living thing while the Goddess watched. All the Mysteries of light and life were hers to create and control, but death and darkness were unknown to her. A time came when she could no longer abide this. She knew where the border lay between life and death, and searched that border until she found the passage by which things moved from one into the other."

As he spoke, Aaron paced clockwise around the circle, gesturing dramatically with his hands.

"The God sensed that his borders were being probed, and he was waiting at the gate when the Goddess approached. He hid his face behind his helm and barred her way with his spear, but he could not help but be moved by her beauty and her splendor. Thus his indifference was feigned when he demanded that she explain why she sought to move beyond the borders of her own kingdom.

"The Goddess explained to him that she loved dearly all that she had created, and that she wished to see where her creatures went when they left her, and that they were well cared for. The God nodded his great head, but warned her that the realms of death were governed by their own laws, and that the Goddess could not bring anything but herself beyond the brazen gate.

"The Goddess nodded in turn, and stripped off her crown and robes and all her precious jewels. The God was overawed by the Goddess standing naked before him, and bowed himself down and laid his spear and helm at her feet, swearing to serve her always. The Goddess laid her hand upon his shaggy head and demanded that the God lead her down into death."

Aaron paused, staring off into the West.

"The way to death is crooked, but swift, and beyond the River Styx the Goddess found the shades of all the things she had created but which had left her. She knelt among them and wept for joy, and the God stood at her shoulder. She thanked him for caring for her creatures, and bid him lead her back up to the realm of life lest her other creations worry. This he could not do.

"If you are to return to the realms of life, he told her, you must first descend the entire way. And so he led her farther down, past the other great rivers and his guardian Cerberus, beyond the Elysian fields – yet empty for there had been no heroes – and unto the very throne.

290

"There, the Goddess discovered the greatest mystery of all: for she, herself, already sat upon the throne. She had already been there since the dawn of time, which was why she could not leave."

All stood in silence. Then Amber spoke again.

"Thus ended the earliest age of the world, for the revelations of that first descent changed the nature of life and death forever. Then as now, it is the Mother who tends to the garden of life, and it is the Crone who tends to the dead with the Gray God at her side. Every season since that first the Mother descends to the underworld in search of her children. It is autumn now, and passing into winter, and we know the absence of the Goddess. Yet we know that spring has come before and will come again. The Mother descends and becomes the Crone, but in her wake she leaves a promise: that she will return as the Maiden with the Green God at her side, and she will tend to the garden of life and be the Mother once more."

Dominic raised his hands above his head.

"Let us pour out blood-red wine in memory of the Mother, who has left us. Let us pour out blood-red wine to the Crone who awaits us. Let us pour out blood-red wine to those who have died before, because their fate awaits us all."

Amber, Aaron, Dominic, and Jacob each poured out a measure of wine, then passed the bottle back around, drinking until it was empty. When they were done, Dominic pulled a tray of biscuits and another bottle of wine from beneath the altar, and with Amber's aid they opened the bottle and repeated the blade-and-chalice ritual.

"Finally," said Dominic, kneeling at the altar, setting aside a cake and pouring out a last measure of wine. "Let us thank the gods and spirits that have aided us in our quest to find the Liber Caecissima. By your aid, we shall aid another, and undo a great wrong."

"Now," Amber cried loudly enough that even Alexander and Jennifer could hear, "in honor of life and death alike, let us feast on cakes and ale!"

Alexander rolled to his feet with a flourish, and offered Margaret and Jennifer both a hand up. Together, they claimed the book and the blankets and umbrellas, and descended to the fire, where the others helped arrange everything to make room for everyone.

Jacob sat down beside Margaret, keeping her between himself and Alexander. Amber flopped down between Alexander and Jennifer. Dominic and Aaron produced enough glasses for everyone then took the ends, as far from one another as possible in the half-moon they formed around the fire.

"That was really beautiful," Margaret said. "Thank you for letting me come. My other options were staying home, the safe-night Halloween party at church, and Sandy's boozefest. None of which could have possibly been any fun with everyone ignoring me."

"Thank you for coming," said Jacob. "It's really good to have you here.

"It's our pleasure," added Dominic. "I'm glad you're finally getting a chance to see what witchcraft looks like when it's not desperate and full of monsters. You know, the part where it's actually a religion."

Margaret giggled. "I'll admit that I had a very different image in my mind."

That won a laugh from Jennifer. "Amen to that, sister."

"Were you expecting goats and virgins," Aaron asked.

"At least a few black candles and skulls," Margaret admitted. "Don't you guys watch television?"

"You'll find that some places," Dominic admitted, "but my coven is super strict on dead animal parts. There was actually a push to collectively go vegetarian when I was younger. The compromise ended up being no animal parts in ritual unless we knew who'd killed it and how."

"That makes sense, I guess," Margaret said.

"To be honest," said Amber, "we've seen more high weirdness since you came to us in August than our entire lives prior."

"Oh."

"To be clear," added Alexander, "I, for one, am cool with that. I have always wanted an epic life."

"Thank you," Margaret said, carefully not looking in his direction, lest she see Jennifer's face and Aaron's. She could hear his grinding teeth, her sharp intake of breath, quite clearly.

Jacob snaked an arm around her waist and she leaned into the embrace.

Dominic stood and squeezed her shoulder. He said, "I have a couple things to take care of on my own before we formally close the circle. Don't have too much fun without me."

Aaron clenched his jaw as he watched Dominic wander off into the woods. Was he actually going to go do private rites, or was he just disappearing to get high? Why did it even matter? Dominic had made it clear several times that no matter how good the magic was, they would never be together again.

He spat, and got up to tend to the fire, snagging another cake and opening a bottle of beer on his way back to the blankets. This time he sat next to Jacob, and poured a beer for each of them.

"Thanks," said Jacob.

"May I," asked Margaret, just finishing her wine.

Aaron wanted to say no, but filled her cup anyway.

"Thank you," she said. He grunted.

"I also want to thank you for everything you've done so far. I know you don't like me, but you've still taken so many risks to help me. Thank you so much."

Aaron grunted. "Don't worry about it," he said, looking away.

"The same goes for all of you," he heard her say. "I don't know what I would have done without all your help and support."

"You're welcome," said Jacob in that warm voice he'd started using with Margaret. *'Dominic used to talk to me like that'.*

"You're my friend," said Jennifer.

"What else could we do," said Amber.

Alexander didn't say anything, but Aaron could picture the smug face he must be making.

"Would you like to go for a quick walk," Jacob said suddenly. For a moment Aaron thought it was a universal invitation. "I know it's dark, but I can show you a couple of my favorite places before we need to leave."

"I would like that," Margaret said.

The two stood and set off in the direction of Venus Mound, leaving no one between himself and fucking Alexander Dixon.

"A walk does sound like a good idea," said Amber. "Alex?"

"Sure," Alexander said.

"Jen? Aaron?"

Aaron just grunted and shook his head.

"No, thank you," said Jennifer.

"Okay," Amber said. "We won't be gone long."

Aaron watched their retreating backs, his stomach a conflicting storm of envy and hate.

Jennifer scooted over toward him, snagging another bottle of beer on her way.

"Well, that was sudden," she said.

"Indeed."

Jennifer raised her bottle. "Here's to flying solo."

Aaron raised his bottle in return. "At least we're here to tend the fire."

Old World Magic

MONDAY, NOVEMBER 2ND

There it was in front of them, halfway through the Book of Secrets and written in clear Middle English script: the ritual described vaguely by Mirrors and Veils. Simple circle construction. No expensive or hard-to-find components. No need to wait for any astronomical event more significant than the next full moon, less than a week away. Straightforward Latin incantation by a single speaker, and four other people to shut up, stand still, and hold candles.

Completed by human sacrifice.

"Well," Dominic asked, dumbfounded. "What do we tell them?"

"The truth," Aaron decided, eventually.

"You're not suggesting…"

"No," he protested unconvincingly, "but they should know."

That was true enough. Hell, maybe Alexander would convince them to sacrifice Anthony Domiano.

'*Goddess,*' Dominic shuddered. '*I can't believe I even thought that.*'

Dominic was exhausted. They'd been up all night sifting through the grimoire, resisting the distractions of those few rites and treaties they could actually read. He had been ecstatic when they had finally found the "Rite to Release a Victim from the Mark of the Wolf". The shock of disappointment was almost physically overwhelming. Human sacrifice. Mirrors and Veils had hinted as much, but hope had overwhelmed his sense. If Aaron hadn't been there, he would have cried. He considered screaming instead.

Aaron, never as dedicated to helping Margaret as he had been, was taking defeat with greater equanimity. Without asking, he pulled the grimoire from Dominic's hands, a thoughtful look on his face. Dominic didn't have the strength to protest. The white mists of Aaron's aura curled brightly around him, his eyes shone with focus.

"Get everyone over here tomorrow," he said, reopening his note pad. "We might be able to work this."

"How?"

"I'll tell you tomorrow," Aaron scribbled furiously, reducing the ritual to a crude outline and a few quotations. "I need to sleep on this."

"Aaron. I don't want to get anyone's hopes up any more than we already have."

"We're going to need to talk to them anyway."

Dominic sighed. His head hurt. He was exhausted, but the coffee he'd been slamming to get himself this far was probably going to keep him up all night. He didn't want to argue anymore.

"Fine. Here or the coffee house?"

"Here. I don't want Caitlyn in on this."

Dominic felt an indignant urge to defend the woman, but Aaron was right. Caitlyn was too wary of Margaret to be helpful. Besides, she was still holding out on them. This was their deal. Maybe their destiny.

Aaron sat alone in his room with his black mirror in his lap. His notes sat beside him, but he'd already been over them twice. He played it out over and over in his head, until he could almost see it in the mirror – a holographic projection across the surface. The five of them arrayed in a circle, with Margaret and the sacrifice in the center; the invocation, the transference, the climax, and the closing. There was more to the ritual, but it was tinsel: a knife in the heart and a prayer for the soul of the sacrifice – the scapegoat, if Aaron had read the ritual correctly.

Alexander had already volunteered himself as the sacrifice, when Dominic had first mentioned the possibility of the ritual.

Aaron didn't have to say anything. Dominic was on the verge of giving up. Aaron didn't have to let Alexander Dixon be a hero again.

On the other hand, he could be a hero, too, this time. He had found the solution. After they'd come this far, could he really turn back? After consulting the dead and stealing the book from its dream-vault, could he refuse to actually use it?

The ritual played out in his mind over and over again.

What would the pack do to them for moving the Mark? Would Dixon be able to resist the bloodthirsty call of the Mark the way Dunn had?

None of it mattered. The ritual called to him, like destiny. The feeling was even stronger than it had been before the graveyard ritual. Over and over, he played the ritual in his mind's eye, watching it reflected across the surface of the mirror; he knew exactly how it would go.

'*We will begin by putting Jennifer in the South ...*'

TUESDAY, NOVEMBER 3RD

The boys had forgotten something, but Margaret couldn't bring herself to tell them. Their books marked the full moon for tomorrow, but she felt the call tonight, as well. The sky was overcast, but she could see the moon peeking in and out from behind the wind-blown clouds.

Part of her, goaded by the Mark, was angry at them. They were the witches, the supposed experts, how could they forget this? How dare they fail her in such a banal fashion? Surely this was a sign of more and greater failures to come.

Part of her was, of course, afraid. She had almost grown accustomed to the whispering urges, the overpowering sensations, and to the strength. Especially the strength. In time, she would grow used to the monthly assaults by the pack – assuming they didn't grow bored and move on, or provoke the wrath of the monster-woman who had befriended Jacob and Dominic. Could she stand to be just a girl again? Could she stand it if they failed again?

For the most part, however, she was resigned. Perhaps it was God's will that she should endure the transformation a final time: a trial of faith and endurance, or penance for going to heathens for help instead of the Church. More likely it was a simple, honest mistake by young men as far in over their heads as she was. She would take this night with her forever.

It was colder than it had been last month, making it impractical to face the change naked again; the ratty old pajamas she'd chosen to sacrifice were too threadbare to keep her comfortable while she waited. She looked up to the moon, shining behind the clouds, and pulled her coat about her more tightly.

Her breathing was slow and deep, like Jacob had taught her. In ... two ... three ... hold. Out ... two ... three ... hold. She imagined each breath as fire spreading out to her limbs, an illusion that pushed away the cold until she could concentrate. She offered a silent, wordless prayer for protection and forgiveness, and reached out to the moon.

The silver light flowed through her until it touched the Mark, coiled in her belly, and she changed.

It hurt even less this time, a fluid transformation that – until she began to move – felt more like a shift in perspective than anything else. Her first steps brought pain, like the ache of sitting too long at the block, tense with anticipation. There was only one balm for that pain, only one way to extinguish that fire.

She ran.

She knew where the werewolves awaited her, and she ran toward them as if drawn by a magnet. She found them gathered in what looked like a semi-permanent encampment by the river, tucked deep beneath the concrete porch that stuck out from the Riverfront Mall. Glass littered the ground – there were a few intact empty bottles, but mostly they were broken – identifiable by her human mind, but appearing mostly as small, sharp-edged obstacles to her werewolf vision.

The male that had tried to rape her was nowhere to be seen. The other males gave her wide berth. Michael sat separate from the rest, his eyes on the encampment and his thralls, but his ears swiveled all around. The second biggest wolf, Michael's lieutenant, had his nose to the ground, but there were too many scents here for Margaret to sort one from another. The wolf-witch sat as far from the other leaders as he could, watching everything with a bowed head and a sulky back.

Finally, the lieutenant moved up to Michael and communicated something that Margaret could not perceive. Michael stood and howled.

We hunt!

They charged down river, flowing out from under the great concrete edifice that overlooked the south side of the river. Michael led them down river, following the tracks first forged by deer then left by hikers and bikers and countless drunken revelers.

Autumn was hard upon them and game was growing thin. The animals by the river had been half-tamed by the proximity and careless generosity of humanity, but after three full moons only the wariest and least appetizing beasts remained. Scent trails crossed and re-crossed their path, but nothing large enough to bother digging out of its nighttime den. The night birds were silent, and even the insects stilled at their passing.

Still they followed Michael, confident that he led them to a feast. The scent of unwashed man came to them, and Michael howled. The man-scent was drenched in fear and whiskey. The pack veered off-trail, down to the riverbank. Margaret followed, caught up in the movement and hunger of the pack, but uncertain how this scent might lead them to food.

They ran, howling, following the river and the scent of man before turning back up a steep hillside, skirting the edge of a deep ravine lined by twisted girders and wire fencing. Up and over, the trail led back around and down under to the edge of a cavelike recess. Inside, a man lay drunk, sick, and trembling.

Michael pulled the pack up short, not quite invading the sick man's shelter.

Margaret. Michael barked at her. *This one is yours.*

She yelped in horror and surprise.

Kill him, the pack howled.

No, she growled. The thought sickened her human mind, but it excited the Mark. She had already been hungry.

Now that hunger grew, and a savage bloodlust rose beside it. She fought, but the Mark fought back.

Kill the man, Michael growled at her, stalking toward her.

Kill him, the pack howled, circling in so that they and Michael stood between her and escape and nothing stood between her and the trembling man. *Kill him! Kill him! Kill him!*

Images of the act danced before her eyes: the scrawny man, fat-looking in layers of threadbare sweaters and coats; the fear in his eyes as she approached; the spore of his fear in her nostrils; the taste of his blood in her mouth. All that was human and faithful in her cried out against the command. The Mark that ran through her blood and burned in her bones cried out to submit, to obey its master and its nature. The Mark needed life, and life trembled before it.

Kill!
Kill!
Kill!
Kill!
Kill!

The werewolves barked the command in steady time. Without knowing how she had gotten there, Margaret found herself on the narrow path into the hermit's retreat.

Kill!
Kill!
Kill!
Kill!
Kill!

They howled the command in complex harmony. One menacing step at a time, she backed the trembling man into the deepest recesses of his shelter.

He raised his arm to protect his face.

She lunged under it, finding his neck with her jaws.

She bit. Flesh tore. Blood filled her mouth. Life's blood fed her Mark.

The force of the blow sent her prey floundering over the unstable edge. Bouncing off the rocks and wrought iron protrusions, he fell into the cold stream below.

The wind changed, then, blowing off the river in a mad series of gusts: the scent of power and malice came from upstream, more potent than anything she had imagined, and brought the whole pack to a stop. To her werewolf eyes, the figure was nothing but writhing shadows, and the entire pack stepped back away from it. But it did not speak, did not move, did not interfere.

The pack howled in victory, and descended to feast.

Mourning Moon Sacrifice

WEDNESDAY, NOVEMBER 4TH

It was fitting that the ritual be here, in Margaret's family barn: it brought the Crew full circle. The rest of the Crew, at least: full circle for Jennifer – and for Margaret, herself – would be the lawn of Holy Cross Lutheran Church, but that would be ... inappropriate. Blasphemous. And likely to draw the attention of the police.

So Jennifer took her place in the South, at the back of the barn, as Aaron directed. Amber, he put in the North, and Jacob in the East. Aaron fumigated each of them with a wand of sage, then took the West quarter for himself. Each of them clutched long taper candles that Dominic had anointed with fragrant oils.

Dominic stood in the center of the circle, with Margaret and Alexander lying on the ground before him, barely dressed and with their hands and feet tied. Dixon was breathing slowly and deeply, his eyes half-glazed and his undershirt straining over his muscled chest. Margaret, in her thin night gown, was less serene, breathing heavily with her eyes squeezed shut.

The whole scene struck Jennifer like something out of a horror movie.

'*What am I doing here?*' Jennifer shook her head and crossed herself. '*How did it come to this?*'

Dominic chanted in Latin, gesturing toward the quarters and waving various instruments over the two supine figures. A wand, a censer, a knife. He mixed salt and water in a bowl, and poured a measure of it over each of them, earning a gasp and a cry. It was too cold to be naked, let alone wet.

A palpable tension built in the air as Dominic continued to chant, waving his blade over Margaret. A mist began to rise within the confines of the circle, and Jennifer was frozen by fear. A light gleamed around Margaret.

Dominic stood over Margaret, still chanting, and began to wave his knife over her in slow, deliberate spirals. The light around her began to move, scintillating in time with the motion of Dominic's blade, and slowly, slowly, began to flow up out of her and toward that silver point. Margaret thrashed and cried out, her back arching and her eyes glowing brightly. At last, after what seemed like an hour, all the light had gathered into a burning point at the tip of Dominic's knife. The chant ended.

Slowly, carefully, Dominic took a step to the right, standing over Alexander. The light pulsed and his hand shook, as though he struggled to hold it steady against the resistance of the light.

Slowly, carefully, Dominic knelt, reversing the knife as he did so that the tip rested on Dixon's chest. He pressed down slowly, deliberately, and pulled the blade down the bound boy's sternum. The cloth of the undershirt parted and a bright flow of red blood welled up in the candlelight. The light of the Mark flowed into Alexander through the hole in his flesh, suffusing him with the same glow that had surrounded Margaret. Dixon gasped, held his breath, and then loosed a wild, agonized cry that echoed against the trees.

If they had followed the ritual exactly as they hand found it, Dominic would have plunged the knife into Dixon's heart.

'*Did he have to tell us that?*'

Dominic stepped away while Alexander writhed. He began to chant again, gesturing at each of the quarters as he walked the circle backwards, and snuffing each of their candles in turn.

Amber and Jacob rushed forward to help Margaret as she struggled to stand, untying her hands and legs, and drawing her out of the circle. Aaron and Dominic gathered the tools as hastily as they could.

The others all hurried away to what they thought was a safe distance, but Jennifer was frozen in place. She had just seen witches perform a real magic spell. She had just helped witches perform a real magic spell.

She was going to hell.

They were all going to hell.

This was worse than learning that werewolves were real. This was risking her immortal soul.

Almost at her feet, Alexander continued to writhe, making sounds she hadn't imagined a human could make: terrible moans and gurgling cries. His back arched improbably. He strained at his bonds. The hole in his chest closed and the hair on his muscular arms grew thick and dark. His flesh began to ripple and flow beneath the hair, pulling in and out like the tide, and the ropes fell from his wrists. His glossy black hair grew into a mane, and the line of his jaw began to pull.

A hand caught her by the shoulder and, at last, she found the will to turn away. Aaron and Amber took her arms and guided her back to where Margaret huddled under a blanket with Jacob, both of them under Dominic's close supervision.

She found, though, that she could not look away for long. She had helped bring it about. She couldn't pretend it wasn't happening.

Dixon's legs had come free of their binding as well, and he struggled to be free of his clothing. Little human remained about his appearance. Every inch of his skin was covered in shaggy black fur, and the shapes of his limbs were all wrong. He shook himself, and his limbs settled into a more stable shape – but not a more natural one. Margaret Dunn had transformed into a brindle wolf – large and unnaturally intelligent, but a wolf none the less. Alexander Dixon had not. The massive canine monster that stood atop the rumpled, torn pile of clothing where once there had been a human being, bore no resemblance to Margaret's wolf-form. It was massive, easily twice the size of any natural dog, and wolf-shaped only in the most general sense, with massive claws far out of proportion with its body. It stared at them with bright green eyes and a low growl issued from its throat.

Then it ran, vanishing into the night.

A long silence followed. Margaret was the first to find her voice.

"He was a monster. I ... I didn't look like that, did I?"

"No," Jacob assured her. Jennifer nodded mutely, turning slowly toward the others, though a part of her feared Dixon-the-wolf might return.

"I can't believe we did this," Jennifer murmured. "What's going to happen to us now?"

No one knew. Margaret and Jacob clung to each other tightly, whispering. Dominic stood behind them, hands on their shoulders, his face was composed and his eyes sharp. Aaron stood to one side, eyes narrowed but a small smile playing at the edges of his lips. Amber stood behind them, huddled in her own arms.

"But we did it," Dominic said at last. "We've saved Mara."

"But who's going to save Alex?" Amber demanded, plaintively.

"Dixon can save himself," Aaron said, a little too dispassionately. "Just like always."

EPILOGUE

Swamp Witch

C.2200 BC

His senses had grown sharper in the jungle. Three moons ago he could have pointed to the hunter, now he followed a ghostly image through the green lives of the thick, swampy undergrowth. The man's life was silvery, pulsing with vitality, and sheathed in a self-image that Burning Eyes could barely perceive behind the protective web of the swamp-witch's charm. He did not waste his energy unraveling the protection: he might well need it soon.

A half-dozen more warriors were waiting at the edge of the village to escort him directly and silently to the witch's hut. They were not as well warded as the first, and he could see them through their own eyes and each other's. The jumble of impressions was too much to sort through at once, especially with their minds all concentrated on the witch who ruled them. In their minds she was a blend all the most powerful parts of manhood and womanhood, and the image grew clearer as the brought him to the shaded door of her hut. A woman's face pierced both between the nostrils as a warrior and through the lip as a woman; a man's shoulders, muscular and scarred; a woman's breasts, full, ripe and painted with ocher spirals; hunter's magic tattooed and scarred on her legs. In the warrior's minds the witch had both a massive, erect phallus and a dripping, hungry cunt. She was beautiful and handsome and monstrous and awe inspiring. The warriors and their village prospered, untouched by the illness and poisonous snakes and other hazards that plagued the neighboring villages; still the witch terrified them.

She did not emerge from the hut, although she brushed against him with her mind. Burning Eyes neither resisted her nor opened to her.

"Enter, stranger," she called from within, voice low and sultry.

For a moment, as he crossed the threshold, all his senses went blank. The warriors vanished, along with the witch and even the presences of the village and the swamp surrounding it.

For that moment, even the call was gone. He reeled, truly blind as he had not been since the first days after Dream Leopard had first stolen his eyes, almost falling to his knees in shock. Then he was through and the presence of the swamp witch returned. He could hear her breathing and the slow beat of her heart, the crackle and pop of herbs burning on a low fire. He could smell the fire, little more than coals, and the pungent visionary herbs that burned on it.

Now he saw her clearly as she saw herself: not one body bearing the features of both a man and a woman, but two bodies, one male and one female, each bearing the marks of both initiations. Beautiful and handsome, awesome and terrifying. Her power was immense, and she opened it for him to examine. It was more than he had ever dreamed of possessing, but still a single bolt of lightning next to the great storm of power that called to him.

"I am Burning Eyes," he introduced himself. "I am on a dream quest."

"Welcome, Burning Eyes," she said in that wonderful voice. "I have dreamed of you and that which you seek. I have been waiting for you. Sit."

He sat, finding the furs to his left almost by accident.

"I, too, have dreamed of beasts pulling the sun over a river and a great village of stone. I, too, have dreamed of the great Voice hidden beneath a mountain built by men to honor their gods. The Voice has chosen you to release it, and it has chosen me to aid you."

He said nothing, waiting in the smoky darkness, and examining the witch as closely as he could without giving away more of himself than he wanted to.

He had heard of two-souled shamans, of men who also had a woman's soul, of women who took up the male role of hunter or warrior, but there had never been one among his village. One shaman who had come to him for advice had claimed to be two-souled, but White Rain had merely been a lover of all flesh, whether it was shaped in the body of a man or a woman. This witch did not actually have two souls, either, but a single soul in two parts, each with its own self-image. Both halves shared White Rain's love of all flesh.

Although both she and her villagers saw her as young-looking, he could sense a weight of years behind her. She had been ruling this village since before Burning Eyes had been born, possibly since before Dream Leopard. Four, maybe five decades of gathering power and refining its use. No wonder she could see him in the dream. Little doubt she saw through all his guises now.

"Who are you," he asked at last when she did not go on. "What are you?"

"I am She Who Dances with Both the Sun and the Moon. I am the mother and father of this village. I am their guardian spirit and their shadow. I am flesh made of spirit, and spirit made into flesh." He felt her come nearer, heard her approach around the fire pit. "You may call me Sun-and-Moon."

Her presence enveloped him, drowned him in its power and its suddenly exclusive femininity. The image of her male half was packed away, folded up somewhere inside her until it was needed. He had never been with a woman, but he knew the psychic scent of lust. He felt his body respond to it even as his mind wondered what she was really after. She pressed herself against him and whispered in his ear.

"Tonight is the dark of the moon," she said. "Stay until it is full, recover your strength and together we will begin a line of warriors and shamans to challenge the gods themselves." She pressed so close that he had to embrace her lest she knock him down. Her breasts were full, soft and warm against his chest, her back muscled under his hands. The bone in her nose and the ring in her lip scratched enticingly against his face, and the flesh of her belly pressed against his loins. "I will teach you all the magics and mysteries you will need to reach the land of the sun-king and complete your quest. Then you will return and give me another child."

"Yes," he said. Even with his mind clouded by the lust of their bodies, he could hear the truth of her offer. No doubt she was getting the better end of the bargain, but he knew he would still profit greatly.

310

He tried to pull her down beside him so that he could mount her, but she was stronger and kept her position atop him. She stripped him of his talismans and fetishes carefully, always pinning him with hands, or shoulders or hips even as she used her entire body to caress him. She overpowered him on every level, but she did it gently and seductively. Their roles were reversed and he couldn't right them, but she mastered him so completely that she even made him enjoy it. He did not penetrate her, she engulfed him. He did not plant his seed within her, she drew it out of him. Again and again. He lost count of how often she coaxed him back to life before possessing him again until he was utterly spent, unable to move, a twitching and gasping husk of pleasure.

She pressed herself tight against him, kissing him passionately and spreading his legs to wrap them around her hips as she changed. Her breasts flattened into the hard chest of a warrior and a trembling phallus pressed itself against his own, and the spirit that enveloped his as her body had enveloped his was now as potently male as it had been feminine a moment ago.

The witch loosened Burning Eyes with his fingers, coaxing him open slowly and gently and claiming him completely. The feeling was intensely psychic as well as physical, more pleasurable than he had ever imagined and more humiliating than he had dreamed, and when the witch finally deposited his own hot seed, Burning Eyes was unaccountably erect. Using his mouth, the witch brought Burning Eyes to a final, screaming climax.

The blind priest lay trembling until well past sunset. The moon had risen high and dark by the time he came back to himself enough to sense the incredible power they had raised. The air trembled with it and his body ached with the strain of containing so much. The witch was sitting beside him, both images so clear in his mind that he could not say which body it wore. The witch placed a bowl at his lips and poured a potion down his throat.

"When you wake from the vision," the witch said in a man's voice, "You may possess me in turn, and I will begin your true instruction."

BIBLIOGRAPHY

The preceding text makes numerous references to books both real and fictional, some directly and some by cypher. At risk of robbing the reader of a delightful research hole, a selection of the more significant real-world books are listed below:

Betz, Hans Deiter. Greek Magical Papyri in Translation Including the Demotic Spells. Chicago, IL: University of Chicago Press, 1996.

Farrar, Janet, and Stewart Farrar. A Witches Bible: the Complete Witches Handbook. Custer, WA: Phoenix, 1996.

Otten, Charlotte F. A Lycanthropy Reader: Werewolves in Western Culture. Syracuse, NY: Syracuse University Press, 1986.

ABOUT THE AUTHOR

JS Groves is a human with perhaps too many passions.

He has been writing only slightly longer than he has been practicing witchcraft. A bench jeweler by day, he also has a degree in Classical Studies and an inconvenient passion for photography. He has spent his nights and weekends feverishly writing the Book of Secrets (and quite a few other things) for more than ten years.

He lives in Kansas City with his partner and their feline overlords.

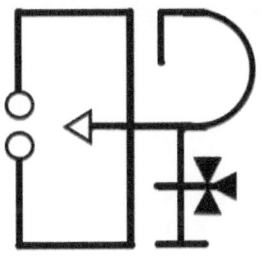

www.ingramcontent.com/pod-product-compliance
Lightning Source LLC
Chambersburg PA
CBHW030244030726
47493CB00023B/576